by vanessa zian

Dog Tags & Lace Series

Midnight to December

Ruby in July

Mine after October

March becomes Dawn

the lifecycle of a crush

vanessa zian

To the real life Lynda, my favorite pen pal and girl crush. The inventor of this book's title—thanks to you this story was born. And to the real life Evelyn, who inspired the best ever meet cute.

In many ways, this book is for all the women in my life, the beautiful souls who teach me things I often didn't realize I needed to know. My girlfriends will always remain my favorite crushes.

Mini-playlist

While writing, I listen to the same one or two songs on repeat. Here are the sounds that aided in this story's creation:

Taven's song: All These Things That I've Done | The Killers
Desiree's song: Creep (live) | Danielle Ponder

content notice

My books weave in subplots of trauma and may be triggering to some, but there's good reason for it. I'm all about the happily ever after, so you will absolutely get that. But my aim is to leave the reader with the ultimate narrative full of truths, no matter what the trauma. We all have experienced some at some point, whether it be "small t" or the "Big T" kind.

We learn by sharing stories. We heal by tweaking the narrative. And we soar when we can join forces and journey together. It's what I'm here for, and I'm so glad you are too.

phase 1: intrigue

. . .

Hope is where it really begins. A seed of hope in the initial spark of interest that pierced your heart, most unexpectedly. You see something you want. Obsess on how to get it. The cycle begins.

one

. . .

Spark

Present Day

desiree

Friday, 7:04pm

IT'S ONE OF those kinds of downpours that sends the outdoor furniture flying, trees swaying and stretching their limbs to some unseen shelter that doesn't exist. The kind where you better find yourself a sturdy structure with a solid roof, or risk getting swept away, wondering why the skies decided to unleash on your vulnerable self so abruptly. Is the universe giving you a sign? Wind like that can feel difficult to believe is anything other than some determined power trying to send you a message.

If there's a message to be heard, though, I'm not paying attention. It's kind of hard to when you're not near any qualifying indoor space that could provide quick shelter, and you're left to power through and brave the rain.

What had started as a light drizzle earlier today at the start of our beachside music festival has now turned into a full-fledged monsoon. The wind had shifted, we should have known the weather report had underestimated something. I'm not sure I've ever seen Lake Erie look so enraged.

I shiver under my poncho, the plastic clinging to my face in a sticky mess as stings of whipped-up beach sand pepper my cheeks. I let my eyes linger on the crowd, laughing at the sight of rowdy concert fanatics courageously raising their arms in welcoming madness, unfazed by the sudden storm. The show must go on, I suppose. Mother Nature joins as lightning dances through the dark clouds just overhead, almost in time with the music. Our revered rock stars remain firmly on stage, lapping up the drama of this pop-up deluge that only adds to the energetic atmosphere.

I scan the crowd in search of Melissa, my best friend and also the current one up for her turn to procure our next round of drinks. She's nowhere in sight, from what I can tell through the blur of rain. A twinge of guilt hits me as I realize I sent her on this errand at exactly the wrong time. Cell service out here is currently mercurial, and besides, the bands are carrying on through the storm, so hearing a damn thing on your ringing phone is unlikely. The only things filling my own ears at this point are the rain managing to seep in sideways past the hood of my cheap poncho, and the thump of bass accompanied by the crash of waves. I consider if I should stay put or try and find some semblance of a roof. Looking around, it seems the other concert-goers are of two camps—either singing along in wild screams of tipsy delight, or scurrying away like a swarm of insects heading for the nearest shadows.

I spin around the memory of Melissa's words in my head, the sales pitch she had given me just three days before. "Come to the festival with me, it'll be fun," she had sung in that adorable yet aggressive way of hers.

Famous last words.

I had tried to fight her on it. I wasn't really in the mood for concert shenanigans. "I'm trying to save money," I had said from my spot on the bathroom floor of my condo.

Melissa wasn't hearing it. "Chris bailed, the ticket is free. And I'm not going alone, so really, if you don't come, you'll actually be wasting money."

"But it's your money," I groaned.

"And you wouldn't do that to me," she insisted. "You're going. It'll cure your broken heart."

I should tell you she was holding my hair back at that moment, I'm sure you can figure out why.

I had moaned into the toilet and flushed down the last of my rum and bile. "My heart isn't broken. I didn't even like him that much."

Melissa gave me two quick slaps to the back. "Oh, I know, sweetie. I'm not talking about Jose, though he sure was easy on the eyes."

I had popped up my body and leaned back on my heels, gratefully taking the tissue she handed me to wipe my mouth. I rose up and rinsed with mouthwash, the tingle of mint doing an excellent job of further filling me with spikes of discomfort. "Don't say his name," I grumbled after spitting out the neon blue liquid. I wiped my mouth and repeated my plead in a whisper. "Don't say his name."

Taven Carlisle.

I couldn't bear to hear Melissa speak it, the name of my childhood crush that my eternally wounded heart was still clinging to hope for. If she said his name, I might be sick all over again.

Because of course Melissa knew that Jose—the guy that just ghosted me after a mere two weeks of dating—of course she knew he wasn't the source of my broken heart. Or the reason for too many rum drinks.

No, Jose wasn't to blame for dropping me. I had become a

basic corpse within the short span of our time dating, if you could even call it that. Had I been in his shoes, I might have done the same thing. It's not his fault that I recently found out that the real love of my life was engaged, and apparently had been for some time. Not only was I late to learn that Taven Carlisle was betrothed, but it was *who* he was engaged to that really got me—the beautiful redhead, a woman who had been in our lives since we were all kids. Childhood sweethearts, the happy couple could call themselves. It was hard to breathe when I realized who his fiancée was, thought about the love story they'd tell. Taven was supposed to be *my* childhood sweetheart, not hers. I tortured myself with looping thoughts of their beautiful little passionate tale, sucking the wind right out of my lungs.

Poor Jose never had a chance.

Jose was more of a rebound guy, only this was the kind of rebound that wasn't really a rebound at all, given that the relationship I was attempting to distract from had barely even existed in the first place. Taven and I had always been complicated like that. And the fabric of our relationship had become threadbare by the time I was twenty-five. I'm thirty now, it's time to move on, right? Surely that relationship should be banished to fading memories.

"Fine," I had obliged to my friend as unwelcome thoughts of Taven consumed my head, yet again. "I'll go to the festival with you." I glanced in the mirror back to Melissa and her fiery green eyes, dancing in victory.

"Great. And you're letting me dress you. I'll make you look hot."

MELISSA DID SUCCEED IN THAT mission, I have to admit. Too bad my red crochet top and high-waisted jean shorts are now hidden under the hideous lime green plastic poncho, and my most obvious accessory is a flurry of goosebumps as the rain and wind are wreaking havoc upon our lakeside beach. I look around the mayhem and blink my eyes to clear away the rain. Still no sign of Melissa. About twenty yards ahead I see something else I'm looking for, though—an unoccupied canvas tent. Perfect.

The logo of some beer company displays prominently on the peaked roof of the tent, barely legible in slinking waves as the wind hits in violent bursts. With my feet fighting against the sand, flips flops filling with a sludge mix, I summon some quad strength and fight my way over to the makeshift shelter, thankful that Melissa had chosen a five-dollar hot pink poncho for herself. At least I'll easily spot her when she returns—no doubt with drinks in hand; she's determined like that. Would she be mad I abandoned our coveted spot so close to the stage? Briefly, perhaps, but she'd get over it. I knew better than to expect her to leave—the show must go on!—and I'm banking on this rain dwindling down the crowds so our stage view won't be at risk.

Under the shelter of the tent I peer over to the drinks stand, my eye catching the quickest blur of fuchsia. I laugh in relief, unsurprised that Melissa remained in line, powering through out there with the other die-hard music fans, all drowning and hell-bent on securing their next rounds. At least when she's done, we'll have some space here in my little tent, all to ourselves.

But my time alone in said shelter is short lived.

It's his voice that I hear first, deep and familiar and dream-like, because clearly I'm delusional. He's saying my name, I hear it before I even register the company of anyone else. It's been five years since I last heard that easy drawl that zapped my insides in the best kind of way.

God, I always loved his voice. Can remember it morphing from schoolboy alto to almost-man tenor, then eventually the deeper tone that I'm hearing now. Deep, yet mixed with something else, something smooth like icing on a cake or maybe even the velvety slips of red wine, not that Taven Carlisle ever drank wine unless absolutely necessary. Stronger was always his poison. But there it is, his voice alright. I wonder if maybe I hit my head, because surely I'm hallucinating.

It's funny that I should run into Taven again all these years later at a music festival. Too coincidental, really, given the venue of our first meeting, seventeen years ago. That particular evening, the night my adolescent self met Taven Carlisle for the very first time, my nerves had been all tangled up, my palms in a permanent state of wet. Not far off from how I'm feeling now at the sound of his voice, calling my name.

He repeats himself as I brave turning to meet the presence I'm now registering just a foot beside me. My heart thumps at how handsome he still is. Dark hair, longer than I ever remember it being, but those same dark and tortured eyes. He has a little more scruff on the jaw than when I last saw him. A short beard, I'd call it. I wonder what else about him has changed. I wonder if he ever thinks about me.

He steps closer, looking like he's unsure if he should hug me or shake my hand or what. I understand the feeling.

I raise my hand in a small wave. "Taven Carlisle."

He grins. "Holy fucking shit."

"I guess you could say that."

"Dazzle—" he says, his old nickname for me, dropping from his lips with something akin to reverence. "It really is you, isn't it?"

As I open my mouth to answer, lightning finds its target in the metal tent pole above us. The last thing I remember is Taven reaching out to me.

Then darkness.

two

Unexpected

Present Day

desiree

Friday, 7:22pm

I WAKE UP on the sandy ground and in Taven's arms, the cool fabric of his jacket on my cheek. It feels good. I like being held by Taven.

There's a continuous ringing in my ears. I can vaguely hear him calling to me, but it sounds like an echo. *"Desiree? Desiree?! For God sakes, Dazzle, answer me!"*

Then another voice. Female. *"Taven? Holy shit, is that you? I go to get drinks and a blast from the past happens, what in the hell! It's so good to see you. Why is she lying like—wait, what the fuck?! Desiree? What did you do to her?!"*

"Fuck, call help!"

"What happened?"

"Lightning, that's what fucking happened! Call 9-1-1!"

I try and croak out a word. "No." I lift my head to get up, but I'm dizzy. And Taven smells like rain and pine and heaven.

Melissa's voice. *"Lightning, what? When?"*

"Just now, how could you miss it?"

"You're fucking kidding me, are we in danger?!"

"I'm here, I'm fine," I say louder. I blink open my eyes to a crowd of people surrounding me, with Taven's face upside down above me.

His voice starts coming in clearer, the ringing subsiding ever so slightly. "Jesus Christ, I thought you were dead. Fuck!" I think I see wetness in his eyes. And raw fear. It makes me smile. But wait, I shouldn't be smiling, I just got struck by lightning. I should play the lottery. My thoughts aren't making sense.

"My leg," I push out. "My leg hurts." I look up and see a woman with a signature red medical bag rushing toward me. She drops to her knees next to me, making a heavy thud in the wet sand. She flashes a light in my eyes and I blink.

"Good," she says. "Okay, what's your name?" Then she yells at everyone around us. "Clear the space, please! You all need to get inside to shelter! Now!" She looks back down at me. "Can you hear me, honey?"

I nod, reluctantly rising out of the wonderful warmth of Taven's lap. I know this is not the thing to be thinking about right now. My head is fuzzy and I can't think straight. But I'm okay. Unless I died and this is heaven, I think I'm okay. "I can hear," I answer her. "My name is Desiree Hope Hatson." I go to stand, Taven rising with me, his arm snaking around my waist to assist. My poncho crinkles within his hold and I think about how ridiculous I must look in front of all these people.

The next several minutes are a blur. I'm taken to the medical area, a tent I never thought I'd need to visit. The medical team guides me from his arms and I'm laid down on a vinyl exam table. Melissa's hands push my soggy, sandy hair away from my face. I see Taven pacing back and forth. His friends are standing to the side, reassuring him that I'm fine and they should get back to the show. He ignores them. My blood pressure is taken. A million questions are fired at me. I tell them my leg hurts, but not to call 9-1-1. I'm a doctor, I'm alright. I sign a paper on a clipboard, agreeing to let the medical staff tend to me even though I just want to go home. I hear Taven explain that one minute we were standing there, then next I'm thrown against the wall of the building beside the tent, before slumping down to the ground. None of which I actually remember.

Taven grabs my hand. I barely feel it, and I don't know if it's because I was possibly struck by lightning, or if it's because the long-lost love of my life is the one holding it. I try to squeeze it back. I barely can, my hand is so weak. "You need to go to the hospital," he tells me. I see the concern etched all over his face.

"No ambulance. Too expensive," I say.

Melissa's hot pink blur comes into view next to me. "The fuck does that matter, Dez? You need to get thoroughly checked out."

"I'm fine," I insist.

Taven reaches for his keys, then slips his arms under my back and legs and lifts me up. "You're going. I'll drive." A group of other guys starts to protest, his friends, I assume. Taven yells at them and tells them if they wanna stay through the storm, it's their funeral.

We leave the medical tent. I tighten my grip around Taven's neck, rubbing my cheek against his jacket. Melissa trots along beside us.

I've never been happier to be jostling through the rain in someone's arms, heading for the grim fluorescent lights of a hospital building.

three

. . .

Curious

Seventeen years ago

desiree

thirteen years old

THE PLACE WAS an overcrowded and unbearably hot concert arena. I ran my tongue over my braces, a nervous habit of mine, and shuffled alongside my parents and older brother. Music thumped in the distance as we made our way through the lobby toward the usher, who paused momentarily to reply to the voice that crackled on her walkie-talkie, before scanning tickets and telling my parents how to navigate to our seats.

We shuffled in down our row, me apologizing with every bump and collide to the attendees already in their seats. The thick air enveloped me in suffocation, the smell of booze polluting the innocence of my adolescent pores. The opening band was still playing, the check-in lady had explained. It was nothing I recognized. I remember being surprised by the small size of the venue. I expected something much larger, more like the massive stadiums I had seen on concerts on TV. The main band we were seeing tonight was on the rise, apparently. I hoped their music would be good. Soulful and emotional poetry to speak to my melancholy spirit, with any luck. I could get on board with that.

I was conjuring hopes of a Fiona Apple-type sound to come, fighting my real wishes of being home and curled up in bed with a book. Had I known what lay ahead of me, I'm sure I would have been more excited. Had I known I'd be starting a new friendship with a boy—our not-so-coincidental meeting about to happen at that concert—I might have worked a little harder to pull a brush through my hopelessly lifeless blonde hair. But I didn't know that yet, and so I followed along with my family and tried to ignore my flared anxiety at the chaotic setting.

Why was my meeting with the new boy not-coincidental? I'll get to that soon.

I saw him—my soon-to-be crush—immediately. You know how it is when you're a kid, surrounded by grown-ups. There's an eagle eye you acquire for anyone else your age, even if you're far too shy to ever utter a word to them. My eyes found him. He looked to be the only other kid there, which made me feel not so out of place.

And a boy, no less.

I immediately wondered if I had the dreaded food particle stuck in my braces, if my hair was a frizzy mess, and if my outfit made me look as frumpy as I felt in that moment. It's like I was auditioning for the part of Apple of His Eye, yet he didn't even know I existed.

As I'm sure you've gathered, I had been dragged to this concert unwillingly. So when I saw him—Taven Carlisle—I was not exactly in the best of moods. Yet my little crush on him was instantaneous. He was cute, he looked to be about my age. My interest began as soon as I laid eyes on him, the pull of intense infatuation, accompanied by a flutter in my belly.

The objects of our crushes always start out being perfect in our minds, don't they? It's all curious intrigue, and you imagine them to be charming and funny and everything you're not, even though chances are they're just as ridiculously awkward as you. But we love to put our crushes on a pedestal.

If to crush is to compress, (or if you want to get technical with it—subdue to the point of distortion), then yeah, that kind of thing tracks. The rock-bottom moments of my Taven Carlisle crush distorted me and sent me into a tailspin of self-deprecating thoughts I'm rather embarrassed to admit.

Just you wait.

The problem with me and Taven was always timing. That, and—in the early days with us—my own insecurities of the gangly limbs attached to the straightness of my thirteen-year-old frame.

But the other big problem with me and Taven was something far worse.

Our parents.

EARLIER THAT EVENING, I HAD been snuggled up beneath the comforts of my blankets, ready to go to sleep. My parents, dressed to the nines, had sailed into my room, beaming.

Mom was already in placate-and-strike mode. "You'll love the music, Desiree. Trust us." I pretended not to see the tiny pill she popped into her mouth, swallowed dry. Her cloud of perfume wasn't doing enough to mask the stale smoke clinging to the fabric of her dress. I loved my mom, but my annoyance with her that evening was making it hard to see the best sides of her. We can do that sometimes with the people we love. See all the flaws as if we need to prove to ourselves that our discontent with them is warranted.

My mom could sometimes look like a washed-up Barbie, which always worried me. Too much Botox, not enough meat on her bones, that kind of thing. My dad, on the other hand, was always very polished and poised. A good-looking man, I could objectively see that. They were a passionate pair, and I often felt like they were a puzzle I couldn't quite make out. All smiles and ambition, but even as a child, I could sense some underlying turbulence.

They had natural vitality, though. My big brother did, too, which left me as the odd one out, lost in the shadows of the family in all my introverted awkwardness. I liked to think of myself as beautifully misunderstood and underestimated. The exquisiteness in the tragedy of adolescent thoughts, in full force.

My dad approached my bed and I turned my head to avoid the stench of whiskey on his breath. He pulled my arm and hoisted me out of my cocoon. "Up you go, don't give me that look."

"It's a school night," I argued.

Dad gave me his signature tinny grin and waved me off. "School? What school? It's just eighth grade, live a little."

Begrudgingly, I quickly dressed and tagged along with them. Followed them into the concert, feeling more like a rag doll being carelessly dragged into bright, bouncing chaos than a willing participant with her own thoughts and opinions.

My brother Dylan came with us, thankfully. An ally in all the madness. I had no doubt that my parents had made us both join them so that Dylan could drive. Which meant my parents could imbibe without caution. Since my father's business venture—medi-spa clinics—had recently taken off, my parents had apparently decided they had too much to lose and risking a DUI was not on the menu. I always hated when they would drink and drive, and I'd be in the back seat, gripping the handle of the car door, praying we'd make it home safely. I never had the guts to protest or express my concerns to them, though. At least now my parents were more careful.

But once at the concert and having spotted the cute boy just one row ahead, I settled into my seat, a spark of hope filling me that maybe tonight wouldn't be so bad after all. The crowd was swaying to the music, and I looked at Dylan, then over his shoulder and to my parents. They were loose-limbed and laughing as my father remained standing, pulling my mother up just as soon as she sat down and prompting her to twirl in a spin.

Their candor unsettled me. I didn't know my parents to be music lovers, but since our lives had recently changed, money now raining down on us in copious amounts, there had been a lot of new "loves" they'd dumped into our world with promises to my brother and me that we would love too.

Let's see, there was the new home we'd moved into that summer—away from all my old friends.

"You'll love it, just wait," my father had promised.

I found the mini-mansion to be cold and loud, every noise echoing off the cavernous walls.

There was the new school I'd be attending—the very next day, in fact. A private one, meaning my old comforts and familiar routines were now obliterated. I pictured plaid and permanently turned up noses, a Rory Gilmore experience in my future.

There were the new earrings my brother Dylan had allegedly given me for my birthday, accompanied by my mother gushing at how beautiful and thoughtful that was. (Later, after the birthday celebrations had wound down, Dylan gave me his real gift, almost apologetically. An enticing box set of special editions from my favorite fantasy author. I could always count on him to know what I *actually* loved.)

Now, it was this band we were seeing.

The concert was the next thing we just *had* to do, we'd surely love it. My brother and I just *had* to attend it with my parents. We *had* to look our best, we *had* to be sure we were seen, the sturdy Hatson family of four, on the scene.

Had to, had to, had to.

Crowds were never my thing, but I was determined to be a good daughter and play along. I would try, for my parents. What choice did I really have? I was a kid; autonomy was beyond my reach.

My father firmly believed in two things—working hard, and meeting the right people. "That right there is the key, ladies and gentleman," my father would say, a glimmer in his eye. "It's the ladder climbing, the zip code jumping. You'll learn soon enough."

His eyes would widen in calculating wonder, as if he had unlocked the secret to everything.

———

THE FRENETIC SWIRL OF STAGE lights popped around us in flashes, filling the darkness in perfectly timed spurts. I fought a yawn and looked at Dylan. "How long do you think this will be?"

"*What?!*" He looked down at me with a bemused laugh.

I cleared my throat and tried to match the noise level. "*How long?!*" I swirled my finger around us. "*This?! Tonight?!*" I was met with a shrug and Dylan's large palm patting my head.

I dropped my shoulders in resignation, my eyes scanning the crowd again, trying to be casual as I landed my gaze on the cute boy, my temporary crush for the night. I couldn't help but study him. He had this little curve in his ear and was wearing a black t-shirt with something printed on the front, though I couldn't make out if it was the band name or what. There was no one else with him, but he was definitely a kid like me. Where were his parents? I pulled my eyes away, willing myself not to stare.

I glanced up at Dylan, and couldn't help but laugh at his permanent slight smile. He was just as lost in the sound of twangy strings as my parents were, swaying slightly and nodding his head in rhythm to the drum beats. He shot his eyes down to me, and he threw me a wink, then leaned down to speak into my ear so he could be heard over the deafening noise. "Relax, Little Dez! Try and have some fun!"

"I am!" I insisted. I tried to slip in a smile in return.

He wrapped an arm around my shoulders, and I instinctively glanced back over to the kid, wondering if he at all noticed me. He was looking at the stage, drumming his fingers on his leg, oblivious to anyone around him. It made me wonder how often he went to concerts and what kind of music he liked.

Dylan gave me a slight squeeze. "Good! And tomorrow's going to be fine, don't worry about it!"

"Aren't *you* worried?" I shouted back. Switching schools in middle school was one thing, but for Dylan, it had to be worse. He was getting ready to start his senior year of high school.

He turned his eyes straight ahead, then pulled away from me and crossed his arms over his chest, expression now forlorn. "Nah," is what I think he said, but I couldn't really hear him anymore. I studied him, already knowing what he was thinking. *One more year and I'm out of here*. He'd play football, showcase his talents at his new and smaller school, then be swept away to college. I dreaded thinking about it.

My eyes wandered back to the cute boy, and I watched as who I assumed to be his parents finally made their way down the narrow space between seats and towards him, drinks in hand.

His father was sliding past the other people in the row, stern-faced and silent as people rose around him to allow him to pass. His mother, a tall and sturdy woman with dark hair like her son's, was dressed like she had just walked out of court. She had on a button-down shirt dress nipped at the waist, with a stylish suit jacket draped over her shoulders. She stopped just short of reaching the object of my imaginary affection, her face twisting to what I think was supposed to be a smile. She turned to face behind her, grinning now at—

My mother.

That's when it dawned on me.

So that's why we were here, for these people, whoever they were. The mom passed her drink to her husband, then turned back to my beaming mother. The two women air-kissed, then attempted an awkward hug over the row of seats. I strained to listen to them, but I only caught about every other word of their exchange.

"Here...looking for you....so great!..." a bubbling of laughter, my mom doing that signature hair adjusting that she does. She pointed a finger in my direction. *"Daughter...Dezzie....same age... Taven!"* Her attention shifted to my crush.

"Wonderful....soon!" the other woman exclaimed. More laughter. The men were on the other side of their wives, so I had to lean forward to see them, but it was all more of the same.

I looked back at the cute boy, who now had a name—Taven. He was looking at me and smiling. *"Hey,"* he said to me in a similar shout that seemed to be the necessary tone of the evening, accompanied by a small wave.

My heart thudded. His parents knew my parents. This wouldn't just be a one-time meeting where I could longingly gaze at the adorable boy in front of me, never to be seen again.

This was someone I'd have to get to know. Someone who would see my insecurities. Someone I could fantasize about on a regular basis. It meant I was entering official crush territory. Phase one: intrigue.

I smiled back at Taven and hoped to God it looked sweet, and not lopsided as I tucked my lips around my teeth to hide my braces.

It was hard to see much, you really only got quick flashes of red whenever the maniacally moving lights landed on something. But from what I could tell, Taven had friendly eyes. His face revealed the slight awkward spray of pimples that mirrored mine, which made me feel better. He was still in that boyish phase right before the transformation of several inches of height and a deepening voice. You know how it is at that age, the guys surrounding you are all either still boys, or suddenly looking far too much like men, which would leave me a stammering fool when forced to talk to them.

Instinctually, I glanced over to my parents, then back to Taven. That's when his small smile turned to a full grin, and he rolled his eyes. I loved that eye roll. It said to me all kinds of things about our joint discontent, like we were in on something together. He pointed a finger in my parents' direction, said, "*Your mom and dad?*" as he raised an eyebrow.

My cheeks flamed as I mutely nodded. I glanced up at Dylan just in time to see him shaking hands with Taven's dad.

I looked back at Taven. "*Same,*" he said, shrugging a shoulder in understanding, perhaps. "*You're Desiree, right?*" He knew my name. That felt wonderfully exciting, yet terrifying at the same time. What had he been told about me? And by whom?

I gave another silent and slightly stunned nod. He put his hands in his pockets and looked down at the floor, probably bored to tears with me, wondering if I had any verbal communication skills. When he looked back up he said, "*Have fun,*" and then returned his attention straight ahead. I cursed my awkwardness at not having been able to utter a single word to him in return.

A few minutes passed, all with me in a personal battle with my eyes as they wandered every two point five seconds toward Taven. I was thankful his back was to me so I could admire his profile without notice, enjoy the swoop of his dark hair, cut short at the sides with a small wave at the top. His hair looked far too perfect for a boy our age.

The glow of his phone screen caught my eye, and I chanced a peek at it. It was one of those fancy new iPhones, a small tablet right in the palm of his hand.

I tried my hardest to be subtle as I watched him, the glow a beckoning call to me. I itched to know who he was talking to in the clear bubble stream of text exchanges.

I watched as Taven's fingers typed furiously away, wondering what he was writing, who he was writing to, fantasizing he would type that frantically to *me*, that I could be the one to receive such fervent attention. I had only just gotten my cell phone (one of the few perks of our new lifestyle), and would take far too long to text people, overthinking my responses to the point of setting the phone down and walking away.

But there he sat, just ahead of me and taunting me with his presence. I watched his shoulders bounce with a chuckle at whatever was happening on his screen. Then he exited out and a Lock Screen popped up. It was a photo of him, his boyish arm draped awkwardly around a beautiful girl.

four

Wonder

Seventeen years ago

desiree

thirteen years old

TURNS OUT THAT Taven had a girlfriend, if you could even call it that at that age. Evelyn was her name. She was a pretty redhead that seemed to have a permanent place in Taven's young heart, and in his phone by way of countless photos and selfies.

We attended different schools, Taven and I, but in the early weeks of eighth grade, our parents had thrown us together as a consequence of their newfound business partnership. My parents were money-driven entrepreneurs, through and through. They had a handful of medi-spa clinics, and Taven's parents were some sort of investors with an empire of their own.

My mother, of course, was the one to explain to me the significance of this partnership. "Your father made an excellent contact with the Carlisles, Dezzie. The Carlisles are worth millions, maybe more."

We'd been shopping for clothes, which no longer meant scouring through racks under unflattering fluorescent lights. Now, shopping with my mother meant sitting with champagne on a pink velvet sofa under soft lighting that made her look ten years younger as overly friendly sales assistants brought us armfuls of garments, each softer and shinier than the last.

I stepped out of the dressing room in yet another tiny dress, this a deep espresso with a subtle iridescence. It barely covered my butt. "So?" I asked.

My mother grinned. "A bit short, but I love it."

I rolled my eyes. "No, I mean why is the Carlisle's bank account something I should think about?" I looked in the mirror, noting with some bloom of hope that the dress did in fact give me a little shape. "I don't care about money."

My mom sighed and stood before me, smoothing down the flyaways of my hair before examining the sight of me in the mirror. "That's easy to say at your age."

I nodded, a feeling of guilt creeping in. I didn't want to seem ungrateful. I just didn't understand what she was getting at.

"Look, Dezzie," my mother said, spinning me by the shoulders to face her. I saw something in her blue eyes. Sadness, perhaps. "It just means that the Carlisles are people to keep close to us. You'll be seeing a lot more of them. It's for the business, sweetie."

"Right."

"You know," she said, her eyes shining with an idea. I already dreaded what that might be. "You don't have a date for your dance."

I stepped backward. "It's not that kind of dance, Mom."

She waved my explanation away. "I was thinking maybe you could ask Taven."

"He has a girlfriend," I admitted, despite the pain it caused to say it out loud.

She let out a sharp laugh as she looked past me to admire herself in the mirror. "He's thirteen. It's not a girlfriend."

"Actually, he's fourteen," I argued.

That caught her interest. She raised an eyebrow at me, then turned me around to face the mirror. "So you guys have been talking?" I watched in the reflection as the corners of her mouth lifted. She nodded. "Good, that's good. Just be careful. We can't have any adolescent drama, you understand that, right?"

I nodded and fought the urge to confess that she didn't need to worry, because Taven and I hadn't really been talking. I just paid attention to things. Overheard Taven's mom share a few vital tidbits about her son that I clung to, as if knowing about him would make me closer to him.

I turned away from the mirror and faced my mother, an older version of myself with her pale hair and eyes. "I like this one," I conceded. "I think I'll take it."

"Perfect," she agreed.

My mom, against my will, would later ask Taven's mom, Lynda, if he was available to accompany me to my dance. Turns out he was busy. I ended up not even going, being the new girl and having no real friends to speak of, much to my parents' dismay. The espresso dress hung abandoned in my closet, tags swaying like dropped flags at half-mast.

***

OUR WEEKENDS WITH THE CARLISLES quickly became a regular thing. It was sailing on the Carlisle yacht, an introduction to their fancy club, followed by lazy dinners of champagne (for the adults), and sparkling water for the kids (yuck, though I would politely pretend I loved it. By the end of September, when tired and parched from the sun ripping the moisture right out of my skin, my brain learned to associate the tingle of bubbles with reprieve from dehydration).

I used the forced social occasions as an opportunity to stare shamelessly at the beautiful boy that was Taven Carlisle. He would attempt to talk to me, but I could barely utter a cohesive sentence to him. I could probably count the number of words I actually spoke to him out loud, but it didn't matter. Being in his presence felt like enough. I was happy just listening to him, or watching him interact with other people, allowing myself to daydream and wonder what being in his inner circle might feel like.

We slipped into the cooler weather of fall, and on Halloween, my parents insisted that we get dolled up in coordinating family costumes. (Dylan, with his quick new group of friends, was not required to attend.) My mother was all extravagance in a faux fur coat accompanied by a slim black cigarette holder, dressed as Cruella de Vil. My father was her henchman wearing a newsboy hat, and I was dressed as a "cute" Dalmatian. I know, awful, right? We attended the famous Carlisle costume party, and Taven had grabbed my arm to pull me away and slip us up to his room (his own apartment, really). His touch felt like a gift.

I cautiously stepped in, looking down at my white polka-dot tights, the matching micro tutu and bodysuit, feeling like an idiot.

Taven wore a grim reaper costume, and he pulled down his hood and settled his scythe next to the door before closing it.

I took in the sight around me. The queen-sized sleigh bed, the dark gray walls, the mini-living room area with a futon, bean bag chairs facing a massive TV.

"Cute costume, by the way," he said, his eyes scanning me up and down.

My cheeks heated and I ripped the puppy ears headband off my head, tossing it on his bed. "Thanks."

"Just...make yourself comfortable. Have a seat."

"Okay."

"Guessing you didn't really wanna hang out down there, right?"

I glanced up at him through my tinsel faux lashes. He was grinning at me and my stomach did a flip. I was nervous in his presence, and his smile wasn't helping. "Not really."

Taven nodded and plopped himself on a bean bag. "Didn't think so. You like Gears of War?"

"Sure," I lied. It was a video game I knew, but had only ever played it a couple times with Dylan. I internally committed to making it my new favorite game.

We played in silence for a while, him wrestling with his controller, me slipping off my shoes and sitting cross-legged in the other bean bag, getting more and more into the graphic action of the game and feeling less sweaty-palmed and anxious. I was grateful for the distraction, and to finally have a chance alone with Taven, not under the watchful eyes of our parents where I felt permanently stuck in the role of baby of the family. Maybe here now, I could just be me. I could create a dazzling display of the fabulous cool girl I desperately wanted to be.

At some point, he paused the game, the screen frozen in a frenzy of pixelated action. He typed something into his phone, and the next thing you know a suited staff member came knocking on the bedroom door, a silver tray of snacks in his gloved palms. I half expected to hear "Master Carlisle" escape the guy's mouth, but I was relieved when he gave a quick nod, saying, "Your requested snacks, Taven." The man nodded toward me. "Desiree Hatson, right?"

I nodded and said, "Hi," confused how he knew my name.

Taven grabbed the tray from the man. "Desiree, this is Alfred."

"Alfred?"

Taven chuckled. "Kidding."

"Oh," was all I said.

Taven placed the tray down, explaining, "It's a Batman reference. Alfred the butler?"

Not-Alfred shook his head, smiling. "You think you're so funny. I'm Mike," he said, turning to me. "I work for the Carlisles."

I nodded, hopelessly confused and wishing I could think of something funny to say in return. Instead, I settled on, "Oh, okay. It's...it's nice to meet you, Mike." Was I supposed to shake his hand? Is that the thing to do with the help? I had no idea.

Mike gave me a mock salute. "Anything you need when you're here, just say the word." Then he turned on his heels and disappeared through the doorway, pulling the door closed behind him with a click.

Taven and I settled back down onto our beanbags, the coffee table in front of us serving as our dining spot. He handed me a small plate, piling it with some kind of spring rolls and sauce. I hesitated before taking it. I dreaded the idea of eating in front of him and making a fool of myself, but I told myself to get over it.

"There you have it," he said, shoving half a spring roll in his mouth and grinning, looking adorable. "Guess you're part of the family now."

<hr>

Taven and I eventually settled into an easy rhythm whenever there were gatherings at the Carlisle Manor, as I had come to call it. If it wasn't video games, then we'd talk about movies or books, or hang out with a couple of his other friends he was allowed to invite over. On nights when the universe wanted to remind me that Taven's heart belonged to someone else, I'd get to pop in and say hi to the famous Evelyn, mystery girl, as I listened to him talk to her on video chats. She seemed sweet and a little quiet, a shinier and prettier version of me, but I guess she went to some boarding school and they didn't get to see each other all that often.

Yes, her being geographically far away absolutely made me happy.

My crush on Taven pretty quickly catapulted itself into the depths of obsession. I was a goner.

As a crush develops, you get to that point of deciding you *need* to make this work, make him truly see you. If to crush means to compress, then a developing crush means squeezing the hell out of any opportunity to get to know as much as possible about the person.

I was obsessed with this mission. I loved when he shared little reveals with me, like how his parents grounded him for playing video games past 8pm and how annoyed he was with them. I'd roll my eyes in joint frustration, as if my parents were just as strict, even though they definitely were not. I needed to know what Taven Carlisle liked, what made him angry, what he found funny. It was like I was stocking up my own personal filing cabinet in my brain of all the information on him that I could, convinced that if I could just crack this code and get to know him in and out, then I'd be able to morph into exactly what he wanted. He'd magically realize that his dream girl—me! —was sitting right here in front of him. I could then ensure that any time we hung out, I checked every box of perfection so that I'd leave his room and he'd instantly be filled with regret, and he would, beyond his control, run after me, take me in his arms and demand to know where I had been all his life.

When you set your mind to something, it's pretty difficult to turn it off, no matter how badly you want to. No matter how badly you wish you could quell your ridiculous obsession, and just enjoy your time with him as it was.

That's not how it happened for me.

Instead, it was me stealing glances at him whenever I could, his permanently immaculate haircut sending me spiraling in a sea of admiration. I'd quickly look away whenever he caught me. Rather than have the initial pull of my crush subside as I got to know Taven better, got to see him as more of a three-dimensional human being with flaws, I instead found that my adoration for him only grew stronger. I found the messiness of his room fabulously laid back. Found the way he loudly barked out a laugh at movie lines—some barely even funny—adorably positive.

Sometimes his older sister, Jacqui, would join us, and watching the two of them made me like him even more. She was older than us by two years, but as Taven's body was rapidly morphing, he was already a couple inches taller than her. He had a clear protective nature when it came to his sister, calling the guy she was dumped by a "dick" and offering to kick his ass if she wanted him to. Or if she rushed into his bedroom, needing anything whatsoever, help with finding something or an opinion on an outfit, he'd happily oblige. His brotherly nature was not combative like some siblings can be, but more like the way Dylan was toward me. I'd often have to remind myself that Taven was the younger sibling, not the other way around.

I liked his sister. Jacqui was bubbly and quirky, and had matching dark hair, like her brother's, but with caramel streaks. At sixteen, her body was already a womanly figure, something I envied, but she didn't seem to know her own beauty. It made me less intimidated, which was good because I was committed to being her friend too, making sure I was extra sweet with her, exaggerating my own interest in anything she had to say just as another way to get in closer. Taven was going to see how wonderful I was, it was just a matter of time, I told myself. I wanted it so badly it hurt.

He was easy to talk to. He knew how to side-step my awkwardness, even succeeding in pulling me more and more out of my shell. He'd share with me his struggles with school, the pressures put on by his parents, and I'd feel like I won the lottery to be on the receiving end of his confessions.

Then I'd go home and cry into my journal, begging God to tell me why I had to be born so horribly plain. Why couldn't I be pretty and perfect and sweet like Evelyn, some phantom I had never even met in real life. I was convinced Taven was only nice to me out of necessity, thanks to our parents.

Soon came the holidays, all spent together. The Hatsons and the Carlisles, taking over the world one business conversation masked as friendship at a time.

THE NEW YEAR CELEBRATION WAS when I knew I was really in trouble.

Some people make New Year resolutions. You know, eat less candy, be better about doing assignments on time, that kind of thing.

Taven had bigger ideas.

We were in his sister's car when the concept was drummed up. Apparently at the Carlisle Manor, some guest wanted some particular kind of alcohol, and one of Taven's older cousins was doing the pickup. Jacqui and her best friend had quietly excused themselves to tag along, eager to get out of the house for a minute. I was surprised when Mr. and Mrs. Carlisle didn't object, but I guess when the champagne is flowing, our usual moral codes drop down a notch or two.

Jacqui insisted that Taven and I join as well, and I fought my nerves as the five of us squeezed into her BMW, with me in the back seat, pinched between Jacqui's liquored-up, giggling friend and Taven. It was dark out, and with limited sense of sight, I felt a heightened sense of smell. All I could focus on was the sweetness of a fruity scent—Jacqui's friend's perfume was nauseating.

I shifted closer to Taven, turning his way and grasping for a whiff of whatever cologne he had on.

When we pulled into the liquor store, Jacqui, her friend, and the cousin jumped out, instructing Taven and me to stay in the car. I was relieved, scared that if I went in, they'd offer me a lollipop at checkout.

The car was still jostling from the doors slamming shut when Taven turned to me. "Is it just me, or was her perfume about to make you throw up?"

I laughed with relief. "Oh my God, yes! Why do you think I was leaning to your side?"

He patted my leg, and I wished I didn't have the added layers of my pea coat and sparkly nude tights in between his hand and my skin. "I just thought you wanted to get closer to me."

"Ew, you're so gross," I said, instantly regretting sounding so juvenile.

"Ouch, Dez. That hurts."

"Don't you have a girlfriend? You shouldn't talk like that." I pulled my lip between my teeth, proud for not flirting in return, but also knowing full well it was only because I had no skill in the art in the first place. I was almost fourteen, but still felt worlds away from being old enough to charm any guy with cute flirtation.

He pulled his hand back from my leg. "Evelyn's in California, visiting family while on her break, remember?"

I nodded, then shifted uncomfortably in my seat. I looked around at the red leather of Jacqui's car, wondering what kind of car Taven would opt for when he would be gifted one just before his sixteenth birthday.

He snapped his fingers, startling me. "I have an idea."

"I'm all ears," I said. "And a little worry."

He grinned down at me, I could just make it out in the glow from the shopping center lights. He was dressed up in a suit beneath his coat, and all evening I had been staring at him in disbelief at how *grown-up* he looked. I was wearing the short espresso dress that had been abandoned from the dance I never attended, a gold bolero over top, and I had felt pretty while I was getting ready. But seeing him in his suit made me feel painfully like a little kid. I hoped my glow-up would arrive any day now.

"When we get back to the house, we're going to come up with Bingo cards for goals we have for the New Year."

"Bingo cards?" My mind whirled to rows of old people in a nursing home, and a guy in a top hat sitting at the front with one of those number spinner things.

"Yeah. Fun ones. We'll fill them in, and as the year goes on and you get five in a row, you get prizes."

"What are the prizes?"

He shifted in his seat and draped his arm on the doorframe, looking at me with a grin. "Anything we want. But here's the catch."

"Oh boy."

"No, listen. It's really good."

"I'm sure it's great."

He twisted around again, facing forward. Patted my leg once more. "I fill in yours, and you can fill in mine."

Liquor obtained and back in the safe confines of his room (though with two mini shot bottles of Fireball, given to us by Jacqui), we settled in our beanbags and got to work. Taven downed his Fireball and set out two sheets of paper, lining up a ruler and drawing out straight lines. I watched him curiously, wondering if he ever drank anything before, but I was too shy to ask.

I took the tiniest taste of my drink, surprised at the sweet cinnamon. "It's like eating a red-hot."

"You've barely even touched it, how would you know?" he teased.

"I can't drink this, Vin. I'll be…" I couldn't even say the word.

"Drunk?" he offered.

"Yes!"

He shoved yet another tray full of snacks towards me, this time mini crab cakes and some sort of pastry. "Eat and you'll be fine. Never drink on an empty stomach."

I grabbed a crab cake and let the salty flakes crumble in my mouth, scared of what my miniscule sip might do. I already felt warm, though I knew that was absurd.

He handed me one of his freshly made Bingo cards and a pen, and told me to have at it, not to hold back. I looked down at it, this giant black grid and its crooked star right in the middle. He had written "Taven's New Year Bingo Card" across the top, which made me smile. It seemed boyish somehow.

I went to work scribbling away the most ridiculous things I could think of. "Sky-Dive" and "Go Streaking" and "Steal a Piece of your Mom's Jewelry—see how long she takes to notice." I was itching to be as creative as possible, but filling out twenty-four squares proved harder than I thought it'd be.

When we finally finished, we traded papers. I looked down at mine and started laughing. "Finish my Fireball?" I squeaked. "I could do that right now." I took another sip, almost finishing the bottle, then instantly washed it down with several gulps from my sparkling water, delivered in a champagne flute upon our arrival.

"Cheater," he said with a kick to my foot.

I drained the rest of it and slammed the mini bottle down, crossing off my square. There. I scanned the rest of the sheet and noted his recommendations. Some were funny (Eat So Many Marshmallows You Throw Up, Barge in on Dylan and His Girlfriend, Fail a Test on Purpose). Others kind of made me sad

(Make a New Friend, Say "no" to Your Parents—with attitude. Sneak Out of the House).

When we both realized we had "Go Streaking" on our cards, we laughed and made up some elaborate scheme on how and when to do it, knowing full well I'd never in a million years go along with the plan.

There was one square in particular on my card that had my mind spinning, obsessing over why he wrote it. "Share a secret." Could it be an invitation for me to admit my crush? Was that the thought behind it? I glided my finger along the square, heart thumping as I wondered if I should say something.

"What's on your mind, Dez?" I looked up to find him staring at me, grinning. "Got any good secrets?"

I studied his face, feeling like I was staring for too long but unable to look away. He wiggled his eyebrows at me and in that moment, I knew he was teasing me. Taunting me, even. Yet I wanted to share my secret with him, even so. Even with the rejection I knew I'd get. Sometimes our hearts like to betray us like that, humiliate us all in the name of clinging to false hope.

I pulled my eyes away from him, back down to my paper, and shook my head no.

TAVEN AND I CONTINUED WITH good old-fashioned mischief that night, and it was the most fun I think I'd ever had. We snuck sips of bubbly when no one was looking, then dared each other to stand outside in the cold without jackets on for as long as we could, laughing as the clouds of our breath puffed around us. I was a ball of jittery shivers, yet my young little heart was feeling warm and flushed. I was spending time with Taven in a way that felt natural and fun. I told myself that could be enough.

When we made our way back to the party, everyone was

counting down with the host on TV as the ball made its descent in Times Square. We shuffled our way to a corner off to the side, adults around us towering above, but I felt safe with Taven beside me. I looked up at him and we locked eyes, giggling and a little buzzy. He mouthed out each number in the countdown, and I was mesmerized watching his lips.

Four

Three

Two…

For a moment I thought he might kiss me.

One

But that was ridiculous. Of course he wouldn't.

I was his accidental friend, I reminded myself. Forced upon him thanks to our parents. Yet he kept his gaze on me.

When I finally couldn't stand the eye contact anymore, I burst into a full belly laugh, shoving his shoulder, asking him why he was looking at me all creepy like.

His lips found my cheek, and he held them there for an agonizing yet glorious moment. They were damp with champagne, yet soft and warm and sent a vibration humming through me and a flutter in my belly. "Happy New Year, Desiree Hatson," he said as he pulled back. Something passed over his expression, and I had the urge to kiss him back, but I didn't.

"Happy New Year, Taven Carlisle."

I KNOW HE KNEW I liked him. Even *I* could see how obvious I was, but I couldn't help it.

Over the course of the rest of eighth grade, Taven sprouted a thousand inches, his chest and shoulders broadening out, and I couldn't help but fantasize about what kissing him would be like. But we remained firmly friends, nothing more.

When we weren't thrown together at some party, we'd text

all the time, about anything and everything. He'd teach me dirty words and I'd blush on the other end of the line. We played online video games together. He had become my best friend, though I tried to remind myself that it was one-sided.

I would come to regret our sharing the day Taven revealed to me that his stupid relationship with Evelyn had leveled up.

We were sitting in his bedroom, it was late May. He had already finished school, and I only had a handful of days left. Our parents had decided to run out for a drink and leave us behind, my mom singing out, "Don't get into anything naughty, you two!" I could have killed her.

Taven looked at me, eyes shining with excitement. "I kissed Evelyn, Dez. I finally did it," he grinned.

I arched an eyebrow his way. "Oh, yeah?"

"Yeah. Not the little kisses. This was like, the real thing. Full on make-out."

"Ew. I did not need to hear that." He had the courtesy to blush a little, at least. My mind whipped to an image of him cradling his girlfriend in his lap, sucking face like two lovebirds. I thought I might be sick.

I repositioned myself into my usual spot in the velvet beanbag chair, perched beside him as he sat on his futon, and I feigned excitement for him. "So you finally got the guts, huh? Took you long enough."

He nodded, a swoosh of his dark hair flopping into his face. "Whatever. We hardly ever get to see each other. I'm so happy school's done, this summer's gonna be awesome."

I nodded in return, not sure how to respond. But I was curious, I had to know. "How was the kiss? How...how did it happen?" I looked down at my phone, hoping I came across as not really interested, just a friend trying to be polite. My ears felt hot and I felt suspiciously on the verge of tears.

He stretched out his legs, clasping his hands behind his head as he stared up at the ceiling, a stupid smile on his dreamy face. "It was at her graduation party."

"Graduation from eighth grade?" I confirmed, willing my eyes to not linger too long on him. I looked back down at my phone. Scrolled through some nail polish colors. Coral, that could be nice. Right? Nice to look cute and girly and remind Taven *I'm right here.*

"No, from law school," he said, grinning down at me. I must have looked confused because he quickly added, "Kidding, Dez. Yes, from eighth grade. Some parents get really into it. Mine don't, but some do. Haven't you gotten any invites from kids at your school?"

That would be a no. I didn't really have any true friends at my school, being the new girl and all. Which, by now, I guess I couldn't really say that, could I? But I still felt it. My fancy private school had some long lines of bonds very firmly rooted, and I preferred to keep to myself. No one there understood me, I told myself. I wasn't like them. So when my mother had suggested a graduation party for me, I had balked, knowing it would be more for my parents as an excuse to show off. Luckily, she had settled on throwing a Memorial Day bash instead.

"Kids at my school don't really do that kind of thing," I lied. Taven knew it was a lie, friendships from both our private schools overlapped, but he let me take the out.

"Well, anyway. It was amazing, and you're the only person I can talk to about it."

"Me? Why?" I twisted the fabric of my t-shirt between my fingers, both thrilled and surprised to hear him say that.

"'Cuz you're a girl. I can't be an ass and talk to the guys about that kind of thing. You know, out of respect for Evelyn."

I rolled my eyes. "Lies. You mean because all your friends already think you've been doing way more than that for a while now, and you can't blow your cover." I may not have had any tight bonds with anyone, but I wasn't deaf. I'd hung out with

Taven's friends multiple times by then. I overheard all kinds of things, I knew how dumb guys were, bragging about doing this and that. Up until now, I might have believed them, but hearing Taven's confession, I had a sneaking suspicion there were more fabricated stories floating around than I realized.

"Oh, shit. Fine, yeah," he conceded. He rose up to a sitting position, resting his forearms on his knees. "Sworn secrecy?" he asked, offering his hand to seal the deal. I nodded and reached for his outstretched hand to shake. "You're my best friend, you know. I hope you realize that, Dez."

I nodded and replied, "You too, Vin."

As quickly as the declaration came, though, it vanished.

Apparently kissing your girlfriend meant you had little time for anything else. With Evelyn back home for the summer, Taven would skip out on the famous Carlisle parties, and I'd be granted permission to sit them out too, staying home alone and curled up with a book. Eventually our text exchanges dwindled, his responses to me taking longer and longer to arrive, each one shorter than the last.

A month later, they stopped altogether.

five

. . .

Awe

Sixteen years ago

desiree

fourteen years old

IT WASN'T ALL bad.

Right around the time Taven was pulling away, quickly dissolving our "best friend" partnership, I gained a new friend.

Melissa Belle had been another recent arrival in school, blessedly replacing my new girl status about halfway through eighth grade. Rumors had been circulating about her. I ignored them all, always feeling a kind of sympathy for her.

The Poor Girl. That's what everyone said about her because she was there on a scholarship. I kept my mouth shut about the fact that not too long ago, by all their standards, I might have been considered the poor girl too.

I hadn't ever talked to her, really. Just a passing hi in the bathroom, maybe. She had emerald eyes and the kind of long dark curls I'd hopelessly battled my curling iron for. She also had excessive curves that you envied, maybe because she owned them. The guys loved her tits, popping out over the buttons of our white uniform blouses, and the girls just wanted to be able to fill out a dress like she could. They would never admit that out loud though, naturally. Thus, Melissa seemed to keep to herself, like me.

On the second to last day of school, with the classrooms all muggy and teen hormone levels teetering between grouchy and full-fledged volcanic, some boy called Melissa fat. Ironic considering the kid was a chubby ginger whose blemished cheeks could rival a Pollock painting.

I had just sat down at my desk, plenty of time before the bell even rang, and there were only two other kids in the room when Melissa walked in. "Hey, look. It's the fat girl," the one kid said to his friend, under his breath, but given how empty the room still was, it ended up being heard. Literally, though, that's what the little jerk said to her, I'm not even kidding. He couldn't even be creative about insulting her.

I watched the interaction from the safety of my seat in the back, hiding my prying eyes behind my upturned water bottle as I pretended to drink. Melissa had just walked by the kid's desk when the horrifically stupid jab was sling-shot to her. If I were her, I would have run to the bathroom and cried. Dumb, I know, but that's the truth.

But Melissa? She stopped in her tracks, put her books down on his desk. "What was that now?" she asked, face red and blotchy.

"Oh shit," said the kid's friend through a laugh.

"Uh," the insulter stammered. "You know, we...we have salads here."

"Right. Appreciate the tip," she said before pulling her fist back.

She punched him square in the face while I watched in

amazement, trying to decide if I should intervene or offer up a kick or something. Not like I'd have the guts to, but it was fun to imagine.

It was just the four of us in the classroom, no one else had filed in yet. Too embarrassed to admit he was hit by a girl, I don't think the kid ever told a soul.

That was Melissa. She could get away with that kind of thing. Still can. Badass bitch was a phrase I'm still convinced to this day was created with her in mind.

After the punch, she scanned the room, meeting my eyes, the question in them clear. Would I tell?

I placed my water bottle down in front of me, lifted my chin and smiled a closed-mouth grin at her.

The kid got up from his seat, covering the side of his face with his hand as if that could erase our knowledge of what just happened. He grabbed his things and scurried to the door, muttering, "Crazy bitch," under his breath.

Melissa sat down next to me, a waft of her perfume consuming me and adding to my awe.

"You're my hero," I sheepishly croaked out.

Melissa nodded once. "Good. Then that makes you my new best friend." Which is exactly what happened.

That, and the whole new girl crush that bloomed for me right then. It made Taven slipping through my fingers a whole lot less miserable.

"Take me to your fancy country club, my sweetheart." Melissa looped her arm into mine, causing the strap of my bag to slip off my shoulder. She replaced it with a light pat, then turned to face the building before us. Her eyes roamed over the stone facade as the rumble of my mom's engine faded away behind us.

"It's not that fancy," I argued.

You have to understand something about the Montgomery Windsor Country Club—it's for a certain kind of people. A kind that I didn't really understand at that point in my life, the summer before high school, but my green little mind sure did understand that it was about more than just money there. I just didn't know what.

I didn't want Melissa to feel uncomfortable. Truth be told, not even *I* felt totally comfortable at the place, though prior to today, I'd only ever come with my parents or brother. Maybe having a friend with me would help.

Melissa gave my arm a squeeze. "Girl, it's a members-only club with like, a bajillion dollar fee to even be able to *look* at the place. It's fancy. You have to wait on a list and get *sponsored* to even join."

I glanced over to her, the breeze catching the swirl of curls framing her face and making her look far more angelic than I knew she was, given her fist skills. "How do you know that?"

"Easy."

"Meaning?"

With a shrug she said, "I called and asked about how to join." She paused our steps, which was good because I was rather shocked to hear that last statement. I stared at her as she plucked a flower from the massive container plant perched beside the glass doors of the entrance, inhaling the spiky, fuchsia petals of the bloom appreciatively before placing it behind my ear. "There. Gorgeous."

I shook my head. "I can't believe you called the club." Call me crazy, but the idea of picking up the phone to call anyone was something I hated. Let alone being a naive fourteen-year-old and calling a very grown-up club like this. *I* would have been a stammering idiot. I had no doubt that wasn't the case for my new friend.

She shrugged. "Of course I did. I needed to know what I was up against."

"Right," I said as we continued toward the entrance.

We stepped in through the glass doors and the blast of air conditioning gave us reprieve from the July heat. The receptionist, Lacey, was smiling at us and darting her eyes to the flower in my hair. I panicked that she had seen the act of thievery and was going to scold us, even though Lacey was the only nice employee of the place.

Lacey beamed at me. "I love the look, Ms. Hatson."

"Ms. Hatson," Melissa gushed with dramatic flair. "See? Fancy."

I rolled my eyes. "Just call me Desiree. And...thanks," I bumbled. We stepped up closer to the marble-topped desk and I fished through my bag to find my card.

Lacey waved me off. "You're fine, Desiree. Do I really need to repeat myself? I know who you are, you don't have to show your card to me."

"I know, I know," I said, my cheeks flaming. "Everyone else always makes me show it. Sorry."

She ignored my unwarranted apology and looked at Melissa. "Bringing a guest today, I see?" she asked as she scooted a clipboard my way and I scribbled in Melissa's name.

"Not just any guest," Melissa crooned, as if Lacey the receptionist was about to hear big news. "I'm Melissa, Desiree's very best friend."

Lacey grinned. "That makes you a friend to me as well then. Here by yourselves?"

I pulled my shoulders back in an attempt to have as much confidence as possible. You weren't technically allowed to be unsupervised at the club until you were sixteen, but I knew other kids were dropped here all the time without their parents. It was the kind of crowd that liked shipping their kids off to boarding schools followed by summer camps, favoring part-time parenting a Norman Rockwell painting would know nothing about.

"Yup," I nodded. "My parents dropped us off, though they'll be back in a little bit," I rushed to add. It was a lie, they had some other plans, and Dylan would be picking us up, but I felt the need to keep Lacey out of trouble in case she was somehow blamed for letting us in.

Melissa looked at me quizzically, and I rushed through the rest of our Lacey interaction with eagerness, relieved when we successfully made it past her desk and through the paneled halls.

I glanced down at the paisley carpet, thinking that in some bizarre way, the club *smelled* like paisley, as if that could be a thing. Everything had a paisley theme around here. If it wasn't the pattern itself, it was the fancy way the bartender swirled bottles in the air before pouring your drink. It was the tear-drop pendants dripping from women's chains around their neck. I started to think of the place not as Montgomery Windsor, but as the Paisley Club.

I shared my thought with Melissa, turning it into a little rhyme. "The Paisley patrons, all swirling and boozy. Some trying to remain polished, others definite floozies."

She laughed, saying, "You're an odd duck, Dez. And I love it. You have all these random thoughts that make you a fabulous human."

I pulled my head back, surprised by the compliment. "Thank you?"

She frowned at me. "Don't put a question into that statement, there's nothing to question. Just say 'thank you' like you know you're amazing, because you are. You're the only girl from school that I actually like."

I loved her already. I aspired to be like her.

We walked through the double doors and across a stone terrace, and Melissa smiled at a bathing-suit clad toddler wearing swimmies bigger than him. A harried-looking young woman raced after him and passed us, whisper-yelling, "Wait up, where are you going? Get back here! Remember what your mother said about listening better to me!" The kid only giggled and ran faster.

"Well, he looks like a hellion," Melissa noted.

"Glad I'm not his nanny," I agreed.

When we made our way out to the pool area, Melissa immediately went into oooing and ahhhing at every opulent detail. "I think I found my new favorite place in the whole world."

There was a massive pool, flanked by hot tubs on high platforms. Meticulous container plants dotted every corner, perfect spills of vines creeping over the edges, skirting the tropical palms and accompanying rainbow blooms. A massive u-shaped bar stood to one side, half raised and sheltered under an awning, the other half sunken into the pool with underwater bar stools running parallel. There were waterfall fountains, a lazy river meandering throughout, cabanas and couches framed with gauzy white panels. In the distance were the greens of the golf course. The wives spent time here with their nannies and children, the husbands making their way back in waves, removing their golf gloves before bending down to kiss the cheeks of their bikini-clad women.

I remember the first time my parents had taken me to the club. Everyone had their own pools at home, I was sure, yet they all still hung out here. I thought that the whole club was more like a resort. I imagined that's exactly what Melissa was thinking now too.

I threw my bag down on a lounge chair, gesturing to Melissa to do the same. "Well, I'm glad we did this, then, if it's your new favorite place." It was my time of the month, and I hadn't mastered the art of tampons yet, so I hadn't really been thrilled with the game plan presented by my parents. But the look of excitement in Melissa's eyes had me happy we came.

That, and I knew I'd probably see Taven. Not that I ever really said much to him beyond a sheepish "Hi" in passing anymore, since he'd declared to me a few weeks ago that our friendship was making his girlfriend uncomfortable. Stupid Evelyn.

I had met her during the club's Hazy Days of Summer bash, the unofficial opening of the pool for the season, even though it had technically been open since Memorial Day.

"So you're the girl Taven always talks about," Evelyn had said, curt smile that relayed, *I hate that he talks about you*.

"Yup, this is my Dezzie," Taven had confirmed, then cleared his throat and lowered his voice. "She's like a sister to me."

Stab to the heart. "Sister" was about a million times worse than "friend zone."

And then later that evening, back at home, I got the text.

T: Evelyn doesn't like how much I talk to you.

D: Why? That's dumb.

T: I know, not like she has anything to worry about.

D: Of course not.

T: But I promised not to text you so much. To make her more comfortable. You understand, right?

D: Sure. Yeah, I get it.

What else could I say?

Since that awful declaration, when I was at the club, I'd hole myself away in a corner with a book, hoping to be invisible while Taven's parents and mine perched themselves by the poolside bar. Thankfully, my mom stopped pushing the me-and-Taven thing, I guess feeling confident that her "right people" friendship was securely in place.

But as beautifully as my comfort around Taven had grown, obsessions and all, it pretty quickly vanished after that declaration. In my mind, he had gone back to some mysterious place of intrigue, topped with a whole lot of "He doesn't want you, he chose her" insecurities. Snap, just like that, I was back to feeling unsure and uncomfortable around him, like every flaw I had was blasting through speakers at full volume. The connection I thought we had was apparently all in my head, and I felt like a fool.

Melissa snapped her fingers in front of my face. "Yo! Earth to Dez!" I looked down at the small table next to us and watched as she unloaded her bag with gummy bears and a Vogue magazine, setting up shop like she'd done this a million times before.

"Sorry, lost in thought."

"I can tell," she laughed. "You want some gummy bears?"

I shook my head and ran my tongue over the smoothness of my teeth, now braces free. My stomach was in knots, wondering if Taven would be here today and if he'd be curious about the new friend I had with me.

I scanned the area, looking for his signature swoop of hair. There were several women engaged in conversation as they occupied the chaise lounges near the pool, but far enough away from the splash zone that circled the water's edge. There was a line at the bar, both on land and in the pool, and I could hear the bartenders complimenting the guests as they prepared drinks. I was about to give up my search when I heard a familiar laugh.

Sure enough, there he was. With a group of guys, a few older ones too, maybe, all roughhousing in the shallow end. Playing some basketball game. And no Evelyn, to my relief.

I tried not to stare, I really did. I'm sure I was subtle behind the veil of the heart-shaped glasses Melissa had insisted I wear.

Melissa stripped off her dress beside me to reveal her curvaceous body in a black bikini. Our plan to come here had been last minute, so she had to borrow one of my mom's swimsuits, since there was no way mine would fit her. Even my mom's was a bit tight on her, but Melissa didn't seem an ounce uncomfortable. "Come on," she said, nodding her head toward the deep end and the two steaming hot tubs perched above. "Let's be very fancy in there. You can dangle your legs in the water while I soak. Sound good?"

I liked how assertive Melissa was. It made being her friend very easy, I didn't feel pressure to be funny or interesting. She could do that all on her own, and in fact, I found she inspired a more relaxed side of me whenever I was around her.

When Melissa had an idea in her head, she went with it. I had always felt like I had somehow missed a step in the maturity game, but being around her made me feel like maybe high school wasn't going to be so scary after all. Maybe I was ready for the final stages of being a kid.

We were about five minutes into our soak, my calves tomato red from the heat, when I noticed Taven heading our way. I had to bite my cheek to distract myself from staring.

Melissa nudged my leg. "Hot guy alert."

I kicked my legs around in the bubbling water, willing it to ease my nerves. "I actually know him," I said with the tiniest semblance of pride. "His parents and my parents are good friends."

She smirked in a half-smile. "Lucky."

Taven crouched down beside me, saying, "Hi, ladies," and my eyes flicked to the scars on his knees, the signature marks of a former boy and his adventures. "Like the new look, Dez," he grinned, those beautiful dark eyes of his scanning my face, the heart sunglasses, the spiky flower still tucked behind my ear. "Dazzling, Dez. Maybe I'll switch up your nickname."

I smiled sheepishly. "Melissa's styling me like her own personal Barbie doll."

Taven turned to look her way, saying something about how his sister used to do the same thing to him. I tried not to be jealous as Melissa threw her head back and laughed about wanting to see pictures, and him telling her, not on his life. Their banter was so easy. It had taken me weeks, hell, *months* to talk to him like that. Boom, first meeting and Melissa's there.

I stumbled my way through proper introductions, my heart thumping furiously the whole time. Despite my jealousy, I was glad I had Melissa there to take the pressure off, though I hadn't mentioned to her anything about my crush. I had a feeling she would see right through me and figure it out. I kind of *hoped* she would, anyhow, then maybe back off any flirtation attempts. It occurred to me, however, that I didn't know her well enough at that point to know whether or not she was the steal-your-guy type. The thought scared me. I couldn't imagine the rage I'd feel if all this time, I'd quietly sat around waiting for the Evelyn phase to be over, to then lose Taven to the confident radiance of Melissa.

Taven turned to face me again. "So, Dazzle, I came to invite you two over. We're getting ready to start a new round. You guys wanna play?"

Melissa leaned forward to eye up the kids in the pool, her boobs floating immaculately in front of her while I pretended not to notice the quick glance Taven most definitely darted at them. Not that I could blame him. She really did have exquisite boobs, and my mind briefly went to a flash of imagining touching them, followed by a heat of embarrassment and wondering if maybe that meant I was gay.

"With those guys?" she asked, eyeing up the teenage testosterone with clear appreciation. "Absolutely." She climbed out of the tub, water gloriously dripping off her curves, and then she dove straight into the pool, leaving Taven and me. I wondered how her bikini top was going to stay on after a dive like that. When she bobbed back through the surface of water and did a quick tuck of her breasts, I was relieved on her behalf.

"New friend?" Taven asked me, his eyes never leaving the spectacle that was Melissa Belle as she swam right up to his group of friends.

"Yeah, met her right at the end of school. She's nice."

He leaned his shoulder into me, giving me a little shove. His skin was warm from the sun. I craved more contact. "Good for you, Dazzle. A Bingo square conquered." He looked back over to Melissa and the guys, and I followed his gaze. One guy was saying something to her and she placed a dramatic hand on her chest before poking his shoulder and laughing.

Eyes still held on his crew, Taven whispered, "I've missed you, you know."

"Pretty busy with Evelyn, I guess." It had to be said. I couldn't help myself, even though I knew I sounded petty and needy. I wanted him to feel guilty.

"I think you'd really like her if you got to know her."

I looked back up to him, allowing a moment to admire the way his hair swooped over his forehead, a fat water droplet waiting for its moment to drop from the end. I didn't tell him that me not liking her wasn't the problem.

"I uhh...I can't swim," I blurted out, eager to move away from the Evelyn subject. It was agony to hear anything about his girlfriend, and knowing how she felt about me, there was no way I was going to pretend to be her friend, locked in the most horrific third-wheel position of all time.

He looked back to me, eyebrows furrowed. I prayed he wouldn't ask me why I couldn't swim. I had kept my jean shorts on, and was hoping he'd figure it out on his own.

He looked down at my shorts, then scanned my legs, and if I wasn't mistaken, I thought I heard his breath catch a bit. But then he placed his palms on his thighs and pressed himself up to a stand. "That's alright, Dazzle," he said, extending a hand to me to pull me up from my perch. "You can just dangle your feet in on that end and be our judge."

I stood up next to him, very aware that he kept a hold of my hand, even with me now steady on my feet.

"Okay," was all I said.

six

· · ·

Realization

Present Day

taven

Friday, 9:58pm

IT'S AMAZING THE flood of memories that crash over me as I stare at Desiree, looking annoyed yet beautiful in her hospital gown. It was so many years ago when we met, before the rift in our families and the nightmare that ensued. I think about the time when we were sixteen and had snuck out to see each other, after my parents and hers had cut ties. I remember how painful it was in the beginning, and how surprised I was at how much I missed her, like a limb had been cut off. It felt cruel, but everything was so fucked up, I didn't know how the hell to navigate any of it

We didn't get enough time together, me and Desiree. My Dazzle. I bet things could have been different if we had. I bet *I* would have been different. She was always my rock, even in the beginning, now that I think about it. For those three years from thirteen to sixteen years old. Through all the awkwardness of approaching adulthood, through the hell that was my parents breathing down my neck or me fighting for decent grades to get them off my back. It was Desiree that I felt most comfortable around. She could make me feel like I was actually worth something.

It was pretty terrifying as a kid, truth be told, to be in the presence of a girl I think I knew deep down was out of my league. She was smart, she had this subtle sense of humor, and she didn't cater to peer pressure or teenage expectations. Dazzle was everything I could never be.

It's hard to say exactly when I had started to develop a little thing for her, but it was fairly early on. There was that first New Year party we spent together, when the Bingo tradition started. We were mere babies, but I remember staring at Desiree as she walked in with her parents, and she had on these high heels she could barely walk in. It was like that scene from Bambi where he takes his first awkward steps. She was all skinny legs and off-kilter, but something had stirred in me seeing her all dressed up. I saw the preview of the beautiful young woman she would clearly soon become.

For some reason, it scared me. No one was so unconditionally kind to me like Desiree was, or looked at me with a kind of awe like I was *something*. Not even Evelyn, my puppy love girlfriend at the time.

Evelyn was like a hobby, easy and carefree. She was into sports, like me, and we could talk about our latest soccer games or my lacrosse stuff. Nothing crazy, just simple and fun. With Desiree, though, my thing for her caught me off guard, flaring up insecurities that I know caused me to keep her at arm's length those first couple of years. I wanted her near, couldn't ever resist my draw to her, but I was too scared to take the leap—a damn idiot. Why is it that we push away the things we want the most?

It wasn't until later when I finally got the guts to let her know my feelings. Even then, she's the one that ultimately prompted the conversation.

Maybe that's exactly how it was supposed to be.

I sit here now and take in the sight of Desiree Hatson—the blonde hair, soaked and wild all around her, the outline of her hips under the flimsy hospital blanket. Hips I have held and driven myself into over and over again, yet it was never enough. My craving for her has never gone away, like it or not. Seeing her now is a new kind of torture. I want to touch her skin, taste that sweet mouth, hold her and beg forgiveness for all the times I fucked things up.

I realize that I still love her. Like no time has passed. All the affection I've ever held for my Dazzle, lying dormant in the depths of my heart, now all crawling back out.

I'm fucking engaged, I remind myself. Possibly still engaged, that is.

Either way, I can't be looking at Desiree like this. I *shouldn't* be, anyway. I have a good woman in my life, one that I do care for.

I tell myself that I'm just here to make sure Desiree is okay. Then we'll part ways like nothing happened. Maybe we could make plans to meet up. Have coffee. A friendly lunch.

Maybe I could claim her once again, fuck her until she screams my name and is begging for mercy. Spread her legs wide and drive myself into her, mouth on her breasts and cock buried inside her.

Fuck me. Think of Evelyn, of what you're trying to build with her.

I sigh and Desiree blinks up at me with a grin. I instantly feel guilty. "So, you and Evelyn?" she chides. "After all these years?" I swear, it's like she can read my mind. Fucking Christ. She always could, I never could get away with shit with her. Dazzle always saw right through me.

I lean back in my chair, attempting to make myself comfortable in the green plastic. "Yeah, who would have thought?"

"Childhood sweethearts." She looks away, and I study her face for a reaction. I watch as she bites her lip, and her beautiful blue eyes blink in some kind of distant expression. Is she hurt by that, by me and Evelyn reconnecting? Or am I just dreaming that the Desiree I knew as a kid, the one that was my friend before all else, that she would even hold any kind of romantic affection for me anymore?

A snort escapes Melissa's mouth from her spot on the windowsill. "Yeah right." She darts her chin toward Desiree. "That right there was your childhood sweetheart, remember?"

I can't help but smile. I always did like Melissa. "I remember," I agree.

Melissa takes off her poncho, the plastic crinkling and piercing the silence. She walks over to Desiree and grabs her hand. "I can't fucking believe you were struck by lightning, Dez."

Desiree lets out a slow groan, and I inch forward in my seat, worried she's in pain. "Not directly," she clarifies. "So embarrassing."

I reach forward and grab her foot, tucked under a blanket. Give it a little squeeze. "What the hell are you talking about? There's nothing to be embarrassed for."

"Agreed, Dez," Melissa chimes in.

"It was a freak of nature."

It was a zap through some equipment box her calf had been touching when the strike happened. Knocked her clear off her feet and gave me a fucking heart attack. Aside from some redness on her leg, though, and an apparent ringing in her ear, she's apparently fine, thank God. I can't even think about what I'd do if she died right then and there. I'd probably go the rest of my life wishing I had died with her.

That's not the thought to have. I know that.

"What are we waiting on?" Desiree asks, scooting herself up in the bed. "I want to go home. I'm hungry. I need a shower." Her eyes meet mine. "I keep thinking Taven Carlisle is in my room."

I look into the pools of blue and try and read her expression. "I am in the room," I say. I can't tell if the strike is making her loopy or if she's just had too much to drink. Or if she's joking. Maybe all three. I rise out of my seat and stand beside her, grabbing her hand. "Hey, are you alright? Do you remember me there in the tent with you?" I search her face for signs of something. The doctor said her memory might be a bit foggy.

"I..." she starts, her brows furrowed. "Oh, hell, I can't keep a straight face," she grins. "I was really hoping to pull off a whole thing of delusion."

"You always were shit at keeping a poker face," I tell her, my thumb running circles on the back of her hand. So soft, just like I remember. It's like the jolt that ran through her is running through me now, too. I miss holding this hand a whole lot more than I should.

Melissa spins around and heads for the door, saying she'll see what she can do before marching out of the room. A moment later we hear her giving an earful to the nurse or someone, demanding we get our paperwork so we can get of here.

I look back at Desiree and we grin at each other. "I see she hasn't changed. Glad you guys have stayed friends," I add.

She nods. "Yeah, me too. Magnets, I guess. Couldn't stay away from each other."

I release her hand and sit back down in my chair, trying to ignore the headache I feel coming on. The green glow of overhead lights is doing nothing to help. I reach over to the remote beside Desiree and turn them off.

"Setting the mood, are we?" she jokes. "But what would Evelyn say?" She looks at me with wide and innocent eyes, the piercing blue looking even more gorgeous now than I remember.

"When did you become so funny?"

"I've always been funny. You're just choosing not to remember."

"I remember you in a Dalmatian costume looking like you needed to ask permission to even speak, Dazzle."

She rolls her eyes at me. "I was thirteen. A kid. In a new town. What did you expect? I think you pretty quickly learned I was no wallflower."

I smile, remembering those early days with us together. I don't remind her that I knew her back when she *was* a wallflower. Before she hit her strides of confidence, before she had settled into the young beauty that would send me excusing myself to the bathroom to relieve my throbbing dick every five seconds. Still, even before all that, I was crazy about her. I always knew she had a little thing for me, but it took me a lot longer to admit to myself I felt that same thing in return.

I was a coward.

I look back at my Dazzle and let her have the out. "No, you were no wallflower," I murmur.

"Hmm," she hums in agreement. "Sure glad the lightning didn't affect *your* memory."

I can't help but think that there's certain memories I truly wish I could forget. Memories from five years ago in particular. The ones that haunt me when I close my eyes.

seven

. . .

Arrangements

Five years ago

lynda carlisle

Summertime, 9:18am

SHE ARRANGES THE flowers with expertise, a skill she had long ago acquired. All her favorites—lilies, the classic roses, pink dahlias for texture and pops of baby's breath for softness. Sprigs of greens for earthy balance. A holly branch for the symbol of resilience. There was a meditative ritual to these arrangements, and with it came a moment to reflect on where this most unexpected skill of hers all began. She clutches the delicate strand of pearls around her neck as her mind wanders to how far she had come.

Pearls were never something she ever believed she'd own. Didn't even understand their value. Because Lynda came from nothing, that was the truth of it. And when you come from nothing, things like pearls or jewels made for decorative accessories weren't exactly on your radar. For many years, the only things that ever concerned her were food and growth.

You learn quickly how to grow up when you're fighting for your next meal.

The man that helped create her was non-existent (she wouldn't dare dignify him with the title "father"), and her mother, bless her heart, was more in love with needles and pills than putting food on the table. Hunger was a constant companion, and their trailer was a revolving door of seedy men and early encounters of certain demands. She didn't even have breasts the first time a man touched her. "I'll take care of you, you'll see," the man had promised. One of her mother's "friends." She quickly understood what taking care of her would mean to him, to the others that followed.

But Lynda had brains and courage. And when you grew up in the world she did, you learned to utilize your resources.

She learned that with a smile, she could make the uninvited contacts transactional, and so food and the occasional treat from the local convenient store became things she could proposition. Waves of hunger pains in her belly could be spaced out much further.

She learned that if her belly was full, she could concentrate on her studies. Earn good grades. Get in the good graces of teachers that took a liking to her (a non-physical one, thank the good Lord), and so bloomed this little thing called hope, something her surroundings knew little of.

She studied the voices on the radio, their smooth drawl like a beckoning call. They intrigued her. She developed an obsession with watching the mannerisms of the flawless faces on TV, on the news, understanding that looking and speaking a certain way was how you got money, steady meals, shiny-looking clothing that came together as a set.

As her mother's disease became more and more chronic, the lure of college became a real possibility. She knew it was only a matter of time before she was an orphan. Perhaps a government scholarship could be within her reach.

It didn't take long for her mother to succumb to the illness created by her addictions. Lynda became a ward of the state halfway through high school. By the time she was eighteen, she was living in a foster group home for teenage girls. "Bad behavior" may have put her there, though she didn't see how stealing money in a home that promised to take care of you while simultaneously continuing the neglect she was accustomed to was considered wrong.

For once, though, the system didn't fail her when she was in the Jennifer Grace Cottage. She was lucky—she had stumbled into one of the good group homes. There was a young counselor there that had kindness and seemed genuinely horrified by her stories, yet also committed to exhibiting odd and innovative techniques to rewire the damage done due to her "complex trauma." That's what it was called, she learned. For her, though, it was simply life.

For her housemates that showed interest, she'd help them with their schooling. She showed them how to open a bank account when they were frustrated with the poor teaching techniques of the home's classes meant to do so. She became an unofficial assistant to the mother hen of the cottage. It suited her, gave her a purpose and some semblance of control. The girls turned to her for advice and guidance, and she gladly imparted what wisdoms she could to their eager ears.

College proved to be her playground. She studied finance (numbers had always been her strong suit). Analysis of numbers, forecasting, transactions, all things that her mind understood. By the time she graduated, she had internship offers at top firms across the United States.

And then she developed a bona fide crush on someone. Someone that had been her mark, but he slipped past her head and into her heart. He was a businessman, a supervisor on her team, and while he came from a world polar opposite to her own, they connected in their ambition and drive. Their business was a competitive one, to put it mildly. He taught her the ins and outs of this strange new world, a fantasy land for all she knew. Money became a laughable concept to her (how these people *played* with it!) and together they made plans for all the ways they'd achieve their dreams.

While hunger was never a fear she had been able to shake, it was then that she'd realized it was officially an irrational one.

She was free.

LYNDA CAREFULLY FILLS A WATER bottle to later be used to pour into the flower vase. The drive to her destination would be fairly short, thankfully, but still impractical if the container for her bouquet was sloshing around water in her car. Instead, she'd place the flowers in their vase dry, and pour the water in once she arrived. It worked well last time.

As she screws the cap on the filled water bottle, she thinks about her husband, knowing he would laugh to see her taking such care to ensure the perfect flowers be delivered intact. He wouldn't understand exactly why this mattered to her so much. Not his fault, Lynda had purposely kept certain things from him.

She and her husband married young, twenty-two and twenty-eight, respectively. She kept her background vague, happy when the mere term "orphan" quickly shut down further questioning. Rich people didn't like to talk about uncomfortable things, she found. Convenient for her. Her husband's family took her in as one of their own, charitable in that way, and suddenly her old life was a chapter closed. No—more than that. A bad novel that was decrepit and better suited for kindling. This book now was her real story, and she created the narrative with precision.

Years later, she still laughs at her life, living within these means. Who would have thought! A mansion, the best schooling for her children, cars and jewelry and all the fine things. She paid most of it little mind, seeing the opulence as more of a necessity to keeping the appearance, lest the image should falter, careful connections starting to question her authenticity or right to be here, and she'd be left hungry again.

So yes, Lynda dressed a certain way, spoke a certain way. Wore pearls and acquired a green thumb that resulted in the gift of beautiful gardens, something she insisted on maintaining herself despite her husband's urging to allow the landscapers to handle it. It was the one thing she refused, because no one knew how to curate a glorious garden in the way she could. Gardens were something exquisitely within her control. She found peace in strolling through to the area specifically for her cut flowers. Peace in creating beautiful arrangements.

And she would continue to allow such beautiful things, luxuries and the rest of it, to rain down on her family without guilt, because her children deserved better than the life she lived. No one deserved that kind of suffering, and she'd be damned if anyone ever took it away from her.

For Lynda, her crushes were not ones of naive fascination based on whim, but of the obsessions with survival and control. And there wasn't a crush in the world that would ever be out of her league.

THE FUNNY THING ABOUT LIFE is that you just never know what curveballs will be thrown your way. You can have the best laid plans, have made all the right choices, and still, the universe proves to know better. The house always wins.

It was years ago when she got the call that her husband was in the hospital. She had nearly thought the voice on the other end of the line had the wrong number as they explained that her husband was clinging to his life. Attacked in his usual parking garage while preparing to head home after work. Beaten nearly to death by some angry faction or another. Lynda went into survival mode. Were the necessary documents all signed or on file, the finances in order and readily retrievable? There were arrangements to be made and loose ends to be tied, and fast. They had prepared for this kind of thing, in the off chance they were ever in trouble. Being in the business that they were, it was wise to do so, as they were surrounded by wealth and greed. When you take risks with people's money, people that had an obsession with only making more, you never knew when the tides would turn on you. Still, she had thought they'd been smarter, never making deals if she had suspicions or a bad hunch. One wrong move, and these people could be your enemy.

Thankfully, the universe proved to be on her side this time. Her husband lived, despite some damaging blows to the head. The gift of having been found soon after his attack, the doctors explained. Too long in that beaten state and he might not have been so lucky. She realized that they needed to be more careful and focus on their less risky businesses, even if it meant smaller rewards.

She had some contacts in the Midwest, and so they moved to a safe and quiet suburb in Ohio that was neatly nestled near Cleveland. The kids were still relatively young, not yet adults. They'd adapt to their new surroundings. Lynda and her husband would find a new business venture, perhaps, one that could offer them more control over their day-to-day lives, with no one to answer to. It made the most sense. You do what you need to do to protect your family at all costs. It was something she had learned in her group home days, and was further emphasized once she had children of her own. While—thanks to her upbringing—this had initially been a foreign concept to her, it quickly became her mantra.

Hunger would always be a lingering threat in the back of her mind (there wasn't a plate of food in front of her that she didn't finish), but her fear for safety of her family was far heavier. She'd be damned if anything happened to them. Her family was her proudest accomplishment, and they were a team. She'd do anything for them. She'd kill for them.

And so, they built a new life for themselves, this one even more successful than the last. They'd be smarter, pay closer attention to those they kept in their circle. Potential enemies and friends alike, if they had to. More often than not, she would soon discover, they came hand in hand.

eight

· · ·

Bold

Fourteen years ago

desiree

sixteen years old

THE TRANSITION INTO high school turned out to be a breeze. Melissa and I stayed in our same school, just moving to a different building on campus. I tagged along with her on every adventure she would set her mind to. We did drama club together, Melissa scoring the lead role in the fall play, as a freshman, no less. Then again for the spring musical, and pretty soon everyone knew the lead roles were always going to go to her. She was a natural on stage, with plans to make it big one day. I was jealous of her talents, I'll admit. What kid wouldn't be? She had that remarkable little something that I so clearly lacked, yet my happiness for her always subdued my jealousy. I could shine in her proximity.

I remember the first time I had gone to Melissa's house, the small bungalow with grimy buildup on the beige siding, which most likely had once been white. The sidewalk leading up to the brown door was cracked, but there were little planters perched along the rail of the small porch. I found it sweet. A small touch of simple beauty.

Melissa lived with a million people. There were her parents, loud and welcoming like her. Then her grandmother, a rotund woman I don't think I ever saw without an apron on. Her uncle lived there as well, Melissa's mom's brother, and when he had his kids for a few days, her cousins lived there too. I had no idea where they all slept, the house was a split level and we mostly hung out downstairs, where her bedroom was, but I liked the chaos of the place. Her family had a way of making you feel special, like every time I entered, it was a day of celebration.

"Desiree, there you are!" her mother would say. This would usually be followed by her shoving a wooden spoon in my mouth of some stew or another brewing on the stove. Her mom was from Puerto Rico, her dad was French, and I loved the richness of her family's accents. The roll of multiple languages that would pour out of their rambling mouths, a million miles a minute. The Spanish held a dialect beyond the comprehension of my fancy private school education's language classes, but with their animated ways of expression, you felt like you understood everything being said just fine.

I was more comfortable at Melissa's house than any place in the world. Sleepovers there became a regular thing, though she would insist we go to my house as often as possible. She loved the spaciousness, the opportunity to ogle over my brother whenever he was home from college. I'd acquiesce now and then, rolling my eyes as she shamelessly flirted with Dylan, saying she watched his latest football game on TV and thought he was magnificent. He'd wink at me and warn me that my best friend was no good. I'd tell him I agreed.

Melissa worked her way through various crappy boyfriends,

never lasting more than a few weeks. She was a hopeless romantic, and she made it no secret that her crush on Dylan would "stand the test of time," saying she and I were destined to be sisters-in-law one day. I'd groan at how I'd rather not have my brother locked up for sleeping with a minor. Secretly, though, I loved the idea.

I, on the other hand, remained painfully single, my crush on Taven never dissipating. Melissa knew of my feelings for him by then, and she and I would commiserate together on our bad romantic luck.

By fall of our sophomore year, I was happy to be back in the Carlisle-Hatson routine again now that summer was over. Evelyn was back at school, and I got Taven all to myself. I started to notice that Taven talked about her less and less as the school year went on. By Christmas, he never mentioned her at all. Seemingly sensing my reluctance to ask about her, he eventually admitted that they had broken up weeks before. He was so upset, but all I could think was *this is it. Now is my time.*

Melissa wasted no time in zeroing in on the Taven and Desiree love story.

"He likes you too, you do realize that, right?" she asked me one day. We were in school at lunch, and I was picking my way through the salad bar line. Melissa was piling her plate with the oddest concoction of veggies, pickled onions, a pasta salad, two types of dressings (she liked half her salad to be healthy, half to be "fun").

I spooned some corn chowder into a cardboard bowl and considered how to answer. "Sometimes I think he does," I confessed, "but other times I think he just feels a really good friendship with a girl that he can talk to differently than he can to guys. That it's not really an attraction."

I lifted my tray, and we walked through the hall and out to the courtyard. It was late March and we were getting glimpses of spring weather, that perfect time of year in Ohio when the cherry blossoms were in full bloom, pale pink bursting through their buds like they had been there all along.

We settled into our seats and I stretched across the picnic table to steal a bite of Melissa's salad. I had to admit, the chew of the pasta was a nice compliment to the crunch of leafy greens. "Girl, get your own fun salad next time," she teased, a smile escaping her perfect lips. I told her it was more fun to steal hers, and we both chewed away in silence for a few minutes, simply enjoying the warmth of the sun penetrating our sweaters.

"He'll be getting his car soon," I said. Taven had already turned sixteen back in September, but after a string of some C's and D's on his latest report card, his parents were in that mode of rubbing foreheads in frustration with their struggling son. He was forced to hit pause on his beloved sports, a move that caused him to sneak multiple beers one night, calling me and complaining about what assholes his parents were. I listened as he ranted on about how sports had nothing to do with the idiotic teachers that spoke like they were voices hired for putting people to sleep, not meant to inspire young minds. I thought about how much his own private school education was costing his parents, and how sad it was that despite the tuition fees, he was still slipping through the cracks of education.

When his attitude toward his parents was received as a bit too disrespectful, they had "punished" Taven by withholding on the promise of a new car when he got his permit. Instead, they had him do all his driving practices in one of their cars. Once he got his license, he was driving around in his mom's pearl white Mercedes. I knew he hated it, but his anger seemed to have lost its resolve. He didn't complain, even when his friends would tease him relentlessly. He'd shrug it off like it was no big deal. It was just a car, at least he was allowed to drive anything at all. It was that type of thing that only made me fall for him even more.

But the Carlisle plan worked. Taven dug his heels in and ground out the studying necessary to raise his GPA, and as a reward, he would finally be getting the vehicle of his choice. Some sporty-like car, but the make was a Dodge. It would be fully loaded, I'm sure, but still, I found it to be a surprising choice. I had teased him that he should be getting a Bentley or something, and he joked that then I wouldn't ever be allowed to drive it.

I loved how we could talk to each other like that. Both of our families had money, but it was clear that his family had *money, money*. Whereas everyone else at that level could seem like snobby shows-offs (and make no mistake, I found his parents scary as hell), Taven never struck me as someone needing to flaunt it.

Melissa dropped her fork and looked at me. "Getting his car soon?" I looked at her raised eyebrow.

"Yeah."

She tilted her chin toward me. "Ten bucks says he lets you pick the color."

I dropped my fork then too, rifled through my bag and took out my wallet. "Do you have change for a twenty?"

"Inferno Red, Dazzle? That's what you went for?" Taven said as we wandered out of the Dodge sales office and to the open area.

"Yup. Inferno Red." I dragged out those two words as slowly as I possibly could, incredibly proud of myself for being able to say them with a straight face. You should have seen me when I told the sales lady that was the color I suggested for Taven's new baby. You'd have been proud. Something about saying "inferno" felt a bit naughty. He was getting a Dodge Challenger, and when I saw the name of the color as one of the options, I couldn't help but giggle.

He shook his head, running his hand through his hair and to

the back of his neck. "Fuck me, this was a bad idea. I should have never told you you could pick the color."

"You could always rescind the offer, you know. If you don't want to have to say 'inferno' every time someone asks what exact kind of red it is." I sang out the proposition, knowing the rebel in him wouldn't back down.

We were walking around the showroom, five cars neatly on display with paint jobs so shiny, I felt like I was staring at an image from a fake cartoon. Or something a computer generated. I didn't know about Taven, but I was feeling very grown-up as the salespeople fawned all over us. "Waters?" they had asked us. "Sodas or coffee? Our coffee here isn't very good, but I could send someone to Starbucks for you." My cheeks flamed in embarrassment at the clear All-Hands-On-Deck for the rich people display, but Taven maneuvered through like he himself was the man behind the money, not some sixteen-year-old kid. Mr. Carlisle had made some calls and let them know his son would be coming in to finalize the details of his car to be ordered, customized for him. Everyone there must have been thinking how spoiled this kid was. It made me uncomfortable, but I was determined to keep my chin held high and not be overly giggly.

I paused in front of a sensible black sedan. "You know that Melissa called it?"

Taven was one car over from me, examining the price sheet on a large SUV. "Called what?"

"This," I said, waving to the space around us. "She said you'd let me pick the color. Bet me ten bucks on it, not even realizing you already had."

"Why would she say that?" he asked, his tone surprisingly quiet.

I studied him across the glare of light reflecting from the hood of the car in front of me, squinting as I tried to read his expression. My heart rate picked up speed, and I realized how badly I wanted to broach the subject. What subject was that, even? A subject of an "us," a declaration of my crush, *something*.

He stepped away from the SUV and started walking toward me, slowly, staring down at the glittering white tiles of the showroom floor. I followed his gaze down, stepping closer, pausing just in front of him. I stared down to the black leather of his boots, then to the pale blue polish of my toenails peeking through the strap of my sandals. *Say it, say something*, I begged myself.

Finally, I let the words slip out in a croak. "Because she thinks you like me. Like—more than a friend."

Two and a half years of memories of our friendship came swooshing through me. The moments playing video games in his bedroom, or hanging out poolside by the club. The Bingo cards we did that first year, then again our freshman year of high school, then again this past year.

I looked up at him. "Does that count as saying something uncomfortable to someone I care about?" I asked him, referring to one of this year's squares.

He met my gaze and pointed to his chest with a smile. "I'm someone you care about?"

"Yes."

"And that was uncomfortable for you to say? That I might like you?" His eyes were shining, and I felt the tiniest bit of hope. "As more than a friend?"

"Yes," I breathed out.

He nodded once. "Then it counts."

We stood there like that, frozen in our spots as if the glitters in the tile had somehow seeped out and turned to glue. I didn't know what to say next. Wasn't it on him now to fill in the giant emotional blank laid out before him? I scanned over his face, the cupid's bow of his lips, wondering what they tasted like. Wondering if he ever thought about kissing mine. When I looked back up, his brown eyes were even darker than usual, wolfish. He smirked at me like he knew exactly what I had just been thinking. I licked my lips, and he let out the slightest low rumble of a hum, mouth twisting up into an appreciative grin. My stomach flipped at what I hoped was passing between us.

Our moment was interrupted when the saleslady came up to us.

"Alright, Mr. Carlisle?" Her heels clacked as she walked up to him, a stack of papers and brochures in her hand. "You're in luck. Inferno Red with all of your specifications is available to order, at the price your father negotiated. Should be ready in less than four weeks."

He pulled his eyes away from mine and faced her. "Oh, yeah? Great. Thanks."

She looked over at me. "Your girlfriend has good taste."

Taven didn't correct her.

nine

. . .

Inferno

Fourteen years ago

desiree

sixteen years old

WE DROVE HOME from the showroom that day in Mrs. Carlisle's white Mercedes, and Taven stretched his arm out across the center console over to my lap, grabbing my hand to hold. He'd never held my hand before while we were driving. It was definitely his declaration of something. Right?

Still, I felt uncertain.

I glanced over to him, but his eyes remained firmly on the road, his other hand gripping the top of the steering wheel.

What if I was misreading this, and it was all just comfort? Or excitement for his new car he just ordered? What if this wasn't him saying he did in fact like me in that way, but just a "There, there, kid. You're cute." kind of gesture?

My mind was spinning wildly, and suddenly I wished he

hadn't held my hand at all, because this was all feeling like too much anxiety for me to handle. I had an instant stomachache, and my throat was desert dry. The car felt hot. I rolled down my window a bit for some air, but then regretted it because we were on the highway and it was entirely too loud. But if I rolled the window back up, would that be weird? Would he ask me what I was doing? Then what would I say?

I was effectively freaking out.

That's how it was with Taven. One minute I'd slip into a space of wonderful comfort with him, the next I'd be whiplashed back to the awful pain of Phase One—mere intrigue with the object of my affection firmly rooted in a space of mystery. It was maddening.

The entire car ride home, my mind replayed the conversation in the showroom over and over again, a track on repeat. Intrusive thoughts ran rampant through my brain. Did I just screw up? I worried I scared him off, and he would soon start to pull away from me again, like he did that awful first summer after he had French-kissed Evelyn and I was thrust back into a zone of nothingness in his world. I played the whole thing out in my head. That I had presented the idea of him liking me, that he'd momentarily thought it was cute of me, and was now realizing how dangerous that was to our friendship, since it was always painfully obvious that I liked him. I thought of all the conversations we'd had over the past two years or so when he'd ask if I was seeing anyone, and I'd tell him there was no one of interest to me, just one guy, but I didn't think he liked me back. All the little tests I'd set up for him, none of which he passed. He'd always dodge my bait and change the subject.

I thought about the day he told me he and Evelyn had sex, losing their virginities to each other the end of last summer. It was Labor Day weekend, and Taven had just turned sixteen, but she was only fifteen! I thought *what a slut*, but I knew that was unfair. They had been together for a while. Of course they'd eventually sleep together! What did I expect? I had been sick to my stomach for the rest of the evening. I couldn't help but fight back tears that my dream of that being us, of me and Taven being the ones to share that special moment were now completely lost.

But still, I forced myself to move on. Continue our friendship and take the scraps of Taven Carlisle that I could. Looking forward to when Evelyn was back at school, and I'd get him all to myself again.

Something glorious happened, though, when I finally found out she broke up with him. She couldn't take the distance anymore or something crazy like that. I wondered if there was some other boy she had her eye on. Taven had actually cried in front of me, and I think it was the first time, for the briefest moment, that I didn't like him. Sure, I was madly in love with him, but seeing his tears for some girl that dumped him was disgusting to me.

And here we were now. Him holding my hand on a car ride after picking out the stupid color Inferno Red, for God's sake. I said a silent prayer that this would all be okay. That I didn't just ruin everything between us. Saying nothing and holding our friendship would have been the smarter move. My mind kept spiraling and screaming for Taven to *say something*, but of course, I ruined the logistics of that by stupidly rolling down the window.

After what felt like hours of the tornado swirling in my brain, Taven pushed the button that rolled up my window. I kept my eyes on the highway, the giant billboards advertising all the ways various companies could offer you products and services to make your life better.

With the car quiet again, he spoke. "What are you thinking, Dazzle?"

How to respond...quick, think of something good to say. Sadly, "I don't know," was all I could come up with.

"Yes, you do, don't lie to me."

I looked down at our clasped hands, noting how firmly he was holding mine. "Fine," I finally said. "I'm wondering why you're holding my hand."

I looked up at him and saw the grin sweep across his face. "Isn't it obvious?"

"Not to me."

He raised our clasped hands and kissed the back of mine. I nearly died. "I'm holding your hand because Melissa's right. I do like you as more than a friend."

My view of the road narrowed to a pinhole at hearing those words escape his mouth. There was a loud drumming in my ears, maybe the sound of my own pulse, who knows. "Really?" I squeaked out.

"Don't play dumb. You know I have for a while now. I just didn't know what to do about it. I wasn't sure if you felt the same."

Did I know? I had hope, sure. Read into every little thing that might have indicated that he liked me. But I always went straight back to convincing myself that was impossible. "What do you mean, for a while, or that you didn't know what to do about it? Why not?" I couldn't wrap my head around what I was hearing. It didn't make any sense. *How long is a while?*

"Because of our families," he explained. "Their friendship. I knew us being a thing would be awkward."

Us. A thing. I had died and gone to heaven. Was this really happening? "We don't have to tell them," I offered.

He glanced over to me, his brown eyes framed by the pinch of his brows. "What? Fuck that, I'm not going to hide this."

I didn't know if I was just an idiot not getting something, or if I was just overthinking or what. "Then why didn't you say something sooner?"

He shrugged, and I took in the sight of his rounded shoulders hidden beneath his t-shirt. It was lacrosse season for him, sports no longer being withdrawn as punishment by his parents, and time spent in the gym was turning him even more into a manly God in my eyes. And here he was, talking about an us. Little by little, I allowed myself to believe this was real.

He gave my hand a little squeeze. "Dazzle, will you please confirm that you feel the same way?"

The sweet idiot. Of course I did. "Yes," I whispered.

"Good," he said. "In that case, I guess I was just waiting for the right moment."

I laughed. "Sure am glad I chose Inferno Red, then."

He let out a groan. "Stop, you're gonna give me a fucking hard on if you say 'Inferno' one more time."

Me? Capable of turning him on? I had to think fast, relish in this opportunity. I turned in my seat, placing my other hand over our clasped hands. "Vin, look at me."

"Can't, I'm driving."

"A quick glance, come on."

He caved and darted his eyes over to me. "Inferno," I said as slowly as I possibly could. I blushed, I couldn't help it, but I was going to give this all the courage I could.

"Fuck me."

I wanted to repeat what he said. Say something sexy like, "You want me to fuck you?" But I was too chicken.

I watched him as he smirked, shaking his head. "We're about to move way too fast, aren't we?"

My stomach summmersaulted at hearing him talk like that. I smiled and straightened myself in my seat again. "I guess we'll find out."

WHEN WE GOT TO MY house, I think we both did a silent prayer of gratitude that no one was home. As I unlocked the front door for us, I called out "Hello" just to triple check, but thankfully, no one responded. I looked up at Taven, nervous as to what to do next. "Are you thirsty?" I asked.

He put his hands in his pockets and shook his head no.

"Wanna go watch a movie in my room?"

"Sure," he said. He followed me up the stairs, around the hall and to my room, a spot we didn't spend too much time in. Most of the time our parents were together, it was at the Carlisle Manor, a mansion that made our six-thousand square foot home seem humble. It was the Carlisles who threw the best parties, had the best catering, the valet parking, etc. My parents envied their wealth, I knew, but they were happy to ride the coattails of their friends and simply have them in their company.

We kicked off our shoes and settled onto my bed while I flipped through some channels. I looked over at Taven, silently begging him to put his arm around me. We had spent countless hours together, but we also had such a firm routine in the ways we interacted. It made today's declaration of mutual interest and of starting something more together feel like meeting him for the first time all over again. Normally we'd sit on our sides of my bed with space between us. Did we even know how to snuggle? Would we kiss well? I had kissed a couple boys, at a school dance or hanging out at friends' houses, but I hadn't kissed anyone I truly liked enough to make a habit of it. I was nervous that Taven, a far more experienced kisser, would find me horrible in that department.

And then another thought popped into my head—would we jump straight into having sex? Would I lose my virginity today? I didn't really see why we would wait, we knew all there was to know about each other already. It seemed strange to take it slowly.

Suddenly the only thing I wanted was Taven's mouth on me, and for him to strip me naked so I could feel all there was to feel of his skin on mine.

"Hey," he whispered, grabbing my hand and pulling me

toward him. I snuggled into the crook of his arm—*this is really happening!*—and tried to make myself relax. He pulled my chin to look up at him. "Is it okay if I kiss you?" I nodded mutely and he leaned his head down, his lips reaching mine.

He started slowly, almost easing us both into this new thing between us, and my heart beat wildly in my chest. He had put gum in his mouth, and I was thankful that the minty taste would mask what I was sure was my not-so-fresh breath. I squeezed his shirt, twisting myself to better face him and get more comfortable. When his tongue slipped in my mouth, I moaned and then was instantly embarrassed by the sound. But it only seemed to further ignite him, and he powered on, and next thing you know I was straddling him while my mind was shouting, *"I'm making out with Taven Carlisle!"*

It was surreal, yet comfortable. We paused for air at some point. His hands explored my body, under my shirt, then slipped under my bra. Aside from that, though, we took it slow and did as much as we could with clothes on.

The next several weeks continued on like that. Now that he had a car, we had the beautiful freedom of seeing each other whenever we wanted, like a pass that sent us hurtling toward the autonomy of adulthood.

But his parents ensured we still knew our place.

They weren't having their son unsupervised with his girl-friend, and they demanded his bedroom door stay open when I was over. We weren't allowed at each other's houses if parents weren't home. So we did what we could in the swirls of our fren-zied hormones and attraction to each other. It was all so absorbing and intense—lots of making out, nothing too extreme. A hand job on one day I was feeling brave in my room, where my parents didn't care if the door was closed. We'd carry on with some touch and exploration, but never sex. I was too nervous, and truth be told, I think Taven was, too.

It's funny, now that I think about it, it's like over the course of that spring, our friendship took a back burner. When we were together, we were either making out, or watching a movie, or hanging out with our parents and counting down the seconds until we could be alone and make out again.

My parents were thrilled with the match, naturally. My mother promptly put me on birth control, even though I assured her we weren't having sex.

When his parents insisted I start coming over for family dinner on Sundays whenever I was available, I was fearful of their judgment. The first couple times, I barely said a word, pushing my food around on my plate in nervous discomfort. We'd sit in their massive dining room, the table a long display of silverware and china, fresh white floral arrangements adding the only warmth to the cavernous space. The walls had some kind of fabric on them in a wild geometric pattern that I found dizzying. Classical music would play from some hidden speakers throughout the room. Jacqui, Taven's sister, would make eye contact with me from across the table and wink, mouthing to me random quips in response to whatever her parents had just said, and I'd stifle a laugh. Taven would hold my hand beneath the table, but I had the distinct feeling he was just as nervous as I was. I wondered what dinners were like when I wasn't here. Were they this stoic and quiet?

His mom would make Taven drive me home promptly afterward, stating she knew exactly how long it took to get to my house and when exactly she expected Taven back home. All this said right in front of me, every dinner I was there. I'd look at Mrs. Carlisle—Lynda, as she insisted I start calling her—(though really I just avoided having to say her name at all), and I'd wonder if she was this strict when Taven was with Evelyn. He would later tell me she was.

Toward the end of tenth grade, Lynda asked me about my college plans.

"I'm not really sure yet," I replied over a meal of pork chops and roasted vegetables, some syrupy and sweet glaze meticulously poured in a zigzag design over top. I fiddled with the linen napkin in my lap.

Taven looked over to his mom. "Don't go grilling her, we still have two years left of high school."

Lynda paused her movements, a forkful of pork held midair. "Which will be over before you know it. And while I realize you think life is just one big game full of fun, all of this," she said, scanning her eyes around the room and beyond, "doesn't just fall into your lap, Taven. It takes planning and hard work."

"Maybe I don't want all this," he countered. I could feel his hand tense as he squeezed mine.

His dad huffed out a laugh. "Everyone wants all this, don't be naive."

Jacqui chimed in, tone light as she tried to steer the conversation. "And what exactly is all this?" she said through a smile. "A home and comfort and what not? Because I sincerely doubt you guys need to worry, Taven and I have had the best role models to teach us the ways."

I looked at her, trying to convey my gratitude for her attempt to placate and avoid an argument. I cleared my throat, deciding it would be easier to focus on the original subject. "My parents want me to go for pre-med. You know, follow in their footsteps and open a specialized clinic, which would be nice. I haven't really decided if I'll go that route, yet, but it's an option." I didn't add that my only reluctance was that I saw how hard my parents worked, how their stress levels were permanently set to high.

"It's a good plan," Mr. Carlisle offered with a nod. (Unlike Lynda, he had never offered for me to call him by his first name, Bill.)

Lynda grabbed her wine, sipping before adding her two cents. "Agreed. I've spoken with your parents about it. Though it's funny, isn't it?"

"What is?" Taven asked.

Lynda set her wine down and dabbed her mouth with her napkin. She looked at me and said, "Your father has always had to contend with his limitations for his spas, given that he's not a physician. With a doctor in the family, he could expand services and offer true medical services. Something he's well aware of."

It was a jab, and I knew it. My father hated his clinics being called anything other than "clinic" or "medi-spa," the "medi" being a very important term for him to put at the front of the label. But he was no doctor, nor was my mother, so what Lynda was saying was true. My father couldn't truly open up a medical clinic without some kind of partnership with a medical professional. My parents made good money, obviously, but there was an element of prestige that seemed to taunt my dad when it came to the more respected true medical professionals he encountered. It was his insecurity, and Lynda just had to bring it up.

I sat up straighter in my seat, pulling my shoulders back. "Well, I have the math gene from my parents, and I've always been good in any kind of science. Medicine is a respectable field. I'd be happy to step in to help my family carry on a business they've worked so hard to make happen." I kept to myself the fights that business often caused, the increasing frequency with which I noticed my mother's pill-popping, or the times she'd send me out to get her cigarettes, now that I could drive. The seedy gas station spot I'd nervously enter, because she knew that was a spot that wouldn't card and would sell them to me. The Carlisles didn't need to know any of that, it was none of their business.

Lynda smiled. "You're a good girl, Desiree, wanting to do right by your family." She nodded. "Shows good character."

It was a compliment, yet I felt sick to my stomach.

ten

. . .

Alternatives

Present Day

taven

Friday, 10:34pm

I STEP OUT of Desiree's hospital room to speak to Melissa in private. She looks at me quizzically, wondering what I'm up to, I'm sure. I might be wondering the same thing.

The doctor had told us Desiree could be released, but that she needed to be with someone for the next forty-eight hours, in case any other symptoms came up. No more music festival, just rest. We were to watch for things like dizzy spells, forgetfulness, hearing issues given the ringing she was having in her ears, or shortness of breath. Desiree had pushed back, stating that she was a pediatrician, she knew what to look out for and didn't need babysitting, that she just wanted to get back to her house and rest. Melissa had laughed and patted her leg, telling her,

"Over my dead body am I leaving you alone. I'll stay with you." Desiree insisted it wasn't necessary.

Desiree and Melissa were staying at a hotel for the weekend, some spot that was no-frills and meant only for a place to crash. I cringed when Melissa informed the doctor of where they were staying, knowing it was a shitty place. Poor planning and everything else was booked, Desiree explained when I asked why the fuck they were staying at such a shady motel.

Desiree still lives in our hometown, about two hours away from here. Melissa, an actress with sporadic momentum, lives in New York. She was in Ohio for a few weeks, staying with her family between jobs.

All this gave me an idea. When the doc delivered the information that Desiree needed monitoring, the thought popped in. I'd take Desiree back to my place, keep an eye on her. I live much closer, she wouldn't have to drive home late at night, I told myself.

Really, I'm just hell-bent on this unexpected encounter not being the last we see of one another. It's been five years since I've laid eyes on her. It's like she's brand new to me all over again. I need more time with her, have to get to know this full-fledged woman who's always had my heart. And now that the idea has entered my mind, there's no way I can get it out.

I lead Melissa to a quiet spot at the end of the hall, and she crosses her arms and waits for me to speak. When I hesitate, she starts the conversation for me.

"What are you up to, Carlisle? Why the clandestine meeting here?" Her eyes dart over to a passing nurse as she waits for me to explain.

I run my hand through my hair, nervous to share my proposition. "Let me take Desiree back to my place," I finally say. "It's late, your hotel is no place for rest and relaxation, and my house is only thirty minutes from here."

She looks back at me, a baffled expression clear on her face. "What? Your place?"

"Yes." It's killing me that Melissa's looking at me like I'm crazy. Like Desiree isn't one of the most important things to me in the world, despite the hell we've been through. I don't like that her best friend's expression is full of doubt.

She narrows her eyes at me. "Why would she do that?"

I try and think of some kind of good excuse. "Because," I shrug, hoping it appears casual. "It's a shorter drive to my place. In case Desiree doesn't feel well sitting in the car." It sounds weak, even to my own ears, but it's all I can come up with.

Melissa shakes her head, eyebrow arched. "She seems alright."

"But she lives alone, right?"

That part hadn't passed me. I perked up with hope when the doctor asked if Desiree lived with anyone, and she responded no. I hoped that meant she was still single. At the very least, it meant she wasn't married. "And she doesn't have a...a significant other or anything like that?" Melissa shakes her head no once again, and I feel about a thousand pounds lighter. "Then I'll take her back to my place and keep an eye on her."

She glares at me, and I'm reminded of how vocal Melissa could always be with her opinions. "And how would *Evelyn* feel about Desiree Hatson staying with you?"

Shit. I know it's a bad idea on that front. A twinge of guilt creeps in, but I try and push it aside. I'll figure Evelyn out later. She's out of town and doesn't live with me anyway. Right now, all I know is that Desiree Hatson, *my Dazzle*, popped up in my life with a goddamn lightning strike, she's in need of care, and I'm going to be the one to give it. That's it, there's no budging on that.

I rehash some semblance of that explanation to Melissa's startled eyes, hoping she gets it.

She unwinds her arms with a sigh. "God, you two are exhausting, you know that?"

I let out a nervous laugh. "I think I know better than anyone, other than her, how exhausting we are."

She pulls her thumbnail up to her mouth, contemplating. "You realize if her dad finds out she so much is talking to you, let alone staying with you, he'll probably disown her. He blames your family for ruining him back when he was still in Ohio."

I slip a hand in my pocket and lean against the wall, willing myself to settle the anger that flares up at hearing Melissa mention Frank Hatson. "Funny," I say, gaze focused on the exit sign at the end of the hall. "I think it's my family that has every right to be the ones hating *him*, not the other way around."

Melissa pops her hands up and to her sides in defense. "Look, I don't know what the hell happened between your parents and Frank, some business deal gone bad bullshit or whatever, nor do I care."

"It's more than that," I whisper.

She looks up at me, expression stony. "What's that supposed to mean?"

"It's a long story." I drop my head down and consider how to sidestep this most unwelcome detour in the conversation. "Forget I said anything."

A few beats pass. Some more scrub-clad staff scurry past us, and I wonder what I'm going to do if Melissa decides to veto my idea, all because she thinks she's protecting Desiree from me or the wrath of her father.

She finally lets out another sigh. "Whatever. I have a feeling I don't even want to know."

"You don't."

"The point is, this is fucking weird, Taven."

I step forward and gesture down the hall to Desiree's room. "She had an accident," I press. "Why is me wanting to take care of her so hard to accept?"

"Because you haven't seen her in five years, maybe?" She widens her eyes at me as if to tell me I'm an idiot. "That, and you're suggesting taking her back to your place *where you have a fiancée—*"

"Evelyn doesn't live with me," I cut in. "And things have been a bit...tense." She glares at me. We stare in silence at one another.

I look away. "I apologize for interrupting. Go on, you were saying?"

She lets out a sarcastic laugh and shakes her head. "I don't even know. I just can't believe you're here. I mean, what are the odds?" I breathe a little relief at the small smile she gives me.

"Apparently lightning and running into each other again are our odds."

"Insane odds," she concludes with an eye roll.

"Agreed," I say. "So, what do you think? Run with it?" I look her square in the eyes, my expression pleading. "I'll take care of her, I promise. You can pummel me if I don't."

"That does sound like fun. You deserve a pummel or two." I only nod, waiting for her to make some kind of decision, knowing this is only step one. Step two is getting Desiree herself on board. Her rejecting the idea and throwing me out of her hospital room is far more terrifying to me than the woman before me.

Melissa finally speaks. "My head is saying take my girl home and get her far away from you and this proposition to take her back to your place, but..."

"But?" I ask with hope.

"But my heart is whispering a little something else."

I smile. "What might that be?"

"Can I ask you something?"

"I have no doubt I couldn't stop you if I tried."

She smiles at that, a genuine smile that shows me a glimmer of the friendship we all once had years before. As a bunch of kids, no care in the world. "Glad you still know me," she says.

"Most people never change who they are at the core," I say through a smile.

She raises her eyebrows. "That's what scares me." I know what she's insinuating. That she's worried I haven't changed. I don't bother explaining that I'm still me, just the best version of it.

"So what are you trying to ask?" I prompt.

Melissa was always a bit of a gatekeeper for Desiree. As kids, and it's clear she is again now. Which makes me happy for them both, really. There was a time during college when Melissa wasn't talking to Daz, and while my girl would put on a tough front, I know it hurt her.

I also know that Desiree has a boundless amount of forgiveness in her heart, something I love about her. I selfishly hope that forgiveness could extend to me. Maybe we could start fresh, though I realize it's a big request. But we've had time. Space. And now here we are, back to the beginning, two adults with an opportunity to get to know one another yet again. There's hope in that.

Melissa looks up at me, eyes narrowed. "Answer me this, Taven. Do you still love Dez?"

I pull my head back, surprised by the forwardness of her question. "I've never stopped loving her."

"Yeah, okay. But I mean like, *really* love her? Fiancée and drama bullshit history aside, do you *love* her?"

"Yes," I say without hesitation.

"And what do you expect to happen in the next forty-eight hours exactly?"

I lean back against the wall and breathe in the smell of antiseptic. "I want to say that I'm taking it minute to minute here, just following my gut and that I have no fucking idea, but I guess that's a lie."

"So what's the truth?" I look at Melissa's face and see an even bigger smile breaking through.

I go for broke. "That I'm madly in love with her," I blurt out, surprising myself at how quickly and easily the words come.

I think about the nights I've spent holding any other woman in my arms, yet wondering where Desiree was or if she's okay. Reaching for my phone to call her and chickening out, knowing she deserves better than me. My mind runs through the countless times I'd had my chances with her, and screwed it up, letting messes, initially fueled by our families, get in the way. And then later, my own messes.

I look back at Melissa and search her eyes from some kind of understanding, or belief in what I'm trying to tell her. "Mel, I've always been in love with Desiree, since I was sixteen years old, and probably even before," I admit. "I'm hoping tonight is a sign from the universe that we are meant to figure this thing out once and for all. And that I have exactly forty-eight hours to undo a cycle of fuck-ups and bullshit that has kept us apart. To undo damages done by our families. To clarify things and make it right."

Melissa lets out a whistle. "Tall order. That all?"

I tell her that's all. And that it's everything. And I have no fucking clue what I'm doing.

She tells me to give her my keys, that she'll be right back, she's going to their hotel to pack Desiree's things.

When I return to the room and approach Desiree with the plan, by some strange miracle, my Dazzle says yes. Says there's no other place she can think of that she'd rather be.

It shouldn't surprise me, because whenever we're around each other we've always been right back to the natural rhythm of *us*, no matter how much time had passed in between. But I'm surprised and relieved, nonetheless. I tell her so, and Desiree tells me I shouldn't be. We exchange a silent look of mutual understanding.

Evelyn's name never even comes up.

phase 2: making every second count

. . .

Initial interest and curiosity has settled. There's now urgency you feel in making this thing happen. The panic consuming you at the thought of it not. You're nervous at each encounter or opportunity, and reckless in your behaviors. The dopamine crash happens, and you're addicted to the object of your desire.

eleven

· · ·

Urgency

Five years ago

lynda carlisle

Summertime, 12:02pm

SHE MAKES THE drive in silence, flowers tucked safely beside her, nestled in a cardboard box used for transport. There was no need for music to fill the empty cabin space of her car. No need for a podcast to fill her mind with ideas and insights, not right now. She took this drive in silence, each time she'd done this. She had been finding that it was one of the few times she allowed her mind to spin through the memories and the bleakness. While Lynda didn't like to have to do so—what's in the past is over, not much sense in dwelling on it—she did in fact recognize the value in processing now and then.

She thinks about when she first met the man that would later become her enemy, unwelcome as the memory often is. It was clear from the start that the husband she had been introduced to had a crush on her own husband.

She knew the behavior all too well. The excitement in the men meeting, the similar drive and ambition, sparking their competitive natures. The introduction of the families, kids thrown together to solidify the connection. Then the business talk that progressively became more and more inappropriate and locker room-esque. Hell, her husband may have had a crush right back.

She patiently played along, not wanting to outwardly express her concerns to her husband about this new man in their lives. One had to be more subtle than that. A woman needed to finesse her husband with seeds to be planted, always leading him to believe an idea had been his own. Lynda was a master at this game.

It was how she herself had landed her husband, all those years ago.

A smile sweeps across her face as her mind wanders to this unexpected memory. She turns her blinker on to merge onto the highway, thinking about how she had fallen in love.

They had met at work, it's true. But it was no accident that she landed on his team. She had done her research, and knew the various teams she might be placed on when she received the internship offer. She knew everyone's ages, schools attended, general background and family wealth. She also knew that William Carlisle was single and handsome, which seemed like a winning combination.

At the orientation, she bumped into him with her coffee, effectively spilling it all over his pristine suit. A subtle blush, her apologies for being so clumsy, explaining how nervous she was. Men liked innocence like that, and William proved to be no different. She feigned surprise when he mentioned that he pushed to have her on his team. After the fool she made of herself to him? My, why thank you, sir. Thank you so much, Mr. Carlisle. He insisted he call her Bill.

Lynda made sure he felt like a hero in her eyes, and pretended to act embarrassed any time a little comment slipped from her pink lips that might have leaned into flirtation. Silly young intern, flirting with her supervisor. Please forgive her, forget she said a thing.

A drink? Oh no, she couldn't possibly.

He insists? Well then, alright. Just one drink.

What she hadn't expected was to have her fake crush turn into a real one. To fall in love with him. One drink really was one drink, Bill was perfectly polite about it. She started to worry he did not in fact find her attractive at all, that he was simply being mannerly.

In the second phase of a crush, a person tries to make every single moment together count. It's your chance to get to know the person, have them get to know you and hope they fall just as hard as you have. You find little opportunities to touch, sending a little zing of electric deliciousness you hope they receive as intended. Because the spark exists there for you, like it or not. Reciprocated or not.

It was maddening for her at first. This was not something she was used to! Men always pursued her, usually unwelcomely. After years of learning which moves to accept and which to fight off as best as she could, this was new territory for her. Lynda didn't like it one bit. She felt off-kilter and unsure in his presence, suddenly thrust into an agony of longing for him that was terrifying.

He was smart. He treated his team with respect, but never let them get away with a mistake without learning something from the mishap. Bill's instincts were sharp, and he worked hard to not only do his job to the best of his abilities, but to be a mentor to those within his circle.

He never once behaved inappropriately despite her leaving

ample opportunities to do so. She learned that nice men did exist, and that they needed a little more coaxing before they'd finally take the plunge and make a move.

In the end, he confessed to have feelings for her, but only when pressed. His work integrity made him unsure of this, however, and so Lynda was moved to another team. Thus, a personal relationship finally ensued.

She'd never had to work so hard for something she wanted rather than needed.

SURELY YOU CAN UNDERSTAND, THEN, why Lynda felt she had to work extra hard to protect her family. She wanted to rescue her family from the dangers of their city, but she knew she couldn't force the issue. She would have to suggest moving away and then wait for her husband to agree. Bill didn't like quick changes, but Lynda argued that you never knew when there would be an opportunity to be had. He countered that you never knew when that opportunity came with risk.

It's one of the things she initially loved most about Bill—he was a master at this art much like she was. They both understood that risk was part of the game, and in truth, it thrilled them for many years. However, money makes people do crazy things, she quickly learned, and the addiction for more is limitless. Her husband's unexpected attack in the comforts of his parking garage had been the final straw in her mind. No more chasing in a game that had become too dangerous. Her husband had his hesitations in leaving behind the world he knew so well. They fought like cats and dogs about what their next steps would be, him yelling that she was being ridiculous, one bad moment wasn't enough to uproot everything. Her begging him to be reasonable, knowing that his hunger for the game would be something he'd struggle to let go of. Her proposal to leave the familiarity of the wealthy New York neighborhoods he knew and loved in favor of the suburbs and a new business focus wasn't exactly a welcomed one.

She came up with another idea.

Her plan had been simple and effective. A networking event in the Midwest. A fresh start with contacts she had forged, making her husband believe they were a result of his ability to charm.

Bill could hardly say no to her enthusiasm.

She had learned of the event and knew of the businessman who would be speaking to a crowd of eager listeners about a new venture. Lynda worked to ensure that the man and her husband would run into each other at the hotel bar later, suit jackets unbuttoned and ties loosened.

She sat quietly in the background as she watched each man stroke the other's ego, sure they had found kindred spirits in one another. Her plan was working. Bill expressed interest, even toying with the idea of moving to the area deemed ripe and ready for the new business. She finally felt like she could breathe a little. She'd succeeded in pulling her husband out of his comfort zone, and in turn, she could keep her family safe.

Naturally, once the move happened, the two families would become close on a personal level. While it wasn't her first choice, thanks to her difficulty in trusting people and for the sake of putting the past behind her, she understood it would have to be that way. One didn't rise to success without partnerships built on loyalty. Both families had something to offer with their skillsets and assets, but it was clear to her which man was more cunning. It brought her some comfort to realize she and her husband would always have the upper hand.

Thankfully, Lynda did come to find that she enjoyed their company. The wife was a sweetheart, of course, though the husband would continue to grate on her nerves now and then. Never mind that, she could side-step his arrogance, particularly when her irritations were tempered with a glass of wine. The important part was that the plan was working, the businesses were proving to be a success, and her husband's thirst for the next challenge was still meeting its match. They had continuing plans to grow, and their lavish lifestyle of comfort and warm meals was never at risk.

As long as she kept a careful eye out, they would be okay. She knew, too, that she could trust her gut. It had never proved her wrong in the past.

When the two families' children began dating (teenagers—so many hormones, she was hardly surprised), she quietly supported, though her apprehension was evident. Things could get messy when the passions of youth were toiling their way through hearts. Perhaps she feared the kids' inevitable breakup and heartache. She tried to remind herself that young love was fairly innocent, and she need not worry.

twelve

· · ·

Panic

Fourteen years ago

desiree

sixteen years old

"DYLAN, I NEED your help. Can you come get us?" I asked as I cradled my phone in one hand, patting Taven's back with the other. He was moaning and curled up on the floor in the fetal position, periodically shouting out a Taco Bell order.

Melissa was standing in the doorway of the bathroom, curly hair long and tousled around her shoulders while she spun one of the strands around her finger. "Should we just take Inferno and go get him some food?"

"No!" Taven shouted from the fuzzy cream rug beneath him. "No one drives my baby!"

The music of the party was muffled and thumping from downstairs. A gaggle of girls walked by us, rolling their eyes at the drunken guy on the floor. I could hear sloppy kisses of kids making out, and Melissa turned her head to yell at them. "Get a goddamn room!" Meanwhile, her own lips were swollen from having just been doing the same thing, and she looked back at me and smiled, hiccupping through a giggle.

I heard Dylan curse on the other end of the phone. "Dez, what happened? Are you okay?"

"I'm fine," I assured my brother, who sounded slightly inebriated himself. I knew that tone, it was his big brotherly concern, but mixed with a little slowness in the cadence of his speech. "Taven and Melissa and I are at a party," I explained, "but I think Taven's pretty messed up. I don't know what to do. And he drove us here." I hated sounding so pathetic. The kid sister that rarely ever did anything reckless, now calling in a mild panic.

"Whatever you do, don't let him drive."

I looked down at my ridiculously hot boyfriend, now looking ridiculously pathetic as he was crying out other food orders, ones from a slew of random fast-food places. The broken towel bar he had managed to yank off the wall lay haphazardly across his body. I kneeled down beside him to lift it, rising and assessing the wall damage. "Don't worry, I'm not even sure he could find his car right now," I told Dylan as I tried to press the rounded edges of the rod into the crumbling bits of drywall. "Let alone try to drive it."

Bits of dust dropped down onto Taven, coating him in white powder. "Such a mess," he muttered out, wiping the debris from his face.

"You look like you caught flurries of snow," I said.

I was trying to sound soothing, but the little nagging feelings of worry had already crept in. I was at the house of someone I didn't know, having dragged my best friend here with me, all because I wanted to be the cool and chill girl for once. Go to let loose? Tell my parents I was going to Melissa's, while instead chugging cheap alcohol procured from some unknown source?

Sure, I could do that for my boyfriend—the one who was now drunk and out of his mind. When we're in the throes of our crushes, we can sacrifice bits of ourselves. Against my better judgment, I had done just that in hopes of showing Taven that I could be a good time.

This was fine, I tried to tell myself. I'd figure this out, but I couldn't help the pit of dread in my stomach, and I suddenly just wanted to be home and in bed. Stupid as it was, I was hard-wired to be a worrier. Kids did this kind of thing all the time, right? Why, oh, why couldn't I just be as easygoing as everyone else? What was wrong with me?

Taven raised his hand. "I could find Inferno anywhere," he whispered below me with gusto, like it was a secret spy message wrapped in a reassurance of his loyalty to his country.

Melissa grabbed the phone from me, holding it up to her ear. "Hello, sweet Dylan," she purred. I felt the tiniest bit of comfort in her calm presence. Everything was fine. Melissa would know what to do. I was freaking out for nothing. We'd figure out a way to get out of here. "Can you come get us, pretty please?" she asked my brother. "I think I'd be alright to drive, but Taven won't let me." She stumbled a little, then added, "Actually, maybe I'm not so okay." I waited as she took another step out into the hall, slowly pacing as she listened to my brother. I heard her say, "That's not really an option," and I wondered what the suggestion was.

This was not exactly how I wanted my night to go. Five minutes ago, Taven and I had been holed up in a guest room, tipsy with hands on each other's bodies in the dark and forbidden upstairs of the parents' house of one of Taven's school acquaintances, someone I didn't even know. I had reached for my good old red plastic cup of cheap booze, ready to boldly take a swig and try and make this moment count, feeling so in love with my boyfriend that had just rescued me from prying eyes.

Earlier, when we were downstairs in the kitchen amidst the

main mayhem of the party, Taven had been taking shots, something I refused to do. He was laughing and trying to get me to join in. "Come on, Dazzle! Cross off a Bingo square, take a shot!" He was grinning and looking devilishly handsome, but still, I refused. He was having fun enough for the both of us, so I quietly sipped my mixed drink, content to let this Bingo square sit unfulfilled.

It was when one of the guys from his school came up to me, pressing a shot glass to my lips, that I started to get uneasy. "One shot, Taven's girl. I won't tell." The kid had a glint in his eye that gave me the creeps. "I have a feeling you'd be real fun, wouldn't you?" he said.

I pushed the glass and his hand away from my face. "I'm really okay," I said, eyes searching for Taven. I saw his smile drop as he looked at the kid hovering way too close to me, and was relieved when he slammed his drink down on the counter, before marching over to us.

Taven yanked the guy's shirt, pulling him away from me, saying, "Don't fucking touch her," then he grabbed my hand.

The guy backed away, laughing. "Alright, Carlisle. Take it easy. Just want your girl to know she's got backup options when she's sick of your dumb ass."

I squeezed Taven's hand in panic, trying to pull him out of there, worried a fight was about to start with the dramatic cheers of the crowd egging them on. "Ignore them," I pleaded to him as I led us to the doorway, looking behind me at the crowd of guys all shouting out random phrases, saying Taven's girl is hot, does he share, just one taste.

He paused his steps, turned to face them, and I was about a half a second away from freaking out.

Taven slowly let a smile sweep over his face. "You guys think you're so fucking funny, don't you?"

"Uh-oh, Carlisle's mad," one guy taunted.

"Ignore them, please," I repeated, trying to keep my voice

firm. His eyes were dead-locked on them, refusing to pull away, chilling with the lifeless smile on his face that looked anything but happy. If looks could kill, his would have.

I pressed my palm into his chest, pushing him backward and out of the kitchen. "Look at me," I said as I steered him down the hall. I put my hand on his cheek and forced his eyes back to mine. "Hey, look at me." I smiled, willing myself to act natural. "They're just trying to rile you up. Don't let them. Then they win."

He studied me for a moment, contemplating how to respond, I think. I knew his pride was bruised, but the last thing we needed was him in some house party fight, returning home with a black eye. His parents would kill him.

He finally nodded, saying, "How do you always know just what to say?" and I breathed a sigh of relief.

I pulled us down the hall, toward the bottom of the stairs. I guided us up and then down through another hall to an empty room, our own little hideaway. I closed the door behind us, glad to be out of the mayhem and deafening noise, unscathed and ready to steal away a quiet moment.

I stepped forward and kissed him, slowly, savoring our peace. His mouth was hungry on mine, and he reached behind me and flicked off the light. He guided us back to the bed and I laid myself down on it, heart beating rapidly, partly from the rush of the interaction downstairs, and partly from the knowledge that Taven and I were actually in a room by ourselves with a closed door for once. It felt like a sacred moment, and I wanted to make it count. I was tipsy and in love, and Taven was in love with me right back.

Within five minutes, I realized it was only *me* that was tipsy —Taven was full-blown trashed. I had clearly underestimated how coherent he was, so when he said he was dizzy, I pulled down my shirt and grabbed his hand to pull him off the bed, the weight of his body nearly crashing us both down as he stumbled into me. "Sss...sis fine, I just need some food," he said.

It scared me how quickly he had gone from being normal Taven, to this pliable substance of flesh and bones. I thought of my mom, and the way she could have nights of one too many, sitting on the couch with a far-off stare, swaying and apologizing to no one. Lucid enough to recognize her drunken state, but too far gone to do anything about it. It didn't happen often, but when it did, I always pitied her vulnerability.

So when it was clear Taven was a lot more drunk than I realized, I hurried us down the hall, pushing open doors to a closet, then an office where another couple was on their own mission. Closed that door and ran past Melissa, who was pressed up against a wall with some party guest conquest of the evening. I eventually found the bathroom. Melissa cried out over the shoulder of her guy, "You guys alright?"

I had shoved Taven into the bathroom and that's when he grabbed onto the towel rack to steady himself. The next thing I know, both he and the silver bar with its neatly displayed bundles of teal terrycloth came crashing down on the floor, with Melissa rushing in behind me to assess the noise.

Now we were here. Melissa was pacing the hallway and consulting with my brother, and I was rubbing Taven's back and hoping he would just get sick and be done with it. I scanned around the vanity and my eyes found a neat stack of small Dixie cups. I turned on the faucet and filled one, handing it to Taven. "Drink this," I said.

He waved me away. "No more shots."

"It's not a shot," I said, nervous that he was serious and actually thought it was. Was he that far gone? "It's water, you just saw me fill the cup."

He lifted his torso, leaning up against the wall and rolling his head to the side as he closed his eyes. "I don't do water. Water's for assholes. Just get me a beer, I'll be fine." I looked at his slumped shoulders, panic rising, wondering how the hell we were going to get out of here so I could get him home safely without his parents finding out. They'd ground him for life, I was sure of it. I could kiss being able to see him goodbye. I was simultaneously mad at him for being dumb enough to think multiple shots was a good idea, yet aching at the sight of my guy so messed up.

I drank down the water myself, figuring I might need to sober up if Dylan couldn't come get us. I looked back at Taven. "You sure you don't want some?" I said with as much flirtatious teasing as possible. "It's so refreshing, so delicious. You should really try it." *Please, for the love of God, Taven. Pull yourself together and drink the water.*

He waved me off again, slumping his way back down on the floor, and I was nervous he was going to pass out. But then, eyes still closed, he muttered out, "I fucked up."

I rubbed his back, relieved he was talking. I told him it was okay. Just a little too much to drink, no big deal, like I did this kind of thing all the time.

He shook his head ever so slightly. "No z'not. You're too, too good, Dazzle. Deserve better. Z'not me. Why me?" he asked in a whisper.

I pushed the hair away from his closed eyes, thinking how someone could look so peaceful, yet be saying such sad things. "I deserve you and you deserve me, got that?" I hated seeing him beat himself up like this. My anger evaporated as I listened to his slurred and dejected words.

"Why do you even love me?" he breathed out. "You shouldn't love me, Dazzle." It was the last thing he whispered before dropping the full weight of his head onto the floor, passing out.

WHEN MELISSA RETURNED TO THE bathroom with my phone, I looked up at her in hope. "Well?" I asked. "Can Dylan come get us?"

Melissa shook her head. "Nope, said he's too far away. So he's calling your mom instead."

I looked at her in horror. My mom was not an option. She'd tell Taven's mom, and the wrath of Lynda was something nobody wanted. This was my own personal nightmare, right here. I had to protect Taven and keep him out of trouble. He did not need this. "Call him back!" I half-shouted to Melissa's startled face. "Stop him!"

Melissa raised her hands. "Relax, my God, what's gotten into you?"

I darted my eyes over to the slump of Taven on the floor. "This. This is what's gotten into me." I was on the verge of tears, feeling desperate that tonight was going to blow up in my face when the Carlisles decided to ship off Taven to military school. I could see it now. They wouldn't be understanding that their son had just gotten a little carried away. They wouldn't give him some sweet lecture on drinking and pat him on the back, saying, "There, there. We all make mistakes."

No. The Carlisles would be furious. They'd yank all privileges like the carrots they constantly dangled in front of Jacqui's and Taven's faces. His phone, his car, any activities that weren't strictly school related. For people that constantly hosted elaborate parties for themselves, champagne flowing with an air of carefree living, they were highly hypocritical when it came to the ways they parented their children. I had seen enough over the years to know they treated their kids like juvenile delinquents that needed constant reprimanding.

Melissa crouched down beside me, her expression softening as she recognized the panic I was feeling. "Dez, sweetie," she said, brushing the hair away from my face. "Your mom will be cool about it. Dylan said so." She flashed her eyes down to Taven.

"And besides, he's passed out, and I sincerely doubt either of us want to be stuck here all night."

"It might be better than the alternative," I said, already hating the idea, especially with my boyfriend out cold.

Melissa smiled. "Yeah, but...that dude I was just hooking up with is a horrible kisser," she said with a tipsy giggle.

I groaned, realizing I was surrounded by no one of any help.

This was exactly why I never did this kind of thing—house parties that were broken up by cops, kids laughing at the stories the next Monday at school while I internally shook my self-righteous head, wondering what the appeal was. It all sounded like stupid child's play that I had no interest in, or so I told myself.

Yet curiosity was somewhere on my mind, I suppose.

The curiosity was killed now, that was for sure. I was screwed, stuck with my boyfriend on the floor, my mind spinning with fears of how drunk is too drunk, and whether or not he'd need his stomach pumped. I tried to think back to the slideshows of warning signs of alcohol poisoning I'd seen. I was the kid to actually listen to those school presentations of guest speakers and police officers coming in to talk about the dangers of teenaged drinking. While every other classmate cracked their jokes under their breath, I had been fighting tears when that nice couple came in to talk about losing their son to drunk driving. The anguish on the mother's face, giant blown-up photos of her son behind her trembling body. The father, placing his arm around his wife, holding back his own tears unsuccessfully. My heart hurt for those people, and for the boy who lost his life to the promises of a simple good time. I feared ever putting my parents in that position.

Yet here I was, at some guy's party and ignoring all of my own usual good decision-making skills, all out of my desperation to get some alone time with Taven. His parents had continued to remain incredibly strict about us being together. I was still never allowed to be at his house when no one was home, and the

Carlisles insisted my parents enforced the same rules at our house. We didn't go to the same school, and Taven was always so busy with sports, all of which left me craving any seconds of time with him I possibly could. I was kicking myself for being so dumb, yet at the same time, wishing I was wired to more cooly handle this kind of thing.

I should have planned better, I shouldn't have been drinking. Jacqui was away on a school trip, Dylan was two hours away at college, and now my mom was going to have to come and get us. My first real attempt at letting my hair down, and I had messed it up. Go figure.

My mind started running through all the possible scenarios of how this would go, how my mom might react. Would she be mad, or would she be happy we were trying to be responsible? I really didn't know, it was my first time ever being truly tipsy, maybe even drunk.

I was pretty sure I'd never drink again. I clearly wasn't very good at it.

MELISSA AND I SLOWLY MADE our way down the stairs and out of the house with Taven's nearly dead weight between us, having miraculously been able to wake him up, but just barely. Once outside, I tried to suck in as much fresh air as possible as we huddled together down the driveway where my mom's car was waiting for us. We piled into the back seat, and my mom handed me a large empty cup. "In case he gets sick," she explained, then she pulled off. I couldn't read her expression or decipher her tone, but at least we were out of the party.

"Inferno!" Taven wailed as we drove past his car, parked on the street. "Nobody better touch my fucking car." I stared at him, horrified, and jabbed him in the ribs with my elbow.

Melissa leaned forward in her seat and patted my mom's

shoulder, hiccupping. "Don't worry, Mrs. Hatson. Taven never usually curses, I promise you." She grinned her signature smile, and my mom rolled her eyes, but I saw the smallest lift of the corner of her mouth. Being in the familiar space of her car, seeing her tiny smile—it all gave me a sense of comfort I was embarrassed to admit I needed.

"Sure, sweetie. Okay," she said.

We pulled into a gas station. My mother handed me her credit card, instructing me and Melissa to go in, grab some bottles of Gatorade, fried chicken, and French fries. She turned back to Taven. "Will that work for you?"

He was leaned against the window, eyes closed, but he curled his thumb and index finger into the "perfect" sign.

Melissa and I ran in, got the goods, and brought everything back out to the car. My mother drove us home, silent. I wondered what she was thinking. If I was going to get a lecture or what. I wouldn't blame her if that's what happened. I deserved it.

We pulled into our garage and made our way into the kitchen. She instructed the three of us to eat, then handed us each two Advil, diligently watching as we took our pills.

"What's Taven's curfew?" she asked.

"None tonight!" Taven chimed in with victory.

I picked at a fry, painting swirling patterns with it through some ketchup. "He was supposed to stay the night at a friend's house."

My mom nodded, satisfied with that answer, I suppose. She said she was going back to bed, and instructed us to keep an eye on Taven and call her if we needed anything.

All I could think was how much trouble was I in, and where were we all going to sleep?

Melissa and I ended up crashing in my bed, and Taven insisted we leave him be on my bathroom floor. At some point I woke up to the sound of him getting sick, but when I tried to wander into the bathroom to check up on him, the door was locked. I lightly tapped, but he ignored it.

I stared at the closed door, a heavy sigh escaping me, hoping he was okay. It broke my heart to hear him like that and not be able to help him. I wanted to at least offer him some comfort, but I knew him well enough to know he was probably embarrassed and wanted to be left alone.

Being on the other side of the door made me really sad for some reason. It was almost like a strange feeling of rejection. I was picturing him there over the toilet, miserable as he tossed up fried chicken and a sickening combination of alcohol. I wanted to be with him and make him feel better, but I couldn't. He'd shut me out.

THE NEXT DAY, I WAS the first of the three of us to wake up. I wandered down into the kitchen where my mom sat at the table in her robe with a cup of coffee, staring at her phone. "Grab yourself a cup," she said, eyes glued to her screen. "You might want some today."

I didn't usually drink coffee, but I did as instructed and poured myself some of the sludge, followed by a heavy dose of cream and sugar. "Top off?" I asked, lifting the pot toward her, and she raised her mug for me.

I filled her coffee, replaced the pot and sat down in front of her. I was itching for her to say something, but she remained quiet. "Where's Dad?" I asked.

"Tennis at the club," she said, still not looking at me. I waited for her to say more, to share whether or not she had mentioned last night to him, but she said nothing.

When I finally couldn't take it anymore, I broke our silence. "Thank you for getting us last night," I said.

She looked up at me, blue eyes looking sad, and put her mug

down. "I'll always come get you anytime you need me. I hope you know that."

I nodded, feeling guilty. "You're not mad?"

She sighed and leaned forward in her seat, reaching for my hand. "I'm not mad. You're a straight-A student who makes my parenting job easy. If anything, I'm happy you're allowing yourself some fun."

"Maybe less fun, next time," I said, sipping my coffee and feeling incrementally better.

My mom sighed. "You're young. I was once young too, trust me. If a night of too many drinks is the worst you do, then I'm lucky." She released my hand and rose to a stand before walking to the junk drawer, pulling out her cigarettes. "Come on," she said. "Step out with me."

We walked out to our deck, overlooking the pool, newly opened for the season but still too cold for any real use. It was late April, and I pulled my cardigan closer against my chest while my mother lit her cigarette, a strangely comforting smell that I loved, bad as it was. I watched her profile as she let out an exhale of smoke. "I see drinks are now on your hobby list. Hopefully not cigarettes too?" she asked, holding up hers in reference.

I didn't have the heart to tell her that no, because her own habits had succeeded in turning me off from the whole thing. While I'd probably forever associate the smell with my mom and all things nurturing and sweet, I knew better than to fall into my own addiction of them. "No, I don't smoke," was all I said.

"Good." She took another drag and turned to me, waving off the smoke that wafted toward my face. "Desiree, sweetie. I'm glad you reached out to Dylan last night, that was a smart move. Next time, if there is a next time," she said, eyebrow raised at me, "you can just call me, alright?"

I nodded, not sure if she was mad about last night or hurt that I didn't call her first. Maybe it was both.

"How's Taven doing?" she asked.

I answered truthfully. "I'm not sure, he locked himself in the bathroom, but I know he got sick."

"That's for the best."

I leaned against the railing and sipped my coffee, trying to clear my fuzzy head. "You didn't tell his mom, did you?" I asked, praying that my mom wouldn't feel obligated to rat him out.

The smoke swirled around my mother in mesmerizing waves, and she looked back out to the yard and trees beyond. "No. I don't think she'd be too happy to learn her son had been imbibing so carelessly."

"Thank you," I said with relief. It wasn't enough to convey my gratitude, but there were no words to express my fears of the formidable Lynda Carlisle thinking her son was even more of a fuck-up than she already seemed to think he was. Or worse, for her to see me as being a bad influence.

My mom took one final drag of her cigarette before jabbing it out in the sand filled crystal ashtray she kept outside. She crossed her arms and looked at me. "Desiree, I didn't keep my mouth shut for you, or even for Taven. I did it for Lynda, because I know her and I know how much this would worry her."

"Oh," was all I said. I looked down at my bare feet against the wood of our deck, feeling more guilty by the minute.

"I'm not a stranger to kids and house parties and drinking. I get it. I raised your brother, remember?" she says, and I look back up at her to see her giving me a little half-smile.

"Couldn't have been easy," I joke.

She laughs. "Well, your brother has a very naturally charismatic way of talking himself out of trouble. He's like your father in that sense, I suppose."

"Two peas in a pod." I couldn't be sure if my mother had a favorite child, but if she did, it would be Dylan. Not like she made it obvious, but she seemed to relate to him better. My parents and brother were the fun and carefree types. I was the quiet goodie-two-shoes. I knew I made my parents proud, but I also knew they wished I were a little more...something. I was constantly being told to lighten up or stop being so sensitive, to quit taking everything so seriously. They meant well, I know they did. I just felt like an outsider sometimes, the misunderstood, quiet, and sensitive soul.

My mom was slowly nodding, her expression pensive. "You and Taven strike me as a little more...I don't know. Fragile, perhaps. Maybe it's because you two are the babies, and us mothers subconsciously keep you in our minds as younger than you are."

I looked down at my coffee, mindlessly blowing on it and watching the ripples of brown liquid. "That makes sense," I said. "But you don't have to worry about me."

She sighed. "Not yet, but give it time." I looked up at her with a frown, but she just smiled, leaning her elbows back on the railing. "Relax, it was a joke."

"Very funny."

She ignored me and continued. "My point is, I may not need to worry about you, but I do know Lynda worries about Taven. She thinks he's not as driven as Jacqui, or as focused as both Lynda and Bill are hard-wired to be. These are her words not mine," she clarifies.

I was immediately defensive. "Yes, he is. Taven has all kinds of dreams of what he wants to do with his life and the adventures he wants to have. Just because he's not some straight-A student doesn't mean he's a screw-up," I said, irritated at the insinuation.

My mom raised up her hands. "Don't kill the messenger, I'm just relaying what she's shared, that's all. But don't make it a habit of thinking I'll always keep my mouth shut to her, okay? This was a one-time thing. And I don't know if Taven just got carried away last night and will live and learn or what, but what I do know is you both need to look out for each other, okay?

Especially when it comes to being out at random parties and downing whatever alcohol is available, not knowing who bought it or what the hell you're even consuming. You're both entirely too young to be making drinking a regular habit. It's a slippery slope, Desiree."

I groaned, putting my coffee down and resting my arms on the deck railing, laying my head in them. "Last night was not a regular thing, I promise."

I knew I deserved a lecture, but I hated every minute of feeling like I disappointed her or that she needed to worry about me. I felt horribly small and mortified, listening to her attempt to give me life lessons I never wanted to think about in the first place. I never even really drank before last night! But I couldn't exactly say the same thing for Taven, so I figured I'd rather not say anything at all.

"Fine," she said. "I'm glad to hear that. But Desiree—look at me, honey," she said, pushing my hair from my face and running her hands through it, combing it down my back. I turned to face her, still keeping my head down. "I feel the need to remind you how vulnerable a young girl can be, especially if she's been drinking."

"I didn't take any drinks from anyone. I poured them myself, or Melissa or Taven poured them. And he wouldn't poison me, I'm pretty sure," I said, trying to keep my tone light, but knowing how painfully immature I probably sounded when she was trying to give me a valuable warning.

My mom continued stroking my hair, a look of tenderness and sadness in her eyes. "I know he wouldn't, sweetie. But remember this—if he's passed out drunk somewhere and you're a little tipsy too..."

"Yeah?" I asked when she faded off.

She sighed. "And harm comes your way, who's going to be there to protect you?"

thirteen

. . .

Addiction

Present Day

desiree

Friday, 11:37pm

MELISSA SQUEEZES ME in a hug as I rise out of the hospital bed, grateful to finally be getting the hell out of here. After the whirlwind of the past several hours, I can think of nothing better than getting into a hot shower, washing the sand and stale remnants of the festival off of me and plopping myself into a warm bed.

At Taven's house.

Yes, I have agreed to head back for my forty-eight hours of obligatory babysitting to my ex-boyfriend's place. Does that make me nuts? Maybe. But the idea of actually being able to spend some one-on-one time with him fills me with an uncanny giddiness. A chance to clear the air and at the very least, have my friend back.

In some ways, it feels like Taven and I have yet to know the grown-up versions of one another. Our early twenties were so tumultuous, so many curveballs thrown our way that it hardly feels like we were ever able to exist on any solid ground. Even five years ago, during our brief time back together when I thought *for sure* we were both ready, it was nothing like I thought it would be.

I have a feeling this time could be different. Even if he's just in my life as my friend, I have to have it. Okay, fine—there's an annoying bit of my heart that aches for more, stupid as that is. I can't help it. You know how it is, that nagging little piece of hope you just can't seem to let go of.

But I'm reminding myself that he has a fiancée, and maybe hearing about his new, settled life with Evelyn will help me. Maybe I just need to spend some time with him, and we can catch one another up on all we've missed. Maybe I just need to see for myself that Taven's really okay, and I can move on from him, once and for all.

I think about the past five years of my life since Taven and I were last together. The truth is, I've kept dating safely on the casual side of things, never taking any relationship seriously. I'd get freaked out when anyone got too close or wanted to declare exclusivity, as if the idea of it came with handcuffs and a chain. It's like this block has existed in my heart, and I recognize that it's a block placed there by Taven Carlisle.

It's time to get rid of it.

"Are you sure you want to do this? That this is a good idea?" Melissa whispers in my ear. I glance over her shoulder to Taven, sure he can hear her. He gives me a little wave, saying he'll step out to give us some privacy.

I pull back away from her. "Mel, it'll be fine. *I'm* fine."

She arches an eyebrow. "Fine stands for 'fucked up, insecure, neurotic and emotional.'"

I smile. "Okay, so then we're on point."

"That's what I'm worried about. He's your kryptonite. Your addiction."

"Maybe a little," I agree.

"And look, I'm all for a wild-haired idea—"

"For as long as I've known you," I interrupt.

She gives me a little nudge and whines out, "I just *worry* about you, kid. I can't help myself," she adds as she crosses her arms.

"I'm a big girl. I got this. Besides, I thought you already gave your seal of approval," I say, my eyes darting over to my bag on the chair.

Imagine my surprise when Taven and Melissa had wandered out of the room to discuss something, and next thing you know, Taven is walking back in, saying he gave her keys to his car to go pick up my things from our hotel. I teased him that I didn't know him to let other people drive his cars. He said he made an exception. He wants me to rest and recover at his place, which is closer than me heading all the way home. All so he could keep an eye on me.

I had stared at him for a moment, wondering if he was for real. His expression—his beautiful, handsome face—was firm. Dark eyes holding my gaze like he wouldn't dare look away. That look said a million things, like I could see the years of all our shared moments passing in the space between us. I looked at his crossed arms, covered with new tattoos.

I had been with him when he got his first one. I had loved that day.

He was waiting for my answer, dead serious.

Back to my place. I want to keep an eye on you. I can't let you out of my sight until I know you're okay.

Oh, really?

Really. Please, Dazzle. Let me take care of you.

My skin tingled. I threw caution to the wind and agreed.

Was I crazy? Maybe.

I blink away the image of him before a blush betrays me and I look at Melissa. She gives me a little smile and shrug, saying, "I just don't want you getting crushed all over again." It's yet another one of those moments when her facade is down, and she seems so innocent. A peek behind the curtain of the Broadway actress who usually exudes such confidence.

I heave out a deep breath. "Can I tell you something?" I ask her.

"Anything." Her green eyes smile with a bit of sadness, and I'm wondering what's behind that look.

I tuck my hair, windblown and wild from the rain, behind my ear. "In college, when you stopped talking to me," I say, scanning her face for her reaction. It's a subject we rarely bring up. I continue. "That was a really hard couple years of my life. Not just because of my mom getting sick, but also because of how much I missed you. I half-wondered if I was in love with you, that's how badly it hurt," I add, my tone teasing.

She lets out a gentle laugh, but drops her head down in defeat. I shake her shoulders to force her to face me again. "Hey, look at me," I say. "I'm not here to blame or rehash or anything, I know you had your reasons."

Melissa had gone for her bachelor's in New York, destined to be the star that she viscerally was. Like any friendship that spans the course of many years, it was a time of quiet distance for us. We went from best friends that saw each other daily to casual acquaintances that were swept up in our own lives, the geographical distance making keeping in touch difficult. Until one day, we stopped talking altogether. I suspected that the new guy she was seeing was toxic, and she later confirmed that to be true, but still, it hurt like hell at the time. I didn't know what exactly had happened to cause our distance—the emotional distance. At the time I felt horribly naive in thinking our friendship would last forever, never veering off course.

I twist one of her dark curls through my fingers. "What I'm trying to say is this—when you and I finally reconnected, life got better, you know what I mean?" She nods, but remains uncharacteristically quiet. I continue. "You know the history with Taven."

"That I do," she agrees. I look at the scatter of freckles under her eyes and smile at the memory of the summers together that earned them. The sunscreen, then later, the tanning oil we thought was a good idea. The drinks on the beach, the lounging by my condo's pool. All of my favorite moments with Melissa.

I sigh. "I just can't help but think that maybe this, right now, maybe this is finally our time. And I want him back in my life. I just do," I shrug. "I want to offload the things I should have said to him and never did."

She nods with understanding. "I agree, I think that would be good for you."

"It's time."

"But back in your life as what, exactly? Where do you hope he'll fit in?"

I plop down on the edge of the hospital bed. "You mean other than as the long-lost love of my life?"

"Well, I already knew that."

I puff out my cheeks with an exhale. "It's no secret, I guess."

"He's in love with you too," she says, and I pop my head up at her in surprise. "He said so, earlier. When he approached me about taking you home with him."

I can't help the smile that sweeps across my face. "He said that?" *Don't cling to hope. He can just be your friend again. That's better than nothing.*

Melissa's jade eyes go wide, her eyebrows raised. "Why the hell do you think I actually went and got your stuff?"

"Figured you did it just because you knew I'd go for it."

She rolls her eyes. "Doll face, I wouldn't let your heart get burned all over again for nothing. Yes, I had a feeling you'd go for it. Fun little unexpected weekend to reconnect, just you and Taven."

"I'm pretty transparent, I guess," I mutter.

She ignores me. "I wasn't going to let you do that to yourself, though, before seeing where he was at. If he felt the same. Which he does, so that's a start. But now what?" She puts her hands on her hips, and I look behind her to see Taven pop his head in through the doorframe, then back out again.

"He's *here*, Mel. I have to have him back. Even if it's just as a friend," I add.

She tilts her head to the side. "You could do that?"

"Sure." We both know that's a lie, but she lets it slide. "Look, I thought losing my mom was the hardest thing of my life," I say, my mind slipping to those last moments with my mom, before cancer took her away. "But not having you two, my *people*, that's just as hard," I explain. "Maybe even worse, because parents die, and we expect that. Not quite so young, I mean I wish I had more time with her."

Melissa reaches out and touches my arm. "I know, babe."

"Although, at least her sickness brought you and me back together," I say with a smile. She nods and I imagine she's thinking the same thing I am—that there's a silver lining in the darkest of experiences. You just have to be open to finding it. I place my palm over my heart. "There's people that just stay with you forever, no matter what. Always in your heart. Even when you and Taven both weren't in my world, I still held onto the love for you in the very core of my being, you know what I mean?"

She nods and says, "Me too," and I think I see her eyes welling. I give her stomach a little poke. Tease her and say there's no need for tears, and sure enough, she blinks and one makes its way down her cheek.

She quickly wipes it away, though, saying, "Well, *this* wasn't what I imagined for the fun-filled weekend I had planned."

"Life rarely ever goes as planned."

Melissa opens her mouth into a smile. "I'm sorry. For all of it, you know that, right? Dumb fool, I was."

I stand and give her another squeeze, her soft frame feeling like the best comfort in the world. I can feel the guilt in the tightness of the squeeze she gives me in return, and I want her to know there's no need for it. "We were both stubborn asses, not just you," I say as I release her. "But we're older and wiser now, for the most part."

"Mostly," she agrees.

"Mostly," I nod.

I step past her and go to grab my bag from the chair, and slip the strap over my shoulder. "Listen. I realize this is a screwed-up idea, to go stay with Taven freakin' Carlisle. If it were anyone else, I'd laugh at the suggestion."

"But it's Taven," she whispers with understanding.

I nod. "Exactly. It's Taven." My chest rises in a heavy sigh. "And I'm sick and tired of pretending he's not my other half. Other than you, of course."

"Of course."

"I have to see where this goes. I have to try, one last time."

She steps closer to me and kisses my cheek. "I get it. See what happens, if you guys can figure something out." She shrugs. "I'm a phone call away if shit goes south."

I lift my mouth in a side smile. "You mean like if Evelyn shows up?"

She laughs. "Yeah. Like that. Or anything, really."

"Let's hope your phone remains quiet, then."

"Fingers crossed." She grabs my hand and spins around one of my rings. "You want to know why I really agreed? Not just because he said he was in love with you."

I study her eyes, wondering if she had the same thought I did. "Then why?"

She sighs and drops my hand. "We were at a music festival. A party spot. Drinks flowing everywhere." I nod, knowing what she's going to say. "I couldn't help but notice that Taven's sober."

Sober.

I grin. "Neither could I."

fourteen

· · ·

Secret

Fourteen years ago

desiree

sixteen years old

THE SECOND HALF of high school had been hell, thanks to the explosive family break-up that caused the end of the Carlisle-Hatson era. My family had been forced to sell their businesses, and they were back to square one.

Taven and I had officially been boyfriend and girlfriend for only a couple months.

My mom had come into my room one night, explaining that things were about to change. I was sitting on my bed, books spread out before me while I studied for the next day's final history exam. She wandered over to the window and placed a lowball of amber liquid onto the windowsill. I watched as she slid open the window, letting in a small breeze that caused my curtains to flutter gracefully. My mother reached into her pocket for her cigarettes, then lit one, her cheeks sucking in with an inhale before blowing the smoke out through the screen.

She never smoked inside.

I studied her face, waiting for her to explain what was going on. I noticed the circles under her eyes and my belly twisted in knots of dread.

She finally spoke, her gaze held firmly out the window. "We've decided to cut ties with the Carlisles, Desiree." I continued to watch the flutter of the curtain, confused, waiting for her to explain what that meant. The smell of the smoke made its way over to me, and I grabbed my pillow to squeeze against my chest, leaning down to inhale the floral scent of fabric softener in attempt to chase the stink away.

My mom plucked the lowball from the windowsill, put it to her lips, and tipped the contents into her mouth. She pulled it away and ashed her cigarette in the glass with an aggressive tap. I noticed the tremble in her hand. "They've done some inexcusable things, and because of that, we need to make some changes."

I scrunched my eyebrows in confusion. We had just been over there last weekend. Taven and I had been rounding our way through the bases on his bed, wondering how long we could get away with the closed door we were risking in the house full of people. If this was it—we'd finally have sex.

We didn't, though. Our time was cut short by the sound of my mother's voice down the hall, telling me it was time to go. Taven and I had scrambled off each other, worried we were about to get caught. I straightened my clothes and jumped into the hallway just as my mother was approaching, her face red and expression stern. When she saw me, she turned on her heel and told me to follow her, which I could barely hear over the sound of my heart pounding. She led me back down the hall, through the foyer, and to the front door. Mike held the door open for us without making eye contact.

The entire car ride home my mind was spinning on how close Taven and I had gotten, wondering when we could meet again or how we could actually get some time to ourselves. We had gotten pretty swept away that night. I was nervous my parents knew what we were up to, not that they wouldn't expect it. Still, it wasn't exactly a confrontation I wanted to have with them, and as the three of us drove away, I was in a panic that they were about to give me a lecture. But they didn't. In fact, they didn't say a word the whole ride home.

Apparently, it may not have had anything to do with concerns about me.

I narrowed my eyes and stared at my mother's profile as she took another drag of her cigarette. "What do you mean, what did the Carlisles do?" I asked, my voice weak.

Her gaze remained focused on my bedroom wall. "It's none of your concern, but just know that we are through with them."

"Okay," I quietly nodded, having no idea what "through with them" meant exactly.

She squeezed her eyes shut, then opened them, raising the cigarette and pointing to me. "I mean it. This is serious, Desiree. That means no more Taven."

I whipped my head up to look at her. She couldn't be serious. "But—"

"I mean it," she snapped. "Nothing to do with him anymore. You two are done." She closed her eyes again. "You have to be done. I'm sorry."

I tossed my pillow aside, holding my breath, wanting to scream as I watched her chest rise and fall. I wanted to shout that whatever the hell was happening with Mr. and Mrs. Carlisle had nothing to do with me or Taven. That this was ridiculous, there had to be some misunderstanding. I wished I could be more like Dylan, who was always more vocal, never having a problem standing up to our parents and saying his piece. What would he do right now? He'd probably yell at

Mom and tell her to stay out of his life. I'd seen him do it before.

I'd also seen my mom cry in response, and my heart would pinch with sympathy for her despite myself. Trying so hard to tame her son who knew what he wanted and went for it, without hesitation.

My mom took a deep breath, collecting herself. When she opened her eyes again, she picked up her makeshift ashtray and walked toward me. She sat on the edge of my bed and squeezed my knee. I could see turmoil all across her face. She was stressed. Upset. Hurting, maybe. "This is not a joke," she said. "Things are...complicated, honey. And I know you don't want to hear this, but that includes Taven."

"Mom, what are you talking about? What's complicated, and what's Taven got to do with it?" Alarm bells were ringing in my head. Had Taven done something that I didn't know about? Was he in trouble?

"I don't want to get into details that you don't need to know."

I inched my way closer to her, desperate to understand what was happening. "Did Mrs. Carlisle tell you something about him? Because he's a good guy, Mom. You have to know that." I was irritated and hurt at the idea that my parents might be viewing Taven with the same disdain his own parents often seemed to.

"It's not about that, Desiree," she said, her voice beginning to rise. "You're not listening to me."

My irritation was quickly rising to confused anger. "Explain it to me, then! Explain why the hell you think I'm supposed to stop seeing him when he's done absolutely nothing wrong—you can't do this!" I was yelling now, something I never did when it came to my parents. I was simultaneously high off my newfound anger and afraid of the repercussions.

"Enough," she snapped, her eyes wide and tormented. I

went to speak up again, but the look on her face stopped me. She looked almost like she was in physical pain, her shoulders hunched over and her face scrunched like it hurt to breathe. It scared me.

Something was definitely wrong, and if I wanted to be able to get through to her, I had a feeling getting in an uncharacteristic screaming match wasn't going to work in my favor. I swallowed whatever it was I wanted to say.

She softened her voice. "Enough."

I looked at her in a staredown, willing myself to find some semblance of defiance, prove to myself and her that I was old enough to stand my ground or hear whatever it was that she felt was causing the ridiculous idea of me no longer seeing Taven.

But I was incapable. Inept. Misunderstood and wildly insignificant in a household of personalities far bigger than my own. I'd always be the baby, just like my mom had said the morning after she picked me and Melissa and Taven up from that party, a memory that mortified me.

I didn't talk back to my parents, ever. I respected them too much, I suppose. Feared having them upset with me. At Melissa's house, loud and vocal arguments were the norm. Mrs. Belle yelling at her to put her things away before she causes someone to fall and break their neck, did she want to kill everyone in the household? Melissa yelling back, "I said, *in a minute!*" lost in whatever it was she was doing, and I'd be scurrying over to the pile on the stairs, running it down to her room, eager to placate.

Or her mom yelling at her to change her shirt, nobody needed to see a young girl's breasts. Melissa yelling back that her mother shouldn't have given her *an impossibly big rack, then!* and I'd stand there in quiet shock and discomfort at the exchange. Then Mrs. Belle would kiss both our cheeks, tell us to have fun and be safe while throwing a sweater in Melissa's arms, knowing full well she'd never wear it.

It wasn't like that in my house. I didn't have a confrontational bone in my body. I was a "yes" girl, quietly obeying and hoping my goodness would be recognized and loved. Feeling hopelessly invisible.

My mom softened her voice. "All you need to know is that you are not to see Taven or speak to him ever again, do you understand?" She looked at me, waiting for my response. "I'm so sorry, honey. I really am. But it's the way it has to be."

I simply nodded, wanting to be done with the conversation. My mind was spinning knowing full well not seeing Taven again was never going to happen. It wasn't even an option—I was in love with him, and he was in love with me. My world *was* Taven Carlisle. It was that simple. I couldn't wrap my head around what on earth could have happened that would make him not being in my life something my parents thought was necessary.

So I sat there quietly and played along for the time being, thinking of what I was going to do.

I'd ignore her demand. Whatever stupid blow-up our parents had was beyond my concern. I didn't care what mishaps were happening between them. It had nothing to do with Taven or me. I couldn't wait until my mom left my room, knowing I would immediately grab my phone and text him to see what the hell was going on.

But when I did, his response was not what I expected.

T: I'm sorry. I can't talk right now. Things are really bad, I can't explain.

And that was the end of that.

As you can imagine, it was a dark time. I texted Taven every hour for days, pleading with him to get back to me. To tell me what was going on. I'd apologize, not even knowing what I was apologizing for. Then I'd spiral and go into anger mode, telling him to fuck off if he couldn't even have the decency to talk to me. I felt like a discarded piece of trash, convincing myself that the Carlisles had somehow decided my family was beneath them, and Taven was swept up in it too. So many insecurities and feeling like I wasn't interesting enough, special or good enough for him—they all came flooding back. I sobbed until my nose was sore from tissues and my belly ached in pain, as if my broken heart had dropped to my stomach and was spreading its disease. I couldn't imagine ever feeling whole again. I *needed* Taven. I needed him so badly, I loved him so much, and he wanted nothing to do with me. I wasn't enough for him to defy his parents.

All my efforts to reach him went unanswered. I felt like a desperate fool, and in truth, I was. I'd take my Honda Civic and grab Melissa, forcing her to go drive with me to the Carlisle house, creeping past the gates and hoping I could peer in and see something. I secretly hoped he'd magically appear, hop in the car and we'd drive off and run away together, as silly as it sounded. I'd stalk his social media accounts, starved for glimpses of what he had going on, but there were no posts, no comments or activity of any kind. I'd drag my best friend to the Paisley Club, hanging by the newly opened pool for hours on end, dreaming that he'd show up and he'd throw me fully clothed in the pool, laughing that this had all been some terrible joke. Gotcha! I'd get lost in these fantasies, loving the alternative to my actual reality.

Sometimes my fantasies would go from hopeful to dark, and I'd imagine these elaborate stories of what was happening in Taven's world. That he was swept up in an arranged marriage. That the Carlisles had him courting some beautiful hotel heiress princess, a new family they were joining forces with. A life that had been planned for him all along, and he was blindly following along with it, falling madly in love and planning the wedding of the century to be had when they both turned eighteen. I was obsessed with torturing myself with dreams of showing up to this fictional wedding, hand in hand with a prince of my own, and Taven would see me walk in. He'd stand at the altar and declare he couldn't go through with it. He'd apologize to his mom and dad, then come running down the aisle to beg for me, dropping to his knees and saying he couldn't live without me. In this fantasy, sometimes I'd go along with it and drop to my knees right with him, kissing him and telling him I forgive him. Other times I'd remain standing, dramatically holding my chin up high. The music would swell and I'd grab my new man and say, "Taven Carlisle, I once thought you broke my heart. But the truth is, you freed it." Then my love and I would turn on our heels and walk away, leaving Taven weeping on the ground, cursing his family and then crying out that he'd never love anyone the way he loved me.

fifteen

. . .

Subterfuge

Fourteen years ago

desiree

sixteen years old

OVER THE NEXT couple of weeks, things within the house got worse. My parents would hole themselves away in their bedroom, muffled shouting traveling down the hall, and I'd sink onto the floor of my room in sedated numbness. I wondered if they were splitting up, but I was too wrapped up in my own heartbreak to even care. They put the house on the market, explaining that money was tight for us, because the Carlisles pulled out their investment in the business. I was given a warning that I'd be transitioning back to public school for my junior and senior years.

The new girl yet again.

Had it not been for Melissa barging into my room and force-feeding me milkshakes and fries any chance she could, I might have lost my marbles.

The dust was starting to settle after the Carlisle-Hatson fallout when Taven finally reached out to me.

I had shed countless tears by that point, my heart completely split open to the point of a physical pain. I couldn't eat, showers felt like a chore, and I prayed to God asking Him to fix this. To go back in time and fix whatever it was that had happened to turn everything upside down.

So when the text came in from an unknown number one day, saying it was Taven, I thought I was dreaming.

> D: What number is this?

> T: Texting from a friend's phone. My parents check mine.

> T: I'm sorry I didn't reach out sooner. Could we meet up?

I was apprehensive, but what could I do? Clearly he had been given the same "stay away" command I had, but what did that mean for us? Did he still care about me? Had he ever even loved me?

Whether he did or not suddenly didn't matter. I'd take what I could get. I'd make this count, see him again and make him remember just how wonderful I am, how wonderful we are together. Make him see that nothing else matters.

I typed back as quickly as I could, having no idea how long this window to Taven would be open.

> D: Yes, any time. When? I'm free now, I could sneak out. My parents aren't home. Can you pick me up?

My hands were shaking, I was desperate to make this interaction happen. We just needed to *see* each other, and then everything would be fine. We could go back to being us. We just needed to figure out a way to communicate. He could get a cell phone that his parents didn't know about, we could create new emails or fake Facebook accounts and talk that way, anything we needed to do.

My parents had sold my car at that point, despite my begging them to let me keep it, promising I'd figure out a way to make the monthly payments. I had watched them hand over the keys to the eager palm of its new owner, some college kid. I felt like I was watching my freedom get ripped away.

Without transportation of my own, Taven would have to pick me up if we were to meet. In Inferno. A red car that was entirely too easy to spot. My mind spun around wildly thinking of all the ways we could make this happen.

My phone dinged as I paced around the room trying to determine my next steps.

> T: I can be there in twenty minutes. Could you walk down the street a little just in case?

> D: Yes! Yes, I'll head out in a minute and meet you by the stop sign at the front of my neighborhood.

I ran a brush through my hair, changed outfits twice, only to put back on the jeans shorts and tee that I was originally wearing. My thoughts were all over the place as I darted down the street, whipping my head left and right to ensure the coast was clear and I could get away without being seen. I waited at the stop sign, praying my parents wouldn't pull up any time soon. Finally, the beautiful purr of Inferno arrived.

When I got in the car, Taven was quiet. I was quiet, too, because I didn't know what to say. Something had shifted in those weeks of radio silence, and he now felt like a stranger to me all over again.

I wondered if it was because he knew his parents had messed up, and he held some guilt over the ruin it had caused my household. Did he feel bad? Did he know how terrible things were for my family? But I didn't want to ask what was wrong, because the last thing I wanted to do was bring a dark cloud over our precious borrowed time together.

As we pulled away from the curb, I finally broke the silence. "Where are we going?" I had expected him to take me back to his house, but that wasn't the direction we were headed in. I peeked over to him, to my Taven, noting the gray baseball hat sitting backwards on his head and covering his always impeccable hair. The hat was new, one that I had never seen him in before. I hated that anything new had entered his world without me knowing about it. Even something as ridiculous as a hat.

"I don't know," he answered, his tone quiet. "I figured we'd just drive around for a bit."

I looked out my window and the blur of trees whizzing by. I thought about how the time that had passed since we last saw each other felt like an unrecognizable blur as well. "How's Jacqui doing?" I asked, wanting to fill the space with some kind of conversation. "Is she getting excited for college?"

I didn't want to ask about his parents, because in my eyes, they were enemy number one, though for different reasons than my parents. To me, Mr. and Mrs. Carlisle had screwed up to the point of ruining the single most important thing to me, and now I was stuck in a car with him feeling like none of our history had ever happened at all.

Taven slid his hand down the steering wheel and for a moment, I thought he was going to reach out and grab mine. But he didn't. He only rested it on the center console. "Why are you asking about Jacqui?" he asked.

I frowned at him. "Because she's your sister and I haven't seen you guys in forever?" Really, it had only been a few weeks, but with the mayhem of my household, with everything changing yet again, it felt like another life.

He huffed out a sarcastic laugh. "Right."

I folded my arms over my chest, confused by his impassive demeanor. "And because I really couldn't care *less* how your *parents* are doing, if I'm being honest." My tone was bitter. I wanted to be more calm about it, scared of pushing Taven away if he was siding with his parents in all this, but I couldn't help myself.

His eyes darted over to mine, saying something that I didn't understand, and I regretted having mentioned his parents at all.

"What did you hear about everything, Desiree? What makes you think this is my parents' fault?"

I glared at him. "You're kidding, right? Your parents pulled out of the business."

He ran a hand down his face. "I know. But...it's hard to explain."

I hated that answer, or lack of one. "Well, are *your* parents in a state of constant fighting? Is your house up for sale right now?"

"What? No, why?"

I picked at a loose thread in the ripped part of my jeans shorts, twisting it around my finger. "Because *my* house is up for sale. I'm going to have to change schools again. We're stopping our membership at the club, they're dissolving the business, and I'm pretty sure my parents are on the brink of divorce. All because *your* parents pulled out their investment. So yeah, that's what my life is looking like right now." *A shit show*, I thought.

I didn't care about the money or the school or the club, none of that truly mattered to me, but I wanted to convey to Taven that because of the crumbling of our parents' partnership, my family was spiraling, and it appeared that his wasn't. And I felt like I was the one being punished through it all. I wiped a tear from my cheek and stared out the window, wishing I could go back in time to when everything was perfect.

Taven finally grabbed my hand, and I flinched with surprise. I wasn't sure how to even feel comfort in it. Like I couldn't trust it. "I'm sorry, Dazzle," he whispered. "I'm sorry all of that is happening to you." All I could do was nod. I wanted to stay mad, but I wanted him more.

We drove around a little while longer, shifting the conversation to safer topics. He asked me how my last weeks of school had been, how Melissa was doing. I allowed myself to relax a bit and told him about her dreams of going to New York to pursue acting. How I knew she'd succeed, because she was such a natural. How Dylan was thriving in school and how his football scholarship would allow him to stay there and graduate.

Taven eventually asked if I was okay. I wanted to scream and cry and tell him that I was definitely not okay, but I held back, not wanting to be a dramatic mess. Instead, I assured him it was fine, that we were halfway through high school and the next two years would fly by. I thought about how not too long ago, Dylan had to switch schools as a senior in high school, and now he's living his dreams. He'd been fine, and I could be too. I'd figure it out.

We avoided any more talk about our parents, which I think we both knew was best. I didn't like how angry I felt towards his family, and I knew it wouldn't do us any good to try and get in the middle of it.

When he approached the front of my neighborhood, it was nearly dark. He pulled over and put the car in park. I reached for the handle to open the door, but he told me to wait, so I dropped my hand back in my lap. I waited for him to say something. I wondered if he was going to kiss me. My stomach was in knots, and I hated how foreign it felt to be with him again.

He finally put the car back in drive, spinning the wheel around and whipping Inferno into a U-turn. "Fuck it, I'm taking you back to my house," he said. "Tell your mom you're at Melissa's or something."

My pulse quickened at the prospect. I worried my parents wouldn't believe the lie I was about to tell, but I didn't care. I'd do whatever I could to get more time with him. "Okay. But what about your parents?"

Taven shrugged. "They're not home."

***

THERE'S OFTEN A PRETTY CLEAR moment when you realize your parents aren't perfect. As a kid, you think they hung the moon. Even when they're telling you "no" for something. You're mad at them, sure, but mostly because you love them and hate that they don't seem to know what exactly you need or want, or aren't willing to give it to you. It's hard to love someone so much and feel disappointed by them.

It was probably Dylan that first gave me clues that our parents had flaws. When I was ten or eleven, and Dylan was fourteen, I had heard him crying in his room. He had been fighting with Mom over something. I didn't know what exactly, but I remember feeling mad at her for being mean to Dylan.

I had quietly knocked on his door, and I heard his muffled sniffle on the other side. "Can I come in?" I asked.

I heard some ruffling and then eventually, he opened the door, and I saw how red his eyes were. "What do you want?" he quietly asked.

I remember not being sure why I had even knocked on the door, but I loved my brother and felt like I needed to *do* something to make him feel better. "Want to build a Lego set with me?"

He rolled his eyes and stepped back from the door, but left it open for me. "I don't feel like building some stupid unicorn, Dez."

I looked down at my hands and twisted them around my shirt. "We could play something else."

When you're ten, you're not exactly gifted in the art of consoling someone. I didn't know what else I could offer him, but I knew I wanted to understand what had happened. I felt like there was something I didn't know about, which bothered me. "Why is Mom mad at you?" I finally braved asking.

He sat down on the edge of his bed and looked up at the ceiling. "It's hard to explain."

"Why?" I pressed. "What did you do?"

He looked back over to me. "I didn't do a fucking thing."

I remember being startled to hear him curse like that. Especially with the door open, and our mom already mad at him. I glanced behind me, waiting for her to come storming in, yelling or screaming or something. But she never did.

I think Dylan felt guilty, then, because he reached over to grab my shoulders. "Look, I can't explain it, but I think some changes might be happening."

"Like what? What happened?" I searched his eyes, dark brown like mine, and looked at the disheveled mess of his sandy blond hair.

"Dad messed something up," he said. "Something big, okay?" I nodded as if I understood, but I most definitely did not. "And Mom's being an idiot about it."

I winced, not liking hearing Dylan talk like that. It's a tough spot to be in, when you adore your big brother and the easy way he seems to make friends, the natural way he's good at everything, the way he's always looked out for you. But you also love your parents, and the idea of them making big mistakes feel scary and unsafe. Confusing. "So that's why you and Mommy were fighting?"

He nodded, and I could see how sad he was. I longed to fix whatever was wrong. "Yeah. But it doesn't matter. I'm starting high school soon. Couple more years and I'll be out of here."

That declaration was like a gut punch. It was hard to imagine being anything other than a kid, living under our parents' roof. I was in fifth grade, middle school was right around the corner. But still, to think about being a grown-up one day felt like light years away. The thought of Dylan not living with us had my stomach twisting.

I thought about how I wanted to be ten forever. I never wanted to grow up. And I hated the bubble that burst in thinking that our mom and dad might be flawed people that had done something bad beyond denying me a sleepover with my friends or a trip to the trampoline park.

I hated thinking I couldn't trust them.

I WASN'T SURE WHY THAT memory had popped in my head as Taven drove us in Inferno back to his house. I guess it was my own guilt in betraying my parents by heading to enemy quarters, to the Carlisle Manor. I wished I could be more rebellious, more assertive like Melissa and Taven were, but it just wasn't the way I was wired. I liked things neat and uncomplicated. I hated getting in trouble.

But my pull towards Taven was stronger, it seemed. I could do this. I could break the rules and make my treasured moments with him count.

He pulled us up to the gate, then down his long driveway, and as the sprawling stone of his house revealed itself before us, my pulse quickened. What if his parents came home? What if I got caught being here? I didn't want to think about what would happen, and a pit of dread filled my belly.

We walked into his room, and I slowly relaxed as I took in the familiar space. The bean bag chairs, the TV. The collection of his vintage cars lining his bookshelves and the spill of his laundry over the top of his hamper. This was Taven's room, and I was safe here.

He sat down on his futon and pulled me over to him, having

me straddle him while he nuzzled his nose in the crook of my neck. I was glad I sprayed a few dashes of perfume before I ran out of the house. "I've missed you so much it hurts, Dazzle," he said. His confession soothed me. He hadn't chosen his family over me, he just didn't know how to reach me without getting caught. When he started placing little kisses on my collarbone, I melted in the familiar touch of my Taven. I started rocking my hips, wanting to savor every precious minute.

We kissed for a while, and my palms relished in the comforting spikes of hair at the nape of his neck. I pulled off his baseball cap and ran my fingers through the silky softness of his hair, always longer on top. I breathed in the spice of his shampoo. By the time I leaned back and pulled my shirt over my head, I had decided this was it. We were going to do this. I would lose my virginity to Taven Carlisle, right here and now. I could feel his erection between my legs, and my heart was racing as I continued to grind my hips into him, thrilled with the idea of finally doing this.

He grabbed my cheeks and looked at me, the chocolate brown of his eyes looking so tender, I wanted to cry. "I love you so much, Desiree. You know that, right?" I nodded and told him I loved him too. I unclasped my bra, exposing my top half to him. Then I reached for his shirt and pulled it over his head, dropping it beside us.

Our movements became frantic. More kissing, hands exploring bodies, me fumbling through the button of his jeans, willing the rest of our clothes to disappear as fast as possible.

And then his father's voice interrupted us.

My heart dropped to the bottom of the floor, down through the foundation of the house, beneath the ground and to some depths of hell I was terrified of. We never even heard anyone come home. Never heard him coming down the hall. Too caught up in our moment, I guess. Too blind with our feelings for one another.

"Get dressed," Mr. Carlisle said. I covered my face with my hands as Taven threw some article of clothing over my naked torso.

"Dad, fuck," Taven said, and I could hear the misery in his voice.

Mr. Carlisle ignored him. "Desiree, I'd like to see you in my office when you're decent. And then I'll be taking you home."

sixteen

. . .

Fragile

Present Day

taven

Friday, 11:59pm

I'M NERVOUS AS hell for some unfathomable reason as I pull up in front of the hospital. Desiree and Melissa are standing on the curb, waiting for me. I step out and shuffle them both in my Bronco, and we chat out some pleasantries of the night, how the rain's died down, how Melissa is going to promptly buy some lottery tickets because clearly, Desiree is on a streak. I drop Melissa off at their shitty motel with an offer to find her someplace nicer, but she waves me away.

"I'm a big girl, I'll be fine," she assures me. She says she'll just stay the one night, then head out in the morning. It feels weird to abandon her like this, but my eagerness to get Desiree alone is stronger than my chivalry.

When we pull onto the highway, I glance over to her. She's

leaned against the doorframe, her eyes close, but I see her smile. "Are you watching me?" she asks.

I laugh. "No."

She opens one eye and looks at me. "Don't lie. Eyes on the road, Vin."

I shake my head and keep focused on the road, wondering what the hell I'm doing. If I'm about to blow everything up or about to make everything I really want truly happen. I think about the times me and Desiree actually got things *right*, and try and dwell on that.

I'm not really on social media, only for my business, and from what I can tell, Desiree isn't either. Maybe she has a fake name on there as a way to keep her personal and professional lives separate, but I'd never been successful in finding her. I wish I had. I wish I knew more about what her current day-to-day life was like. How did she fill her time? Did she still love to read? Did she travel? Or was she, like me, a slave to her work and her career?

All these things are questions I want to ask, but for now, I decide to let her rest. There will be time for that this weekend. I hope.

When we pull up to my garage, I open up the door closest to my house. She stretches her arms out and I hear her let out a whistle. "This all yours?" she asks, her eyes scanning the structure and the multiple doors of the garage, the building nearly the same size as my house.

"All mine," I confirm.

"So you did, it, huh? Successfully living out your dream?"

I nod, pride swelling in my chest. Desiree was there when the dream was born. There when my actions threatened to wreck it. "I'm determined, if nothing else," I say.

"Like your father."

"Like both our fathers," I add, then regret bringing up Frank

Hatson. Bitterness fills me at the name, but I try and push it aside.

"So," she says. "Is this your main car? This Bronco? Or do you drive all your cars around depending on the day?"

I park and turn off the engine, turning toward her. The dim lights overhead frame out her silhouette, and I momentarily think I'm dreaming that she's really here, in my car. In my garage, one of the places where I'm happiest. She's wearing this tiny little top, cut low between her breasts. No bra. I want nothing more than to run my fingers down the slopes of skin and slip underneath the fabric. Feel the peak of her nipple and hear her whimper. Feel the way her womanly frame has filled out since the last time I was between her legs.

I try and shake away the image. She really does have the perfect name. I feel nothing but desire when I'm around her. "This is my favorite to drive," I explain. Then I smile at her, eager to share this next vital piece of information. "Ask me the name of the color."

Her lips pull into a smile, and I want so badly to lean over and kiss those lips. Instead, I reach for her hand and pull it to my mouth, kissing her knuckle with as much restraint as possible. She doesn't stop me. Always so trusting of me, my Dazzle. I tell myself it's a friendly kiss of her hand, nothing more. Her finger-tips are cold, and when I pull her hand back from my lips, I put my other palm over top to warm her fingers.

"What's the name of the color, Vin?" She twists and gives me her other hand to warm, slipping it in between mine. I cradle them both like they're a baby bird I'm holding.

"Remember Inferno?" I ask.

Her blue eyes stare at me with amusement. "How could I forget?"

"Well," I say, so happy that I finally get to actually share this little moment with her. Not gonna lie, I fantasized about having this conversation with her countless times since buying my

Bronco. "When I got this car, I thought of you," I explain. "And how you picked Inferno Red."

"I loved that car."

"It's a couple down," I say, nodding over her shoulder to the row of cars beside her. "Still have it, still love it."

"Really?" She twists her head over her shoulder, but my other cars are blocking the view. "That, I have to see." She turns back to face me. "Tomorrow? A ride for old time's sake?"

My cock twitches at hearing those words from her lips, and thinking of the fact that there will be a tomorrow with her at all. But I clear my throat and try and focus. "Absolutely. But first, I should tell you that you inspired me picking out *this* car, and its color."

"Oh, yeah? How so?"

I kiss her hand one more time before reluctantly letting go. I unbuckle my seatbelt and grab my phone and wallet from the console. "Because, Dazzle. It's called 'Eruption Green.'"

"Eruption," she repeats, dragging the word out in the most adorable attempt to be sexy I've ever heard, followed by a flush of her cheeks. She laughs, and the sound of her laughter has my chest warming. Such a familiar sound that I've missed. Her little chuckles that sound like chimes and make me want to bottle them up to hear forever. Fuck, I've missed her laugh.

But more importantly, I've missed *her*. And hearing her laugh has me feeling more confident that having her here with me for the next forty-eight hours is going to be alright.

seventeen

. . .

Cracking

Fourteen years ago

desiree

sixteen years old

I STEPPED INTO Mr. Carlisle's office with trepidation. Taven stood beside me, holding my hand, and I wondered if he felt as nervous in his father's presence as I did. While Mr. Carlisle had requested my presence alone, Taven had insisted he join me, which I was relieved by. His parents made me uncomfortable, seeming more like headmasters at a school than warm and nurturing caretakers, and the prospect of being in a room alone with him was utterly intimidating.

I knew that Taven felt constant pressure from his parents. He felt like he didn't have the same studious temperament that the rest of his family had or expected of him. I knew that he had tutors when he was a kid, and more recently, Jacqui would tutor him and turn the lessons into understandable snippets that he could retain. But Taven never asked me for help. I had a feeling his pride kept him from doing so. Anytime I offered, he'd wave me off, joking that he could think of better ways for us to spend our time.

I think he just feared me seeing him struggle, and that broke my heart. I had debated adding "Ask Desiree for Help with School Once in a While" on one of his Bingo squares, but then thought better of it, not wanting to set off insecurities.

The thing was, Taven was smart in a way I could never be. I'd stand in the garage with him and watch him tinker with Inferno for hours. There was one day where he had the entire engine on the concrete floor, and I wondered how the hell he was going to put it all back together. I remember being nervous when he started the car to test whatever latest gadget he had installed. I imagined the car blowing up, and when he could see my fear, he pulled me close to him. He leaned into my ear and whispered, "Dazzle, I got this, baby. Relax. I know what I'm doing."

The engine purred to life and I beamed at the grin on his face, seeing the boyishness in his pride, knowing whatever sound or response he was hoping for was there.

He also had a love for certain aspects of history. What started as a love for vintage cars became an obsession with the Industrial Revolution, how Ford had enabled cars to be available to the masses. When I'd struggle with boredom over a school history project, he'd go into all the behind-the-scenes of random tidbits of information about how this or that came to be, telling stories in this animated way that made it feel like an adventure. He had a freakish gift for memorizing random facts. I would tease him that he just made that up, but then I'd go online to confirm, and sure enough, whatever the thing was would be correct. Taven's mind was meant to explore and figure out in a hands-on way, but the confines of a classroom seemed to do nothing to serve him.

His parents never tried to understand that. Instead they

would relentlessly scold him, serving punishments on the silver platter of withheld privileges, one of which was occasionally me, prior to the family blow-up.

But there we stood, hand in hand in front of the formidable William Carlisle. Taven's dad. A righteous man, from what I could tell, with many opinions about the "right" way to do things. He was almost militant in that way. And now we were confronting him, two kids about to be in trouble not just for the half-naked twist we were caught in, but for seeing each other behind his back.

I looked around the room, wanting to avoid eye contact. It was bathed in warm browns, a small space in comparison to everything else in the house. The walls were lined with books, there was a massive brick fireplace running from floor to ceiling. Leather couches and club chairs coated in caramel luxury, a small mini bar. The whole thing reminded me of the office from *The Godfather*. I wondered momentarily if the Carlisles were involved in that kind of thing. I knew they had built the house a few years ago, but I couldn't remember where they were originally from. Did they even have mafia in Ohio? I had no idea.

Mr. Carlisle spoke first. "Taven, I thought I said I wanted to speak to Desiree alone."

I could feel Taven straighten his spine beside me, and I had this urge to hug him and tell him he didn't need to be brave in front of his father, all for me. That his father didn't mean a damn thing to us, but of course, that wasn't true. It was the wishful thinking of a teenaged kid.

"Sir, I can't think of a single thing you would need to say to Desiree without me being here too."

My blood felt thick in my ears. I could smell cigar smoke, and I prayed it would mask the scent of my perfume. I suddenly felt like a kid pretending to be a grown-up with the stupid perfume on. I was standing right there, but the two of them were talking as if I weren't. I felt small and inconsequential, even as Taven stood by my side.

I could feel his hand squeezing harder, and Mr. Carlisle's eyes dropped to our bundle of sweaty palms and nerves before looking back up again. "Fine," he finally said, the muscle in his jaw twitching. He leaned back in his chair and told us to have a seat. Taven and I stood frozen. He ignored our disobedience of the command and looked at me. "How is your mother doing, Desiree?"

I pulled my head back. "My mother?"

"Yes. How is Holly?"

He was asking about my mother. Holly Hatson. I pictured my mom's tired eyes and stringy hair, the way her clothes were hanging from her slim frame far too loosely. I felt protective of her. I pulled my chin up and said, "She's doing great, actually. Really well." Mr. Carlisle could go fuck himself if he thought I was going to indulge him with the tales of how she was falling apart, thanks to his slimy business schemes.

He narrowed his eyes at me, clearly not believing a word of it. I hated him in that moment. Did he really want me to share all about how shitty things were since the Carlisle-Hatson fall-out? Would that give him some sick satisfaction? Money and power and casualties, I guess that was his thing.

Taven stepped forward, dropping my hand. "Dad," he said, then he cleared his throat and said, "Sir."

"Taven, I would like for you to step out of the room, please."

"No."

My heart fluttered wildly, feeling like I was in the lion's den and about to watch a cub get mauled. I wanted to reach forward and pull Taven's shoulders back, tell him we should just leave, and then run away in Inferno and never come back.

Mr. Carlisle glared at Taven. "I would like to speak with Desiree alone. Now. I don't bite, and this is a matter that requires some privacy. Surely if this is someone you care about, you would want to respect her sense of privacy?" He raised his eyebrows, the crinkles in his forehead becoming more prominent.

Taven stood firm. "Privacy for what, what do you want with her?"

"I would like. To speak. To Desiree. Alone." I stared at Taven's father, unblinking. I held my breath, not sure what was going on. I had a feeling in the pit of my stomach like something bad was about to happen. I'd never spoken to Mr. Carlisle alone before. Every instinct in me told me I didn't want to start now.

"There's no need for that, Dad," Taven pleaded. I didn't want to know why he had such desperation in his voice. "Just let me take her home."

Mr. Carlisle's eyes zeroed in on his son. He spoke slowly. "It was understood that you were not to see one another again, remember? And yet, here Desiree is. Which means you have put me in a difficult position, Taven. One that has me wondering if I will continue to need to question whether or not my *son* is sneaking around against our orders. No matter what, I need to address some things. So that we can put what has happened behind us."

I could see Taven's nostrils flaring, his chest rising and falling in heavy breaths. But he remained silent. Mr. Carlisle continued. "You're young, both of you. I know you think what you have is more important than what is best, but you'll see. You have your whole lives ahead of you to make your own choices." His voice was restrained, I could tell. He was becoming increasingly agitated. "And your loyalty to this *family*, Taven," he said. His fist met the desk before him in a startling slam, and the pens in their crystal container rattled, along with my nerves. "That loyalty is paramount. I thought that was understood."

Taven stepped closer to him. "It doesn't have to be that way. You know that. She has nothing to do with any of this. You can't punish us out of spite."

"Is that what you think this is? Spite? Taven." Mr. Carlisle's furrowed his eyebrows as if confused. He softened his tone. "I'm sorry. To you both, but this is what's best. It's time you go your separate ways, and that's final. It's very simple."

Taven stood back and crossed his arms over his chest. "That's impossible," he said, tone steely. "Desiree is pregnant."

"She *what*?"

"And we're keeping it."

My jaw dropped and I looked at Taven in shock, my eyes growing about a thousand times wider. I looked back at Mr. Carlisle just in time to see him closing his. "No, she's not. Please tell me she's not," he whispered, pinching the bridge of his nose.

No, I most definitely was not. Though now I wished I was. I wished we had actually had sex and were reckless and that I could be the knocked-up teenage girl, carrying Taven Carlisle's baby. It was a twisted thought. But I couldn't help but fantasize that if I were pregnant, there would be no way our families could keep us apart. I'd have the baby, we'd figure it out and be a beautiful family of three and live happily ever after.

I loved how determined Taven was. The balls he had. To come up with something like that on the fly, lie straight to his father's face all in the name of getting more time with me. I could never in a million years do something like that. I'd be a blubbering mess trying to get through the lie.

Mr. Carlisle rose from his seat, leaning his palms on his desk. I tried to read his expression, but couldn't. Rage, I imagine, though he hid it well. "Is this true, Desiree? How far along are you?"

I had the urge to cry. It would have been an appropriate reaction, tears at the confessions of our indiscretions. But my tears were threatening me for other reasons. For feeling trapped and having no idea what to do or say. "I...uhhh. I don't really know," I mumbled. My mind spun up a plan, we could go have sex and try to get pregnant! Then it could all be true! I suddenly felt sick, my mind whiplashing me in a thousand irrational and terrible thoughts. I was miserable having to stand here like this. Like a criminal standing before the judge. I wanted to run away and climb under the covers and get back to some semblance of simple normalcy, because this was all feeling like too much, and I was cracking.

Taven stood beside me and placed his hand on my back, rubbing in gentle strokes. "We just found out. And we're keeping it." I fought the urge to look at Taven and expose my disbelief in him standing here, spinning this lie. My face was hot, and I didn't dare say a word.

Mr. Carlisle swore beneath his breath. "Does your mother know?" he asked me. I shook my head no. He leaned back in his chair, rocking it in a gentle rhythm. He ran his hands over his face, and I looked at the simple gold band around his fourth finger. "This is exactly what your mother and I feared, Taven." His voice was muffled behind his hands, and for the briefest moment, I felt sympathy for the man. I heard more sadness in his voice than rage.

He dropped his hands and pulled open a drawer in his desk. I watched with both fear and curiosity as he pulled out a white envelope. He opened it and pulled out a slip of paper. A check, from what I could tell. I expected him to be yelling now, or demanding I go take a pregnancy test this instant and prove it, or throw us both out of there or *something*.

His silence was far worse.

Mr. Carlisle held the check in front of him for a moment, contemplating something before finally raising it to me. "The first thing you need to do is tell your mother, Desiree." I nodded, no words able to escape my mouth. "And you are to give this to her."

I slowly stepped forward and took the paper from him, my eyes widening at what I was reading. A check to Holly Hatson. For a hundred thousand dollars. It had already been filled out, and my mind raced with what this could be for or what it could mean.

Taven came up beside me, leaning over to see. "Dad, seriously? Hush money bullshit?"

Hush money? I had no idea what he was talking about. Hush money for what?

"Watch your mouth, son."

I heard Taven huff out a sarcastic laugh. "Let me get this straight. You think you can fix everything with some check, have the Hatsons go away quietly and never return. Problem solved." He scrubbed his hand over his face. "That's a fucking disgusting insult..." It sounded like he had more to say, but he only shook his head as his voice faded to quiet.

I studied his face, trying to understand. I saw the indignation, hurt, and anger shooting from his eyes to his dad who had just completely humiliated both me and my family. Did he know something I didn't?

"That is not what this is," his father insisted.

"What is it then?"

"A gift."

"For what?" Taven demanded, arms extending out beside him. "What do you suppose that would do?"

If I thought I felt like a piece of trash earlier—when I thought Taven was done with me—then I now felt like a damn swampland filled with the waste of the upper echelons of civilization. A check for a hundred grand. Just like that. Pay us off and move on, like that's all my family was. Money-hungry simpletons that could be commanded with the simple stroke of a pen.

Mr. Carlisle looked at Taven. "*Son.* May I remind you that you insisted on being here. *I* would have preferred to give this to Desiree in private."

"So you could humiliate her without an audience."

"As I said, son. It's a gift. One that your mother insisted on."

Lynda? Why would Lynda insist on this so-called gift? I felt downright nauseas with confusion. Like I stepped into another universe or something. One where I was faking a pregnancy and accepting hush money gifts from wealthy titans.

Taven sneered. "Like hell it is. You're unfuckingbelievable." He locked his hands behind his head, pacing. He dropped his hands and pointed at the check in my grasp. "It's a payoff to *exit*. You think it's all that simple?"

"It's a chance to help. To make things right."

My eyes darted back and forth between the two of them, trying to understand what was happening. Did Taven know something I didn't? Did his parents do this kind of thing a lot? Use and abuse people and then pay them off once they had their fill?

Taven crossed his arms over his chest and moved over to the back of the couch, surprising me by leaning on it. He dropped his gaze to the ground, seeming to relax his shoulders just the tiniest bit. "Dad," he said, his voice now quiet. "If you want to help Holly, you should speak to her directly." Taven looked back up at his father. "Don't do it like this."

I couldn't wrap my head around the scene happening before me. Help Holly? Not Mrs. Hatson, but Holly? As if Taven and my mother were equals as opposed to him being the teenaged boy dating her teenaged daughter.

And why would Mr. Carlisle want to help my mother? I thought they pulled all their funding and were through with us. Could my mom and Taven's dad have had an affair? Was this all some sordid turmoil that Taven's dad was trying to clean up? I couldn't begin to believe that. I saw the way my mom looked at my father. Like Frank Hatson hung the moon. She was head over heels for him, had been since she was "green behind the ears," as she was always so proud to say.

I had no idea what was really going on, and I was suddenly exhausted and had zero desire to know. We needed to get out of here. *I* needed to get out of here. A strange fear was bubbling inside me, and I worried I was in danger. Alarm bells were going off in my head to *run*, but at the same time, I couldn't move.

Mr. Carlisle rose from his seat and stepped out from behind his desk. "That's enough of your input now, son," he said before turning to me. "Desiree, you've always struck me as a good kid." He was buttering me up, I knew it. I detested it. "That check is for your mother," he continued. "She won't speak to us, so I trust that you will ensure she receives it. And as for the latest development—" *Our baby*, I thought. Not a development. Though it was a baby that didn't exist, so what difference did it really make? It was good to know where this man would stand, though, if it did. "I will speak to Mrs. Carlisle and we'll go from there."

Then he put his hands on my shoulders and looked me directly in the eyes. They were dark brown, like Taven's. I struggled to bravely look into them, instead choosing to scan the small curve of his eyebrows.

When he spoke, his words surprised me. "It will be okay, Desiree. Alright? Whatever you decide, it will be okay."

Then he dropped his hands and dismissed us, telling Taven he could drive me home after all.

Explaining what was done was already done.

eighteen

. . .

Reckless

Fourteen years ago

frank hatson

Springtime

HE HAD FALLEN hard and fast for her, a chemistry neither one of them expected. Frank didn't believe himself to be someone who would step out of his marriage to Holly, but then again, it certainly wasn't the first time another woman that wasn't his wife had caught his eye. He found women to be beautiful creatures that mesmerized him and tortured his soul with their curves, their smiles, the batting of eyelashes that he knew damn well was far from the innocence it pretended to convey.

His own mother had coddled him, which at first he found endearing. As a small boy, her constant praises and unconditional love were the heartbeats of his ego. She was beautiful and beloved by all in their family's circle, and he felt like a star by proximation.

But she also suffered from restlessness. A pull in her heart to be free from the confines of domestic living as the wife of a local politician.

It was a snowy evening the night she left him and his father, claiming a need to run to the store. His father had warned her it was unsafe. The roads were icy, and he told her whatever it was she needed could wait. Turns out the thing she needed was an escape, and ice wasn't going to stop her. After two days of her absence, with reassurances from his father that his mother just needed some space, little Frank stole his mother's abandoned nightgown from beneath her pillow. He'd clutch it to his small chest and cry into it each night, wondering what he had done to make his mother leave.

Her moods could be mercurial, it was true. Winter proved to be the most challenging. She'd fade away into the shadows of her depression, and no matter how many sweet drawings her son created or plates of toast and berries he concocted—his chubby fingers working carefully to not burn himself—nothing could pull her from her darkness other than time.

That snowy winter was the first time he remembered his mother leaving. There would be others. His father always took her back, explaining to his son that a man's job is to stand by his woman. He wondered why it wasn't a woman's job to stand by her man, vowing that one day, he'd find a wife who would.

Which he did, thankfully, and at times Frank felt ashamed at the loyalty his wife so clearly exhibited, when he himself proved to struggle. At times he wondered if his wife had ever cheated too, and he'd carefully monitor her spending, certain he might catch something that looked off. He was sure he would catch her red-handed by way of a hotel bill or repeated phone calls to some unknown number. It should have eased his mind when nothing ever revealed itself. Still, the anxiety of no guarantees threatened his sanity.

And then there was *her*. The mistress he never planned to

take. It was one thing to give in to a momentary attraction now and then. It hardly counted when his loyalties remained firmly to his wife and family, anyone could see that.

But those goddamn eyelashes she had. They batted their way first to his cock, and later to his heart. The first time they made love, he nearly wept at the beauty of it.

Their exchanges had often teetered on flirtatious, the times they'd see one another, always surrounded by party guests and too much champagne. He thought he was imagining it, but there was no mistake in the flush of her cheeks when he'd compliment her dress, or her necklace that was dangling between her breasts, begging to be admired. There was no mistaking the times she joined him out on the patio while he snuck a cigarette, claiming to need some fresh air. They would chat and laugh at the ridiculous new hat so-and-so was wearing, how the hat surely required a town council meeting and permit, ostentatious as it was. He would leave her company with a lasting smile on his face. So beautiful, so easy to talk to, so clearly in admiration of him.

They ran into one another at the club one evening. She was there with some friends, he was catching a quick drink before heading home for the day. He smiled warmly at the table of beautiful young women, offering to pick up their tab, only for them to all laugh and wave him off. The tab was the least of their concerns, as attached to platinum credit cards as they were. When she excused herself to the ladies' room, he was sure that was his invitation. He followed after her to the dark hallway around the corner. Was there waiting for her as she exited.

You startled me, she said.

He brushed her hair behind her ear, apologizing. She looked at him, eyes unblinking and lips slightly parted, pink and full and inviting. *Forgive me*, he said. *I'd hoped you stay a little longer, have a drink with me.*

I don't think that's a good idea, she said. He dropped his hand, irritation sweeping through him.

Then he realized, of course it wasn't a good idea. Too many eyes at the club. They needed to go somewhere else. Someplace private.

His office.

I have something I wanted your opinion on, he said. *A marketing campaign that could use a fresh take. You'd be doing me a great favor.*

Her gaze dropped to the floor, how adorable she was when trying to play coy!

I'm sure you have other people for that, she said.

Ah, yes. But none with the natural gift for cleverness like you have. The slogan's not quite right.

My cleverness?

Don't pretend you don't know how witty you are. Take a look?

She nodded, making a quick excuse to her friends, leaving the Windsor Montgomery Club with Frank, surely not the first time the club had been a catalyst to sordid affairs.

Once they were in the safe confines of his office, dark and empty after hours, he decided to ease her mind. He imagined she was feeling guilt at their obvious mutual attraction. He made himself a drink. Offered her one. She accepted, and he loved the flush of her cheeks after just a few sips. He would go slowly, feign frustration, lean down for a kiss that doesn't quite meet her lips. *Christ, me and my stupidity, apologies, sweetheart.*

It's alright, she would assure. *It's not just you.*

Am I crazy to think there's something between us?

No, you're not crazy.

It was all rather perfect.

He turned away then, timing it just right. His back to her, a confession of the challenges of his marriage, the fights he and Holly couldn't stop having. They were on the brink of divorce, it was only a matter of time. But he was a jackass, he shouldn't be burdening such a sweetheart with all of his miseries.

When he felt her hand on his shoulder in a gentle caress of comfort, he knew he was in for it. She didn't just feel attraction toward him, but she cared for him, too.

He started slowly, kissing her temple, first. Just one gentle kiss. Then her cheekbone. The tip of her nose. The soft flesh beneath her ear, and his kisses continued down her neck, her breath hitching with each contact. He was a skilled lover, knowing just which spots to give attention, and she was aroused as a result. All from his touch.

When his lips finally made their way to hers, she eagerly returned his kiss. He savored the moment, tasting her sweetness like a succulent cherry to be cherished.

A stroke of his thumb over her nipple, taught beneath her dress. His hand slipped down to the hem, and he lifted it one tortured inch at a time, the silkiness of her thighs causing his erection to grow with each passing second. His cock nearly burst through his zipper as he pushed her panties aside, his fingers making their way through her slick heat. She was soaked, all because of him. He didn't enter at first, choosing to gently circle instead, her hips grinding into him and her grip tightening on his shoulders. *Please,* she whispered. *Oh, God, please.*

Yes, sweetheart. That's my girl. Be patient.

Please, more. I need more.

He rewarded her by slipping his fingers inside, groaning at the feel of her, so tight around him. He could only imagine what it would feel like when his cock finally entered her.

Fuck, she whispered. *My God, that feels so good.*

I want to fuck you, sweetheart. Please tell me I can fuck you.

Her eyes were closed, head held back as she bathed in her pleasure. *Yes. No. I don't know.*

Yes, you do. It's alright. He quickened his movements, relentless as he worked her.

I need you, she cried. *I need more.*

He wouldn't make her wait. Partly out of fear of her stopping him, partly out of his own greed. He cleared his desk and gently laid her back down on top, pressing his hips into hers so she could feel his arousal for her. He pushed her dress up past her breasts, using his mouth to shove her bra below, exposing her beautiful pink nipples to him. He kept his fingers inside her as he maneuvered his mouth over one peak, swirling his tongue and delighting at the gasp she made with every move.

He pulled away from her to undo his pants, working fast to keep her in the moment. He stroked himself, his fingers wet with her arousal, leaving him nearly trembling with the feel of her slickness along his throbbing cock. *Look what you do to me, sweetheart. You feel this?* he asked, taking her hand and wrapping it around his cock. *That's what your pussy does to me, that wetness is all from you, you feel that?*

She remained silent, only whimpering and rocking her hips, begging him to enter her. He placed the head of his cock at her opening, the heat radiating was maddening. This was it, this was the moment.

With one push, he entered her completely, covering her mouth at the startled cry she let out. A virgin, his sweetheart had been a virgin, and she willingly gave herself to him. He placed his mouth on her breast, wanting to comfort her, seeing the tears in the corners of her eyes. He sucked and teased her perfectly pink nipples as he began gentle strokes, her pussy tightening around him.

It was beautiful. She was beautiful. When her whimpering cries of discomfort subsided, he quickened his pace, holding onto her hips and losing himself as he buried himself deep, as deep as he could go. She lay slack beneath him, but he couldn't slow down. It was too much, she was too much, and she had captivated him to depravity. He was helpless to her.

When he shot inside her, he thought he'd entered another dimension. She was so incredible and pure, and now she was his.

She had given him a gift, his sweetheart, and deserved pleasure, and he'd be sure to give it to her. When he pulled out from her and she began to rise, propping herself on her elbows, he told her he wasn't done. That now it was her turn.

He was going to show her what it was like when a man worshipped her. He placed his mouth over her sex, working in skilled strokes with his tongue until her legs gripped tightly against his arms. When she trembled beneath him, begging for him to stop, that it was too much, he continued. *Wait, oh my God,* she cried. *Oh my fucking God. I can't. I think...fuck. Holy fuck I'm going to...*

He pressed on, fucking her with his mouth until her body convulsed, beautifully unraveling as he tasted every last drop of her arousal, mixed with himself. This beauty that met her pleasure with his touch.

With one final flick of his tongue, he released her, then hovered over top of her to take in her startled expression. *You're so beautiful,* he soothed. *You came so beautifully, sweetheart, did you feel that?*

I felt it, she said, and he kissed her so she could taste herself and the love they just shared.

Frank, she said.

Yes, sweetheart? He loved the startled look in her eyes, the disbelief and innocence and fear, combined with the flush of her cheeks, her pussy swollen with pleasure from his ravishing.

We can't tell anyone about this, she said. He could hear the worry in her voice, creeping in as the reality of what they had just done settled in.

Shh, he soothed. *It'll be alright. No one will know. No one will ever know, it's just between us.*

Which, of course, was a lie, these things inevitably come out. One reckless evening when he was caught with his pants around his ankles and his sweetheart on her knees. A party guest wandering in, nosy in their curiosity to explore the rest of the house. A quick scramble to dress, a pull of Holly's arm, instructing him to get Desiree, that they had to leave, *now*.

But that night in his office was how Frank began his affair with his mistress. A girl of eighteen.

Jacqui Carlisle.

nineteen

· · ·

Avoid

Fourteen years ago

desiree

sixteen years old

THE RIDE HOME after leaving Mr. Carlisle's office, check in hand, was a confusing blur.

I don't even know how to explain it. I had been whiplashed from the adrenaline high of hearing from Taven, finally. Rushing out to see him, deciding tonight was going to be the night that I gave myself to him. It felt like a physical need, one I was sure I'd get fulfilled, forever binding me to Taven Carlisle no matter what. It felt so simple! Beautiful and pure and simple!

Until the utter humility of getting caught, wanting to withdraw into a cave and never be seen again, followed by standing there, having to face his father. Hearing Taven blurt out some lie that he had knocked me up. The spark of hope, such foolish hope wanting him so badly that I momentarily thought this was actually a good idea, which, of course, I logically knew was insane and irrational. I was locked up in a mental straightjacket of my own emotional bargaining, born out of desperation for my longing to be with Taven, no matter what.

And then, boom. A check was handed to me, and something about Taven's reaction to it, like he understood it was some payoff, had me feeling like he had a better understanding of what exactly happened between our parents. Meanwhile, I had no clue.

None whatsoever.

I couldn't help but think about the past three years with him, with this crush that I'd craved and longed for, working my hardest to savor each moment with him while secretly hoping that in all our time together, I could do the impossible and actually make him like me. This perfect boy, could I make him find me so magnificent and irresistible that he might reciprocate my feelings for him?

It felt so stupid to think about now. He's just a regular old person, like anyone else. Flawed. Occasionally reckless. Afraid of my parents to the point of parking down the street to pick me up. Afraid of his own parents to the point of spinning up some lie in order to be able to see the girl he claims to love.

And apparently, a guy who was capable of keeping secrets from me.

I had the realization that I had no idea what was going on. It was like I had waltzed into an underground game and didn't even know it or realize how long I had been there.

I felt physically sick, though I wasn't sure exactly what part of all those emotions were to blame. A part of it was this lie thrust upon me, this child's play of a lie that I knew deep down I didn't actually want any part of. And my head was throbbing with the question marks of this check in my hand and what the hell was actually going on.

I started to feel like I just wanted the simplicity of our lives from years prior. When we lived in our small and modest house, when my parents' business was just a tiny spot, offering massages and face creams and electrolysis to remove those dreaded hairs in dreaded places. Life was good then.

Now, I was starting to see that there existed some game of backhanded deals and bodies in trunks, only the body that felt like it had been thrown in the trunk was mine. It felt dark and suffocating and scary, way more than my young mind could handle, and I wanted out. I suddenly hated that my family ever got wrapped up in things with the Carlisles. Clearly, it was a dangerous thing, playing with the Carlisle fire. I wanted to be as far away from them as possible.

I felt used, that's the term. The high of finally seeing Taven again had crashed, and reality had settled in, prompted by a hundred thousand dollars.

I did not want to be a teen mom.

I did not want to be tied to the Carlisles forever, always in their debt and never feeling secure.

I did not want to play along until some mystical pregnancy happened, peeing on sticks in front of my mother as I'm sure she'd have me do. Demanding why I hadn't taken the birth control she had insisted on, even though in actuality, I had.

It was all so ridiculous, I fought the urge to laugh out loud. Feared that laughter would make its way to heaving sobs, fueled with shame and embarrassment at how idiotic and naive I had been.

I knew nothing, *nothing* about the world or secrets surrounding me, or hell—even about myself.

I looked over at Taven, driving Inferno like always, and I willed myself to still see him as the image of utter perfection. But sadly, the image had started to fade. My love for him was still there, despite it, but his pseudo-perfection was turning into something far more realistic, and that scared me a little. I felt unready for this, for the complexity of his flawed humanity.

I thought about that night of the party when my mom had brought Melissa and Taven and me home after Dylan called her. And Taven had locked himself in my bathroom. I remember staring at that door, feeling the blockage he had created. It was my first real glimpse of a vulnerable side of him. And tonight I was seeing yet another layer of it, the one that's underneath facades created to hide his true feelings. I didn't know what to say to him in this new light, so I stayed quiet.

It was Taven that eventually broke our silence. "Tell me a secret," he said, his voice filling the dark cabin space of Inferno, lit only by the neon glow of the dash.

I whipped my head to look at him, glaring. "Really? A Bingo square? Now?"

He went to reach for my hand, but I pulled it away. I felt cheap and I didn't want his attempts at comfort. "Don't touch me," I mumbled out, my words barely above a whisper. Because still, even after all that just happened, even with my recognition of him as a basic kid in high school with darker shadows of his own, I *wanted* him to touch me. I only wished I didn't. I resolved to remain strong.

"What are you thinking, Dazzle?"

I chewed on my lip, gnawing away like it might unearth some answers I wasn't even sure I had the right questions for. I saw the lights of passing shopping centers, and wished I was one of those people in the stores right now. Quietly running their evening errands after work.

I sighed, fighting the tears that I knew were coming. "I don't know," I answered honestly. "I just know that I feel like shit."

He cursed, sliding his hand down the wheel and reaching for my arm, yanking with force when I resisted. "Please, just let me hold your hand," he pleaded.

I locked my arm in place, looked down at his hand grasping on for dear life to my elbow. He had never been forceful with me, and I could feel the moment he realized he was being forceful now. Could feel his grip instantly soften before he retreated his hand completely, balling it into a tight fist and giving it a thump of frustration on the console between us. "Fuck," he breathed out.

I scanned his face, his beautiful profile, that perfect wave of his hair, long on top like always, with an indentation from his gray baseball cap, now discarded in his room. I looked at the tension wrapped up in his fist between us, then the white knuckles of his other hand, gripping the steering wheel. He was upset. And I had just rejected him.

I caved. I placed my hand over his fist, coaxing it to uncurl, and locking our fingers together. His palm was warm and familiar, and I allowed it to warm me, even if just for a moment.

The thing was, I couldn't stand seeing him tormented. I hated even more that I knew I was the one person that might be able to cure that. I hated it because it felt good to hold that power, and it seemed wrong of me to like that.

And I admit, I felt lonely. I wanted to be strong and choose myself and my own needs, yes. Mainly because I was starting to realize that the intensity of our feelings for one another, set to high volume with the fallout happening around us, was beginning to take us to a darker place that filled me with anxiety.

Yet having Taven and holding his hand, even with everything going on—it was better than the cold loneliness of battling my thoughts on my own.

Our fingers now linked and in their rightful place, he gave me a small squeeze. "Let me just say, I'm so, so sorry about my father."

"Taven," I said, attempting to be soothing. "Why? It's not like *you* had anything to do with that."

He shook his head in frustration. "Because. I just...I don't know what he was thinking. It was fucking embarrassing, watching him give you that check."

My tone slipped into sarcasm, though I didn't mean for it to. "For real? So sorry it was so uncomfortable for you."

"Stop it, don't be like that. You know what I mean."

The guilt swept in then, because I did know what he meant. His own frustrations with his parents' money, the responsibilities both he and Jacqui could often feel as the heirs to the Carlisle name and fortune. The way Taven struggled to feel good enough, and his own discontent with the running theme that money is the answer to everything.

I sighed and willed myself not to direct my anger toward Taven, not on that front, anyhow. I was mad at our parents as a whole, I was mad at the situation, and I realized that of all of the hurt I was feeling in that moment, it was a fairly minimal amount stemming directly from Mr. Carlisle himself. I may not understand his reasonings behind this supposed "gift," but I did understand that it had nothing to do with me.

Still, I couldn't fight the unexpected frustration and irritation I had toward Taven. I wanted reassurances from him, not empty apologies on his father's behalf. I wanted some semblance of acknowledgment that he had been keeping something from me, not avoidance and random side exits on a ramp to a fake pregnancy.

I let go of Taven's hand and crossed my arms over my chest, willing myself to create emotional distance from this boy I so very painfully loved. It was a step, at least. I could feel a slow wave of understanding that distance would be an unfortunate necessity. I didn't like the crippling discomfort in everything going on, and the tiny seeds of wanting out had been planted.

I wouldn't be able to see him again anyway, that much I knew. Where the hell were we supposed to go from here? Two kids with zero control over our lives, ultimately. With a heavy heart, I realized I needed to start getting used to that. That was the bitter truth.

My feelings would dissolve in time, I hoped. I tried to tell myself they would. Over and over again I repeated that line in my head, while staring out the window as the world swooshed past us.

My feelings will dissolve.

My feelings will dissolve.

It won't always feel like this. It won't always hurt so much. I gripped with all the might I could to those phrases, jumping through mental hoops to sit in the decision to let Taven go, knowing it was the right choice.

My feelings will dissolve.

They had to. That's what happens with young crushes, right? Hot and heavy intensity that dissolves with time and distance? I had held Melissa's head in my lap several times, telling her the same thing when some boy or another broke my best friend's heart. *Don't speak to him, create space so you can get over him. Talking to him will only make it worse and stretch out the time it'll take to heal.* And she always did, she always healed.

I wished Melissa was with me now. I told Taven to take me there, that I wasn't ready to go home yet.

"Why?" he asked. "Talk to me, Desiree. Please." His voice was strained, and I knew he could feel that I was pulling away.

I tried to keep ahold of my anger toward him. This would all be easier with anger as my fuel, as opposed to the love I felt for him. I was mad at him, right? He said something dumb and now roped me into a bigger mess than everything had already been. I clung to that. "What were you thinking, telling your dad I'm pregnant?" I asked.

Even the word itself felt disgusting in my mouth, like a kid trying to sip her parents' Scotch. Bitter and something you recognize you're just not ready for yet. You feel like a fool when everyone's looking at you and laughing, going, "Told you so!"

My tears started flowing then, quietly spilling out of my eyes and down my cheeks. The pain of realizing you're not as mature as you think you are, and that you have far too many years and life lessons ahead of you before you can call yourself a grown-up. I may have been only a year and a half from officially being one, yet I felt inexplicably small and inept.

"Wishful thinking, I guess?" he said, his voice teasing, which made my tears fall even harder. I heard him curse under his breath, looking over to me and realizing I was crying.

I covered my face with my hands and sobbed into them, embarrassed. Yet at the same time, I felt vindicated that he could see firsthand how much he was hurting me. "*Please*," I sobbed. "Don't joke like this is nothing."

"I'm sorry," he whispered. "Fuck, I'm an idiot. I'm so sorry. It just blurted out of me, I don't know."

I sucked in a deep breath, staring up at the ceiling of Inferno and willing myself to push out the jumbled thoughts in my brain. "What am I supposed to do now, Taven?" I blubbered. "Pretend I'm pregnant? That's your big plan?" I was raising my voice in strangled cries, unused to feeling anger like that, but finding some joy in it, too. There was a sick power in my emotions tumbling out of me like this. It was confusing.

"Look, it's gonna be fine. Not a big deal. We'll just say you had a miscarriage or something."

I turned my head to face him, sure my face look liked a wild mess of hysterics. "And if your parents tell my parents?" I was queasy at the thought. "Don't you think they'll want me checked out, and then surprise! Your daughter's still a virgin, Mrs. Hatson," I added, in case he had some grand idea of changing that fact. Like hell would I be giving up my body to him now. "Oh, and she's definitely not recovering from a miscarriage."

He banged his head against his headrest, and I could see his chest rising and falling. "Fine, I fucked up, is that what you want to hear? Does that make you happy?"

"Admitting it is a start."

"What are you so *mad* about? It's not a big deal! I'll tell my dad I made it up."

"Yeah, right. No, you won't."

He glared at me. "What's that supposed to mean?"

He wouldn't admit he made it up. I knew him better than that. Taven would spin truths that were fitting to his narrative, always finding ways to get himself out of trouble. I thought back to the little fabricated tales I heard him tell his parents to escape punishments. That test he failed was given on a day he left early for a game, and the makeup one was ten times harder. I remember looking at him in sympathy for his bad luck, but when his parents weren't looking, he turned to me and grinned with a wink.

I thought about that time he told me his dad had found a bottle of booze in his room. How he assured Mr. Carlisle that it must have been from his friend's girlfriend, he didn't even realize it was there. Definitely not his, he believed him, right?

All those little white lies I knew he told his parents were coming back to me in one fell swoop. I thought about when he had told all his friends he had been making out with Evelyn, only to later reveal to me the real time he had his first kiss with her. Was he telling his friends the same thing about me? That we'd slept together, that he'd taken my virginity and all the details of some makeshift beautiful moment? Did it matter, did I even care? Previously I might have thought not, let him do whatever he needed to do. I loved him blindly like that.

But now I wasn't so sure.

It felt like the glass was shattering on the three years of affection I had held for Taven.

I remembered when he was the perfect guy in my eyes. The dreamy veil of rose-colored glasses I wore that found each and every thing about him nothing but alluring. The glasses were off, and in their place were spectacles that held lenses of mistrust securely in front of my eyes.

There were probably all kinds of little white lies I didn't know about. It sickened me to realize that.

And then tonight. He knew something I didn't about the Carlisle-Hatson blow-up, something concerning *my family*. Wouldn't I have a right to know about that? It was clear back in his dad's office, the way Taven said, "Holly." And his dad didn't correct him. It was odd. Taven knew what was up.

"What's really going on with our families, Taven?" I finally asked. "Tell me the truth."

Another bang of his head on his headrest. I looked at him as if seeing him for the first time while he kept his head held back against the black leather, and I darted my eyes to the road.

His voice was quiet. "I can't tell you."

It wasn't a denial. That was a start. "Why not?" I asked. "And *how* do you know about what's going on?"

I studied his face for a reaction, trying to understand what was on his mind. I saw the frown of frustration mixed with something else. "My parents told me."

"And you didn't think to tell me?"

"It's not that simple, Daz. I can't explain it," he said, glancing over to me. "And please don't ask me to. It's private."

I placed my hand on his arm, hoping that would coax him into opening up. "But it's *me*. And it's my family."

He looked down at my hand on his arm, probably confused by my emotional pushes and pulls. When his eyes met mine, I saw the tenderness in them. "It's to protect you, Dazzle. Trust me on this."

I pulled my hand back, frustrated at the locked door I was facing. I longed to understand what the hell was going on, but the kid side of my brain was feeling almost frightened to.

And most of all, I was heartbroken that whatever it was, Taven had kept it from me. Me, someone I thought might be the one person he was ever truly honest with.

I finally shared the fear I had on my mind. "Are your dad and my mom having an affair?" My tears had stopped by then, and my throat was dry. I took a deep breath in, inhaling the leather and pine-scented air freshener swinging from the cardboard tree on Taven's rearview mirror.

He surprised me with his response. "God, I wish."

I looked out the window, confused and unsure how to respond. It was a no, that much was clear. I didn't bother asking if his mom and my dad were having an affair. Lynda seemed to barely tolerate my father at times, and I didn't think it was any sick sexual tension there. She was cold and stoic, far from a seductress.

My head hurt, the throbs of a post-cry settling in. I remained quiet and we wound our way into Melissa's neighborhood. I stared at the rows of small split-level homes looking tidy and peaceful, the cars in the driveways like little soldiers, awaiting their service.

He pulled up in front of Melissa's house, and I felt a smidge of trepidation at showing up like this. My face was a blotchy mess, I was sure. Like a foolish teen with a broken heart, how cliché. I prayed Melissa would answer and whisk me away to her room so I wouldn't have to face the mayhem of her family.

I looked down at my hands, realizing this was probably the last time I'd see Taven for who knows how long. Maybe forever. We had no way to speak to one another. He'd go back and tell his dad yet another lie—that I'd had a miscarriage, that my parents would kill me if they knew. *She went to a doctor's office and took care of herself, all is fine.* I could already see it. Taven would tell his father that as a way to protect himself, I knew. And I would let him. Because flaws and all, I still loved him, and I understood. That was what would work best for him, and it didn't really matter anyway. I almost envied the way he could fabricate his own realities.

I turned to face him and leaned over to kiss his cheek, remembering that time he had kissed mine at New Years. "You're never going to tell me the truth, are you?" I eked out, my voice quiet. Your family comes first, not me—that's what I really wanted to say.

"Trust me when I say that you don't want to know."

I nodded, told him good-bye.

As I walked up to the brown door and outdated Easter wreath of Melissa's house, I realized that there was one thing I truly did trust about Taven at that moment. That some things were best for me to not know.

phase 3: whatever it takes

. . .

A belief takes over your mind—you'll only be happy if you have this. You're in denial regarding how fixated you've become. You agonize over the vulnerability of being so attached to something so precarious. But the crush has a chokehold on you, and you'll do whatever it takes for that next hit, even risking your own sanity.

twenty

. . .

Denial

Fourteen years ago

frank hatson

Springtime

NATURALLY, HE AND Jacqui denied everything. The gall to suggest such a thing! How could you? Sick, that's what you are, sick for even indulging in such a horrid accusation. And what, you think no better of your daughter? That Jacqui would just fall into the arms of some forty-year-old man, just like that?

Frank could so clearly remember the look on Bill's face. Red and fuming, vessels popping from his forehead like worms that might crawl out from his skin and slither down behind the collar of his shirt.

But Lynda's reaction surprised him. She remained stone-faced. Impassive. It was chilling, in a way, and in that moment, Frank Hatson had the slightest wash of fear.

She didn't do the predictable thing and come at him, yelling and screaming with fists to his chest. Not like his wife did when the accusation first came about.

Holly had been crushed when the Carlisles confronted them both on the matter. She and Frank stormed out of happy hour at the club—lured into a public place, no doubt, so that no one could cause a scene—and rushed home where Holly unleashed her torment onto her husband.

"How could you?" she cried. "To a young girl!"

Frank had gone from enraged at his wife's mistrust in him, to sobbing at the way the snobs of the world like the Carlisles would stop at nothing to take him down. Anything to remove a perceived threat. Couldn't she see that? Couldn't she see the way their jealousy of all they had accomplished was beginning to make them wary of losing their coveted thrones? Of course they needed a reason to pull away. It was the perfect plan! Throw some foolish accusation out there, pull their investment, forcing him to sell off the business and be left in the dust to start again. You can't trust anyone, he told his wife. How well did either of them really know the Carlisles, anyway? Who knew where exactly they came from or how it all started? He had a feeling they had some illegal connections somewhere, the money they flashed was too much to be from just being good with numbers and financial planning or basic real estate investments. Lynda in particular was suspiciously quiet about her upbringing, Frank could smell a weasel like her from a mile away. There's something dark about her, he told his wife. Any halfwit could see that. Couldn't she?

That seemed to sink in with Holly. And Frank knew how to handle his wife. When she was upset, she would make a fool of herself in her hysterics. He'd ride out the waves of her emotional crisis until they passed, and she'd drop to the floor in a fit of tears. His arms would be wide and waiting for her as he soothed her in his lap, stroking her pale hair with assurances that everything would be alright. She would sniffle out her apologies for losing it on him, how wonderful and patient he was with her distraught tantrums, how was it that he could love a fool like her so much?

But Lynda Carlisle was a different breed. She wasn't the sort to do that kind of thing. And it was that obvious undercurrent of poise, power, and control that Lynda exhibited that shook Frank to his core. He didn't like it.

From day one, he had been leery of her. Bill was his speed. The two men clicked right from the start. They'd slapped each other's backs with their handshake when the final papers were signed, the Carlisle investments solidified for Frank's clinics. Bill was eager and excited for the expansions to come, a new wave of beauty combined with healthcare. They'd find a physician for future sites, grow their services, Bill would see to it. They would build an empire on the cutting edge advances and technologies that were sure to offer the latest in bottled-up youth and preservation.

And then it was all yanked away. How stupid he had been to allow himself to get caught up in the siren spell of the daughter of the people who had a chokehold on his wallet. He wondered if he loved her, if Cupid had speared his heart and made him blind with his obsession with Jacqui. That had to be it, someone had cursed him and forced him into ruin.

Oh, how Jacqui cried when he severed ties with her.

But I love you! she had said.

Yes, I know, sweetheart. I love you too. But we can't continue, I have a wife and children. You can't possibly ask me to leave my family, can you? You wouldn't do that, break up a loving household, would you?

The way she shook her head no, her tears spilling down her beautiful face. Jacqui was so lovely. A curvy girl, and at the age that he knew brought about insecurities in a young woman, which made him fall for her even more. So blissfully unaware of the natural sexual appeal she had. He had thought of her as a muse of sorts. The type of youthful beauty he hoped to sell to the masses. He had been on his way to his fortune, and then his muse had caused it all to disappear. As in the world of drugs, never take your own product. What a fool he had been.

No matter. Frank was nothing if not cunning. Resourceful. He would start fresh, Desiree would be starting college in two years. He'd groom her for her future as a plastic surgeon, and he'd get his second chance. Make the right investments, secure a new network of contacts, and begin again.

Dylan was worthless in the business sense, that much Frank already knew. A meathead who was finding his glory in football, which his father found peculiar. Dylan's charm was much like Frank's, sure, but his mind was wildly different than his own. No crafty spirit, nor the brains like Holly or Desiree.

It wasn't until the scholarship offers started rolling in—the wining and dining from Division One schools all there to recruit his son—it was only then that Frank could see the appeal in Dylan's future. He had Frank's athletic build. Maybe Dylan was more like Frank than he realized.

Yes, Frank could be the father of a football star, that would suit just fine. The money Dylan would get once he was drafted would be Frank's get-out-of-jail free card. Frank wouldn't hold onto hope for a first round pick, as he wasn't a dreamer in that sense, but even bottom of the barrel would receive a lump sum.

Everything would be just fine.

twenty-one

. . .

Limerence

Thirteen years ago

desiree

seventeen years old

When I stepped out of Inferno the day Taven's dad gave me the check, I made a vow to stay away from him and the Carlisles. I could do this, I could be strong and walk away from someone who had more fun keeping secrets from me and spinning lies than he did proudly and honestly professing his undying love, no matter what. It's hard to explain why exactly Taven's approach had grated my nerves so much, I logically understood that he was just a kid living under his parents' roof and surviving the best ways he knew how.

But I wanted more than that. I wanted the fireworks of young love, the self-sacrifice of choosing *me* openly and honestly, no matter what the consequence was from his parents. And he didn't deliver. It was as simple as that, crushing as it was.

When I saw my mother the next day, I handed her the check.

She looked like shit, I remember that very clearly. Bone thin and hair in the limpest bun on top of her head. I had hugged her before handing her the check, wanting to soften the blow of the humiliation I was about to bestow upon her, and I remember feeling worried I might break her if I squeezed too tightly.

The tension at home had been palpable, and I expected my mom to be angry that I had been at the Carlisle's. But instead she offered me a sad smile. I nearly died with shock. She timidly accepted the check, hands shaking as she muttered a quiet "Thank you" that both confused me and pinched at my heart.

Something was troubling her, but she wouldn't tell me what. Taven had confirmed that it wasn't an affair our parents were having, but still—my teenaged mind couldn't wrap my head around all the secrecy flooding my house. It all felt very dark and mysterious, and I approached it like this puzzle I needed to sort through.

I know now that at the time, my mom had been diagnosed with bladder cancer. I was seventeen when she and my dad finally told me and Dylan.

The Carlisles knew from the beginning, apparently. This was something my mother told me in private, my father never wanted the Carlisle name uttered in his house again. Was that why they pulled out from the business? Too risky with my mom's health issues? I had no idea, though it didn't seem to make sense to do so. While the Carlisles were ridiculously strict and borderline elitist, they didn't strike me as *cruel*, per se. Sure, if my mom's health had scared them off, it would make sense why my father was so vehemently against them. But then why this check? It didn't make any sense.

The good news was that the cancer had been caught early. My mother would be fine, for now. She and my father quietly shuffled her to treatments and surgery without telling me or

Dylan until several months later, when she was in the clear. My mom could be secretive like that.

I had no real feelings about them not telling us, other than hating that I missed out when I could have been a help. But there was nothing to be sad about, she was perfectly healthy now. I suppose I could have been angry they didn't tell us when it was happening. Dylan certainly had that reaction. But not me. It didn't seem like there was any real point in the anger after the fact.

Instead, I dove deep into studying all about bladder cancer, silently cursing my mother's smoking habits that continued even now, though also knowing it was a habit many years in the making. Very difficult to stop, and for my mom, downright impossible. Holly Hatson was like that. She wanted nothing more than harmony and peace, always, no matter what elephant in the room existed. "Ignorance is bliss" had always been one of her favorite phrases, and my dad would laugh at her and pat her ass, saying, "It better not be, woman," before smacking a kiss square on her giggling lips. Her philosophy would drive me nuts —I've always been one more inclined to answers and under-standing.

But not my mom. Answers for her came through the cosmos, a unique way of accepting that the universe would throw at her what she needed. She held an uncanny trust in that process, choosing to pretend that the cigarettes that were perma-nently in her brown-stained fingers weren't slowly killing her. She took her chances.

And I got sucked into a world of cancer. Dangerously so.

There was almost a sick satisfaction I got when I found out about her illness. Not because I wanted harm for my mother—that was the last thing I wanted.

No—this satisfaction was in the excitement of it.

It was something to hold onto, something to fixate on and

absorb myself in. I started wondering if I had cancer blooming in my body somewhere. Was that a lump in my breast? I'd have my mother check, insisting she take me to the doctor's, only to be reassured I was perfectly healthy. It disappointed me in a way I dared not admit out loud. I recognized how crazy that was, but I couldn't help it. I wanted something that made me distinctive. The Cancer Girl. People pouring out their prayers and well wishes in my name.

With Taven no longer in my life and with my mother's precarious health—recurrence a constant fear—a fixation on my own health became my thing. A craving of sorts to have something *happen* in my life that made me more interesting than the next person. Maybe I wasn't good enough for Taven to defy his parents and continue seeing me, but boy, he would feel so guilty when he learned I was sick.

I'd fantasize about getting some diagnosis, how I would find a way to tell Taven, how he'd rush over and demand to be able to take care of me. I'd even gone so far as to writing a fake letter to him, telling him of this phantom diagnosis.

Dear, Taven. You might want to sit down for this. I have something to tell you, and it's not easy to say.

I have cancer.

It's okay, I don't want you to worry about me. (A total lie.)

A broken person gets bad news and blames the world on their bad luck. A wise person gets bad news and finds the light to be found within the experience. And that is the path I'm choosing, to find the light and meaning in all of this. Please know that and take comfort in my ability to make the best of this terrible situation that I wouldn't wish on anyone.

-Yours always, Bingo forever, Dazzle

It was insane, I know. I was seventeen! Broken-hearted and losing my mind, what can I say.

Then there would be other times when I'd give up on my

broken heart, and I'd flip flop on how my fantasy would play out, much like the fantasy I had concocted of Taven and the arranged marriage. I'd decide Taven wasn't it, and I'd read *The Fault in Our Stars*, the book where the girl has cancer and meets the boy in a cancer group. I'd imagine that could be me, too. But in our story, my fellow cancer patient and I would both heal and recover and live happily ever after. We'd have the most beautiful love story of all time, forever in our hearts and in the fabric of our history and most unusual meeting. "We kicked cancer's ass! But at least cancer gave us one thing—each other," me and this mystery boy would say, staring longingly in one another's eyes in front of a crowd of admiring listeners.

That story felt wonderfully satisfying.

WHILE MY HEALTH REMAINED INTACT, I did eventually hear from Taven. It had been several months since I'd seen him that night I received the check. Once again, he texted me from his friend's phone, and then called me a few minutes after I responded.

I answered. I figured talking to him about my mom's cancer was as good an excuse as any. I was hurt that he hadn't reached out to me sooner, assuming he knew my mom had been sick if the Carlisles apparently knew. But I couldn't help myself. I wanted to, at the very least, feel his guilt first-hand when I confronted him.

When the phone rang, I scrambled to answer, ready to finally hear Taven's voice again. He was drunk.

Sure, I had seen him drink before, at that party we had gone to or when he'd sneak some concoction at either the country club or from his parents' liquor cabinet. We were teenagers, it was to be expected.

But this felt different. The Taven I was speaking to felt like an alternate version of the boy I knew and loved. In there somewhere, but shrouded in a guise of turmoil and circus clowns. I could practically hear the upbeat yet slightly disturbing carnival music through his words.

"My Dazzle, you speak to me, finally!" he crooned on the other end of the line. I could hear laughter in the background from his group of friends. It irked me.

I plopped down on my bed and stared up at the yellowed ceiling of our townhouse. "Not like you made any efforts to reach out to me," I pointed out.

Still, even through my hurt and annoyance, my mind was plotting out ways I could go and see him. Maybe Melissa would give me a ride. She could borrow her grandmother's car. We could make this work.

Taven chuckled when I presented the idea. "A secret meet-up. Great idea, Daz. This time we'll run away together and never look back!"

"Where would we go?"

"Hawaii. Then I could stare at you in a bikini all day." This elicited hollers and "I wanna come!" from the boys in the background. I smiled at the small fan base the idea of me in a bikini acquired, I couldn't help myself. "Plus," he continued, "I hear Hawaii is nice this time of year."

I flopped over onto my stomach, bending my legs at the knee and slowly pedaling my feet back and forth in comforting consideration. "Hawaii is nice all times of year," I said.

There was some bang in the background, then a loud group of cheers and boys' laughter. I strained my ears to listen for girls' voices, but could hear none. It relieved me.

When I asked him why he didn't reach out to me about my mom, he claimed he didn't know if I knew yet. That his parents had explained that Dylan and I were to be kept in the dark about it for the time being. He didn't want to be the one to spoil it and give me that kind of bad news.

It made sense. Damn him, it made sense.

And just like that, over a sloppy and drunken phone call and the cacophony of rowdy teenaged boys, I slowly started to forgive Taven.

twenty-two

. . .

Acquiesce

Twelve years ago

desiree

Eighteen years old

IT WASN'T UNTIL college that Taven and I saw each other again in person.

Through the rest of high school, I was stuck waiting for times that I could hear from him from a friend's phone, but that routine got old quickly. We'd talk over backup social media accounts, chatting for hours sometimes, then other times, go days and weeks in between. Sure, he could have come to pick me up if he wanted. I could sneak out again and we could just drive around. We had at one point made tentative plans to do so, but I think we both felt that there was something nice in just talking to one another again. A friendship, like it had been at the beginning. It felt more comforting than in the agony of the intensity of our feelings for one another, far more intense when we were actually in the same room.

After our respective high school graduations, me graduating top of my class, we both headed to Philly. I had just started a pre-med program, and he was going for a bachelor's in history, much to his parents' dismay, I'm sure.

Yes, we had strategically planned to get out of town together.

The decision to move to Philly together started as a joke, at first. We had talked about the potential schools we'd attend, but never did I think he'd actually choose based on where I was going.

The first two years of college, however, he once again had a girlfriend. He was almost sheepish when he told me about the girl he had met through a freshman orientation for his program.

It's not that we had stated explicitly that we planned to go to college and be together romantically, exactly. We didn't consider ourselves boyfriend and girlfriend during the last months of high school, though the undercurrents of flirtation were always there when we talked. But it's hard to date someone you never see, can barely talk to since his parents monitored every little thing Taven did. I figured he had been seeing other girls while we were still in school. He never told me about anyone, though, so I imagined it was never anything serious.

Still, I had in my silly naïveté expected that once we got to Philly, we'd pick up where we left off. When he first saw me, he gave me an awkward hug, then mumbled out that his new girlfriend and I better get along better than Evelyn and I had.

Well played, Vin, I thought. *Well played.*

I was heartbroken, yes. Here I thought we'd finally be doing this thing, be a real couple for once, and apparently he just saw me as a friend. I relished in the wounded spirit that I was, sickeningly enjoying the tragedy of romance within my tormented soul.

I dated here and there, but not much. My heart belonged

to Taven, always. Like I had done before with Evelyn, I figured I'd wait until the time was right. At least his new girlfriend wasn't nearly as exotically pretty as Evelyn and her red hair, and I had a sick satisfaction in knowing that. She was a plain Jane, much like me. Whereas Taven was the life of every party, his new girlfriend (Christine was her name), was the shy sidekick quietly standing by. I felt surprisingly unthreatened by her.

I was in the beg, barter, and steal phase of my crush. The emotional bargaining of taking what I could get. For me, that meant stolen moments with Taven where there was always a charge to them. There was a sly happiness I had in that. We had even kissed again at one point—okay, more than one point—but one of us always stopped it. "But Christine," we'd say, like we were oh-so-virtuous in remembering the sweet girl who had stars in her eyes every time she looked at Taven.

"Christine," I'd say one final time, breath panting and victorious at the bulge popping out of Taven's jeans for me. "She's good for you," I would add.

"And I don't want to ruin our friendship," he would say, me nodding as if that made the most sense. Sure, our friendship.

I'd look at him and wonder why he wouldn't just make it official, this obvious thing between us. We were *so good* together, obviously felt something so strong that had started back when we were mere kids. Couldn't he see that?

And then understanding would settle into me, as it always did. A bitter truth I hated to admit.

That it was complicated.

That our families were enemies, and there was no escaping that, as much as we loved to pretend it didn't matter.

In the end of the day, I could never bring him home and announce with any enthusiasm the great love of my life, back in my orbit yet again. I had a feeling my mom would eventually be able to accept, but my father never would. He would spit on the

Carlisles if given the chance, probably worse. The Carlisle name was never to be spoken in our home.

And Taven couldn't bring the disgraced name of Hatson into his home either—the daughter of parents his own family had solidly severed ties with. Looked down upon. A useful tool to them for a moment, perhaps, but now beneath them. It would be asking a lot from both of us to try and ever make a relationship work, one that wasn't plagued by necessary secrecy.

I also knew of Taven's struggles with making his family proud. He was eternally trying to live up to the expectations of his parents. My heart hurt for him and that struggle, and the thought of actually claiming me as his once again would not help the matters of his precarious relationship with the great Mr. and Mrs. Carlisle. I tried to respect his need to stay on his parents' side, painful as it was. When you're in love with a prince, you're bound to be trampled on by the rules of the monarchy.

So I'd look up at Taven's full lips, swollen from sneaking kisses to mine, and I'd know that this was the way it would have to be. There were no other options. I'd convinced myself that this could be enough.

I'd take what I could get, the ultimate emotional trade of any time with him in exchange for my constantly crushed heart.

twenty-three

. . .

Confession

Ten years ago

desiree

twenty years old

"I HAVE A confession to make." Taven sipped his coffee, and I shifted on our park bench, nestled along one of the winding brick pathways of our campus. I draped my arm over the back and turned to face him.

"What's that?" I asked.

He turned to me, and I took in the signature swoop of his hair, always longer on the top, trimmed short at the sides. We'd known each other for nearly eight years at that point, and I never knew him to have a different haircut.

"It's one I'm hoping you won't be surprised to hear," he said. His tone was serious, and I felt a little nervous at what he was about to say.

As was always the case with Taven, I was firmly back in my

hope fantasy. My hope could subside to a dull ache when he was with someone, but would come full force when he was single.

He and Christine were finally through. They had both done a study abroad in Spain together over the summer, which had terrified me. Melissa was in New York and was too caught up in her acting career to stay in touch with me, so I cried to my roommate Katja with the fears that Taven and Christine would fall madly in love over paella on the beach. He would ask her to marry him. They'd have some romantic clandestine overseas wedding, and I'd have to find a way to slowly poison the new Mrs. Carlisle so I could take my rightful place.

Katja, ever the optimist, would laugh and tell me it was a good plan. Then she'd hand me the tissues and hold me in her arms, saying that one of these days, I would need to let him go.

But that's not how the summer in Spain went down, thankfully.

Apparently, Taven went buck wild with vats of Spanish wine and sunshine, and poor Christine was not one for that kind of thing. She ended it, and when they returned, I cleaned up Taven's newly bronzed but stupidly broken heart.

I was stuck in a mental loop of convincing myself that this was it. I figured now's the time, the day he'd finally confess his love for me. Confess the matching agony we both felt, trying to stay true to our families when really, we were destined to be together. In this particular fantasy, we would kiss, probably in the rain after previously attempting to walk away from each other, but then we'd both realize that you can't sever the cord of true love. The kiss would lead to more, and Taven would guide me inside to my apartment, to my bed, and finally, *finally* enter my body and make it official, once and for all.

I was still a virgin, my silent vow to hold out for the man I felt in my heart was my person. We would do this. It would be the chance to continue what we had started as kids.

I hated so much that my hope could never just die. It lingered around, torturing me.

I sipped my coffee and smiled over its lid at Taven. "Is this confession that you need to find a new hairdo?" I reached over and rustled my hand through his hair.

It was fall of our junior year, and the leaves were in that beautiful space of fiery oranges and reds, fluttering around us and the red brick buildings of campus. Students walked by with their scarves and laptop bags, and the air smelled like new beginnings.

He combed his hand through his hair to smooth out the mess I made. His dark eyes were pensive, but he said nothing.

"Come on, Vin. What's this big confession?" I prompted. I stared at his profile, the scruff on his cheek, broken up with a small scar on his jawline. God, he was hot. The boyishness was gone, and in its wake was the makings of a young man with sculpted shoulders and a beard that could be full if he wanted, but he kept it trimmed short. My attraction for him only seemed to grow stronger every year, and my heart beat rapidly with the damn incessant flicker of hope.

He cleared his throat and finally spoke, turning to face me. "I'm thinking of dropping out of school." I watched as his eyes darted back and forth between mine, looking for my reaction.

I loved that he sought my approval. I hated that his confession wasn't a love for me.

I pulled my head back in surprise. "What? You're kidding."

"I'm not."

"But why?" I frowned. "That seems...like a bad idea."

It was all I could think to say as I internally watched my hope fantasy flitter away like a flyer in the wind.

I tried to focus on what he had just said. His idea of dropping out of school. This was big, and our friendship required my friend hat.

I knew he didn't quite have the same love of school and

learning that I always did, but I didn't think he was miserable, exactly. "You're halfway done already, why the hell would you stop now?"

He shrugged. "Because I have no idea what I even want to do with this degree. I thought it'd be interesting, that I'd dive into interesting war stories or figure out some secret of ancient civilizations, maybe go into teaching with it. But in actuality it's boring as all hell and I can't imagine this being my world for the rest of my life."

I leaned back in my seat and crossed my arms over my chest. I didn't like it.

"You're mad about it," he said, reading my mind.

"No, I'm not."

"Yes, you are."

I sighed. "It's not like I'm mad *at* you, I'm just...I don't know."

"But you are mad," he confirmed. He cursed and turned away from me, throwing his head back and closing his eyes to the sky. "It's a dumb idea, you can say it."

I studied him and the tortured look on his face, so full of self-doubt. I felt bad for conveying my own doubts. It wasn't what he needed. I reached over to his face and rubbed my hand through the soft spikes of hair along his sideburns. "Hey, Taven," I whispered, hoping my tone was comforting. He kept his eyes closed, but leaned his head into my hand.

I tried to explain. "I'm not mad and I don't think it's a dumb idea, okay?"

He opened his eyes and glanced at me. "You don't?"

"No," I reassured. "It just caught me off guard, that's all." *That, and I hoped your confession was that you still love me.*

"It's not some impulsive decision," he said. "I've been thinking about it for a while."

I nodded and withdrew my hand, facing forward in my seat once again. "I guess I'm more mad at your parents for forcing you to go to school if that wasn't really something you wanted to do."

He reached for my hand and laced our fingers together, patting the bundle on my thigh. "It's not my parents. They want what's best for me, and I went along with it thinking college would be fun." He grinned. "And it definitely has been."

"Don't I know it," I chided. There may or may not have been some late-night drunk calls where I'd have to go pick him up and let him sleep it off in my dorm room or apartment. "So glad college has all been such a blast for you."

I was irritated, but couldn't quite pinpoint the source of it. Maybe it was his cavalier attitude about the whole thing. Maybe it was because his schooling was paid for, whereas mine was not. I would graduate with student loans, then pile on more for med school. I'd be in debt until I was three thousand years old, all thanks to my parents' bad luck and worse business decisions. Dylan, my big brother NFL football star, had offered to pay, but I wouldn't let him. He worked his ass off to be where he is, and I didn't want him blowing it all on me or my education, especially when I was on track to have a whole lot more schooling ahead of me.

Besides, I liked the idea of my independence, doing this all on my own.

And yet, here I was, doing exactly what my parents always wanted me to do and pursuing that good old title "Dr.", all so that my dad could resurrect his bizarre dream of the prestige of medicine. I tried to tell myself that it was also out of my own love for the field. You never knew if my mom's cancer might return, and it sure would be nice to have the added bonus of my medical expertise to tackle that if or when it happened.

I stared down at our clasped hands and focused on the feel of his pulse against my wrist. "If you drop out, then what?" I asked.

"I haven't made any final decisions yet. It's just a thought, but I wanted your opinion before I do anything."

"Okay?"

"Look, I mean—why continue to waste the money on an education I have no plans to utilize, right?" He released my hand and sipped his coffee again, and I wrapped both my hands around the cardboard of my coffee cup, willing its warmth to seep into my skin. I sipped the pumpkin-flavored concoction, noting that it had way too much nutmeg. I regretted falling prey to the seasonal fad.

"What do you want to be when you grow up?" I asked him after a minute. "Don't overthink it, just say the first thing that comes to mind."

"A mechanic," he said without hesitation.

It didn't surprise me. He and Inferno had continued their love affair, with Taven always tinkering and doing this and that. That car was his baby, and he treated it with care. "Your parents will be thrilled, I'm sure," I joked. I watched as a guy zipped past us on his bicycle, rolling off the brick pathway and into the grass to pass the slow group of walkers in front of him.

Taven shrugged. "They'll be pissed at first, but oh well. Doesn't matter. I'll open up my own shop. Maybe even get into a side business of vintage car sales."

"Vintage car sales?" I wouldn't even know where to start with something like that. But Taven could do it. I know he could. He always had that natural ease with people, he could figure it out, make the right contacts and that kind of thing.

He nodded. "Yeah. I may not like school, but I *do* like being comfortable financially," he grinned. "One thing my parents have definitely taught me is not to take that for granted."

I envied him in that moment. Taven back to his usual cool and chill demeanor, so confident in the things he wanted. Me, on the other hand—I'd be second guessing every single little thing, destroying an idea of what I wanted to the point of it being unrecognizable, and I'd be thrown right back into a blank territory wondering what my original dream was in the first place. Like now, did I even *like* medicine? Or was it just something I was doing solely for my dad? My mom too, though she wasn't as pushy. I knew she loved the idea, though, of me being a plastic surgeon, probably already planning out the work she'd have done. And I wanted to be able to give her what she thought she needed, happy to just have her alive and well. Still, I couldn't be sure if it was actually my passion, or if was simply absorbing my parents' dreams.

Taven stood up and grabbed my elbow, pulling me up as well. "Come on. Let's go get really drunk. We need to celebrate."

"You deciding to quit school requires celebrating?" I asked.

He nodded. "Yup. I feel a million times lighter already."

"Then I guess we'll go get really drunk and celebrate."

Let this be a lesson to you all—when the crush of your life disappoints you with a confession that you hoped would be that he's in love with you, but instead was his decision of a newfound path in life, and he now wants to get rip-roaring drunk, don't go along with him.

Trust me on this.

twenty-four

. . .

Agonize

Five years ago

lynda carlisle

Summertime, 1:16pm

FLOWERS IN HAND, cradled in her arms like a delicate baby, she steps up to the grave site. The emotion she holds each time she has visited never ceases to surprise her. Emotions are not something she is used to, yet here they are. With her every time she has taken in the gray stone of Holly Hatson, beloved wife and mother, just as she imagines Holly wanted it to say.

It's difficult to describe the attachment she feels toward Holly, even now when her old friend no longer walks the earth. Some relationships are like that, she realizes. A visceral connection, like it or not.

It would have been so easy to cut Holly out of her world and her heart nearly a decade ago. Forget she ever existed and then move on with her life. She tried, Lynda truly tried. The claim had been sickening, a moment in her life she will not soon forget.

It was at a lunch when a woman broached the subject. A frequent guest at Carlisle parties, this woman was more of an acquaintance than anything else. Lynda winces to remember the conversation.

Your daughter, Jacqui.

Kneeling before a man.

Lynda had started to laugh at first. Tried to play it off that she wasn't infuriated that her daughter had been caught pleasuring some high school boy at the Carlisle's most recent party. Kids will be kids, oh the rash actions of young love.

Not a high school boy. A man, the woman repeated.

Frank Hatson.

To this day, all these years later, Lynda's stomach still roils at the thought. Because as soon as the woman uttered Frank's name, Lynda knew in her heart it was true. She excused herself quietly and scurried to the ladies' room, fighting the contents of her lunch as they were threatening to evacuate her body.

She would kill him. She would kill Frank Hatson, make it look like an accident. Her fingers clutched the granite vanity as she stared at herself in the mirror. The perfect reflection of poise and grace, pearls and all. The life she had carefully formed for herself and her family, a far cry from the life she once knew. No one to hurt them, only comforts and happiness to be had.

Except, that wasn't the case. Lynda stared at her reflection that day, her chest rising in explosive breaths as the color continued to drain from her face.

God, please God, make it all go away.

Where had she gone wrong? What kind of mother raises a child that falls prey to such sick and evil forces? Her mind reeled with the epic mistake she had made in allowing this man to enter their lives, their home. The *lavishness* she and her husband had shared with this man! The gifts and introducing them to their friends, the club, all of it! The generosity she had shown him, all because of her own foolish thoughts, wanting the friendship with a woman she felt so connected to. It seemed so perfect—she and Bill could shift gears and enter into this new business, expand their enterprise beyond the trading days they once knew. And for what!

They didn't need another business. They had commercial real estate investments that paid handsomely, a strategic portfolio that only continued to build wealth. What had she been thinking in joining forces with this man and his ridiculous spa ideas that he so stupidly believed were something special and cutting edge?

She realized she didn't only want to murder Frank Hatson, but she wanted to kill the version of herself that had made that decision to allow him into her life, her children's lives. She could always spot a scoundrel like him, her instincts rarely ever betraying her.

And still, she went along with it, thinking it was a safe backup that could diversify their operations, a hand in something different, something easy. A win-win for both families.

Lynda blinks away the fury from her eyes and places her hand on the cool stone of her old friend's grave. "Oh, Holly," she says to no one. "Why the hell did you stay?"

As Lynda makes her way through the graveyard, carefully walking on tip-toes to prevent her heels from sinking into the lush grass, her phone rings.

She rifles through her purse, retrieving the device and seeing a most surprising name on the screen. The last time she received a call from Desiree Hatson, it was very bad news.

And here she was, calling again.

twenty-five

. . .

Vulnerable

Present Day

taven

Saturday, 1:08am

I CARRY DESIREE'S bag and lead her down the glass encased walkway that leads from my garage to the house. I look over and see her taking in the space as I flick on the lights, her eyes wide and roaming as we step into the mudroom area, then through to the kitchen. It's a warm space with brown hardwood floors, cinnamon cabinets that could probably use updating, but I haven't had the real desire to do so. The granite is black, the fixtures bronze, and I realize how very bachelor-like the whole place is. Built in the '70s, my mid-century modern/farmhouse hybrid has had some updates, and some things left original, like the floor-to-ceiling stone fireplace that runs through the center of the open layout of the living and dining area. I love the architecture of the home, but looking at it now, I can see that it could benefit from some color.

Evelyn had said it would be the first thing she'd do once she moved in. That was before she had made her declaration of wanting to put our engagement on pause. She was having second thoughts. Uncertainties.

I'm sure once she finds out I've brought Desiree back here, it will be the final nail in the coffin. I realize I'm relieved at the thought, and I wonder what that says about me. So many years of fighting an internal war with myself, wondering about my purpose or worth. I like to think of myself as well beyond that war now, yet it appears the one piece of self-deception I've continued is standing right here, in my home. I wonder if Evelyn somehow sensed that.

I place Desiree's bag down at the foot of the stairs and follow her to where she's standing in front of the fireplace, staring at the photos on the mantle. Me and Jacqui as kids, grinning while standing in line for the rollercoaster twisting and turning in the background beyond. A family photo of us with my parents and Jacqui's husband at their wedding.

Then the photo of me and Evelyn, dressed in cocktail attire, my arm around her waist. It was at our engagement party just last year. I had been sober for nearly three years then. Thought I had everything figured out.

A lie, I realize, given the present company that I've invited to stay with me for the weekend. Small lies are a habit I thought I had ceased, but I guess Desiree's often been the source of the biggest lies I've ever told. I'm disappointed to find that I'm still doing it now.

I'm telling the biggest lie when I pretend she's someone I'm over.

Desiree picks up my engagement photo and glides her fingers over Evelyn's smiling face. I note that my own smile looks forced, and I wonder if Desiree can tell.

"She's even more beautiful all grown up, isn't she?" Desiree says.

I step over to her and remove the photo from her hand, placing it down on an end table beside one of my sofas. I have the urge to place it face down, but I don't. "She's a good woman," I say, because it's the truth.

We had reconnected four years ago, when I was temporarily living back at home with my parents, after my stay at rehab. Evelyn helped pull me out of my depression, my shame, the overall loss of any sense of control over my life. Within her company, I quickly rediscovered the ease I had with her back when we were kids. That ease seemed like exactly what I needed at the time. I was rebuilding my self-concept, trying to hold onto the goals I had once dreamed of for myself, scared I was about to lose it all. Fears of whether or not I even deserved happiness were threatening to make me turn toward my old go-tos, but I was determined not to let them.

Therapy allowed my soul to let in some light, little by little. To understand the mistakes that I had made, where they stemmed from, and how to love myself as someone flawed and human, afflicted with an addiction that I used to self-medicate. Evelyn had been a friend through that journey, and when I was confident enough that I was never going back to drinking, we allowed our friendship to turn to something more.

Maybe it was too soon. In fact, it was definitely too soon. Not because my sobriety was new and fragile, but because I still hadn't addressed the one big elephant left in my psyche. My Dazzle.

I try and explain some of this to Desiree, leaving out the part of my continued longing for her. I tell her that I'm sober now and have been for nearly four years. She smiles, and tells me she had a feeling, when she noticed how very obviously not-drunk I was earlier this evening at the festival.

I nod, absorbing the fact that it was something she even

assessed for. Of course it was, how could it not be, given how bad things were the last time we spoke?

But there's a twist in my chest to make Desiree understand how Evelyn had re-entered my world and why. She remains quiet as I do.

When I finally finish my broad-strokes re-cap, Desiree looks down at her hands, twisting them in front of her. "I'm glad you've found your peace," she says. "Before things got any worse."

"I'm lucky."

"And," she starts, then darts her eyes down to the end table and the photo of me and Evelyn. "I'm glad you had her when you needed her."

"I wish it had been you," I blurt out, the words escaping on their own volition.

She looks up at me, a frown filling her face and I ache to make it go away. "It couldn't have been me, though. Could it, Taven?"

I hang my head low, knowing she's right. It couldn't have been her because she might have been the biggest trigger to my insecurity I ever had. Which is unfair to her, so what am I supposed to say?

I place a hand in my pocket and look away, back to the photo from Jacqui's wedding. My father's kind eyes and my mother's terse smile. "No, I guess that's true," I finally admit.

I've always held respect for my parents, even in my more reckless times. They seemed like the epitome of having it all together, and I paled in comparison. I think in many ways a part of me had subconsciously viewed Desiree as that. All put together, always too good for me. That's the truth.

I turn back to her. "I've always felt like you were this mystical creature that I could never live up to, Dazzle."

"Me?" she asks, pulling her head back in surprise. "How so?"

I take a step toward her. "Because," I shrug. "You were this cool girl who didn't put on a front, you were always so comfortable to say exactly what was on your mind, and you have this endless compassion for people, but not in a way that makes you mad when they disappoint you. You can just accept them for who they are. Take Melissa, for example."

She goes to sit down on the couch, scooting back and folding her arms over her chest. "What about her?" she asks.

"I know she hurt you when she stopped talking to you when we were in college. But then you let her back in. You don't hold a grudge, unlike me."

"You make me sound like a doormat," she says, eyebrows pinched together.

"You're not a doormat, that's not what I mean." I sigh, feeling frustrated that I'm not making this point to her. "Look, what I'm trying to say is that I'm sorry. For everything. For what happened five years ago and the hell I put you through. And for the fact that no, it couldn't have been you to pull me out of my struggles, because I respected you too much, as fucked up as that sounds."

She huffs out a laugh. "Sure as hell didn't feel like respect, Taven," she says, voice soft as she glances over to the photo of me and Evelyn.

I turn away from her, hating seeing the sadness on her face. I try and collect my thoughts so that I can properly explain myself, or express my regret or something. I want so badly to get her to understand where I was back then, and where I am now. And how sorry I am for all of it.

But then I realize that's not what she needs. Not yet anyway.

What she needs is a chance to say her piece for once. To not be the quiet one, standing on the sidelines without a voice, trying to keep it all together.

I turn back to face her, saying, "Well then, what did it feel like?" Her blue eyes flash up to me, eyelashes framing them and making her look so beautiful and sweet, it's crushing. But I need to face whatever it is she deserves to finally say to me. "Don't hold back, don't try and sugarcoat or refrain for my sake."

She crosses her legs and leans forward, arms resting on her thigh, looking down at her hands while she twists a ring on her finger. "Taven…"

I walk over and sit down on the coffee table in front of her. "Come on, Daz. Tell me. You never got any kind of closure, you just walked away."

She snaps her head up. "You left me no choice, what was I supposed to do?"

I can see it, the irritation and hurt and anger bubbling up in her. I'm tempted to tell her that I agree, that she's absolutely right, she had no choice and I understand that.

But I know my Dazzle. I know that if I say that, she'll just back off again, and I want to see her actually open up and let me have it. Something that's hard for her to do, so I need to push her.

"I don't know," I say, my tone a bit accusatory. "Maybe stick it out and try a little harder?" My words are harsh. Brash. They're words I don't even agree with, but she needs the nudge. "Do you think you gave up on me?"

She rises to a stand and takes a step away from me. I can see her body tensing. This is good, it's exactly what she needs.

"You have some fucking nerve, saying that, Taven Carlisle."

Now we're getting somewhere. "How so?" I press.

She spins around to face me. "How so? How so?!" she says, voice rising and eyes wide. "Because I *did* try! I tried for months! I confronted you about your drinking, remember that? Multiple times! Sure, maybe softly at first, but then not so soft, and guess what?" she says, pushing a palm into my shoulder in a shove. "You didn't change a damn thing. In fact, you only got worse. Hiding it, lying, staying out, making me feel like I had become second in your life behind alcohol. I had to stand there and watch you blow up everything in your world. Even when you were physically present, you weren't there mentally or emotionally. You just pushed me away like I was the goddamn enemy while you drank yourself into oblivion."

"But you *were* the enemy," I say, biting back a nervous smile, mainly because I'm in awe of finally seeing her get good and angry, just as she deserves.

"Ha! Was I?" She nods and fills her face with a maniacal grin. "Well, there you have it, then, folks! I'm the problem, just like everyone thinks. Like your drinking buddies said, I can only imagine what they said when I finally left. Like your mom thought for years, I'm sure. The girl not good enough for her son. Or like Melissa thought, I guess, because otherwise, why did she drop me the minute she went away to college?"

She paces around the room, hands on her hips. I want to comfort her, the urge is strong to tell her how wrong she is, but she doesn't need empty words to placate her right now. So instead, I watch her as she allows the beautiful fury to take hold, little by little. "What I don't get," she says, "what I can never understand is why everyone seems to think I'm so fucking hard to be around? Got any ideas on that, Taven?" She pauses, staring at me, and I remain silent. She blinks at me a few times, waiting for a response that doesn't come, then resumes her pacing. "It's so fucking *frustrating*, people just don't seem to understand that all I do is try and keep a level head, be the voice of reason now and then. Is that so wrong? But I guess that's boring for some people. So yeah, I walked away from you. Fine. So sorry I'm not okay with a dysfunctional love of alcohol and denial. So sorry I realized I wasn't okay with continuing to lose myself in order to try and save you." She pauses her pacing and looks at me once more. "So sorry that you didn't want to hear some hard truths."

"I didn't like your hard truths."

She widens her eyes at me. "Well guess what? I didn't like looking at a *man I loved*, seeing him coast through his days in a haze, making dangerous decisions under the guidance of a bottle, decisions that put my fucking *life* at risk, Taven!" she cries, slamming her palm into her chest. "Do you remember that? Because I sure as fuck do! It's taken me a long time to heal from the flashbacks that haunted me from five years ago. Memories I wish I could forget of the things I can't believe I let slide. Do you know how scary those times were for me? When you were behind the wheel and I thought we would die, or when you were lashing out and slamming your fist into walls, and I'd be standing there wondering what was happening or what on earth I did to deserve this, completely unable to stop you." She looks at me in earnest, sincerely questioning me, begging for an answer that I don't have. I see the tears filling her eyes. "Do you have any idea how terrifying it was to be so incredibly tied to you at my very core, yet to know that that tie was slowly dragging me down right along with you?"

I sit up straight, pulling my shoulders back to try and face everything she's telling me, as painful as it is to hear. But I remain silent.

She blinks, a tear falls down her cheek, and she mindlessly wipes it away. "I was so scared, Taven, it hurt."

"What were you scared of?" I ask, voice soft. I lean over to the tissue box on the table, handing it to her.

She shakes her head slowly, silent while she dabs at her eyes. "I was scared that I'd never be able to get through to you and make you see the destruction you were causing, which is of course exactly what happened. And I was scared that I was going to lose you. That you were going to get in a car and kill yourself one night, or kill us both," she says, her words choking on a sob. "Or someone else, and it'd be my fault, because I couldn't stop you."

My chest tightens and my breath becomes shallow, seeing her break down like this, knowing it's all because of me. And while I've come to terms with my past and the damage I know I can never undo, seeing the one person that has always mattered most to me fall apart is one of the hardest things I think I've ever had to face. It almost feels like too much, and I have to fight through my own inner demons that want to retreat to a place of self-loathing, knowing that's exactly what got us here in the first place.

But I refuse to do that. Not again.

That was the old me. A false version of myself that hid away and used self-destruction as a comfortable hiding spot.

That me is gone now, I remind myself, and Dazzle deserves to get all that she has been holding in off of her chest, to free herself from the whirlwind of emotions I put her through. So I take a deep breath, knowing I can help piece her back together, and I urge her to continue. "Go on," I say gently. "What else were you afraid of?"

She sniffles, and at first I think she's locking back up again, but then she eventually speaks, her tone softer now. "I used to be afraid you might have an accident at work or something. So many times I'd concoct this image of you blowing something up from a mistake, and I'd worry myself sick, completely ill. I'd be all distracted at school, unable to concentrate because I had seen you walk out with a flask you thought I hadn't noticed. And I felt guilty that I didn't stop you, because I knew it'd just be a fight, that you'd tell me I was overreacting."

I push aside the shame that wants to take over in hearing her resurrect those memories. No place for shame in any of this, it does no good. Thinking of that time, those memories, it fills me with disgust. Yet it's a welcomed disgust, I realize. Because I know just how painful that time of my life was all around, and it feels good to hear it brought back to me through her eyes, and recognize how foreign that version of myself feels now.

It's liberating.

Desiree tucks a strand of hair behind her ear and sighs. "I was scared that I had made a huge mistake in giving us another chance. And scared that I didn't even seem to care about your demons, because that's how much you meant to me. That even though the man I was with wasn't even himself most of the time —he was completely closed off and unavailable—I was still willing to sacrifice myself and my happiness because I was that desperate to be with you." She nods her head now, voice more steady as she lifts her chin. "That's it—that's what I think I was scared of most of all. Feeling myself getting caught up in the agony and choosing that hurt, because it felt beautifully tragic, to the point of sacrificing myself."

I rise to a stand, taking the tissue from her hand and wiping away the last of her tears. "But you didn't sacrifice yourself for me, Dazzle. Remember?" I say with a small smile, brushing a strand of hair back away from her face. "You walked away when you knew there was no way to get through to me."

"Right. And now you hate me for it."

"No, baby" I say, smiling sadly at her. "I love you for it. I love that you walked away, just as you should have. You chose *you*."

She looks up at me, sapphire blue eyes sparkling in surprise. "What?"

I smile fully now. "You chose yourself, Dazzle, and I couldn't be more proud of you or happy for you for doing so. Do you realize that? How much I admire that?"

"But...I thought you were mad at me for that." She furrows her brows, confusion etched all over her face.

I slowly shake my head and pull her in for an embrace, cradling her in my arms like I've wanted to do for so long. I could weep with the relief of finally holding her. "Not even an ounce of me is mad. Not now, anyway. Maybe back then, but that was just misdirected anger that I really felt for myself, not you."

Her voice is muffled in my chest. "You just said I was the enemy."

I squeeze her a bit tighter. "I know, I'm sorry. I didn't actually mean it, I was just egging you on, Dazzle. So that you'd allow yourself to open up and give me the lashing I deserve."

She pulls back and slams a fist into my chest. "You jerk," she says, smiling and wincing all at the same time. "You faked me out?"

"I did, yes."

"But why?"

"Don't you see?" I ask, pressing a kiss to her forehead. I can't help myself, I have to kiss the beautiful woman before me that finally let herself do all the talking, messy as it needed to be. "I faked you out because before, I only pushed you away, never letting you get the chance to be heard. It was so wrong of me, and this right here was me making up for that. Because I'm strong enough to listen, now, do you understand?"

"I don't even know what to say."

"I think you said all the right things already. I hope you feel that," I say, trying with all my might to fully convey my pride in her. "You never got mad, back then. You would always be so patient with me, even when I was nothing but a jackass."

She arches an eyebrow. "I got mad *sometimes*. Give me some credit."

I can't help but let out a small laugh at that. "I stand corrected. You did."

Her chest heaves in a sigh. "Maybe not often enough, though."

"No, Dazzle. There was no getting through to me back then, no matter what you did. That's the truth of it."

I release her and take a step back, grabbing the back of my neck, scared that if I keep touching her, I won't be able to stop, and I don't want to fuck up this moment.

She lets out a heavy sigh, and watching her chest rise and fall like that is stirring up so much within me. The chemistry she and I have always had with one another. A connection that's been there since we were kids. Call me a selfish bastard, but I want nothing more than to touch her, kiss her, do a whole lot more with her within the next forty-eight hours. Especially with all I just saw her bravely do.

Especially with her standing here in that tiny little halter top and tiny little shorts. One pull of the strings around her neck and she'd be halfway exposed to me. I admit, it's a tempting thing to do.

Just not right now.

"Look," I say, running a hand down my face. "I know there's nothing I can do to erase the past, but I need you to understand that you did everything you could to help me, and I'm sorry I wasn't ready to accept that help at the time. But none of it is your fault or because of you, okay?" I search her eyes, looking for confirmation that she hears me, that she knows deep down that's the truth.

She nods. "Okay," is all she says.

"It's taken me a while to get to a place of understanding myself, and I don't just mean in terms of time."

"I get it, I think. You mean it takes a while in terms of digging in deep enough. Getting to the things you needed to sort through," she offers with understanding, and I nod.

"Yes, exactly." And those kinds of things right there that my Dazzle can say—those are the gut punches to my soul. It's why my *need* for her has always been so strong. Too strong. I wonder if I'm finally at a place where that need has been tempered to a better level. A simple want.

When we tell ourselves we need something, it's dangerous. A want is the healthier thing, because it frees us from the desperations of grasping.

I sure hope my affections for Desiree are more at the want level, because here I am, reaching out for her once again. I run my fingers down her face, unable to pull away from the softness of her skin. "It's always been you, Dazzle. It's always been you that's had my heart, do you realize that?" I search her eyes for some reaction of understanding, or that she feels the same way, but I can't read her expression.

"Sounds plausible," she says softly, attempting to joke but her tone betrays her. "I want to believe that," she whispers.

"Well, then do, because it's true."

"Not a little lie?" The corners of her mouth lift, and I smile in return. My Dazzle, always knowing how to call my bluff.

But not this time. This time I'm all raw honesty. My chest tightens as I attempt to go all in. "I'm still in love with you, Desiree. Still completely and madly fucking *in love* with you," I breathe out, like there's a pressure valve being released and the words escape and evaporate with freedom into the air around us.

I take my chance. I lean forward to kiss her, not giving a shit if it's wrong. I lace my fingers through her hair, cradling her head while my mouth presses into hers, and when she parts her lips for me, I'm greedy as I slip my tongue in to taste what I still think of as mine. This woman, standing before me, once again trusting as she lets me in.

I refuse to let her down this time.

We kiss for a glorious few moments before I feel her hands on my stomach, pushing me. I back off and step away, cursing that I went too far and have now upset her. My eyes are closed, because I don't think I can stand to see regret or hurt on her face.

Her voice forces my eyes to open. "Taven," she says, voice shaky and I look to see her hand covering her mouth, the other on her stomach.

"I'm sorry," I say, weak as the expression is. She's heard enough weightless apologies from me. "I shouldn't have kissed you."

"No," she says, but her frown has returned. "It's not that, I've wanted to kiss you for longer than I should really admit, it's just, I don't feel..."

"What is it, what's wrong?" I ask.

She runs away from me, and I dart after her as she races past the fireplace and down the hall. She presses open the door to my office, me on her heels, then turns and crashes into me.

"Bathroom," she huffs out. "I'm going to be sick, where's the bathroom?"

I grab her hand to guide her to the powder room, just one door over, but it's too late. A groan escapes her, and she keels over, lifting her pathetic excuse for a shirt and spewing vomit into it, but it seeps through the woven fabric and onto her legs, her sandaled feet, and my floor. I rush to guide her into the powder room and watch as she hovers above the toilet. I pull her hair back and rub up and down her spine as she empties her stomach in violent heaves before finally slinking herself down to the floor.

I crouch down in front of her. "More?" I ask.

"I'm not sure yet. Just give me a minute." She turns her body, face hovering above the bowl.

I wait a few moments, then eventually flush away the contents and leave her, jogging into the kitchen and grabbing a glass from the cabinet. I fill it with water and head back to her, water sloshing as I go. When I hand her the glass she gingerly sips, then swishes and spits out into the toilet.

She puts the glass down on the floor beside her and leans over, hand walling off the side of her face. "This is the second time this week I've been sick," she says, and my heart pinches at whether or not she's trying to tell me she's pregnant.

I know I'm an asshole when I'm praying that's not the case. Not that it would be a deal breaker for me, but because that meant some other prick had gotten to do what I have fantasized about doing on more than one occasion. Fill my Dazzle with my seed. Watch her belly beautifully bloom with our child.

But no, wait. She had been drinking tonight, I had smelled the sweetness on her breath.

And the doctor said nausea and vomiting might happen.

This could be an expected reaction to the lightning strike, right? Maybe I should call him.

I distract myself and open the cabinet beneath the sink to pull out paper towels and a spray bottle of Lysol. I step out to the hallway to clean up the small mess on the floor, then step back into the bathroom, heart pulling at the sight of her feeling ill. I wish I could take it all away.

I quickly wash my hands, and when she finally looks up, eyes tear-filled and swollen, I step closer to her, placing the back of my hand to her forehead.

She smiles at me weakly. I'm scared she's delusional and I need to call the doctor. "I'm not feverish," she says.

"You sure?"

"Yes, dummy. Just nauseous. And being exhausted probably isn't helping," she explains, and I breathe a sigh of cautious relief.

"You're a hundred percent positive that's all? And that it's normal?"

She nods. "Yes. It needed to happen, I feel better, actually." Her eyes dart behind me, out to the hallway. "I'm sorry about the mess."

"Please. You've cleaned up my vomit an embarrassing number of times before," I say. My tone is light, but the guilt behind it is loud in my head.

She shrugs a shoulder. "Payback."

twenty-six

. . .

Reciprocity

Present Day

taven

Saturday, 1:32am

I LIFT DESIREE into my arms and carry her through the house, past the fireplace and to the bottom of the stairs.

"I'm fine, you really don't need to carry me," she says.

I pause and ease her legs down while keeping one arm around her waist. I pull the strap of her overnight bag over my shoulder, lift her once again as I begin to climb the stairs. "You're covered in vomit. I'd rather not have it all over my floor," I say.

"Yeah, sure."

I smile as I make my way around the corner and to my room, past the king-sized bed and into the bathroom. I note the goosebumps covering her arms and I can feel the tremble she's fighting. I place her down and flick on the towel warmer, followed by the heating lamp and lights, and then finally, the shower.

She scans around the space, and I see her taking in the Durango marble lining the walls, the quartz vanity countertop, the sleek glass of the shower, slowly fogging with steam. "Wow," she says, nodding in approval. "Business must be good."

"No thanks to my parents," I mutter, then immediately regret it.

"How are they?" she asks, a divot forming between her brows. "I mean, how are you guys, do you talk?"

I nod. "Yes. We talk every few weeks, though I think their trust of me will always remain—"

"They trust you, Taven," she says, turning toward me. "And if they don't, that's on them." She startles me with the abruptness of her statement, and I smile at how fiercely protective she's always been when it came to me and the dynamics with my parents.

They had cut me off when they found out about how bad my drinking had gotten. I thought they would cut me off when I had dropped out of school, but no. Once I explained my business plans, proved to them I had researched the ins and outs of the operation I wanted to build, they cautiously supported me, much to my surprise. I had been slowly making steps toward those goals, entered a training program and worked my apprenticeship, my fingers permanently gritty and my clothes permanently fuel-scented. The work was hard, but it was work I understood. There was a routine comfort I felt under the hood of a car, manipulating things that made sense to me.

But I had stalled my progress thanks to my drinking. Doing the bare minimum, nowhere near opening my own shop. Coasting by on their dime.

One day, my card was declined. At the liquor store, no less. I was furious. Shaking. I called my parents, demanding to know what the hell was going on, sure it was their belated disapproval of my career plans, since I hadn't been making the progress I had promised.

When my mother explained she had been made aware that I had a problem, I denied it. I myself hadn't admitted anything wrong with my relationship with alcohol. So I liked to let off some steam now and then, so what? Sure, I had a couple slip-ups. A brawl or two, a crashed car when I had taken the keys from my friend, driving him and some of the guys home one night after a little post-work happy hour. I was the most sober one, I had been doing them a favor, or so I thought. No DUI charges, the cops had been more interested in the old Porsche we were in, loving the story of how we had miraculously soared through the air, off the road, landing in a corn field. No harm done to any of us, just sad the harm done to the beauty of a car.

But that was it. My parents gave me two weeks to move out of my apartment and find a new place to live. They were finished holding my hand as I wrecked my way through life. I was left crashing on a friend's couch and working grueling hours to try and save up for my own place.

I failed. There was a morning when I woke up on the street, freezing and ill, no recollection of the night before. It scared me. I reluctantly went with my mom and checked myself into rehab. Figured I'd dry out for a bit, and everything would be fine. I had just gone too far and needed to hit reset.

I blink away the thoughts of that time, having had my fill of revisiting for the night. I look over to Desiree, gently spin her around, lifting the hair off her back as I pull on the strings at the nape of her neck. The steam from the shower billows around us, fogging up the mirror.

"What are you doing?" she asks.

"Stripping this shirt off like I've been wanting to do all night." No sense in denying it.

"But I'll be naked!"

I meet her gaze in the bit of mirror that's still clear and smile.

"So? I've seen you naked before." I keep my hand frozen, praying she'll give me the okay.

I love the flush that creeps up her cheeks. She smiles and closes her eyes. "Fine. But only because I'm dizzy and that shower looks like a dream."

Victory. I pull the strings and try my hardest not to stroke her breasts as I lift the fabric over her head. "I'll be a perfect gentleman, I promise."

"That would be a first."

I slide her shorts and panties down her legs, careful not to disturb the small burn mark on her calf. I work a little more slowly than necessary, determined to enjoy each and every inch of her skin while I can. She's more curvy than I remember, the luscious hips and rolls of womanhood causing my dick to stir, and I'm clenching my jaw so tightly to keep it at bay, I fear I might grind away my teeth.

She steps out of her shorts, and I bundle her clothes into a ball, throwing them into the sink. I fight the urge to kiss her exposed skin as I guide her into the shower.

I tug off my own shirt and throw it to the side, grinning as her eyes go wide as she scans my bare torso. "As good as you remember?" I ask her.

"Better," she breathes out.

She steps into the water while I remain standing outside the glass door. "Are you joining me?" she asks.

"A moment ago you didn't want to be naked in front of me."

"That was before you took off your shirt," she says, arching an eyebrow.

I smile. "No, I'm not joining you. I'm going to help you get cleaned up, but I'm staying put right here."

"No fun," she says, but then I see her steady herself as she leans a shoulder against the shower wall. Her eyebrows furrow slightly and she closes her eyes, and I curse under my breath. "Nauseated or dizzy?" I ask.

"Both," she admits.

I try not to roam my eyes over her body. The last thing she needs is my raging hard-on right now, the lure of hot water rolling over her breasts almost too much to handle. More important issues at hand. I need to make sure she doesn't pass out while in here. "Dazzle?"

"Yes?" she says, voice quiet and eyes still closed as the steam wraps around her.

She looks so vulnerable, standing there like that, water pouring over her shoulder as she fights off whatever she's feeling. There's a tug in my chest to join her and envelope her in my arms, pull her tight against me and make all her discomfort go away.

Instead I tell her, "I'm going to take off my jeans and step in with you to help you out, is that okay?"

I can do that much. I can be refrained.

She nods, to my relief, dropping her head against the tiles of the shower wall. I do as promised, leaving on my boxer briefs as I step into the shower. I gently spin her around, her back to me. Let the water run through her hair and down her body. "You okay?"

She hums in response, and I get to work. I lift the second shower head from its cradle and run it over her body, fighting the fantasy of torturing her by pressing it between her legs. Another time, maybe.

"Here, hold this," I say, handing her the nozzle while I reach for the shampoo. I squeeze out a small dome of it and lather it into her hair, massaging her scalp, my hands working in gentle circles. I take my time with it, scooping her thick blonde locks in my hands and enjoying the chance to do something for her that's so routine, so part of a daily ritual for her that I've been robbed of for the past several years. It's as if in doing this thing for her, I get to be an intimate part of her life, too. At least in this moment.

I cradle her head and enjoy her quiet hums of appreciation as she leans her head back on my chest. She's nearly limp in my arms. I fight the urge to let my hands wander down her torso, over her breasts. Not now.

After a moment she steps forward. Turns her head around and looks down at my underwear, the fabric now heavy and soaking wet. "You're not naked," she says.

"Trying to be a gentleman, remember?"

"But I'm naked, it's hardly fair."

"And I'm hardly looking." I reach my hand to her face and smooth away a soapy stream from her forehead before it creeps into her eyes.

She lifts the corner of her mouth. "Take them off, Taven. That can't be comfortable." She closes her eyes as I lean her head back into the stream of water to rinse out the shampoo. Then laugh as I feel the nozzle in her hand pressing against stomach, a harsh spray of hot water stinging my skin. "Off. Now."

I focus on lifting the weight of her hair to wash out the remnants of shampoo. "They will be staying on," I say.

"But why?"

"Because right now, it's taking every ounce of strength to not devour this beautiful body of yours. And this last article of clothing is the only thing keeping me from pushing you against this wall, wrapping your legs around me and ravishing you," I answer honestly.

"That doesn't sound so bad," she whispers. I can barely hear it over the sound of the water, but that's what she said, alright.

"Well, Dazzle, too bad for you that I'm a changed man."

"Changed how?"

I take the nozzle from her hands and replace it back on the cradle. Turn back to face her. "Changed in that I'm far more patient these days. And I'm not going to make love to you when you're nauseated and dizzy because you've been *struck by light-ning*, remember that?" I say, my tone teasing.

"But to be clear, that is on the agenda?" Her eyes remain closed but she smiles, and I take the opportunity to scan her face. The small ridge in her nose, the pink and full lips. So beautiful.

I reach for the loofah beside me. "When you're feeling better. If you want." I take some soap into the loofah to lather up, hoping the slight floral scent doesn't rev up her nausea. I study her face and am satisfied by the small smile she holds, so I get busy. Groan quietly in appreciation as I leave trails of white suds over her body—her arms, her stomach, the peaks of her nipples, taunting me. Her breath hitches as I slowly make my way over the soft flesh of her breasts, which are fuller than I last remember.

She lets out a moan. "Lord, I had no idea how fun it would be to be washed like this," she says. "It feels so good."

I don't share out loud what I'm thinking. I wonder if anyone has ever washed her, shared a shower like this with her before. I take her declaration as confirmation that this is a first for her. I like that.

"It feels so good to take care of you, Dazzle." *So good.*

She presses her lips to my shoulder. Tender, like I'm a gift to be revered. "I like being taken care of." She looks up at me, blue eyes steady and full of meaning. "By you."

twenty-seven

. . .

Question

Present day

taven

Saturday, 1:56am

I SLIP THE towel around Desiree's torso, then grab another to wrap around her hair. She steadies it on her head and heads into the bedroom, rifling through her bag and pulling out her toothbrush and toothpaste. I watch as she returns to the bathroom, opens the cabinet below the sink, rummaging through and finding my mouthwash. "I forgot mine," she explains, and I tell her what's mine is yours.

"Are you finally going to step out of those?" she asks, her shoulders wet and gleaming as she looks at me through the mirror and glances down at my briefs.

I peel them off and grab a towel, covering myself while she brushes her teeth, then swishes with mouthwash. I dry off as quickly as I can, enjoying watching her here in my house, doing her routine.

When she's finished, she turns back to face me and readjusts the towel on her head. "Are we going to talk about all the tattoos?" Her eyes scan over the ink on my arms and torso.

I laugh. "If you want to. Sure," I reply as I tighten the towel around my waist.

"You really are a mechanic now, I guess."

"Part of the uniform. None that you have, I noticed." I grab a robe from the linen closet just outside the bedroom door, return to her and drape it over her shoulders.

She drops the towel from around her chest and dries herself off, holding my gaze the whole time. "I've considered one. Something for my mom," she says.

"What would you get?"

"I'm not sure. Everything feels so cliché." She hangs up the towel and slips her arms through the robe, pulling the belt around her waist.

"If you haven't noticed, I have a 'one day at a time' one. Nothing more cliché than that."

She steps forward to me and finds the cursive lettering running along my chest. "You earned it, though," she says as she plants a kiss.

We walk into the bedroom, and I pull back the covers. Prompt her to slip in. "Do you need anything? Some toast, maybe?"

"That might be nice, actually. Yeah." She crawls on the mattress and tucks in her legs beneath the comforter and I smile at how confident she seems in her skin. In herself. Making herself at home like it's nothing. It's good to see.

I take in the sight of her, here in my bed, looking like an angel propped up against my pillows, the towel still on her head and robe peeking out from the top of the blanket. I step toward her and slowly unravel the towel. Lay it out flat on the pillow.

I plant a kiss to her forehead and rummage through my drawers to pull on some shorts before heading down into the kitchen. I pop some bread in the toaster, and pull out my phone as I wait for it to finish.

Nothing from Evelyn. It's been two days since I last heard from her. She's away in London on a business trip, and we said we'd take some space, but I have a feeling she's hoping I'll take the initiative and reach out to her.

Funny that I haven't.

Is what I'm doing right now considered cheating? Probably. Kissing and bathing a woman while you do still technically have a fiancée isn't exactly the picture of fidelity. I realize that before I go any further with my precious forty-eight hours with Desiree, I need to do the thing. End it with Evelyn. I shake my head, thinking about the fact that any time Desiree and I had ever been intimate with each other, it always seemed to be under the worst circumstances. Time to change that.

My mind floats back to the past couple months with Evelyn. I had been slowly pulling away, I know I had. As more wedding plans were starting to solidify, her asking me about this venue or that, a date to choose, small or large guest list, etc., I became more and more hesitant. More regretful at having proposed to her in the first place.

I had been living under the assumption that the damage I caused with Desiree was irreversible, and she would be forever out of my life. I tried to hold respect for her choice to walk away. I had considered reaching out to her as part of my making amends, sure. But I never did, feeling like it was an interaction that deserved to be more than an item on my checklist.

I was sober when I asked Evelyn to marry me. But the truth is I had been high off of the freedom I felt, and I knew Evelyn wanted a commitment from me. It felt like something I owed her. We could make this work, I could be her person, and she could be mine.

But you can't force what's not right, no matter how much you tell yourself it will all work out fine.

The toaster pops up and I plate the bread, smearing butter over top. Such a simple task, making a late-night snack for a woman who is in my bed, not feeling well. Yet I can't deny the pull at my chest in doing so. I feel happy. Content. It's an odd feeling for me, and I recognize that there's not been a single moment when I've made food for Evelyn that I felt quite the same thing. It's hard to explain. I think I've been fighting a restlessness that comes from the idea of years of domestic life that lay past my wedding.

I don't feel that when I replace the image with Desiree.

I walk upstairs to the bedroom, water and plate in hand, and walk in to find Desiree's eyes closed. Her chest is subtly rising and falling. I place the plate and water on the nightstand beside her, pulling the blanket up and tucking her in. She lets out a hum and turns on her side, facing the inside of the bed with her back to me. I run my knuckle down her cheek. "Sleep, Dazzle," I whisper before stepping out of the room.

It's two o'clock in the morning. Seven am in London. Evelyn will be awake and getting ready to pack up, expecting me to pick her up from the airport this afternoon and give her a ride home to her place. I could do it now, I could call her and finish it without ever having to face her.

Except that's what a coward would do. Instead, I reach for my phone and send her a text, wishing her a safe flight.

My phone lights up with her response.

E: Thanks.

E: I've missed you.

twenty-eight

. . .

Risk

Ten years ago

desiree

twenty years old

THE BAR WAS loud and crowded, but I was a few fruity drinks in and feeling fabulously warm. A handful of us were there, celebrating Taven's decision to drop out of school, and I was chatting my way through the philosophies of some cultural phenomenon or another with my roommate, Katja. She had bright blue hair and giant grayish eyes, and I remember giggling, thinking she looked like one of the Bratz dolls that the girls I nannied for would play with. She asked what was so funny and I shared my observation. She nodded her head and thanked me for the compliment.

"Despacito" was blaring in the background, and Katja pulled me by the hand up to the dance floor. "Come on, I love this song!"

Normally I didn't dance because I didn't love the feeling of being on display. That, and I never knew what to do with my arms, but that night, I had decided to let loose. I followed along after her, tugging my dress down my thighs and regretting the decision to wear heels. We swayed along, my eyes randomly finding their way to the bar to where Taven was talking to some brunette. He had just broken up with his girlfriend a few weeks before, and while my friend-zone status with him was tolerable when he was with someone, I couldn't help but feel my crush level up whenever he was single. A quiet ache in my heart that continued thumping away. Me pleading with the universe to let this be our time.

His eyes caught mine and he winked. I smiled back, satisfied that he wasn't too busy talking to that girl that he'd forgotten about me.

I spun myself around, throwing my arms up in the air and shimmying my hips with liquid courage. Katja backed her ass up to mine and I laughed as she slid up and down my body like I was her own personal stripper pole.

It reminded me of something Melissa would do, which made me sad. I hadn't spoken to her in months at that point, my last text asking if I'd done something to make her mad going unanswered. My mind wandered to where she was now, if she was out dancing with some new replacement best friend, or if she was snuggled up with a guy, falling madly in love and having no more room in her life for me.

So when some random guy grabbed my waist and pulled me close to him to dance, I went along with it. He was cute, with longish hair and a snake tattoo up his forearm. I recognized him from somewhere I couldn't place. We were off campus at one of the tried-and-true places where my fake ID would work, since I was the only one in our group not yet twenty-one. Maybe I'd seen him here before, who knows.

I swayed along with snake guy, secretly hoping Taven was

watching and feeling some stirs of envy. I willed myself not to look his way, to pay him no attention whatsoever. I was mostly successful.

When snake guy crashed his lips onto mine, his tongue darting into my mouth and bringing along with it hints of a lager, I wrapped my arms around his neck and dove in. *Please let Taven be watching.* The guy grabbed my ass, then pulled back, breathing into my neck, "You're so sexy. So fucking sexy."

I was desired. It felt good.

WHAT DIDN'T FEEL GOOD WAS later. After several more songs and one too many drinks, I decided I needed some air. Snake guy offered to come with me, and we stumbled out to the dark sidewalk, hand in hand and sticky with sweat and spilled drinks after sloshing around on the dance floor. The air was chilly, and I pulled my arms around myself in a hug to fight off the cold.

"Here, come on," snake guy said, pulling me around the corner to the small alleyway beside the bar. "Let's get you out of the wind."

"Okay," I said, tagging mindlessly along behind him.

He wasted no time in kissing me. He pushed me against the brick wall of the building, tongue roaming and hips pressing against mine. His hands were everywhere, and I remember feeling like I was his own personal please-touch museum. Not that I minded the exploration, I just wished they were someone else's hands.

When he lifted my dress up past my thighs and over my ass, I laughed as I pushed him back. "Just what do you think you're doing?" I asked, tugging my dress back down. I was trying to keep my tone light, but it dawned on me that following this guy down a dark alleyway was not my brightest idea. Damn drinks.

Messing with my head. I was drunk, more so than I realized, and I stumbled on my heels.

"Easy now," he said through a grin, cradling my arm to steady me.

"Maybe we should get back inside."

The look he was giving me was all predator, and I went to step past him. He placed an arm on the wall behind me, blocking me. "Come on, baby," he said, pressing his lips to mine once again.

I let him kiss me, the sound of his grunts and groans now filling me with disgust and dread. What was I thinking, wandering out here with him like this? All to make Taven jealous, I realized with self-contempt. How pathetic I had been. And now I'm stuck trying to play along with this guy who is quickly becoming far more aggressive than I would have given him credit for. I felt embarrassed at the situation I had put myself in.

I tried not to freak out, figuring I'd let the guy get his kicks in before trying once more to get out of his grasp. Everything would be fine, there was nothing to worry about. He's just drunk and a little pushy, that's all.

When I finally couldn't take anymore, I turned my head from him and tried to pull away a second time. I started to slip past him, only this time he was more forceful when he stopped me, his hand wrapping around and squeezing my arm to pull me back.

I let out a nervous chuckle. "My, eager tonight, aren't we?"

I didn't even know the guy's name. Didn't know a damn thing about what kind of person he was or if he was going to let me off easy. For all I knew, he could have been a serial killer.

He raised his forearm and pressed me firm against the wall, and I stood there in horror as I listened to the sounds of him trying to work to undo his jeans.

"What are you doing?" I asked, trying to hide the alarm in my voice.

He chuckled. The sound was revolting. "Don't play shy, you're fucking hot as hell, Desiree." He kept holding me firm as he worked to undo his belt buckle, fumbling and cursing. All I could think through my haze of drinks was how did he know my name.

"Appreciate that, but please get off me," I said, pushing against him with zero success.

"No one can see, it's fine."

As if that was what I was worried about. Was he serious? "Let me be clear, I'm not interested in doing whatever it is you think you're doing."

He ignored me. Like I had said nothing at all.

I tried again. "Stop it, get off me," I repeated. My voice sounded weak, so I tried again more loudly. "Get off me, *now*."

He paused his movements, eased off me momentarily and I had the slightest glimmer of relief. I had been overreacting, see? He stopped.

What I didn't expect was the slam against the wall that he gave me next.

The force was so startling, I thought I might be dreaming. That had to be it, I was dreaming. Caught in some nightmare. My head hit the brick, and a burst of pain seared through me. "Hold still," he said, his voice like a distant echo in my head. *Hold still, hold still,* as if I hadn't just told him to get off me. There was not an ounce of the previous warmth held in his tone, and even through his force, I still felt confused, like I was misreading the situation.

This is not happening. This can't really be happening, was all I could think.

Please God, I'll do anything. Please let this not be happening.

I should scream, I thought, but it's as if my voice was caught in my chest. There was something scary about screaming in that moment. I tried anyways, shouting, "Help me," but it wasn't loud enough. I felt too shy to be loud, almost embarrassed. Like if I really truly screamed out with all my might for someone to help me, and someone came, they'd all laugh at the ridiculousness of me actually thinking the guy was trying to rape me, right here on the side of a building.

He laughed and covered my mouth, and I tried to breathe out through my nose, but it was hard. I squirmed to free his hand from my face so I could catch my breath, but that only made him push against me harder. "You playing hard to get?" he said, along with some other absurd words, but I tried to tune them out.

I could barely move with him pinning me to the wall like that, so I held myself still, scared to move and have him slam me again and knock me unconscious. He pulled my dress up once more and pushed his fingers past my underwear. I tried to squeeze my legs closed as hard as possible, and he kicked at my knee, using the opportunity to dig his fingers inside me while I squeezed my eyes shut. I thought I might pass out as his disgusting mouth pressed to my neck while he invaded my body.

I struggled with heavy breaths through my nostrils, my mind swirling through a thousand ways I could possibly get out of this. Do I act like I'm okay with this in hopes that I could get him to let his guard down? Then kick my knee into his crotch and run away? My limbs suddenly felt like lead, and I had the distinct feeling that that was a nice bit of hope, that I'd be strong enough to overtake this guy. I had a distinct feeling that his mission was much stronger. I should have shouted louder for help. Good God, why hadn't I shouted louder when I had the chance? I didn't know. I didn't know he would take it this far. Why hadn't I known?

I had tears spilling down and I tried to breathe in as much air as possible anytime his grasp on my face slightly slipped. He continued pushing his hand into me, and I prayed that would be all he'd do. Maybe that would be enough for him.

Maybe I somehow deserved this. After all, I was the one who initiated coming out here, right?

I tried to slink out of my body. *Please, Taven. Come outside and look for me. Please.*

Maybe if this guy tried to undo his jeans again, that could be my chance. I could just hold still until then, save up my strength for my moment.

Unless he slammed me to the ground, then I'd be done for.

When the sound of Taven's voice came calling around the corner, I half denied myself the prayer of hope. That Taven was actually out here, calling my name. I popped open my eyes, but I couldn't see anything, just the sharp angles and shapes of this guy pressing against me. I closed my eyes again, trying to eke out any sound I could from my voice.

And then I felt the most wonderful feeling of absence of pressure, and a gust of air on the front of my body. I stumbled to the side and desperately inhaled all the air I could, scared to open my eyes and still see the guy in front of me.

I heard Taven's voice. Saying he was going to kill him. I heard the scuffle, the sound of thumps of fists hitting flesh.

Taven saying he was going to kill this disgusting piece of shit.

I scrambled to pull my dress back down and opened my eyes to see Taven on top of the guy on the ground in front of me, fists flying as the predator covered his face with his forearms in cowardly retreat. Taven was a blur of movement, punching, then raising the guy by his shirt before slamming him into the ground. He rose up to a stand and kicked the guy in the abdomen, the head, taunting him and shouting, "Aren't you going to fight back, you fucking little shit," and at that point I realized he wasn't going to stop any time soon.

I reached for his shoulders. "Taven, come on. You're going to kill him, we have to go."

"I *am* going to kill him," he said, expression like something I'd never seen before. Something wild and uncontrollable.

"Please, Taven. Stop, we have to go," I pleaded. I scanned around, looking for anyone around to help as I realized there was going to be no good end to this.

I rushed around the corner and into the bar, scanning heads until I found Felix, one of the guys in our group. I pulled him by the arm and rushed him back outside, hearing his startled "What the fuck?" as I shoved him over to Taven.

I prayed to God that Felix could stop Taven before he killed the guy.

twenty-nine

· · ·

Resurgence

Ten years ago

desiree

twenty years old

WHEN WE MADE our way into the quiet darkness of Taven's apartment, I closed the door behind us. We had taken a cab home, both of us silent and stunned as we absorbed what had just happened. Me working to blink away the tears threatening to consume me, and the images of the guy pressing against me, then the sight of him bleeding and lifeless on the ground, Taven's chest huffing out in strained breaths as he finally allowed Felix to pull him away.

I shuffled him into his small galley kitchen and switched on the light, wincing as my eyes adjusted. I guided Taven over to the sink. I had nearly sobered by then, but Taven only seemed to be getting more drunk by the minute.

"Did I kill him?" he asked, his voice a strange slur of what almost sounded like giddy boyishness. Like he wasn't referring to the harm inflicted on someone, but rather a kid asking if he gets to keep the new puppy. "Is this puppy all mine?" was more the fitting words to match his tone.

It freaked me out. I held his hands in the sink and turned on the water, mind spinning over what just happened as I watched the water mix with blood, Taven's and the snake guy's.

He repeated his question, placing his hand over mine to stop my work in cleaning him up. "Dazzle, did I kill him?" His eyes were glassy and the smile creeping over him sent a chill down my spine. It was almost like he wasn't even there. Like the rational human form of him had left his body.

"You didn't kill him. Felix stopped you."

"Damn it," he said. "But I was supposed to kill him."

"No, you weren't."

"I was defending your *honor*." Honor was said like an invention he had created. Honor! Eureka!

"Which was wonderful of you," I soothed. "You have no idea. But I don't need you in jail."

"Psshh. I wouldn't go to jail. It was self-defense. Dazzle defense. I Dazzle-fended you."

"Yes, you most certainly did."

"I should have killed him. I will be having a word with Felix," he said, slurring and swaying.

I gently washed his battered hands, then grabbed paper towels to dry them. I knew I should probably ice them, but I was too exhausted. Instead, I guided him to his room and onto his bed, stripping him of his bloody clothes down to his boxers. He was muttering something, some dirty joke as I did so, but I stopped listening to him at that point. I tucked him in, then went back to the kitchen to grab water and Advil. I popped two for myself and swallowed them down, then poured out three more to take to Taven.

I made my way back to his room and handed him the pills. "Here. Take these."

He hesitated for a moment, I worried he was going to fight me on it, but then he finally sat up. He reached for the pills and threw them back. I handed him the water and he guzzled it down, letting some dribble out the side of his mouth as he pulled the cup away prematurely. "Water's good," he crooned.

I left him to go use the bathroom. I sat on the toilet, willing myself to focus on my surroundings, the navy blue shower curtain, the beige towels on the rack in front of me. I was back in Taven's apartment now. I was safe. I looked at the small cup next to the sink. Taven's toothbrush, his razor, anything I could focus on to push away the feeling of hands and hot breath all over me. I wanted to erase the memory of some guy forcing his fingers inside me.

Was that considered rape? I didn't even know, but I knew I felt disgusting. He certainly got his punishment, that was for sure. I thought about the way we left him battered and beaten in the alleyway like that, and I prayed there wouldn't be repercussions.

I slipped off my dress, not even caring that I was down to my bra and underwear. It didn't matter. I walked back into Taven's bedroom and opened up his dresser drawers, finding one of his shirts and slipping it over my head, trying to ignore Taven's whistles and mumbles of appreciation as he watched me. How my body was gorgeous and to be cherished. "You cherish that body," he slurred. "You protect that body. You don't be mean to it."

He said how happy he was he protected me. How he'll always be there for me. I silently thought how relieved I felt in knowing that was true.

He kept carrying on about what a beauty I always was, how he still remembers the first time he saw me in a bikini. Did I remember that time? he asked me. On his parents' boat, when we were kids? I said I remembered. I let my mind wander back to those summer days on the water. Or by the pool at the club. The warmth of the sun, the carefree laughter of us as kids.

He said he remembered it all like it was yesterday. How I had this one bikini that he loved. How it was white. How he masturbated to the image of me later on that day. In my teeny white bikini.

I smiled.

It felt good to smile. To think of something sweet. It felt good to know I could still smile. I could still remember pleasant things. That hadn't changed or been taken from me.

I allowed myself to fully smile. I didn't need to be scared anymore. I was okay. Maybe everything would be okay.

I slipped into bed beside Taven and curled my back up against his chest as he draped his arm over me. The heaviness of it felt wonderful.

Usually in the past, if we had shared a cab back to his place, I'd pass out in his bed and he'd take the couch, insisting I be comfortable.

But not tonight.

Tonight I just wanted the safety of feeling Taven's arms around me. Drunk and all, his arms around me were the exact comfort I needed.

I don't know when I began crying, exactly. Three minutes, ten minutes after crawling into his bed, I'm not sure. He cradled me in his arms, asking me if I was hurt, and I told him no. "Just scared," I said, my body trembling as he pulled me tighter.

"I've got you, Dazzle. It's okay. I've got you." I listened to his soothing voice and let my tears fall while he kissed my head over and over again. "I've got you."

I didn't want to tell him what exactly the guy had done to me. With my dress hiked up around my waist, and the guy's buckle undone and hanging loose from his belt loops, I'm sure Taven could fill in the blanks. I didn't want to think about what would have happened if Taven hadn't shown up. I realized how close I might have been to having my precious virginity robbed from me, just like that. Outside some bar.

As a feeling of gratitude washed over me, I turned around and searched for Taven's lips. His mouth felt familiar yet new to me, different from the heated and stolen kisses we'd share when he was still with Christine. These kisses were tender, a quiet exchange of our feelings. Feelings for one another, feelings of fear that were creeping in, now that the adrenaline highs were wearing off. I ran my hands through his hair, and hummed at the warmth of his hand finding its way under my t-shirt and onto my skin. The whisper in my ear of him saying, "I love you so much, Dazzle," made my heart beat faster.

I decided that I needed to be naked with him. I slipped off the shirt I was wearing, unclasped my bra, and shimmied off my panties while I pressed myself against the warmth of his chest. I assisted him as he worked his way free of his briefs. My Taven. Naked side by side with me under the safety of warm cotton blankets. I draped my leg over his hips and felt his body against mine, and I inhaled the scent of his cologne, spicy and intoxicating.

I felt his hands on my torso as he gently rolled me onto my back and hovered over me. So gorgeous, this naked man above me.

"Tell me if you want me to stop," he said, his voice gravelly and serious.

"I don't want you to stop," I said.

I spread my legs beneath him, heart pounding wildly at the realization of being so incredibly raw and naked with one another. I twisted my legs around his hips and arched myself up toward his body. His breath was heavy, and I wondered what he was thinking. What I was thinking. I don't know if I was acting out of love, lust, the need to wash away the memories of what had happened earlier that night, or all three. But nothing felt more important than being here with him like this. Under his covers, just the two of us, skin to skin with no barriers between us.

He was kissing my face, my jaw, and I ran my hands up his arms, relishing in the ripple of muscles as he balanced himself on top of me.

"I've wanted to do this for so long, Desiree," he breathed out.

"So have I," I whispered.

"I'm so in love with you," he said, and I hummed as I felt the light stubble of his jaw when he kissed my neck, sending an ache between my legs and deep in my abdomen. "I worship you."

But he didn't enter me. I wanted him inside of me, and I kissed his shoulders with feverish desperation, wanting to experience all of him that I could.

"Please, Taven," I begged. "Make love to me, please." I arched my hips up to him with need.

He held his body still, firm and solid above me as his mouth slowly made its way down my neck, to my chest. I nearly cried out at the feel of his tongue circling my nipple in delicious torture. I looked down, wanting to see the beautiful sight of my Taven, devouring me. It felt erotic as I watched the prick of my nipple disappear into the heat of his mouth, then back out again, over and over as I lifted my hips thinking I might scream with frustration. I steadied my lower half and glided myself over his length, dizzy with the incredible feel of it. We rocked together like that, nearly making love, but not really.

"Fuck," he gasped. "Fuck, I want you so badly."

"Take me, then."

I felt his hands lace through my hair and squeeze, and I looked up to see his eyes pinched closed in restraint. "We can do this, it's alright," I assured him.

"Are you sure, baby?"

"Yes. I'm sure."

"I don't have a condom."

"I don't care," I said, nearly crying out with frustration. I reached between us to grab him when I thought I couldn't take it anymore. I gripped tightly, he felt so good in my hands, firm yet smooth. This is what I wanted. I would steal this moment with him.

I guided him to my entrance, loving how right it felt with him pressed up against me. He groaned at the contact, and I arched my back to urge him forward.

"Fuck," he said, and the next thing I knew, he was pushing himself inside of me. Pressed fully against me, pelvis meeting pelvis. It happened in one forceful shove that left me stunned at the suddenness of it, feeling like I was splitting in half. "Desiree, holy fuck," he groaned out.

Taven was inside of me. Completely in, I thought as I fought the cry I wanted to let out from the pain. "Ow," I said, I couldn't help it, followed by a quick "I'm okay" when he lifted himself up to look at me.

"Am I hurting you?" He pulled out slightly and looked at me with such tenderness, I thought I might burst with the love I felt for him in that moment.

"No, I'm fine," I lied. I wrapped my arms around his neck and kissed him, focused on the feel of his chest pressing against me as I squeezed my eyes shut. He pushed back in and the burn ripped through me, but I continued kissing him as he slowly began to move. Gentle at first, then faster and more furious and groaning.

"Taven," I whispered between kisses and panting breaths. "Yes, Taven."

"You're so beautiful, Dazzle. Fucking Christ, you feel so good," he said, his voice strained. "I can't believe this is happening."

I listened to the sound of his voice and tried to relax. Yes, this was happening. Me and Taven. Finally. This was good. It hurt like hell, but it was good.

I knew the first time would be painful, obviously, but I hadn't expected quite so much.

And as he rocked on top of me, I had the realization that if we had tried this at sixteen, I don't think I would have gone through with it. I hadn't seen many men's penises, but I knew Taven's was big. And there was no way at sixteen I would have been able to do it. I think I would have been too scared at the first sign of pain, and I would have stopped him.

I thought about all the times a young girl must have been in that position. Made a decision to lose her virginity, only to then want to back out. How many times had a guy forced himself to go through with it anyway, caught in the moment and unwilling to stop at her protests, pushing further and further in until she simply stayed still, praying for it to be over? Realizing this was a bigger moment than she thought it was, to do this act, and filled with regret over the decision to put her trust and care into this guy's hands?

These were not the thoughts I wanted to be thinking as Taven worked himself into my body. I reminded myself that I was ready for this, that this was a man I loved, a man I had known since we were kids. A man who nearly killed someone tonight, all to rescue me from harm's way. Yes, this was a man who deserved this gift I was giving him. I was ready for this. I had waited long enough.

So I bravely squeezed my legs tighter around him, and began rocking my hips, ignoring the stings of each thrust. I met his movements and tried to find my rhythm, my nails digging into the flesh of his back as I contended with the feeling, choosing to focus on how deliciously full I felt with Taven inside of me. How right this was. How glad I was that it was him. We were doing this, we were finally having sex.

And then he came inside me, shuddering and vulnerable and beautiful as he hovered over me.

It was done.

THE NEXT MORNING, I CAREFULLY rolled out of Taven's grasp and crawled my naked way out of bed. I found the discarded t-shirt on the floor, slipped it on and went to use the bathroom. It burned, but not too badly. The burn was a strange and comforting reminder that it happened. I finally gave myself to Taven.

I was no longer a virgin.

It felt significant and I wondered if I looked different, if I had some kind of womanly glow to me now. I smiled to myself, thinking about the gravity of what we had shared together.

Then I groaned as my bubble was burst with memories of the hours before that. The shit show that would forever be the story to proceed the night I lost my virginity. Is it possible to be deliciously happy, yet scarred and broken at the same time? Because that's how I felt.

I went to the kitchen to brew some coffee. As I waited for it to finish, Taven walked in carrying a bundle of bed sheets, kissing me on the cheek as he made his way past me and to the stacked washer and dryer in the corner across from the fridge.

"Good morning, gorgeous," he said as he shoved in the linens and threw in a detergent tablet.

"Laundry this early in the morning?" I asked.

He slammed the glass door closed and turned to me, looking sheepish. "I, ughh, I think you may have started you period." He grabbed the back of his neck, and I saw a flush creep up his skin.

I tried not to be distracted as I stared at his bare torso and the sweatpants hanging low on his hips. "Oh. No, um. That's not it."

Had I really never told Taven that I was still a virgin? Didn't he assume I would tell him if I slept with anyone?

He dropped his hand from his neck and stepped toward me, cupping my face in his hands. "It's really okay. I have a sister, remember? Nothing to be embarrassed about," he said before pressing a quick kiss to my lips. He backed away and opened a cabinet, pulling out two mugs as the coffee machine beeped. "Thanks for making coffee, by the way. And for the pills, I think you saved me. Now I'm only at about a level five headache instead of three thousand."

I watched as he poured us each creamer, then the coffee, handing me mine with a clink of cheers. I sipped and let the creamy vanilla and roast flavors soothe me as I tried to figure out how to say what I needed to say. How to tell him what I had assumed he already knew.

I decided to just say it. "Taven, I was a virgin," I blurted out when I could no longer take it. I studied him, waiting for his reaction. His eyes blinked back at me over the rim of his cup. Glued to mine, unable to look away.

"I was a virgin, that's why there was blood," I repeated, more quietly this time.

Still, he only stared at me. "Vin? Did you hear me?"

I jolted when he slammed his coffee cup down on the laminate counter, some of it sloshing over the side. "Christ, Daz! Why didn't you tell me?" His voice sounded pained. He ran his hands down his face.

"I'm sorry, I...I guess I thought you knew that. I never told you about sleeping with anyone."

He dropped his hands and threw them out to his sides. "I figured you were just private about that kind of thing!"

"Are you mad?"

He turned his head to look at me and I tried to read his expression. "Am I mad?"

"Yes, are you mad?"

"A little, yeah."

"But why?" I asked, my voice small.

He regretted it.

He was mad because he regretted it.

I did it wrong.

Or he thought this was a one-time thing and now he's mad because he took my virginity, and he feels some obligation to me he hadn't planned.

My mind spun around all the possible thoughts he was having. "You don't owe me anything, if that's what you're worried about. If this was just a one-time thing."

His face softened at that, and he reached over to me, pulling me into his arms. I inhaled the masculine scent of him, trying to calm my nerves. I felt him kiss the top of my head. "Jesus, Dazzle. That's not what I'm worried about. Last night was *not* a one-time thing, I hope you don't want it to be. Please tell me you don't want it to be."

"I don't want it to be."

"Good."

"Then why are you upset?" I asked, my voice muffled in his chest. I could just hide away here in his chest and never have to face the look in his eyes again. Humiliation was threatening me.

But he pulled me backward and grabbed my arms, looking me square in the eyes. "Because, baby. You deserve so much better than my drunk ass stumbling on top of you for your first time. Don't you know that?" I said nothing, not wanting to admit that no, I didn't know that. He gave my arms a shake. "You deserve better than this dingy apartment for the setting. You deserve a night that doesn't start with," he squeezed his eyes closed, "some fucker fucking with you followed by me damn near killing him." He opened his eyes and looked down at me. "Do you know I dreamed about being your first so many times? *So many times*. For years."

"You did?"

"Fuck yes, I did." He hugged me again and I allowed myself to wrap my arms around his waist as he rocked us back and forth in his tiny kitchen, the sound of the washing machine filling the silence. "I want a do-over," he said. "Last night didn't count. I want to do it right."

I laughed. "It definitely counts, I have the soreness to prove it." I pulled back from him. "Speaking of, how are your hands?"

But before he could answer, I jumped out of his arms at the sound of three loud knocks on the front door. We exchanged questioning looks as we crept to the door. Taven looked through the peephole. He asked who was there, but I could hear the hesitation in his tone. A man's stern voice answered. The police.

Taven Carlisle was requested for questioning at the station.

Taven Carlisle was under arrest.

thirty

. . .

Raw

Ten years ago

desiree

twenty years old

I SAT IN the police station waiting area, a ball of bumbling nerves. The last thing Taven had said to me as he was taken away in handcuffs through a door was, "Call my mom." I had no idea when I'd get to see him again. But I wasn't leaving, that was for sure.

Snake guy was in the hospital. He had a concussion, abrasions that required stitching, and they were monitoring him for internal bleeding. He had been found unconscious and rushed by ambulance, though upon awakening, one name stuck out in his head—Taven Carlisle.

I thought we didn't even know the guy, but according to Taven, he'd "partied" with him before and always had a feeling he was a creep.

I was scared to say anything. Do I tell my story? Explain that Taven had been protecting me, that it was self-defense? But I remained silent, afraid that would be viewed as me corroborating the story snake guy was saying, and that I was just trying to come up with a plausible excuse.

I looked around at the waiting area, which was surprisingly bright with large windows overlooking the parking lot. There were standard simple black chairs, like in a doctor's office, and a long desk area with police officers behind glass windows. The whole place looked like it could have been any old government office building, not necessarily a place where people were taken and fingerprinted and who knows what else. I wondered where Taven was now. Was he in a cell by himself, or sharing it with some big, burly dudes that had far more criminal experience than he did?

At least I had the good sense to act quickly after the police showed up at Taven's apartment. I had slipped back into my dress and heels, then topped it with one of Taven's sweatshirts. I must have looked ridiculous. I took Inferno and followed Taven, who was handcuffed in the back of the police car. I wished so much we could be together for this part.

I had pulled into the parking lot and parked his baby in the last row as far from any other cars as possible. I'd never driven Inferno without Taven in the car with me, and even then, it was usually just when he had too much to drink. I was determined to treat it with care, though. As if that one thing that was within my control could be enough.

Walking into the station was terrifying. I had to be buzzed in —what was I even supposed to say? "Hi, my name is Desiree Hatson and I'm here because my friend—maybe boyfriend, it's not really been established yet, though I did sleep with him last night, so let's cross our fingers—anyway, he was taken here in handcuffs, and I thought I'd just swing by and say hi."

Would I even be allowed to see him? I had no clue. Getting

in trouble wasn't exactly my thing, and I was clueless about how any of this worked. Would there be bail? How long would that take? I wished Melissa was with me. I wished I could call my mom and ask for advice, but I feared her reaction once she learned that I was sleeping with the enemy.

So I prepared myself to follow Taven's orders. His cell phone had been confiscated, so I had to call from my own. I had his mom's number, thankfully, though I don't ever recall a time I had actually called it.

With shaking hands I scrolled through my contacts to her name, took a deep breath, and pressed the call icon.

She answered.

I explained that Taven was in jail. That it wasn't his fault, that he was protecting me. My voice was shaky, and I rambled everything out as quickly as I could.

"Desiree," she said, cool as a cucumber. "Are you in the police station right now? Inside?" Lynda's tone surprised me.

"Yes," I confirmed.

"Please do not say another word."

"What?"

I heard her sigh on the other end of the line, the only indication that she was feeling any emotion throughout this exchange. "Walk outside, please. Did you drive there yourself?"

"Yes, in Inferno. In Taven's car, I mean."

"Good. Go outside and sit in his car. I'll stay on the line. But not another word until you do, do you understand? You're in a police station, dear. Everything is being monitored, there are cameras, you must assume that anything you say is being studied."

I nodded, as if she could even see that, and did as I was told.

Once in the safety of the car, I explained what had happened in greater detail. Every piece I could. She asked questions to fill in blanks, and I answered them. It felt infinitesimally easier to speak here, with the quiet and familiar comfort of black leather and the scent of Taven surrounding me.

When she asked if I had reached out to rape crisis, I balked. "No. Why? Was what he did rape?"

If I'm not mistaken, I heard a slight tsk. "Desiree, your body was penetrated without your consent, and with force. Yes. That is considered rape. The laws vary state to state, but there is no mistaking a sexual assault took place. You need to get a rape kit done immediately."

My stomach dropped. A rape kit.

But of course, it was too late for that. I had sex with Taven afterwards. And now I needed to explain that. To his mother, of all people.

Lynda had been furious to learn of what "idiots" we had been in the aftermath of everything. She insisted I get a rape kit anyway, and I initially refused. The last thing I wanted was to be poked and prodded once again, knowing there would be no evidence other than that I had had sex with Taven, without a condom, and his semen was inside of me.

But Lynda insisted that being evaluated by a medical professional would legitimize my claims of self-defense, convincing me to do it despite my fears. I would follow orders and do whatever I could to help get Taven out of trouble. I went alone, smiling and politely making the most useless conversation with the kind nurses trying to distract me from my hell. A victim advocate offered to hold my hand. I let her. She looked to be about my age, with smooth pale skin and a nose ring, and I wondered aloud how she had gotten into this kind of thing. She explained that she was a volunteer. She was planning on heading to law school and the court experience she sometimes got in this role was useful. She wanted to work to prosecute the bad guys one day.

I didn't have the heart to tell her my greatest crush was currently being considered a bad guy.

I explained to the nurses that I had sex after the incident, and that we didn't use a condom. They asked if I was on birth control, and I told them no. They asked if I was concerned about getting pregnant, and I admitted I was. They gave me a Plan B pill, had me swallow it with instructions to try to keep it down for at least two hours. They gave me crackers to help. I wondered absently where I was in my cycle, if I was now killing a potential baby Taven and I may have created. I hated that I would never know, but I knew it was for the best to be safe.

Lynda called around to the best of the best local lawyers, and I impatiently waited to hear back from her while undergoing tests and examinations at the hospital with the sexual assault nurses. My phone would eventually ring, and I'd answer to hear her cursing that all the best lawyers were in court, and that we'd need to wait. Mr. Carlisle was on a flight on his way to us, and he'd be arriving soon. An hour later, Lynda called to say that a lawyer was able to make it to the station, and I, once again, was ordered not to say a thing other than to explain that I had been assaulted.

Taven was finally put in front of a judge that evening and was released. I was back at the station by that point, and Mr. Carlisle was waiting for us on the sidewalk. I was mere minutes away from falling apart, trying to keep it together and fighting my trembling lips the whole way back to my apartment.

Taven walked me to my door, and I stepped through the threshold and abruptly closed the door behind me with promises to call him tomorrow. I couldn't stand the look of sympathy on his face, and the last thing I wanted was to have my breakdown in front of him.

Katja, my roommate, held my trembling body while I

sobbed over the events of the past twenty-four hours, but as instructed by the Carlisles and the lawyer, my lips were to remain sealed throughout the investigation. Rumors spread fast, and we didn't want the wrong narrative out there.

Eventually, I was told to explain what had happened, under the guidance of Taven's lawyer. Explain that the person found bleeding in a back alleyway had been hurting me, and that Taven had acted in response.

But there was no proof. It was his word against mine. I was seen at the bar with him. Kissing him on the dance floor. Leaving the bar with him. Nothing could prove penetration by the guy. Our friend Felix confirmed that he had to pull Taven off of snake guy, but that he didn't know why the men were fighting.

The best evidence we had with the whole thing was the bump on the back of my head from the guy slamming me into the wall, and a few bruises on my chest and arms and knees, all of which had been photographed with me standing in the hospital exam room raw and exposed.

Taven's argument was self-defense, but because he was determined to have used "excessive force," he was still charged. First offense, no weapon involved, so lower charges and a minor penalty of probation and fines. The guy sued, naturally. There was money to be had, and hospital bills to be paid. All in all, the lawyers kept saying that Taven was lucky.

The whole thing saddened me. And while I know he went too far, I also knew Taven's heart was in the right place. How would his life have been impacted if that had been a felony charge? If he had been working toward some goals that would now be obliterated as a result? It disgusted me to think about.

And I hated more than anything that because of one wrong choice on my part, trusting someone I shouldn't have to join me in getting a simple breath of fresh air, I had been sexually assaulted and dragged through the nightmare of having to share my story again and again, continually reliving it under questioning eyes. I became more numb each time. A repeated cycle of sharing details of the night. How short my dress was, what kind of underwear I had on that the guy was able to slip his fingers inside me. That part was the worst.

Fingers inside me.

How many fingers?

I don't know, I didn't count.

But that's how it was.

Trauma isn't just some big experience that happened. It's the repetition of reliving it that's traumatic too. It's the wound on the mind left behind as a result. And when you're sharing your story with ears that are looking for a completely different objective that has nothing to do with helping you heal, that wound gets picked at and examined until the original damage is now ten times worse.

All because I was made to rehearse with the lawyers, talk to the police, everyone—all to ensure that every detail was exact and told with consistency to help Taven's case.

This is when my spiral of depression began. A slow and steady decline that had me becoming a sliver of a version of myself, locked within my original body.

Once everything was settled, I stopped seeing Taven. I just couldn't do it. I ignored his calls and texts until they eventually ceased. Looking at or speaking with him reminded me of that night, of everything we had been through in the aftermath. I was too ashamed to talk to him when I realized I had used sleeping with him as a distraction to attempt to erase the previous events of that night.

Only, it didn't. It only further fueled my shame, and in fact, because I hadn't sought help in the first place, it made things worse.

How is it that when you've been put in the position of a victim, it's your responsibility to ensure your next steps are done perfectly, no errors allowed? That it's your responsibility to make all the "right" choices, when it was someone else that made one major wrong one? It infuriated me that my way of attempting to cope and survive in the aftermath of that night was now viewed with ridicule. It felt vicious and unfair.

My mom barely spoke of the whole thing once she found out. Lynda had urged me to call her—gave her "blessing" that I could tell her, and I shared this weight I had been carrying around, finally breaking down on the phone with my mom about a week after Taven's arrest.

She told me not to tell my father, that this was between us. She assured me that I was strong and it would be okay. She came to visit me, and we laid in bed together that whole first day, just watching movies and eating junk food. Two women just doing the best they can. She told me she had been sexually assaulted before too, and that it gets better, little by little.

Her words comforted me, as surprising and simple as they were. I was starved for any kind of reassurances by that point.

After my mom left, I went into work mode.

And I stayed there. I spent the next couple years focused on my studies like it was the only thing in the world that existed. No more bars or drinks or guys, just work. An obsession with all things school and my part-time jobs.

I graduated with honors a full semester early.

thirty-one

· · ·

Tenacious

Seven years ago

desiree

twenty-three years old

WHEN I BEGAN therapy three years after that horrific night, it was with reluctance. My mom was sick again, the cancer had returned and spread to other parts of her body. A backache one day, then a headache. I was in the grueling early stages of med school, thankfully back in Ohio and close to home, and had been thrown the curve ball of her illness.

It was Dylan who prompted me to start therapy. My big brother, living his dream as a football star, and he said they had counseling services that he himself had found helpful. When the big brother you idolize makes a suggestion like that, you listen.

When I started therapy, I thought I was going to talk about my current situation. Stresses of an ailing parent, the rigorous world of med school, that kind of thing. Clearly, that's what was wrong with me, right? That's why I was depressed. That's why I couldn't remember the last time I had genuinely laughed out loud at something. Obviously, a young woman navigating a rigorous educational path with an ailing mother was the thing causing my depression. The thing causing my inability to taste food or get out of bed on days I didn't have to. My incessant feelings of wondering what exactly *is* life all about, and what are we all doing here? What was the point of it all? The thoughts that tormented me and kept me in a haze.

But it was the events of three years ago that ended up being the topic that resulted in me convulsing on the couch in front of a strange woman that I had never even met before.

Her name was Ruth, which sounded like an old woman's name, but, really, she was probably about mid-thirties. With gentle prodding, she helped me unearth some haunting negative thought patterns that had become the soundtrack of my life.

I am insignificant.

I am incapable.

I am inadequate.

I am not safe.

"When is another time you remember feeling this way?" she asked one day a couple weeks into our sessions. "Try and close your eyes. Focus on your breath for a few moments."

I took one last glance at the beams of light pouring in through her windows. The yellow glow that made the golden seat of her chair create the essence of an angel. I reluctantly closed my eyes, feeling vulnerable, and I focused on the feel of the fabric beneath my hands of my own seat. It was difficult to concentrate at first, but eventually an image popped in my mind, and I shared it.

"I remember being a kid, and my brother Dylan got his first football trophy. I think it was his first one, I'm not sure," I said, opening my eyes to look at Ruth and clarify, lest I be sitting here lying.

She smiled at me. "It's okay, just follow what your mind is telling you. Whether or not it was his first trophy or fifth doesn't matter. What matters is that it sticks out to you."

I nodded and closed my eyes once more. "I remember my parents doing a big dinner celebration for him at a restaurant. We didn't often go out to dinner at that point, it was before they came into real steady success, so it felt exciting.

"But also sad in a way."

I heard her voice, soft as she prompted me further. "What was sad about it?"

"It all was special, but it was for him. I had never done anything to get a trophy. I got good grades, but you don't get trophies for that kind of thing. I remember seeing the reflection of light off of this gold and maroon monstrosity and thinking *I* wanted something like that. Some physical thing to prove to the world that I'm significant too. That there's something special about me."

There was guilt as I made the confession, because Dylan was my big brother and had always been someone to look out for me. He would include me when his friends were over, letting me play video games with them, or "referee" and keep score when they were playing whatever game outside. Having him be the main focus of what should have been a positive memory, which was now feeling very depressing, felt like a betrayal to him. I shared that with Ruth.

"It's alright, Desiree. You can love and appreciate your brother, but also envy some of his achievements."

I considered that. I hated the sound of the word "envy," it seemed too harsh or selfish or something. But I couldn't deny it was accurate.

We went on to process my sexual assault, armed with the new understanding that I lean towards an underlying pull to be significant in some way. I not only felt unsafe that evening, but insignificant as well. Nobody special, nobody worth treating well. Just a body to be used. Nobody whose story is worth fully believing. My mistrust in the victim advocate kindly smiling at me, assuring me she was there to help me, and me feeling insignificant, then too. No real concern for me, just concern in trying to get evidence to help a case.

In the work that followed with Ruth, I reprocessed that entire evening.

It was in a specific session prepared for revisiting the memory, meant to aid in desensitizing me to the painful images that remained burned in my brain, in my night terrors, in the flashbacks that haunted me.

We started slowly, me just holding the image of the experience of being pressed against a wall. I was to view it as if I were watching it on a movie screen, not like I was reliving it.

As I let my mind wander to that image, my body shook, hands and shoulders trembling as I braved the exercise. While I knew what I was experiencing was visible, I still verbalized it to Ruth.

"I feel my body shaking. I feel unsteady."

She prompted me to describe the emotions and the thought patterns associated with them. "I'm helpless. I don't matter," I said, my convulsions becoming stronger. I sat with them and allowed my body to tremble as I faced the visions of that night. I could do this.

I powered through.

I described to her what I saw, how I imagined seeing myself in that back alley, but there were no buildings around, just darkness. Ruth urged me to continue. I was still trembling and felt the threat of tears, but none came at that point. In fact, as uncomfortable as it all was, it also felt good to finally allow myself to face this thing. Little by little, the image became less disturbing. My trembling slowly subsided.

Eventually, the image of me in the alley started changing. I saw my body growing larger, like an unearthly entity, towering above the guy. I was transforming like some goddess in a Greek mythology story. I looked beautiful and strong and powerful. My trembling stopped, though tears were now pouring down my face.

I am significant, I repeated silently to myself.

I imagined him bowing down to me, begging for mercy while I continued to slowly grow in size and rise above, my dress erupting into a golden gown, with layers of fabric that covered him up. Then the lump of his body beneath the fabric disappeared.

I am significant.

I am powerful and in control.

Taven appeared in my vision. He held my hand, growing beside me. Dressed in armor like a Viking ready for war.

I remember being surprised that Taven appeared in this bizarre process. I hadn't talked to him in over two years, by that point. But there he was, holding my hand, strong and powerful and by my side while the world around us morphed from a dark back alley to a city rooftop, and we were looking out at the glowing stars in the night sky above us. They were as clear as if we were in the country, only we were overlooking some city night skyline. I could see the old country club perched there in the city, like that's where it always was. The dots of lights from windows. So many beautiful glittering lights, all around us, perfectly punctuating the darkness.

I am perfectly me.

I am safe.

I am significant.

And then a final thought.

I matter.

thirty-two

. . .

Connections

Five years ago

lynda carlisle

Summertime, 1:21pm

SHE ANSWERS THE phone as she slips into her car, stifling hot with the sun radiating through in the short time she had been at Holly's gravesight. With a sigh, she goes through the general pleasantries, though she and Desiree both know it's merely superficial politeness.

At Desiree's hesitation to reveal the real reason for her call, Lynda prompts her. "Are you and Taven seeing one another again?"

"Yes," is all Desiree says.

"For how long?" The last she knew, Desiree had stopped talking to Taven not too long after his arrest. Now here they were, a few years later, reconnecting.

Lynda hears Desiree's heavy sigh. "It's new. It was new, I

mean. It had only been a couple months, but I've ended things, because I just can't." Her words come out in a strained rush, the girl's voice trembling. "It's a lot to explain, it started after the funeral. My um...my mom died, did you know that?"

Lynda fights back the emotion she feels at hearing those words come from Desiree's mouth. Yes, of course she knew. It's why she's visited Holly's grave three times already, since attending the funeral was impossible. She doesn't share that with Desiree, though. "I did hear that. I'm so sorry, Desiree."

"Thank you. She gave it a good fight." Lynda hears pride in the young woman's tone.

"I imagine she did."

She waits for Desiree to explain the reason for her call. "Listen, there's something else I need to talk to you about. Something about Taven."

"Well, dear. I figured as much. Since I would not exactly say you are one to call me often, this can only mean one thing." At Desiree's continued silence, Lynda reminds herself to have patience. Such a timid girl, that one. Clearly calling with bad news, but unsure how to present it. Lynda decides to throw her a bone. "Let me guess, my son is in jail again."

"Not exactly."

"But he is in trouble, I presume?" Lynda looks at her nails, the perfect manicure she receives promptly every two weeks. The pale pink. Timeless and classic. She wipes a speck of pollen off of her ring finger.

"Not exactly," Desiree repeats. "But...he does need help, I think." Lynda hears some rustling of papers on the other end of the line.

"For God's sake, Desiree. Spit it out, what do you think it's like for a mother to sit and hear that her son needs help, without any quick relief of an indication of how, exactly? Is he or is he not in some kind of legal trouble?"

Lynda's mind rolls back to five years prior, the last time

Desiree Hatson had most unexpectedly called her. *Mrs. Carlisle,* she had said. *I'm sitting at the police station. Taven is being arrested for something. Assault and battery, I think.*

Defending his Desiree. And going too far. How Lynda had reeled at the news. A dumb boy, getting carried away in his aid, showing off for a girl. And not just any girl, but Holly and Frank's daughter, of all people. How had they still been in contact? She figured their youthful flame would have long fizzled out by then. Imagine her surprise to learn that no, it very much had not. In fact, they had been attending the same college together. One Taven would soon say he was dropping out of.

Well, with a misdemeanor under his belt, she could hardly fight him on it, could she? A mark against him that would not fare well for employment. All she could do was hope to God her son had a decent plan to dig himself out of this hole. The relief she found in the fact that he did. Such a boy, still, the way he presented to her and her husband his dream! A garage. Vintage cars. Finding them, refurbishing them, selling them to the highest bidders. Certainly not her first choice, wasn't that the very world of blue-collar grime that she had worked so hard to leave behind?

But her son knew nothing of that.

With reluctance, she realized it would be a good fit for him. Always tinkering, starting from when he was a small boy. She had imagined his skills would move him toward engineering, but there was no denying that school was not his strong suit.

A good trade could still be respectable. Even her husband could see that. And their son was a late bloomer, what more could they do? So they supported his dream, with hopes that his arrest and charges would be a good lesson for him. Stay out of trouble, choose your circle wisely, and focus on yourself. Whatever it takes.

She thinks about all of this as she listens to what Desiree is telling her now.

That she and her son recently got back together, but it didn't last long, because Desiree couldn't do it anymore. But she's worried about him and doesn't know what to do.

Desiree believes her son has a drinking problem.

Bottles buried in the trash bin. On his breath early in the morning. Reckless driving, nearly crashing more than once. A problem much worse than Desiree had realized, and she doesn't know how to help him. She can't help him. She hopes Lynda can. Please assure her she'll help Taven.

All Lynda could think was how hard she had fought to get away from the addictions surrounding her in childhood. Only to brew an addict of her very own.

thirty-three

. . .

Ludicrous

Present Day

taven

Saturday, 11:04 am

WHILE I HAD tossed and turned all night, listening for every sound or soft moan dropped from Desiree's lips in fear she was feeling worse, I woke up feeling surprisingly fresh. I had turned over to her, watching her stir as she slowly woke up, eyelids fluttering as she registered where she was. She turned to me and smiled, murmuring, "Taven Carlisle is in my bed."

I tucked the hair that was falling in her face behind her ear, saying, "Actually, you're in my bed." It was the best damn start to my day I'd had in a long time.

We had moved to the couch after a breakfast of coffee and toast, and now we sat together, listening to rain tap lightly on the roof. Nothing in comparison to the monsoon of last night. The floor-to-ceiling windows of my family room showcase the view of hills and trees beyond, light speckles of raindrops only adding to the beauty. Desiree sips some juice, and I watch her as she admires the view. I can't help but think how gorgeous she looks. How happy I am to have her here with me now. How shocked I was last night to see her, a wet mess in her oversized plastic poncho. And then how scared I was when she dropped to the ground like she did. Today she says she has a mild headache with some continued subtle ringing in her ear, but she overall feels better and assures me she's okay, to my relief.

I ask if she wants to take a walk.

"In the rain?" she asks, startled by the suggestion.

I nod over toward the window. "It's barely a mist. I have a raincoat you could borrow. No thunder or lightning on the radar. I looked."

She laughs, and tells me she'd love a walk.

We walk side by side down the long slope of my driveway. I'm tempted to hold her hand, just in case her headache gets any worse or she starts feeling dizzy, but I resist the urge and settle on just staying close, scanning her face periodically for signs of discomfort. We continue in silence on a path past the couple small homes of my neighbors. It's a rural area, and I point us toward a walking trail across the street and through some woods.

"It's so beautiful here, how did you find this place?" she asks. She flips the hood of my coat up and over her head, and I smile at how outrageously large the whole thing is on her. The rain is more of a gentle misting now, thankfully, and the sounds of birds chirping in the distance offer a sweetness to our walk.

"I had been renting out storage space from a friend's garage, because my shop didn't have the room to expand, but there had been a couple rare vehicle finds that I had to have. I was living in a shitty apartment at the time, saving up and just looking at list-ings for a while, looking for anything that could double as storage for cars we were working on that would take a while. Finding specialized parts and things can take some time."

She nudges my shoulder. "I still remember you taking apart Inferno and me thinking you were crazy for messing with a perfectly good car."

I laugh. "What can I say, I like a project." She shakes her head as I continue on. "Anyhow, so I had been waiting to find a house that needed a little fixing up, big enough to be a permanent investment but still affordable. And I also knew I wanted decent land. The further out from town you go, the more you can get for your money.

"And then this old mid-century modern house popped up, but it had no garage. Figured it would be pretty cheap to build such a basic structure, so I put everything I could down on the property and went for it. You should have seen it at first," I chuckle. "Leaks and golden wallpaper and this disgusting red carpet throughout."

She leaps over a muddy puddle and laughs. "Oh, the good old styles of yore."

"Trust me when I say that's making it sound far more charming than it was. But I loved the fireplace and the windows, which were in decent shape. Little by little I updated what I could, starting with the master bathroom. That was covered in shiny blue wallpaper, which is even uglier than it sounds, believe it or not. The whole space was blue everything. And it had carpet in it to match."

She scrunches up her nose. "Ew. Carpet in a bathroom?"

"Yeah."

"Well, I sure like what you did with it," she smiles.

I smile too, remembering her naked in my shower last night. "How about you, where are you living?"

She shrugs, and I point us to the right where a small stream runs along the path. The water is higher than usual, and I watch as bundles of leaves and sticks float along by. "I'm a young and poor doctor completing my residency," she says, "so I live in a humble little condo for now. Nothing like your spot."

"Do you like the work?"

I love the grin that sweeps across her face. "I really do. I like making kids feel comfortable in an uncomfortable setting, and I like that I get to switch it up. Some days in the hospital, checking out new babies, some days in the office doing standard check-ups."

"So it's general pediatrics?" I confirm. "Not the plan of plastic surgery?" I fight the groan I feel knowing it was her dad's dream for her.

She nods. "Definitely not. It was my mom who encouraged me to pursue something else, actually."

"Oh yeah?"

Her face falls a little and I direct us over to a clearing with a large boulder, where we sit and watch the stream rushing over rocks.

She tucks her knees under her chin. "When my mom was in her final days, there was something really peaceful about our time together. I had to bathe her at that point, and it was this strange thing to be taking care of her like that, thinking about all the years she had taken care of me. Fixed my cuts and scrapes and made me my favorite foods when I was sick or sad." She smiles, her gaze held steady on the water in front of her as she lowers the hood from her head. "I don't think I ever told you this, but she had this tattoo under her left breast. I remember being so surprised when I first saw it."

"Your mom? A tattoo?" I ask, squinting at the peek of sun making its way between the clouds.

"Yup. It was small and black cursive and said, 'times ten.' All lowercase. That was it."

"More creative than 'one day at a time,' I guess. You never knew she had it?" I ask, smiling and trying very hard not to think of the late Holly Hatson's breasts, but unable to stop the image.

Desiree looks at me with raised brows. "Do *you* know what's under your mom's boobs?"

"Point taken," I concede.

"And we weren't exactly a naked house, so yeah, it was a surprise. She said it was a silly joke, that she got it many years ago, and then she held my hand and looked me dead in the eyes. Told me not to chase my dad's dreams, but to chase my own. Go into whatever field I wanted, even if it wasn't medicine.

"I had started laughing and asking her how the hell I'd pay my med school bills otherwise, and she squeezed my hand even tighter. It kind of freaked me out, actually. I realized how serious she was, and I told her not to worry about that. Promised her I'd go in whatever direction I wanted, but I reassured her that medicine was in fact where my passion was."

I put my arm around her shoulders and pull her into me. I remember when her mom died. I remember how utterly useless I was in the days after her death, when Desiree needed me most.

She adjusts herself into my chest and sighs. "Anyhow, as much as I love being creative and reading and writing and things, medicine was still something I was learning to love, especially when thrown into my mom's illness. I enjoyed the research of the body, what poisons it, how to enhance health and that kind of thing. I loved the relationships we had built with my mom's doctors, and I wanted to do that kind of thing too, but for kids and their families. I didn't think I could handle a specialty with more intense life-or-death cases, though, so went with general pediatrics."

"A good choice," I say, finding her hand and lacing our fingers together.

"I think so."

"What's the worst part about the job?"

Without missing a beat she says, "Doing circumcisions on newborn baby boys," she laughs, shaking her head. "Feels so cruel."

"Sure glad I don't remember mine," I say.

When we get back to the house, I head to the kitchen to make us some lunch. She needs chicken soup, I decide, so I get to work ripping apart the remnants of a rotisserie chicken I had in the fridge while Desiree chops up onions and carrots and celery beside me. I'll need to head to the airport soon to pick up Evelyn, to do the thing I hope she knows is coming, but I figure I'll make sure Desiree is well fed before I broach the subject.

With the soup simmering, I slice up a loaf of multigrain bread. I butter up a slice and cut it in half, plating it and handing it to Desiree. I grab my own slice, and we lean against the counter and munch in silence while I think about how to word this.

"So, I have to head out for a little bit soon here. Two hours tops, to see Evelyn, then I'll be back."

She takes another bite and nods, swiping her tongue along her lips to scoop up a spare crumb. "I know, I saw your phone light up with a reminder earlier. I wasn't snooping, I swear, it just popped up when you were in the bathroom. 'Evelyn Airport, Flight...' something or another. I don't remember the details. She coming or going?"

I stare at her, stunned. "She's..." My words drop off as I try and study her face, surprised at how nonchalant she is about the whole thing. Last night, I was kissing Desiree, yet today, the reality of the other woman in my life has had me restrained all morning. Is that it for us? Does Desiree assume last night was just a momentary burst of affection, now to be diminished?

She stares at me, waiting for my answer. "Coming or going, Vin?" she asks.

"She's arriving," I finally say. "Back from London for work."

She drops the last bit of her bread onto her plate and grabs a napkin. Wipes her hands and dabs at her mouth. "Sounds good. Not coming back here, I'm assuming?"

"No, back to her place," I say. "Wait, you're not mad?"

Blue eyes dart over to me, but I can't read her expression. "I'm not mad."

I turn to face her, surprised at how much I don't actually like that response. "But why not? I've been over here trying to figure out how to tell you that I'd need to run out, worried you'd get freaked out and want to leave, and here you are casually telling me that you already know."

She shrugs. "I mean, it was a little jolting seeing her name pop up on your phone like that. Remembering that you have a fiancée and all. Break or no break."

"I'm sorry," I say, because that's all I can think of in response.

She huffs out a little laugh. "I'm very well used to the women in Taven Carlisle's life, remember?" she says, arching an eyebrow.

"And I at one point got used to a certain man in yours," I remind her.

She rolls her eyes and opens the fridge, pulling out a Diet Pepsi. "Please, you were hardly 'used' to him. You met him, what...two times?"

I run my hand down my face, realizing she has a point. "Fine. Anyhow, I'm going to pick up Evelyn from the airport. I'm going to finalize the end of our engagement." I drop my hands and look at her as she opens her can. "Fuck it," I say. "And the truth is, Dazzle, I was kind of hoping that would give you and me the freedom to figure out what exactly we are to each other. And to maybe even rip each other's clothes off once and for all, and that you'd be okay with that." There it is, there's my truth, laid out before her. My heart starts pumping rapidly as I wait for her reaction.

She sips her drink and then smiles at me. "If you were picking me up from the airport, what would your phone reminder say?" she asks, ignoring my last statement.

I pull my head back. "What?"

"Just answer the question. What would your phone reminder say?"

I pinch my eyebrows together. "The same thing. 'Dazzle, Airport, Flight...whatever,'" I say, waving my hand out to the side.

"Exactly," she says. "You'd say, 'Dazzle.' Not Desiree."

It dawns on me. "That's right."

"Because I'm Dazzle to you."

I cross my arms over my chest, flexing just because, and smirk. "What's your point?"

She puts her drink down and slowly glides over to me. Runs her hands down my biceps. "You don't have a nickname for her, do you? No endearing little inside joke you guys share?" I shake my head no. She shrugs. "I like that," she says, placing a quick kiss on my cheek and walking backwards, gliding her hands over her breasts knowing full well her nipples are poking through her shirt. She dramatically sighs. "So, that solves *that* problem."

"Is there another?" I ask, loving the sly way she's teasing me.

I study her, transfixed by her mesmerizing movements as she drops her hands to her hips and narrows her eyes at me. "Another problem, you ask?"

"Sure. Got plenty more solving I can do."

She steps closer to me, a slow and seductive saunter that's filled with mischief. She stops just shy of touching me, and locks those big blue eyes with mine. "Taven," she says.

"Yes?"

She places a hand on my arm. "Tell me what it was that caused the family fallout all those years ago."

My face falls. The room goes quiet, other than the bubbling of the soup on the stove.

So this was her game, I see it now. Be cool about the Evelyn airport thing, use it as leverage and get me to share the dark secret that I know would only crush her and fill her with disgust, just as it has with my family for all this time. It was never a subject Desiree and I discussed. She'd tried in the past to ask me what I knew, but I'd refuse, downplaying it like it wasn't even worth mentioning. In the past, she'd let me.

I have a feeling she will not today.

"No, Desiree. Not that," I say, my voice quiet.

She leans further into me, her face stern, sky blue eyes wild with determination. "I'm not asking. I'm telling you. Say whatever it was. It was a thousand years ago. It hardly matters now, right?"

"If it doesn't matter then why even bother with it?" I counter, skin crawling at even so much as the thought of it.

"It matters because it was something you kept from me. And I know you were young and trying to do right by your family, but I need to know. Want to know if you'd let me in enough to just say it." She presses her hands onto my forearms and gives me a gentle push, her face twisting in a sarcastic laugh. "Don't make a big deal of it, just say it! Say the stupid and ridiculous thing that caused the great, big, earth-shattering Carlisle-Hatson divide."

I unwind my arm and turn away from her. I face the stove on the center island and lift the lid off of the pot, giving the soup a quick stir. "You don't want to know, Dazzle. Trust me on this."

"You've said that before."

"Good, then you know it's where I stand."

"I can't believe you're still trying to be a vault on this, Taven." She laughs, but she doesn't sound amused. I can hear the desperation in her voice. "This is so stupid, it wasn't even about us, so just tell me! It *was* an affair, wasn't it? Your dad and my mom, is that it? And you don't want to tell me now because you think it'll hurt me, especially with my mom gone, but it won't. I won't care, I promise."

"But you will care."

"I won't, and I have to say, you sitting here still remaining absurdly tight-lipped about the whole thing—still protecting your father and his crimes—it's really making me question whether or not I should even be here right now."

I slam the lid down on the pot and then slam my fist onto the counter. "It was *your* father, okay? Not mine. Yours. Are you happy now?"

I look at her. Take in her wide eyes. "And your *mom*?" she says, disbelief written all over her face. She pulls her head back. "Lynda wouldn't."

I close my eyes, realizing there's no moving past this. "Not my mom, Desiree."

"Okay?"

"Jacqui. It was your dad and Jacqui."

She lets out a huff of disbelief. "Jacqui? She was a kid back then. That's sick."

I tuck my hands in my pockets and lean back against the counter, crossing one ankle over the other and staring down at my socks. Good old black cotton socks. Very basic and normal, as if this conversation is very basic and normal. "She was eighteen," I say. "Still in high school but technically legal. So there was nothing my parents could do."

"No."

I stare down at the grooves of the hardwood floor. Grooves of dark divots in the cinnamon wood, one of the best parts of the original features of the house. "Someone walked in on them together at a party," I say. My words sound far away to me, as if someone else is talking. "Told my parents. Jacqui and your dad denied it all, but then my mom found her diary. Read all about it, every sordid detail."

"No," she says, shaking her head.

I ignore her. "My parents sat me down and told me what had happened. They said I needed to be aware of what kind of man Frank Hatson really was. I didn't want to believe it at first, couldn't even wrap my head around what they were telling me. But, sadly, it was true."

"No," she repeats.

I look back up to her. "Yes, Desiree. That's the truth. I'm sorry to say it. I never wanted you to know this, but that's it. That's what caused the fallout. It was your father." *And my sweet, innocent sister.*

She stands there, mouth opened but stunned into silence.

I sigh. "I'm sorry I couldn't tell you back then. But this was also when your mom had been sick for the first time. Your parents had just gotten her diagnosis, and they were dealing with that as well, and not telling you or Dylan about it yet. Your mom was in denial with the Jacqui thing, I guess, and I was told to pretend I knew nothing, to stop seeing you, and that was that.

"I know this is hard to hear, and I hate that it wasn't just some stupid affair had by our parents, I really do. But think what that was like for me," I plead. "Learning my sister, my big sister who was my *favorite person* in that household, was being seduced by and fucking *screwed*," I say, my voice raising despite myself, "by some fucking old pervert little shit, who also happened to be my girlfriend's father." I pause to take a breath, study her face to see if she's comprehending. I want to see if she can understand why I've kept it from her all this time.

"No," she says yet again. "No, that...that can't be the thing." She folds her body in half, dropping her head toward the floor. "This is not true. That's disgusting," she says, popping herself back up to stand up straight. I watch her as she looks out the window and sucks in a big breath of air. "That's just not true," she says brightly, smiling, and my chest tightens as I witness her denial.

She shrugs and faces me. "It's just absurd." Her eyes dart over to the stove, and then she walks over to the cabinets above the counter. She opens and closes doors until she finds the bowls, she grabs two and hands one to me. "I'm really hungry.

This smells really good. I think we should eat." I watch as she pushes me aside, haphazardly ladling scoops of chicken and broth and veggies into her bowl, then sets it down to take mine and does the same. "Let's eat," she says as she sets our bowls down in front of seats at the island. I slowly walk over to the utensils drawer, pull out two spoons and hand one to her.

She takes a seat on the other side of the island and wiggles to settle herself into it, then smiles up at me. "Smells really good. I fucking love chicken soup, did you know that?" She scoops some into her spoon, then shoves it in her mouth, wincing at the temperature as she realizes it's still just barely below a boil. "Fuck, that's hot. Whoops! A little too eager, I guess." I slide my glass of water over to her. She accepts the glass, drinks half of its contents, and slams it down on the counter before wiping her mouth with her napkin. "Aren't you going to join me?"

I'm not sure what else to do, so I grab my bowl and spoon, and go to sit next to her, my heart thumping as I think about the bomb I just dropped on her. One I swore to myself I'd take to the grave. What good would it do her to know? That's her father, the only living parent she has at this point. Naturally, this would be tough to absorb. I can't say I blame her for having this bizarre, maniacal reaction to the whole thing.

She slaps her hand on the counter and jolts me out of my thoughts. "You know what? What time is Evelyn's flight? You should probably go. You don't want to be late."

My heart sinks. I turn in my seat to face her, my knees bumping against her thighs. "Dazzle, please," I say, reaching for her hand. She lets her hand sit limply in mine. "Tell me what you're thinking."

She closes her eyes. "I'm thinking that my mouth stings with the fucking *burning hot soup* I just shoved in there." She opens her eyes and turns her head to look at me. "And that you should probably leave and go get Evelyn. Right now." I see the shift in her expression. The mask of giddiness dropping down to reveal hurt or confusion or anger or maybe all of it. "Please. Just go, Taven."

I consider her request. She wants space, I get it. Space to sit and try and process the whole thing, without me breathing down her neck and constantly asking if she's alright.

"Fine, I'll head out now," I say. "Just tell me you'll be here when I get back." I stroke my thumb over her hand, willing it to soothe her and calm her down. "Don't leave because of this."

She pulls her hand out from mine. "Oh, no need to worry about that. I have no car here, remember?" She looks back down at her soup, fills her spoon with chunks of chicken and broth, then gently blows on it before taking another bite.

phase 4: madly, deeply or misery

. . .

You're nearly ready to give up, deciding you're destined to be miserable and without the thing you want. Your crush is beyond your reach.

But if you're lucky, you feel something else. A subtle whisper in the wind. The clouds shift. Golden rays beam through. There's a glimmer of hope. A newfound peace settles within as you realize your hand is being held. You can feel it—you're falling in love.

thirty-four

· · ·

Slipping

Five years ago

desiree

twenty-five years old

MY MOM DIED on a beautiful day in March. She always loved flowers and gardening, so it seemed appropriate that she would die when the tulips were popping up from their time in hibernation, and the drowsy evergreens were reaching their next growth spurts. I had made sure all of her favorite flowers were at the funeral—lilies and dahlias, roses because they were classic. I arranged one special vase on my own (surely not as well as she could have), but it was my last little gift to her. For all the inner demons I know my mom secretly fought—demons I'd never know about, it seemed—memories of her arranging flowers beside the kitchen were when she seemed most at peace.

When my mom became sick again, I had reached out to Melissa. One final plea to her, because even though it had been several years since we talked, I needed my original best friend. I missed her mom's cooking, the sancocho stew that was a weekly staple, the flurry of activity that was always in the Belle household.

It was one thing to no longer have Taven in my life. But entirely another to not have Melissa, because it was her family as a whole that I missed as well.

She came. When I reached out and shared the news, Melissa was on the next plane from New York, as if no time at all had passed within our friendship. Nervous as I was to make the plea, I somehow knew she'd be there.

She stayed as long as she could, helping with my mom's wig selections and assortment of medications to be administered. She joked about the night my mom had to rescue her, me, and Taven from that party. When my mom was the one giving us pills, the foolish teens who couldn't hold their alcohol.

Melissa would make my mom laugh with the wicked gossip of Broadway stars and behind-the-scenes affairs, acting out how so-and-so made moves on one another in dramatic declarations of love, only to then have a scorned wife wander onto set, throwing drinks in faces.

Whether or not these stories were real didn't matter. Melissa was the entertainment we all needed during that time.

My father stood quietly by my mom's side in those final days. I'd never before seen him crumble like that. His trembling shoulders and soft sobs, whispering to his wife of all the beautiful places they'd go together when he joined her in the afterlife, all of it squeezing at my heart. Thirty years of marriage together, how was he going to survive without his rock? he'd ask her. I'd gently close the door and let them be. Even through my parents' ups and downs, the time they'd briefly separated only to find their way back to one another, I could tell how much they loved each other. As hard as it was to lose my mom, I remember thinking it must be even harder for my father to lose his life partner.

I thought about how wonderful it would be to have a love like that. I wondered if I'd ever get that one day.

TAVEN SHOWED UP AT THE funeral. I'm not sure how he knew about it, my guess is that Melissa reached out to him, but there he was. I hadn't seen him in several years, since everything went down after his arrest.

I almost didn't see him at first. He was tucked away in the back, hiding from my father, no doubt, but I caught a glimpse of him as I made my way down the long aisle of the church, behind my mother's casket. I had always imagined running into him again, dreamed of seeing him at the grocery store or in town somewhere, knowing he was back in Ohio. I was active on Facebook and Instagram at the time, and would peruse his social media accounts. I would go down a rabbit hole of stalking the girl I noticed consistently commenting on the occasional posts that he made. I ached with questions on who the petite brunette was with him in the beachside photo, that kind of thing. Eventually, I stopped looking altogether. It was too hard.

So when I saw him there in that pew, head down and trying not to be noticed but staring straight at me, I gave him a small wave. And when he texted me later that evening, asking if he could see me, I said okay.

I was dating someone by that point. A nice guy from a pleasant family that I met at the hospital, Parker was his name. I brought Parker along with me to the bar where Taven requested we meet. I admit, I had hoped to make Taven jealous.

Parker was a handsome surgeon, and when he asked me out initially, I thought I'd faint that everyone's favorite hot doctor had taken a liking to me.

I couldn't resist his smile, his persistence when I initially declined, unsure of how to turn on the charm with him and certain he was just making his way through all the fresh faces in my class. I learned he was divorced, and not known to be a player, so eventually I said yes. He later admitted he hadn't been looking for anything serious initially, but my rejection had him desperate for more. Little did he know I had just been shy.

I thought we made quite the pair. He treated me well, never made me question whether or not I was on his mind. He consistently texted me "Good morning" every day, knew my favorite snacks and always had them in stock at his house. Even Melissa liked him once they finally met, and she wasn't one to readily let just anyone in.

When Parker and I met up with Taven, the bar was painfully quiet, just the usual bar flies perched in their seats and watching some game on the screens surrounding the place. Parker and I made our way in, and I spotted Taven, sitting by himself in a booth in the corner.

As soon as Parker and I slid in to join—Parker shaking Taven's hand and playing along nicely with this man from my past—I could see that Taven was drunk. He was wearing a black hoodie sweatshirt and kept fidgeting around with its strings that were dangling on his chest, lifting one and jabbing the air with it every time he had some great point he was trying to emphasize. "That's right!" he'd say, darting the thing at us. "It was, it was," *dart, dart,* "that spot on third street!"

He was cracking every inside joke he possibly could with me, asking if I still wear heart-shaped sunglasses, or if Bingo was still my favorite game. He mentioned the new tattoo he wanted to get, and did I remember that guy—that hilarious guy—at the studio when I went with him to get his first one?

"I remember," I said, working carefully to not down my wine entirely too fast despite my desire to want to take the edge off.

"What was the tattoo?" Parker asked, ever the polite one as he sipped his beer. I think he was amused at seeing this ex of mine make a fool of himself, clearly putting on a show. I felt embarrassed for Taven, yet also longing with a desire to make Parker see the wonderful person that Taven truly was behind the drunken facade.

I glanced over at Taven, a smile escaping me. He held my gaze and smiled too, his first genuine one of the night, and a little flicker of the old connection we had erupted.

"Well, Dazzle?" he said. "Are you going to tell Parker what my first tattoo was?"

I looked at him for another beat, then grinned and turned to face my boyfriend. "Taven and I used to have this tradition of making Bingo cards at every New Year. We'd fill them in for each other for goals or things we had to do throughout the year."

"Except with these ones," Taven cut in, "they were really more like dares."

Parker pointed between us. "But you would come up with Desiree's and she'd come up with yours?"

"Exactly," I said. "And one year, we were nineteen, I think?"

Taven nodded once. "Yup," he said, with a poke in the air of his hoodie string.

"I filled in a square to have Taven get a tattoo, and let me pick it out."

Parker stretched his arm out around my shoulders. "This should be good, what did you pick?"

I looked at Taven and noticed when his eyes dropped down to Parker's hand, fingers slowly rubbing the skin on my chest, slipping in between the neckline of my shirt and grazing just above my breast. He looked back up at me and I saw it, the flare of something. Anger. Jealousy.

I tried to ignore the flip in my belly at that look and carried on. "I had him get a heart tattoo that had 'mom' written in it."

Taven kept his eyes on me, poker-faced as he said, "And I did it."

I couldn't look away from him. A million thoughts were passing between us, memories of that day, visions of Bingo cards, every single one of mine that I've kept since I was thirteen years old. I wondered if he still had his. I had a feeling he did. His eyes held mine, and I could see the thoughts behind them. *I see you, Desiree*, he was saying. *And this guy right here will never know you or love you like I do. It will always be us.*

Parker broke our spell. "What did your mom think of the tattoo? Was she flattered?"

Taven downed the rest of his drink and slammed the glass on the table. He leaned back and said, "She told me it was trashy, and I should get it removed."

That was the last memory we shared that evening.

***

THE NEXT COUPLE OF WEEKS were a slow slip back into the cycle of my perpetual crush on Taven Carlisle. We met as a group one more time after that first meeting with Parker. Melissa was in town and came with us that night, along with a couple of Taven's old friends from high school. Tensions were high, testosterone was clearly in the driver's seat, and the little jabs being thrown between Taven and Parker were getting worse as the evening carried on.

First it was Parker ordering my food for me.

Taven scoffed. "What, man, can't let the lady order for herself?" he probed.

Parker was smooth with his response. "She can order for herself, just thought I'd be a gentleman and order for her since she's clearly mid-conversation with her friend at the moment."

Melissa and I exchanged a look. Then she stretched her arm

over to Parker and patted his hand. "And you know us girls hate to be interrupted."

Then it was asking what kind of car Parker drove. A Ford F-350. "You work in construction? Haul a lot of shit?" Taven asked with a grin, knowing full well Parker did not.

At one point Taven was making fun of Parker's specialty—surgery, saying the doctors that felt the need to be fancy were the ones that went for surgery. Parker pointed out that it was still a pathway I was considering, and Taven looked at me, saying, "Dazzle's always been fancy all on her own."

At the end of the night, Taven was helping me slip my arms through my coat. Parker rushed to my side. "I got that, man."

I glared at Parker. A warning for him to step back. Drinks had been flowing and no one needed to poke any bears. "It's just a coat, babe," I said.

"Yeah," Taven chuckled. "Just a coat, *babe*."

Parker was not one to be goaded. He was the rockstar of medicine, destined to make chief or director one day, with the kind of cutthroat ambition that didn't take kindly to anyone he felt might stand in his way, professionally or personally.

Including jealous exes. "Watch your tone, Carlisle," he said.

Taven laughed. "You're pretty serious about Dazzle's coat, aren't you?"

Melissa cut in then, shoving Taven in the chest. He stumbled backwards, knocking over a barstool. "Let's get you home, shall we?" she sang out.

The car ride home with Parker was tense. A lot of it was him telling me he didn't like Taven, that he was clearly still in love with me, and that I needed to stop talking to him. I played the "my mom just died" card, explaining that in my time of mourning, having old friends around that knew her in her prime was comforting to me. We got into a huge fight, one that left me in tears, so when I decided to go to Taven's apartment at two o'clock in the morning, I think we both knew nothing good was going to come of it.

I didn't know where he lived, so I texted him to ask for his address. He wrote me back immediately, still awake, and by the time I knocked on his door, my heart was pounding, and I was wondering if I was about to make a huge mistake. Yet there was nothing that I wanted more than Taven's reassuring arms around me.

When he opened the door, his apartment dark and his silhouette framed by the low light of the small entryway, I knew I was doing this. His hair was disheveled and hanging over his forehead, he looked almost vulnerable to me. The look on his face was one that told me he could hardly believe I was here.

We stood like that for a moment. Unmoving, lips parting, wondering what to do or say next. He was wearing sweatpants, no t-shirt—as if I needed a reminder of what all that skin and muscle looked like. I was done for.

I stepped through the doorway, and next thing I know he was pulling me against him, his face pressed into my neck and he breathed in, whispering, "Dazzle. God, I've missed you so much." I was gliding my hands around his torso, up around his back, relishing in the feel of his smooth skin. He smelled so good, felt so warm. He inched his way to my face, my mouth, kissing me with a passion that had been building up in the few short weeks since seeing him again.

He closed the door, mouth still locked to mine, then pushed me back against it with rushed enthusiasm like I might disappear if he waited too long.

He pulled off my jacket. Ripped open my blouse, then stood back to look at my body, eyes animalistic as he scanned my chest, my stomach. He said nothing, he didn't need to. The hunger in his eyes told me he needed this as much as I did. I reached up and slipped my fingers through his hair, feeling the same softness it's always had. I pulled him back to me while his mouth dotted kisses up and down my chest, my stomach, a bite on my hip as he shoved down my jeans.

I stood there with my blouse hanging on my shoulders, my bra and panties still on. "Taven," I cried out when he pressed his mouth between my legs, the heat of his breath through my underwear lighting me up. He inhaled the scent of me with a growl that left me so utterly desired, I thought I might come right then and there. He pressed his nose up and down, taking me in.

"I've wanted this right here for so long, Dazzle."

I whimpered as he continued worshiping me at a maddeningly slow pace. "Yes," I breathed out. "Please." I stood there weak and ravenous for him. He slid a finger up and down over my panties, planting kisses along my belly, reverent with his touch.

"Mine," he said. "All mine, baby."

"Yes," I panted, clawing my nails into his scalp. He glided his hand down my thigh, then lifted my leg over his shoulder.

He planted a kiss between my legs. "I want to taste you. Here."

A warmth flushed through me at the thought of his mouth on me. "Please," I whispered. He pushed aside my panties, amping up the feel of the heat of his breath on me. I was flushed and impatient, wanting his mouth on me but loving the torture of his painfully thorough exploration. I begged him to take me, to taste me or fuck me or something, until he finally gave in.

There it was. The delicious feel of Taven's tongue on me. Pressing all around, teasing me but not hitting that spot I was craving. It didn't matter. He would get there, and I would enjoy this torture for all I could.

When he fully covered me with his mouth, I gasped and squeezed my eyes shut, taking in the only sensation that mattered.

He guided my hand to my breast, looked up at me and said, "Touch yourself, Desiree."

I did as I was told, pushing the cup of my bra down and releasing my breast. He watched me as I circled my nipple, then his head was back between my legs, and the two sensations combined were so intense, I was panting and dizzy.

He was relentless with his work, quickening his movements as I continued touching myself, massaging my breast with one hand, holding on to his hair with the other. I could feel every move of him stroking up and down, sucking and invading and I started trembling, barely able to stand.

It was too much, yet everything I needed, and I could feel myself blooming beneath him, getting close. I kept hold of his hair, crying his name out over and over again with his tongue working in torturous circles, squeezing my nipple and pulsing my hips into him.

He stopped. Released me and pulled back, and I begged him, "Please don't stop, I'm so close." I looked down to see him grinning up at me.

"But I'm about to make you collapse, Dazzle." He placed a soft kiss on my thigh.

"I want to collapse," I breathed out. "I'm fine. I'm steady, I promise. Please."

"Please what?" he said, gently biting me.

"Please put your mouth back on me." I was on fire at that point, aching with painful need.

"Are you sure?" he teased.

"I'm sure. Fuck, I need you. I need more. Please," I whined.

He gave me one light flick of his tongue and I jolted with the feel of it, everything lit up and felt exquisitely sensitive. Then another, then another and I squeezed his hair and bucked my hips closer, grinding into his face and begging for more.

When he slowed down once again, I thought I might scream with frustration.

I looked down at him. He softened his smile, slowly running two fingers up the skin of my inner thigh, a chill sweeping over me. He stopped just before pushing into me.

"Is this okay?" he asked, and I nearly wept with the sweetness of what he was asking. Knowing what had been done to me before, wanting to make sure I was okay with it now. I nodded. "It's okay," I said and then I closed my eyes in sweet relief when his mouth was on me again, fingers inside me and working their magic until I truly did need to steady myself. I released my breast and reached my palm to the wall beside me, screaming out in wave after wave of ecstasy, coming right there in the entry hall of Taven Carlisle's apartment. I was screaming out his name, my mouth pressed down into my shoulder to attempt to muffle my cries as my pleasure ripped through me.

My legs were weak, and when I was finally able to catch my breath, blinking away the stars behind my eyes, he rose up before me. Cradled my face and kissed me.

"You taste like a goddamn piece of heaven," he said, "just like I knew you would." Then he lifted me up and carried me to his bedroom. I lay limp in his arms, still spinning with how incredible he just made me feel. How hard he just made me come.

We stepped in his room, and I lazily scanned my eyes around the space where Taven Carlisle slept. The room was simple, though nicer than his college apartment. A dark bedspread, the color of which I couldn't quite make out in the dimness of the lights. Navy or charcoal, maybe. Two nightstands, a candle on one, and I tried not to think about why he had a candle in there. Who else he had seduced into his bedroom with the scent of teak or maybe sea salt and soft glows of a flickering flame. I decided none of it mattered.

He laid me down gently and I watched as he held my gaze while he pushed down his sweats, his cock springing free and taunting me. I had a moment of a belly flip of nerves, remembering his size and the feeling of him inside me years before. I felt the anticipation mixed with the slightest apprehension.

I wanted to taste him like he had tasted me. I leaned forward and crawled my way over to him, his mattress creaking quietly beneath me. I paused in front of him to admire this bit of Taven Carlisle that I'd missed more than I ever dared to admit. I took him in, slowly, and loved the taste and feel of him filling my mouth so perfectly.

"So beautiful," I could hear him whisper above me. I looked up to see him watching me as I moved up and down and took in all I could. I slipped my fingers through the patch of hair surrounding him, inquisitive in the chance to get to study him up close, and he groaned above me as I stroked my tongue up the length of his shaft. I was high off the feeling of him growing even harder in my mouth with each pull. I felt powerful in his growls of pleasure and appreciation, all because of me.

He stopped me before he could finish. Instead, he pushed my shoulders back and shoved off my blouse, then my bra. He slid my panties down my legs, dropping them and saying, "You're perfect, Desiree." I felt no self-consciousness, no embarrassment as I watched him admiring my naked body beneath him.

He stepped forward and pushed me back on the bed. I propped myself onto my elbows and watched his naked form as he walked over to the nightstand, pulled out a condom, and unrolled it over himself. My belly fluttered in anticipation of what was about to happen. I needed him inside me so badly, I shivered with the thought of it, feeling my nipples tighten and my skin tingle.

His eyes held mine. "We're going to do this nice and slowly," he said. He pointed to the mirror beside the bed. "You're going to watch me make love to you, you understand?" I nodded. "And you're going to watch yourself as I make you come so fucking hard with me inside you."

I looked over to the mirror, took in our naked bodies, mine laying before him like a sacrifice about to be made. I said okay. He could do this, I knew he could. I had yet to have an orgasm in that way, just never something I was able to do, but I somehow knew tonight I would.

True to his word, Taven started slowly. I stared at him in the mirror in fascination as he positioned himself between my legs, kneeling and starting his mission, pulling my legs close to him, then pressing himself against my entrance. I felt him there, but kept my gaze on the mirror, and he was looking down at me, one hand stroking my leg. "You like watching yourself, don't you?"

"I like watching you," I said.

"Good."

And then he leaned forward and gently pushed himself into me, all the way in and I closed my eyes, holding onto his shoulders, allowing myself to take in every inch of Taven I could. "You okay?" he asked.

I breathed in deeply, the sandalwood scent of his cologne calming as he stretched me in a way I hadn't been since that one and only time with him. "I'm okay," I assured him. It was Taven inside of me. This was okay. This was right.

He cradled my neck with his hand and turned my face back toward the mirror. "Open your eyes, Dazzle." I did as instructed. "Do you see yourself? Do you see how beautiful you are?"

I loved everything I saw. Our intertwining bodies, the way my breasts gently rolled, the flex of sculpted muscle as he began to move on top of me. Worked himself into me. I loved the trust I felt with his hand on my throat, locked in and holding me steady and making me watch us.

We rocked slowly together like that for a while. It was tender kisses and soft moans, and I thought, this is perfect. This is everything I will ever need. I never wanted to stop doing this exact thing right here.

It was so much. So incredible, and I whispered, "I love you," emotion in my voice as I watched the two of us moving together. "I never stopped loving you."

He kissed the tears escaping my eyes, whispering, "I've *only* loved you, Dazzle. It's only been you," and I looked up at him and wrapped my arms around his neck, kissing him as deeply as I possibly could, still only wanting more.

At some point he paused. Slipped an arm beneath my hips and lifted my lower half up, holding me tight against him, completely filling me to the hilt.

"Move, Desiree," he said. He hovered over me, still holding me firmly in his grasp as he whispered in my ear, "I want you to move those beautiful hips and fuck me, riding me like this, you understand?"

I nodded, pressing my heels into him and moving as instructed, riding him from beneath while he held me in the tight lock of our embrace. I turned my head and watched myself in the mirror, taking him like this, my movements greedy, aching with the relentless pressure of him inside me.

With each rock I could feel myself climbing higher, feel every inch of him sliding in and out of me over and over again. I could feel it, I was actually going to come like this.

"Holy shit. Taven," I cried out. "It's so good." I closed my eyes and focused on the mounting pleasure I felt with each move.

He kissed my temple, and I felt him tugging my hair, the tightness on my scalp aiding in the sensations I was feeling. "That's right, Dazzle. Just like that, baby."

I moved again, loving the slow and steady climb I was making with each gentle push of my hips on him until I was right at the edge, crying out, "Taven, fuck me, please!" I needed him to pound into me with a desperation I'd never known I could feel. "More."

He released me and slammed into me again and again, bringing me to my release and I breathed out, begging for more, riding the wave of an exploding orgasm as he twisted my hair in his grasp, yanking my head back. It was the best fucking feeling I'd ever experienced, and I screamed out that I'm coming, don't ever stop, that I'm coming. He drove into me, and I thought this wave would never end. That this feeling knew no limits and I was blind with my orgasm. It was the best kind of high, and then he was shuddering on top of me, swearing and saying my name with his own release. I was stunned with the feeling of it all.

When it was over, he stayed inside me like that for a while, kissing me and telling me he was never letting me go. That I was the only thing in the world that mattered. I told him I wasn't going anywhere.

I didn't know at the time that I was lying, because in that moment, there wasn't a single thing in the world that I could think of that would make me walk away from him.

It was my Taven, in my world again. Making love to me. He'd given me the most intense orgasm I'd ever had, the best sex of my life. No gadgets, no frills, just beautiful sex in its purest and simplest form.

Ecstasy was followed quickly by the firestorm of a new hell when I realized that I had thrown away my relationship with Parker for the love of my life—a closet alcoholic.

thirty-five

. . .

Shift

Present Day

taven

Saturday, 4:43pm

I CRUISE ALONG the highway with Evelyn in the passenger seat beside me. The white dashed lines of the road pass us by and I mindlessly watch them, switching lanes and passing cars in my hurry to drop her off. Then I can get back to Desiree. My Dazzle, who just learned something terrible about her father and is now stewing in the realization of it. I need to see her and make sure she's alright. I want to help her sort through whatever feelings she's having about it.

I think about how I used to use drinking to cope with things I wanted to push down and ignore. When you struggle with addiction, you often think about what the trigger is. And what is the turning point on the path of destruction? For me, there were many things—all the internal fears of whether or not I'd actually find any success, anxieties of living up to the doubts I felt from my parents. Thoughts that I held no worth, that I was incapable of building anything of value, that I would be a failure.

Then there was the time that I ran into Frank Hatson. It was at a grocery store, the summer after high school. I was just getting ready to head off to Philly for college, where I knew I might finally get my chance with Desiree. And there he was, her father, mere feet away, and I wanted nothing more than to march up to him and feel the sweet satisfaction of my fist meeting his face.

Holly came around the corner. I saw her smile at him, and I was frozen in my tracks, seeing the mother that looked so much like her daughter. It stopped me, and I turned on my heels and walked away, chest tight and breaths short. The wind felt like it had been knocked out of me, and I walked outside and gasped for air, wondering what was happening to me.

When I got home, I reached out to Jacqui. I didn't understand the reaction I was having, and she was the only person I could think to talk to, though I hated bringing up the subject at all. My sister was soothing, telling me I didn't need to carry this on my shoulders. She said how sorry she was for everything. She blamed herself, and she said she knew the several weeks of her attachment to Frank Hatson was the reason me and Desiree were apart. I had been furious that some fucker made her think she was to blame. He had taken advantage of her innocence, couldn't she see that? She admitted that for a couple years, Frank had been progressively more flirtatious with her. It disgusted me. The last thing I wanted her to do was blame herself, yet I also understood.

We can be really skilled at beating ourselves up for our mistakes, living with regret and messages of "You're a fuck-up, everything bad that happens is your fault." I knew that feeling well.

To this day, there's little I regret more than not being able to see any sweet justice served to Desiree's father.

EVELYN'S EXHAUSTED. I CAN SEE it in the circles under her eyes and in the frown on her lips. We head toward her place, politely talking about meaningless bullshit. Our conversation is limited to safe topics like how her trip was, the long flight with the elderly couple beside her flip-flopping between random bickering and mini naps complete with snoring.

She fills me in on all this, and she never once asks me how last night's concert was. I'm guessing she just forgot, which is fine by me, but I know she's also jet-lagged and not at a hundred percent. Meaning I should probably hold off any real conversation with her. I noticed she didn't have her engagement ring on, but her text saying she missed me has me confused as to where exactly she stands.

I think back to when Evelyn initially mentioned having second thoughts about marrying me. It was several weeks ago. She had been spending a lot of time with a coworker, someone she realized she had crossed some lines with in the way of flirting and extended communication outside of work parameters. She came to me and told me everything, wondering if she was ready for marriage. Yeah, I'll go ahead and admit, it hurt like hell to hear that.

But there was also a part of me, this little gnawing part, that thought maybe it was for the best, so the reassurance I offered her was half-hearted. While I do love her, and will forever be grateful for her steadfast loyalty as she stood by me through my darkest hours, I also never felt the same raw intensity for her that I share with Desiree.

I also know that there's something dangerous about trusting a spark you have with someone. I've considered whether or not that kind of spark is in fact healthy, or if it's the desperate pull toward something that's ultimately not good for you, all wrapped up in the appeal of a revved-up state of existence.

That's also how drinking was for me.

It was this itch, a burning itch to crack open a beer, just one or two, just a little something to take my mind off whatever thing was stressing me out on any given day. I would tell myself drinking was a good thing, that it was helping me. Soon one or two became three or four beers, and when that proved to not be enough, it was a shot washed down with a beer. There, that was better. I'd feel nice and light and buzzy, not a damn care in the world.

And then that turned to liking feeling light and buzzy several days a week, drinking no longer something reserved for weekends or social events. I'd be stuck on a project at work, decide to reach for a drink to calm down my frustrations, dripping with sweat and grimy with engine soot. I'd be at a party drinking politely along with everyone else, but sneaking sips from a flask any time I thought no one was looking. My tolerance was high, and my itch was strong.

I understand now that I'm someone who likes *more*, always. When one drink feels so refreshing, I'd decide more would be even better. More could translate to other things as well—more projects, more cars, and when I was single, more women. Drinks by the bar followed by taking home the cute blonde that had been flirting with me all night became a favorite pastime.

My rock bottom should have come in the way of a potential DUI. One I managed to get out of, but once at the station, I called Desiree, even though she had walked out at that point. I was locked behind bars once again, sobering up and dying from an exploding head and scared I might lose my license, yet I *still* wanted more to drink. I'd slipped up, sure, but I could keep it together. No more liquor, I'd just stick to beer, everything would be fine. I have since learned that clinging to a belief that *this thing* is the only thing to bring me any real happiness is a lie, but it took me a while to get there.

My addiction to alcohol was progressive. The limits I'd set for myself after one embarrassing or dangerous incident or another were shorter and shorter-lived each time. I'd look at the timeline between major slip-ups—ones where I was thrown out of a bar after some fight, or waking up in a woman's bed having no idea how I got there or if I used a condom—and realize they were turning into the norm. I'd laugh and joke with the guys at the shop, sharing the tales of my drunken shenanigans, but soon the stories started getting less funny and more fucked-up.

But the saddest incident will always be the day Desiree left me. She was in my kitchen, counter lined up with rows of empty bottles she had dug out of my trash bin and collected from the trunk of Inferno. I was furious with the insinuation, yelling at her as she cried and asked when things had gotten so bad. She was telling me some story from the night before—behaviors of mine that I didn't even remember, and I sure as hell wasn't ready to hear it now. It scared the shit out of me to imagine what she was telling me was true.

I walked right out of my apartment and headed straight for —you guessed it—the bar. Telling myself she was crazy, I was fine. Internally I was filled with shame at having put her in danger, and embarrassed to have my secret exposed by someone I idolized. I was self-conscious that she was back in my life, a doctor in the making, and I was still living off my parents' credit card.

It took my parents cutting me off, and eventually my mom showing up and pulling my ass into rehab to finally get myself healthy again. I'm ashamed to admit that. Somehow the disappointment in my mother's eyes was more than I could handle, and it became quickly evident how clueless I was at managing money and living life on a budget. I had to give sobriety a real shot and get it together.

I wish it could have been Desiree that I stopped for. I always wondered about that, why this woman I loved wasn't enough to get me to stop. I hate that she's asked herself that, too. I'm glad she got to finally say her piece last night, let out some anger, but I know it's not that simple to clean up the damage and hurt. It's something I want to address with her again, because she needs to really, truly know that she *was* enough, I just wasn't ready for it. That's the truth.

I subconsciously believed she was too good for me, and I couldn't handle it. I was convinced she was going to wake up one day and realize she could do better, that she'd break my heart eventually. This amazing and smart woman, someone who just left a damn doctor for me. Left a fucking surgeon. I resented her for making that choice. Misery wrapping around me and pushing her away, just to be safe, to beat the inevitable.

After my parents stepped in, I was broke and eventually crawled my way back to their house, tail between my legs. I was stuck living with them at twenty-six years old, like a kid under their watch, under the iron fist that I had always been dying to get out from under. That felt like the lowest of low points for me. It was fucking humiliating. And sadly, it worked. Suddenly dependent under their roof, a couple bucks to my bank account and alarmingly sober, I used my anger to fuel my drive.

I saved up. Got a shitty apartment of my own, yet I was strangely proud and wanted to celebrate. I drank a little. I had been sober for several months at that point. Clearly, I was fine. Just a couple beers. No big deal.

Evelyn was back in my life at that point, as a friend. I hadn't told her that I had a few drinks now and then, convincing myself that it was just to keep her from unnecessary worry. When a few drinks became a few too many one evening, I passed out. I woke up the next afternoon with no recollection of the night before. I had sworn to myself I could still handle alcohol. Instead, it was handling me.

It was Evelyn I called to confess my relapse. Evelyn that went with me to that first AA meeting, where I quietly listened and didn't say a damn thing, still convinced that these people had an addiction much worse than mine. I had never woken up in a ditch, nearly frozen to death, at least, or handcuffed to a hospital bed. My fuck-ups weren't so bad.

But I went to a meeting again anyway, then again, and soon some of the stories I heard sounded a whole lot like things I had been through too. We were all just a bunch of retired partiers from various walks of life, but not so different. We had been maneuvering with a belief that alcohol served us, until we could finally understand that it in fact did not.

I listened to guys that were sober for mere days, then some that were sober for twenty-five years, still coming back here, just to ensure they stayed on the path they really wanted. I remember inwardly rolling my eyes at them at first. Twenty-five years seemed like a pretty clear indicator you'd be alright, why the hell still show up?

This one day a guy came in—he'd been sober for nearly a decade. He said he slipped up, got behind the wheel and nearly killed someone. He was crying in sobs. I stared at him, stunned and in disbelief. That someone could be sober for that long, yet still lose themselves with a drink—it scared the shit out of me.

It clicked then, that this drug is dangerous, and I wanted nothing to do with it. I finally stopped believing the lie that alcohol was a good thing that I would always miss. It wasn't.

All this rehashing of my journey to say, it's taken me some time to trust myself again.

WE PULL UP TO EVELYN'S house and she turns to me. "Help me unload my bags?" she asks, and I tell her of course.

We walk in and I help her get settled before giving her a

quick kiss on the cheek. I tell her to rest and call me later this week. Now's not the time to break things off or make any major decisions. I mean here I am, stuck in this limbo, helping unload luggage with a woman I asked to marry me, and all the while the love of my life is waiting for me at home.

It's fucked up, is what it is.

With Desiree now aware of everything with her father, I'm thinking I need to just get through the rest of the weekend with her as platonically as possible. Make sure she's feeling alright, no sudden memory loss or nausea symptoms popping up, and then take her back home and clear my head.

I'm getting ready to walk out and do just that when Evelyn calls my name.

I turn back to her, watch as she reaches in her purse and pulls out the ring I gave her. I stare at her, the wild red hair that she always has neatly tucked in a ponytail, now long and loose down around her shoulders.

She steps toward me. "I don't know how to say this, Taven, but I want you to take this back."

I stand there, frozen and stunned. *She's giving me the ring back. She's officially ending it.* My heart pounds at the realization. Here I am, one foot out the door, too chicken shit to break her heart just yet, and she's doing it for me.

She wants me to take the ring back. It's over.

"Say something, Taven." I see the concern all across her face. She's known all along she wants out, hasn't she?

Eventually, I verbalize the only words that I seem to be thinking. "But your text. It said you missed me." I wince at how stupid that sounds. How hypocritical, even. This is supposed to bring me relief, right? So why am I questioning her on it? Her work trip— was the guy she had mentioned been with her? I imagine wild nights they had in their hotel room, overlooking London and Big Ben and whatever the fuck else might be there.

Evelyn sighs. "Taven, this might be hard to hear, but I

thought I was texting someone else when I sent that. The guy I told you about." She looks up at me through her eyelashes, and I see the guilt on her face. I guess we're both prone to relapses.

And I guess she wasn't with him in London after all.

"Right," I slowly draw out. "You thought it was him, not me."

A nod. Maybe a tear, if I'm not mistaken, but she blinks it away and looks up at me. "I'm so sorry. I realize that's an empty string of words at this point, but...well, if I'm missing someone that's not you, then I think it's pretty telling that this here isn't working.

"And maybe it never was supposed to, Taven, if you think about it. I think I came back into your life at a time when I was lonely, and you were working through things, and we got swept up in that. *I* got swept up in that, because I do care about you, and I think I just loved the fairytale of the two kids that reconnected all those years later and fell in love after a dark time."

I huff out a laugh. Replace the woman in that fairytale with someone else, and I'm completely guilty of getting caught up in that too.

Evelyn's crying now, telling me over and over again how incredibly sorry she is, how she hopes one day I can find it in my heart to forgive her, that she should have never led me on like she has and how she was a coward for not speaking up before, but she's speaking up now and please, could I forgive her?

I step toward her and pull her into my arms for a hug, not liking seeing her fall apart and punish herself like this when I've been far from the perfect hero. "It's okay, Evelyn. Really, it's okay."

I don't mention Desiree. I don't mention the woman she knows I've always held a soft spot in my heart for, because it feels like that would be some cheap attempt at me throwing it in her face just to hurt her right back. I won't do that to her.

I hear her voice, muffled in my chest. "You'll be okay? You won't drink again?"

I pull her back. "Is that what you're worried about?"

She shrugs guiltily. "A little." I look at her and realize she's probably been holding on to this out of fears that I'd step off my path.

"Evelyn," I say into her shining green eyes. "I'm never going back to that, I know that in my gut in a way I can't really explain, but it's the truth. And it's you who helped me get to that point," I say, giving her shoulders a little shake. "But you don't owe me your whole damn life because of it. That's on me to keep up with, not you."

"You promise?" she asks.

"I promise." I hug her again until she calms down, and I reassure her that we're going to be fine. That we're better as friends, and maybe in time, we will be again.

She says she'd like that.

thirty-six

. . .

Expose

Present Day

desiree

Saturday, 5:00pm

"I STOLE HIS car," I say as I shove past Melissa, into the Belle household where, like always, some dinner in progress is filling the air with scents of garlic and herbs and other deliciousness that normally I'd be all for, but right now I just feel like I could throw up.

She looks over my shoulder and widens her eyes at the car parked on her street. "Inferno! She still lives?"

I nod and race down the steps to her old room, still painted pink like when we were kids. Walls still lined with the cast of *Twilight* and Melissa's personal heroes, Meryl Streep and Lin-Manuel Miranda. There's even an old 8x10 football photo of my brother, and I love that I can still laugh at that, even with everything I'm feeling right now. I love that even with Melissa's success, she still stays here in her childhood home when she's in town to visit, and that it's a time capsule of our best memories. It's exactly what I need.

I flop myself on her bed and squeeze one of her pillows into my chest, feeling just as heartbroken as any sixteen-year-old girl might.

"So what happened?" she asks, standing above me with hands on her hips. "Did Evelyn show up? Demand you stay away from her man?"

"No," I mumble through her pillow. I pull it back from my face. "Something worse. Some horrific lie spun by *his mother*, by *Lynda*, and Taven actually believes it."

A divot forms between her brows. "Oh. I didn't see that coming. What do you mean, what kind of lie?"

I go on to explain what Taven told me, and how sad I am that he actually believes my father could do something like that. But how even more fucked up it would be if we were to actually be together, and I'd be looking at trying to share my life with a man whose mother is hell-bent on ruining my father's name. All because she's always looked down on us and wanted some crazy way to cut ties with me and my family.

Melissa sits down next to me, lays down and curls her body around mine, spooning me gently while her hand rubs my arm. "Where would she come up with something like that?"

I fiddle with the rhinestones on her nails. "I bet Jacqui had a little innocent crush on my dad or something, and Lynda just ran with it."

"And you don't think it's possible that it's true?"

I freeze for a moment, then spin around and turn to face her. "My *father*? And a teenaged girl?" I pull my head back. "Do I believe he ever stepped out on my mom? Sure. But with a girl still in high school?"

Melissa sighs and sits up, then pulls my hands into hers.

"Sweetie, I think it's worth considering that it could be true. Lynda didn't just make it up."

I stare up at her in disbelief, then sit up and tuck my feet beneath me. "Lynda is a fucking snob, Mel. She always has been, and you can't trust people like that. They'll do and say anything all for their own agenda because they look down on everyone around them."

I study her eyes for some indication that she agrees, for a similar hatred toward Taven's mother that I'm fueling by the minute as we speak.

But instead, her expression just looks sad. "But Dez."

I wait a few beats. She is just staring at me, as if attempting to communicate with unspoken words.

"What? What are you trying to tell me?" I implore, my eyes stinging from not blinking.

She continues slowly. "Eleven years ago, when I was just nineteen years old..."

I sit motionless and wait for her to continue.

"Your father seduced me too."

I'M IN COMPLETE DISBELIEF AND shock, just stunned silent and listening with wide eyes when Melissa spills out her story.

The story of how my father had been in New York on business. Melissa was in some off-Broadway play. My father had reached out to her, joked he was sick of hearing me brag about her performance and he wanted to come see the star for himself. He wanted to support his daughter's best friend while he was in town.

It wasn't a big role that Melissa had. My father had brought along some work buddies, and she hoped they wouldn't be disappointed, feeling mounting pressure. She had been struggling with insecurities, the director that she had been developing feelings for, only to sleep with him and then watch him drop her and move on to the next cast member. She questioned whether or not she even had any talent, or if she had gotten the part just because the guy wanted to fuck her.

They went back to his hotel and had some drinks in the lounge. She was hiccuping and realizing she really needed to go, the rest of the men had all left by then, and it was just the two of them. But he was being so nice to her, and she had been having such a hard time adjusting in New York, no longer the big fish in a small pond. Against her better judgment, she agreed to one more drink. Through the blur of extra alcohol, she knew stumbling back to her dorm room was not the smartest idea, so when my dad suggested they go up to his hotel room, she agreed.

She marveled over the view of the city, something she believed would never get old. He came up behind her. He stroked her cheek. He told her there was nothing as beautiful as she was. She turned around, surprised but also intrigued. It was when my parents were separated, she wouldn't be considered a homewrecker, right? One night. She'd allow herself one night with a *real man* to quell her loneliness, and everything would be fine.

She spared me the details of what happened next, but she said when she woke up, she immediately went to the bathroom and threw up, disgusted and ashamed with herself. She ran out of there and back to her dorm room, then proceeded to fall into the arms of the next guy who paid the slightest bit of attention to her. He turned out to be another colossal mistake, emotionally abusive and horrifically possessive.

It's why she stopped talking to me. She couldn't face me, she could barely face herself in those days.

I stare at her as she says all this, wondering what my reaction should be. Mad? Nope, that's not it. At my father, yes. But not her. Scared? That feels a bit closer. Of what exactly, I'm not sure. But there's fear in my chest, I know that.

"Why didn't you tell me sooner?" I ask. "I mean, it's not even my business, but I would have understood."

"Would you, though? Would you have believed me? That your dad fed me drinks and hooked his talons into me like that, and not that I asked for it somehow?"

I think about what she's saying. And I realize with bitterness that at that time, no, I probably would not have understood. I probably would have blamed her.

Because that was when I was young, before snake guy, when I sat on a mighty high throne of self-righteousness. Before I had experienced a similar series of choices that ultimately led to me being taken advantage of. Something that wildly shifted my own views and understandings of the truths about scary things that previously sat in a comfortable box of lies I told myself, labeled That Would Never Happen to Me, with a subheading of (Because I'm Definitely Smarter Than That).

I feel a wave of shame as I realize that. Shame in the way naïveté had me living in a sheltered place of not believing certain things existed in the world. Not close to me, anyhow. I think about when I was younger, the number of times my immature mouth called someone a name behind their back, never even thinking about what that person was going through or had been through, passing judgment on them when I didn't have a damn clue about anything and should have been shutting my mouth.

I think about Melissa and the boys she used to cycle through when we were in high school. So much outward confidence that landed her lots of guys, but how many insecurities was she really holding back then? It never occurred to me that Melissa was anything other than a cool, sexy hopeless romantic who liked to sleep around.

Oh, how I had envied her and that obvious confidence she exhibited when we were teenagers. Oh, how I wanted to hold boys in the palm of my hand like she did, wanted so badly to be a natural shiny star like she was. Yet looking at it with older and wiser eyes, I see the pain she must have had brewing beneath the surface.

After my sessions with Ruth, after my brief fling with Taven when I made the hardest decision in walking away, I reclaimed my sexuality with an adventurous attitude. I never got close to anyone, but enjoyed the luxury of casual sex, armed with a new knowledge of what I actually liked and how to ask for it. Sex was *fun* for me, finally. Might others judge me for that? Maybe.

Because no one knows what really goes on behind someone else's closed doors. We love to judge as a fool hearted way of protecting ourselves, but it only limits our ability to truly have compassion.

I look back at Melissa. I hug her and tell her I'm sorry that my father is a scumbag. She tells me it's alright, it's not my fault. She says she feels better finally being able to get it off her chest.

I release her and push myself back to lean against her headboard. "Was it hard to see him again, when my mom was sick?" I think about how she dropped everything to come back to Ohio at the time. The way she lit up the room and made my mom laugh while lying on her hospital bed.

Melissa shrugs. "Oh, Frank Hatson is just a broken little boy that's starved for love, I paid him no mind," she says through a smile. But I see it. The truth in her eyes. That yes, it was hard. I can't even imagine. But she came anyway. She did it for me.

"Thank you, Mel," I say.

She nods. "Enough about me. What are you going to do now? Or are we just waiting for the police to show up to retrieve the stolen car out front?"

I scoot over to the side of the bed and rise to a stand. "I'm going to drive back to his house, use the time to sort through all the shit I've just learned about my father today, and then I'm going to continue my precious forty-eight hours with Taven."

"Are you sure you're feeling alright?" she asks. "I could drive you if you want."

I shake my head no. I assure her I'm fine, and that the doctors just have to say these things to cover their asses.

She smiles at me. "Well then, way to take advantage of doctor's orders. Now go fall madly in love with your man all over again."

"I will."

"Although," she says, pulling her lip between her teeth. "What about Evelyn?"

I shrug. "What about her? She's no Dazzle to him."

"Cocky bitch," she mutters before smacking my ass and telling me to get out of here. She instructs me to call her when I arrive. I promise her I will as I walk over to the picture of my brother on the wall. "I'm taking this."

She reaches over dramatically, trying to snatch it from my hands. "But no! I love that photo, I'm still holding out for hope!"

"Mel," I say. "This was him in college. He went on to the NFL, remember?"

"And?"

"I'm getting you a new one. Signed." I wink at her and walk out of her room.

And wonder bitterly if my dreams of having Melissa as my sister-in-law are over, since a different Hatson got to her first.

thirty-seven

· · ·

Anticipate

Present Day

taven

Saturday, 8:07pm

I STARE OUT the window, hoping for the moment I see Inferno pulling into the driveway. I had been pacing the house wildly, calling Desiree, calling Melissa, not even knowing if the numbers I had for them were accurate. Desiree's was, though I got no answer. Melissa's was not, so I looked up the number to her childhood home, a house with a landline, and I dialed that. I mumbled my way through a quick hello to Mrs. Belle, hearing the shrieks that she must be having a stroke, that it's 2011 all over again, and my old car is parked in front of her home and now here I am, calling the house. I breathe the slightest bit of relief at her joke, knowing Desiree's safe. She drove up to Melissa's, though I don't like the idea of her driving when just this morning she still had a headache.

When Melissa got on the phone, she assured me Desiree was fine. On her way back to me, in fact, she just needed to process what I had told her. She explained that Desiree didn't even believe me at first, which—call me dumb—wasn't even something I had considered.

To me, I've been carrying around this knowledge of the kind of person Frank Hatson really is all this time. For nearly fifteen years, my family has lived with this dark spot on our collective history, the villain of the Carlisle story, invading our home and our lives. I had to mentally separate that villain from the man that called himself Desiree's father. I couldn't handle thinking of them as the same person. In many ways, I think it was just an added layer of the subtle ways I always kept Desiree at arm's length, back in our early days of college. It was haunting, and a struggle to come to terms with the fact that this girl I loved so much was the product of a man who had damaged my beloved sister. The ultimate tug of war in my mind to try and marry the two concepts of Frank Hatson—father of my girl, and perpetrator. None of that was fair to Desiree.

I hadn't even thought about how completely unbelievable the story would be to Desiree. Since I only worried about hurting her, I hadn't even considered that she might struggle to believe it, and I'd be pushing her away due to her thoughts that I had been buying into some lie.

Thank God she went to Melissa. Thank God Melissa somehow got her to see that it was all true.

When I asked how she convinced Desiree to believe the hard truth, Melissa was quiet. I could hear her breathing on the other end of the line, and eventually she spoke. "Taven," she said. "Just...one of these days, tell your sister that she's not alone in falling into that pervert's trap, okay?"

A wave of nausea combined with a punch to the gut. "How old were you?" I snapped, not meaning to be so abrupt with it, but I was going to fucking murder that bastard if he had done this to Melissa when she was still a child. I almost hoped he had, twisted as that is, because then, just maybe, justice could actually be served if Melissa had some way to provide evidence. A sick spark of hope churned in that idea.

I attempted to calm myself, not willing to let my torment and anger be wrongly unleashed on Melissa. "I'm sorry," I said. "That came out rougher than I meant. You don't have to tell me if you don't want."

"It's alright," she said. "Might as well hear it from me and not make Desiree have to rehash it. But it was after high school, just one time when I was nineteen. Biggest regret of my life."

"No, Mel," I say. "It's him that should have regrets, not you, alright?"

She blows out a sigh. "Thanks, Vin."

I tell her it's all good. That I know all too well about mistakes and regrets and things we wish we could erase.

She says, "But all that living...that's the stuff an actor's emotions are made of." I tell her that she has more grit and resilience than she realizes, and that if anyone can turn a tragedy into an award-winning career, it's her.

***

WHEN THE PURR OF INFERNO'S engine finally roars its way into my ears, I nearly faint with relief. It's dark now, and while I know Desiree's a big girl, I still feel the desire to protect her. I rush out through the mudroom, down the hall of glass that connects the house and the garage, and open the door to see my car idling in front of the open garage door.

The driver's side window rolls down. Desiree's blonde head pops out. "Hi," she says. "I took your car."

I jog over to her. "I see that," I say, smiling. "You can take any of them, any time you want."

She nods and looks toward the garage. "I appreciate that. But I'm kinda nervous to try and pull it in there."

I open the door and grab her hand to help her out. "I got it, no worries. Go head inside." I slide into the car, and smile at the scent of Desiree in here, something that feels so right. I rev the engine a little, showing off, I can't help myself, and she laughs as she watches me maneuver my original baby safely into its spot.

We walk together through the mudroom and into the kitchen. She passes the island and plops down on a seat by the kitchen table. I ask her if she's hungry, and she says she's starving. I walk over to the fridge and pull out the chicken soup we never got to eat. "Do you want some wine or anything?" I ask her.

She looks at me, startled. "Do you keep wine in the house?"

I put the pot back on the stove and turn on the burner, then lean against the counter and slip my hands in my pockets. "Not usually, but I like to be able to offer whatever a guest might want."

She stays planted in her seat, frowning. "Isn't that hard for you?"

"No, Dazzle. Not anymore."

"And you're not tempted to even take a sip or anything?" I can see the skepticism in her face. The worry that she's stepped right back into five years ago. What I wouldn't give to make her feel secure that the me of five years ago is long gone.

I attempt to explain. "I'm not tempted to take so much as a sip, because I no longer believe alcohol serves me. And I understand that my body doesn't process alcohol the same way, say, yours does." I walk over to the table and take the seat beside her, turning to face her. I lean forward, my arms on my thighs. "When you drink too much, what happens to you? Do you get sick? Black out?"

She frowns. "I mean, generally speaking I'm a little more

responsible than I used to be—other than a few days ago, but that's another story."

"So you don't black out?" I ask, trying to ease her into this concept but needing her to understand.

She shakes her head. "No, I don't. A little fuzzy memory, maybe, but I've never blacked out."

I grab her hands. "Well, I do. And it's because I was known to binge drink now and then when I was a dumbass kid, which means today, I might have a drink or two and be totally fine, or I might wake up in the morning with no recollection of what happened. A total blackout. People would sometimes tell me I hadn't even had much to drink on one of those nights, or they didn't realize how bad off I was. Yet just like that," I say with a snap of my fingers, "I could experience a blackout anyway. It's pretty terrifying to realize that something could affect you so completely like that, and beyond your control. At some point I did realize it, though. And it's not something I'm willing to risk ever again." I study her face for a reaction, wait for her to say something, but she remains quiet, so I continue.

"When the urge to drink was strongest, it was when I was most at war with myself. I'm not anymore, not at that level, anyhow. I've learned how to actually *feel* things, even when it's hard or uncomfortable. I don't need something like alcohol to escape what I've got going on. So do I think I could have a beer and be able to stop from going further? Maybe. But it's the blackouts that scare me the most, and I recognize that nothing's worth that risk of losing whole nights and having no idea what even happened.

"I think of it like an allergy," I try and explain. "Not everyone agrees on that concept, but for me it's helpful. So think of it like this—if you were allergic to peanuts, you wouldn't try a bite of one, right? Not even a taste?"

"No," she whispers. My Dazzle puts her hands on my cheeks,

shakes her head again, saying, "No, I wouldn't," and then leans forward and kisses me. I slide her chair closer to me and deepen our kiss, feeling everything she's trying to say in it.

That she's sorry I've had this battle. That she's proud of me. She forgives me.

I plant one final kiss on her soft lips and take her hands in mine. I press my forehead to hers, wanting to get her fed before I end up throwing her on this table and abandoning this damn soup yet again. "I appreciate your concern for me, I really do, Dazzle. It means so fucking much to me, especially with all I know I put you through. Something I vow never to let happen again." My chest tightens as I say the words, nearly choking on them.

She squeezes my hand. "I love you, Taven."

I gently rub my thumb in circles over the back of her hand, trying to catch my breath at hearing her say those words. "Listen," I say, my voice quiet. "I want you to know that I don't ever want people around me to feel uncomfortable, or start feeling like they need to act differently, refraining from their own drinks, okay?"

"Okay."

"Good," I say, pulling away and planting a kiss to her forehead. "So. Dazzle. Answer me honestly. Would you like a glass of wine with your soup? I don't have any here but I would be happy to run into town and get you some."

She raises my hand and kisses it. "No, Taven. I don't need wine to enjoy my dinner. But I would love some tea if you have it."

"Done."

I get up and head to the cupboard, pulling out a basket of options for her to choose from. She smiles and selects a green tea, and I grab one for myself as well.

I contemplate the packets of tea in my hand for a moment

before smiling back and saying, "I love you too, Desiree Hope Hatson." I lean down and kiss her on her cheek. "You have no idea how much I love you."

———

WE FINISH OUR DINNER AND make our way to the family room. Desiree sits on the couch in front of the fireplace, and I throw some logs in, strike a long match and get the fire going.

She hums, "An actual fireplace, I think that might be my favorite feature of this house." She sips her mug of hot tea as I settle down next to her.

"Mine too. One of many, really." I pull her legs over my lap and massage her calves. "How are you feeling?"

She leans her head back on a throw pillow and settles herself. "Mmm, much better now, thank you. I mean, I want to kill my dad a little bit. I still can't wrap my head around everything with that."

"I'm sorry I had to be the one to tell you."

She smiles. "Remember the Bingo squares from when we were sixteen? Say something uncomfortable to someone you care about?"

I make my way down to her feet, pressing my thumbs into the arches. "How could I forget?" I say. "It's where it all started, you and me."

"Still one of my favorite memories, there in the dealership when you bought Inferno."

"Mine too," I agree.

"And after tonight, I'd say you deserve a whole row of squares crossed off for that one."

I nod and continue with her foot massage, pressing in circles as if I could erase away the painful truth she's trying to absorb about her father. I ask her if she'll ever approach him about it, and she says she doesn't know. She's putting it aside for right now. What's in the past is in the past, and beyond her control anyway. Some things in life are hard to accept, but that's all you can do.

She finally asks me about Evelyn. "Did you break her heart today?" It's funny to think how insignificant that topic seems given all we've been covering since Desiree's been here. Predator fathers and the poisons of addiction. A precarious engagement suddenly doesn't even seem that important.

But her voice is quiet, and I can see the bit of guilt she's holding.

I stretch out and wiggle her toes, one by one. "Actually, she broke my heart today." I see her startled response and I pat her feet. "It's okay. The writing's been on the wall for a while now. She just finally pulled the plug."

"What do you think prompted it? Was it me?"

I sigh. "No, baby, not you. Another guy, apparently. Someone she works with."

"Ahh," she says. "The good old work romance. Are you okay?"

"I really am, Dazzle." I turn my body toward her. "There's been someone else that I've liked for a long time now. I just didn't think they liked me back," I say with a smile, hoping she remembers the times she would say that to me, back when we were kids. How I'd know she meant me, but I was too scared to admit my feelings for her.

But it's how our friendship became so strong, and in many ways, I don't think there's anything that can replace the power of that foundation she and I have. It runs through us, steadfast and sturdy, and I think it's the exact reason why I believe we can get through anything together, Dazzle and me. We can get through the pain of what happened with her father and my sister. Through the pain I caused her five years ago. So while I regret hurting her or making her question how incredibly worthy of my childhood crush she was at that time, I don't regret the best friends we became in the process.

She pulls her feet back and crawls over to me, taking my face in her hands. "They like you back. Always have," she says with a soft kiss. "Now go wash your hands so you can make sweet love to me."

thirty-eight

. . .

Crash

Present Day

desiree

Sunday, 10:11am

I'M CURLED UP and reading a book on Taven's patio when I realize I no longer have a ringing in my ear. It feels like the sweetest victory, I had googled stories of people's encounters with lightning and was discouraged by how many have experienced long-term hearing damage. But as I sit here now, Taven beside me and also reading, something I'm shocked to see, I can hear the subtle rustle of the leaves when a breeze picks up. I can hear the nearby babbling of the stream, the distant sound of cars winding through the hills on the roads beyond. It feels peaceful.

Taven asks me what I want to do today, and I shrug. "Sitting here doing this feels pretty perfect. I'm back to work tomorrow." Then something dawns on me. "Wait, did you have tickets for the music festival for the whole weekend?"

He shakes his head no. "I was just going Friday night, knowing I'd have to pick up Evelyn."

I lean back. "Oh, that's too bad. I was going to say we could go. Today's the last day, and I was actually looking forward to seeing The Killers. My mom loved them."

He reaches over to me and squeezes my knee. "I'll make it up to you. A future show to see The Killers, I promise."

I smile. "So you think there's a future with us?"

He laughs. "God, after what I did to you last night and this morning, I sure as fuck hope so. I'm not letting you go."

I laugh too, my belly flipping at the thought of our night together. Of me against the massive window in his living room, overlooking the night sky, back pressed to it while he pumped into me over and over again in sweet ecstasy. Then later, in his bed, him trailing ice all over my naked body, one hand locking my wrists in a hold above my head, a feverish ache between my legs that had me squirming with need, begging him to fuck me.

And again this morning. In the shower. Me on my knees, taking Taven Carlisle into my mouth and bringing him to an orgasm, nearly dying at the sweet relief of finally tasting all of him while his body trembled within my grasp. I felt so incredible doing so, like nothing I'd ever felt before. He told me he loved me, that I was his and he was never letting go.

I look over at him and smile. "We're going to finally do this right, aren't we?"

He nodded. "We have to. It's time."

LATER IN THE AFTERNOON WHEN I suggest we take a drive in Inferno to go visit my mom, he says he'd love to. That he himself had thought about visiting her, but never did.

"How often do you go see her?" he asks me as we make our way into the cemetery. I look at the rows of gray stone, some with fresh flowers, and I inhale the fragrance of the bouquet in my own hands.

"I've only gone once, actually," I confess. "On the first anniversary after her death. It felt too hard, and I just sat there and cried and wondered if something was wrong with me that I didn't visit more often."

"Everyone grieves differently," he says. He reaches over and grabs my hand, and it makes me think of all the times we'd spent in this car, doing this exact thing. Just two kids in love, no idea of all the terrible things happening around us. My mom's sickness. Jacqui and my dad. I wonder if the thing with Jacqui started after my dad learned of my mom's cancer. If it was his way of going insane over it. I can never forgive him for his actions, but I can at least have a better understanding of the torment he must have been feeling. He loved my mom, I do believe that. We all have a variety of ways of either dealing with or avoiding our problems. Taven used to drink. My mom smoked and popped pills. My dad apparently liked young women, just barely out of girlhood.

I think about my own ways of dealing with things. When I was younger, I would just avoid. Never allowing myself to get close to anyone, just keeping everyone at arm's length. It seemed safer that way, though my therapist Ruth would gently push me to see what I was doing. I wonder why I'm like that. Part of it is my own struggles with feeling dependent on anyone, that much I know. I like to feel special, and it's hard to do that at the same time as being vulnerable with someone else, so I subconsciously side-step it.

Taven makes me feel special, though. He always has, the way he looks at me like I'm something incredible, something to be cherished.

Even in those dark couple of months five years ago, when we were back together, and he was drinking. The straw that broke the camel's back happened right in this very car.

We had gone out to dinner, were heading home, and he was driving erratically. I hadn't realized just how drunk he was, but I should have known better. I had already confronted him at that point about his drinking. How I didn't think cracking a beer at 9am was a good idea, and he'd say he had a hangover, to lay off because it was just a light beer to wash away the remnants of last night's Scotch. That the beer would help him go back to bed and then he'd be fine.

So when we were on the highway that night and he was pushing a hundred miles per hour, I was cursing myself for being so stupid. I was gripping the handle on the door and pushing my feet into an imaginary brake pedal, begging him to slow down. On the verge of tears, asking him what was wrong with him, why he was drinking so much. And for the love of God, please slow down.

"You wanna know why I drink so much, Dazzle?" he said, eyes wild and huffing out a sarcastic laugh. "It's you."

I had looked at him, hurt and terrified and confused. "Me?" I asked, trying to make sense of the world literally flashing before my eyes in the fast lane.

"Yeah," he said. "Because I'm just fucking waiting for the day you're going to wake up and realize you could do much better than me. Admit it! You know that's what you think!" He was shouting at that point, swerving and yelling and saying such unfathomable things. I was dumbfounded, wondering what on earth was happening, and how I never saw it coming. "Don't fucking lie to me, Desiree! You miss your fucking surgeon and are regretting pissing your life away with a loser, just thinking how much better than me you are!"

I started crying, pleading with him to know how stupid that was, how not true. He looked at me with something akin to contempt, though I know it was for himself and not me. "Don't do that, Desiree," he said. "Don't fucking sit here and *lie* to me and tell me you don't regret being with me! Don't disrespect me like that! Don't you dare." He lowered his voice and started eerily laughing. I looked at him like he was a stranger that I didn't even know. "Little miss goodie-two-shoes, too good for everyone else. Now with the fucking mechanic! Bet you thought I was better than that, right? I have the Carlisle name, don't I?"

I floated outside my body, realizing he wasn't even talking to me at that point, not really. I remained silent. I had already learned by then that when he was like this, there was not a thing I could say that was "right." Nothing to break through to him. He was yelling at me to answer him, to say all the shit he just knew I wanted to say, but I stayed quiet. He continued to antagonize me, saying the most hurtful things that I'd rather soon forget, and I just prayed that we could miraculously make it home safely. I'd figure out what to do then. I just wanted out of this situation. I prayed to my mom, *Please, Mom, if you can hear me. Please, please. Mom, just do what you can from wherever you are. Please try, so we can make it home in one piece. Help me. Please...show me a sign and tell me you're there...*

I played my silent prayer to my mom on repeat, it was all I could think to do. *Mom, please...* My heart was pounding, I was terrified, misery creeping in at the realization that nothing was as it seemed. I clung to a hope that my mom was out there somewhere, watching over us, and that she could intervene and put an end to this moment before Taven killed us both, and anyone else in his way. It was all I could think to do.

At some point he started to switch lanes, and I screamed for him to stop, that there was another car in the way. He slammed on the brakes, Inferno twisting and careening while I clung on for dear life, the world spinning around me in agonizing drawn-out moments.

We came to a stop on the shoulder. We were facing the wrong direction. I saw headlights whizzing past, horns screeching as I tried to catch my breath, realizing we were alive. We were okay. *Thank you, thank you, Mom,* I said in my silent prayer. I imagined her comforting palm on my head. I heard her voice, telling me it's okay, but to leave, darling girl. That it's time to go. To listen and know that it's time to walk away.

I looked over to Taven, who looked stunned and unable to process what just happened, not like I had, anyway. "Holy shit," he said. "What the fuck was that?"

I popped the car in park and snatched the key fob from the console where Taven kept them. I opened the door, walked a few steps on the pavement where cars were whizzing past us and honking. A car pulled up to us, parking on the shoulder, the headlights blinding me. The driver opened the door and asked if we were okay. I was shaking and terrified, wiping my tears and realizing how close we just came to death. I told the person we were fine, just lost control for a minute, but everything was fine. I tried to smile and reassure him and act like everything was perfectly normal. I worried the guy would look at Taven and question his sobriety. Even in that moment, after everything that just happened, I was worried about Taven getting in trouble. I'd cover for him and get us out of this. Hop in the driver's seat and get us home before this guy could call the cops and make things any worse.

When I turned back to Inferno and made my way to the driver's side, the door was open. Taven wasn't in his seat. I looked ahead to see him walking along the guard rail, I could barely make out his frame in the dark. I panicked, not knowing what to do. I had this other driver waiting to confirm I was alright, Taven's car crooked on the shoulder, headlights piercing the night around me. What should I do?

I got in the car, turned it on and carefully turned it around and back on the road, relieved when I saw the Good Samaritan drive off as well.

I left Taven to walk home, praying he'd make it back safely. I hoped he'd walk off his drunken haze and decide tonight would be his last time drinking.

He did make it home.

But the next morning, he didn't remember a single thing.

I LINK MY ARM IN Taven's as we walk up to my mom's headstone. It's warm outside, the last days of summer upon us, and a light breeze gently blows my sundress against my legs. I kneel down to place my bouquet on the ground, frowning at the fresh flowers already there. Lilies and dahlias and roses, all my mom's favorites. Plus a singular sprig of a holly branch, all beautifully arranged in a vase. From my father?

Taven stands above me. "Who are those from?" he asks.

I look up to him, shielding my eyes from the sun, and nearly fall over when I see Lynda Carlisle walking up behind him. "They're from me," she says. I feel like I must have misheard her.

Taven turns around, the shock on his face mirroring mine. "Mom? What are you doing here?"

"Hello, Desiree," she says with a nod to me, then a nod toward her son. "Taven. I was visiting my old friend Holly, that's what I was doing." She says it as if this is the most natural thing in the world, not like she's admitting to visiting with a woman she had written off many years ago. "I was just leaving when I saw your car pull up. Not exactly a common car to see on the road."

"You could say that," I agree, eyes narrowed and trying to process her presence.

She nods, then looks back and forth between us. "But I certainly didn't expect to see the two of you walk up, arm in arm. Might I ask what's going on?"

I rise up to a stand, heart racing and legs a little wobbly, like a kid caught cheating on a test.

Taven grabs my hand. Lynda looks down at our clasped hands, her mouth in a firm line. "Evelyn called off the engagement," he explains, I suppose hoping his mother forgives what she probably sees as a grave indecency, her son standing here with me, holding my hand.

Lynda tilts her head to the side. "She what? When did that happen?"

Taven sighs and attempts to explain the briefest recap. That Evelyn had paused the engagement some time ago, and finally just recently ended things with him.

He doesn't share that it was just yesterday.

"I'm sorry to hear that, Taven." I watch as her dark eyes consider him for a moment. "Did something happen? Anything I should know about?"

I see it now what Taven was talking about. That he's not sure how much trust his parents hold in him. She wants to know if he's drinking again. She wants to know what he might have done to cause Evelyn to walk away.

I feel his body tense up beside me. "If you're implying that I might have taken to old habits, you can save yourself the trouble. That's not what happened." He diverts his eyes down to me momentarily. "Nor is it because of this, so don't even bother with trying to pass judgment."

I'm proud of him for speaking up. I know it must be hard to for him to have his own mother look at him the way she is right now.

I wish so much that his mother could have the same kind of faith in her son that I do. I can't blame her for her concern, I imagine any mother would have it, but I have a suspicion that Lynda Carlisle is the type of woman to attempt to identify where the problem is. Her default setting. I can see the way that Taven feels like he's in a constant battle of having to prove her wrong.

She heaves out a sigh. "When my son suddenly appears to have a new girlfriend, when just last week, as far as I knew, he was engaged to someone else, you can't possibly expect me to not have some questions. *Especially* given your past.

"And may I remind you that it was me who had to force you into rehab and help you get your life together." She looks over to me. "Thanks to this one's concern for you."

I look up at Taven. Did he know that I'm the one to have called his mom five years ago? Would he be upset with me? I hope not. I'd like to think he would understand why I did what I did, but I would have preferred to have told him myself. I had planned to, just to clear the air, but thanks to Lynda, he's now hearing it from her.

Lynda narrows her eyes at Taven. "Did you realize that it was Desiree that alerted me to your problems?"

He tilts his chin up. "She did the right thing. I have her to thank."

I breathe out a sigh of relief in hearing him say that. I can only hope he means it, and it's not just him keeping face for his mom. Either way, I like that he's choosing us as a united front in her presence. It feels significant. Like we're finally standing together as one, on the same page and ready to face whatever we need to. Together, no secrets or lies, just freely and beautifully us.

His mom's face softens, just the slightest bit. "I agree. I can only hope you never again put her through the hell you once did."

He huffs out a laugh, then releases my hand and crosses his arms over his chest. "Don't you think I feel bad enough about my mistakes already?"

"As you should," she insists.

I just stand there, eyes switching back and forth between them like I'm watching a showdown about to take place, and I'd rather be watching on a screen, not here in the flesh.

He takes a step toward her mother. "I can appreciate that you've always worked to instill good principles in me and Jacqui,

I really can. And I can even appreciate that you hope I don't slip up again, because I admit, I've not always been the perfect son.

"But what I can't understand is why not a single ounce of you holds any kind of question regarding *how* or *why* I struggled so much in the first place. Only questioning how long I could potentially keep my shit together."

"Of course I question why you struggled," she says.

He narrows his eyes at her. "In what ways, as it relates to you? Wondering why your son isn't like you or Dad? Wondering how you were cursed with the kid who would rather be taking apart engines instead of designing the world's latest technologies?

"Because I gotta tell you, Mom. If I were you, I'd be wondering what I might have done wrong as a mother, wanting to know how I ended up with an alcoholic son, or a daughter who threw herself in the arms of a *predator*," his says, spitting out the word, "in the first place."

"Taven," I say, placing my hand on his arm and willing him not to do this right now. In front of my mother's grave. My chest tightens as I look at Lynda's face.

And then I see it. The hurt in her eyes. A mother who loves her child, and realizes she maybe got a few things wrong.

But Taven continues. "You put so much pressure on us as kids, it crushed us. Squeezed the fucking life out of us that we never felt like we were getting anything right, do you realize that? Just when we were doing something good for ourselves, you'd push us to whatever that next level was. An impossible ladder with no end, and nothing ever felt good enough. Ever." His chest rises as he takes in a breath. He unwinds arms and places one around me. "I know I haven't exactly made you proud in the ways I've lived my life, and that I've hurt and maybe even scared you when I've been at my worst, and for that I truly am sorry. I am."

"But?" Lynda offers, and I can't help but smile, because I can see the pride she's feeling in seeing her son stand up to her right now. Even if Taven can't see it, I do. An unmistakable look of a mother's pride in watching her son speak his truth and face his biggest battle—the one within himself.

I've seen it in my work with parents and their children. I've seen it in small moments like when a child bravely takes that needle administering a vaccine. Or when a daughter courageously hears some diagnosis and says, "Okay, what now?" There's fear and sadness in a parent's eyes, but also the undeniable proud look of love. Watching their child grow right before their very eyes. And I can see it in Lynda's eyes now, too.

Taven squeezes my shoulder. "Even if you don't agree with my choices, the least you could do is respect that I'm living the life I'm meant to. And I'm doing it sober, and I'm happy. I'm finally really and truly happy, Mom."

Lynda smiles. "I have more pride and faith in you than you could ever possibly know, Taven Carlisle." She looks to her side, eyes caught on some distant sight. "I didn't exactly have the greatest model for a mother, so maybe I'm not the best at showing affection." She looks back to him. "But I don't ever want you to doubt for one second how much I love you. And all I've ever wanted was for you to be comfortable and secure and happy." She shrugs, and it's such a simple and human gesture that defies the usual statuesque sight of her. "Your happiness is everything to me." She steps forward and kisses his cheek, then steps to me and does the same.

"It's good to see you both. I'll leave you to be with Holly, now," she says as she turns to go.

I look up at Taven, who looks stunned. He expected some backlash from his mother after his rant, I imagine. I'm tempted to laugh at how blind we can all sometimes be to the things that are right in front of us. His doubt in his mother's love and support wasn't just because of her, no matter how stoic her default setting might naturally be. It was because of his own struggles to see all the wonderful qualities he has within. To accept himself fully and completely. It's something I understand.

I call over to Lynda as she's walking away. "Wait," I say. "Lynda, wait up." I jog over to her and place my hand on her shoulder.

"Yes, my dear?"

"It's good to see you," I say, realizing it's not a lie. "But before you go, do you mind explaining what you meant when you said you were visiting with your friend, Holly?"

She stares at me for a moment, then glances back to Taven. When her eyes meet mine again, she smiles. "You really don't know? Your mother never told you?" she asks with surprise.

"Know what?" I ask.

She plays with the pearls around her neck. "A woman of her word, then. Down to her dying days, I suppose." A sigh. "I would have thought she had told you, especially before her death."

"Told me what?"

You'd think I'd be nervous to hear what Lynda has to say, but I'm not. Her face is warm and smiling, like whatever it is I don't know is in fact a good thing.

The breeze picks up and Lynda's flawless dark hair floats gently around her face. She brushes a few strands aside and nods her head toward the small walkway ahead. "Come on. Let's take a walk. And I'll tell you all about the way your mother and I met, and the sister I soon started to think of her to be."

thirty-nine

. . .

Sacrifice

Thirty-eight years ago

lynda carlisle

eighteen years old

THE AIR HAD been frigid that day, the old house creaking and the radiator thumping like its life depended on it. In reality, all the girls that lived within the Jennifer Grace Cottage lives depended on the enveloping warmth of the far outdated radiator. The whole contraption taunted the girls with its pitiful powers that often left the home as frigid as an igloo. Lynda gave the radiator a kick, realizing she'd need to tinker with it again. She had the magic touch, the only one who ever seemed to get it working right.

She was just about to head to the closet in search of the toolbox when the front door opened, a gust of cold air bursting in with it. Lynda looked up to see who was entering, and in tumbled their newest housemate.

The teen girl was horrifically thin, blonde with stringy hair and dark circles cupping the hollow space below her eyes, as if ready to catch tears. Lynda had a feeling that the well of tears in this poor young girl with the small smile and timid wave was all but dry.

Something lurched in her heart for the poor thing. Perhaps it was that the latest newcomer reminded Lynda of her own mother. Frail. Broken. Helpless. A shell of a soul, barely even standing. She wondered what the girl was high on, the marks of self-medicating clear all over her frame.

Lynda was tasked with showing the new girl around. Hope, that's what she said her name was, though the sardonic laugh that accompanied it told Lynda that hope was the last thing she felt.

Lynda could relate.

"I WAS RAPED," HOPE SAID, sitting at the edge of Lynda's bed. Lynda fought the urge to tell the tired and tattered girl to get up and shower before soiling the neat folds of her small cot, the one place she actually considered her own within the home. Now was not the time for her compulsive neatness, though.

"Raped?" Lynda asked, as if it was a word she did not understand. Of course she understood it—had lived it herself, time and time again. Many of the girls of the home had.

Still, the word "rape" was one no one liked to use. Lynda felt herself tensing at the sound of the word's compilation of vowels and consonants. Yet she admired this girl's ability to say it without hesitation.

"Yes, raped," Hope repeated, eyes in a glaze as she stared at the threadbare carpet below them. Finally, her pale and haunting eyes looked up at Lynda. "For the final time, anyway."

It was all she spoke that night. After her admission, Lynda

directed the girl to her own bed, the one on the other side of the small window. Lynda had enjoyed a brief few weeks of having a room of her own in the house, but she did not mind the company of the home's latest newcomer.

The mattress creaked with a piercing wheeze as Hope curled her small frame into a ball, turning away from Lynda. The dots of her spine could be seen through her thin sweater, stretching out across her back like old railroad tracks, desolate and searching for some unknown destination.

Lynda rose from her cot. She lifted the plush blanket she had purchased with her own money and draped it over the girl's body. Lynda felt that Hope needed it more than she did.

HOPE HAD THE KIND OF speaking voice that told Lynda she came from money—more so than anyone else in the home. In the following days and weeks, she opened up to Lynda, explaining that her parents had died two years prior in a car accident, when she was fifteen. With no extended family able to take her in, no friends willing to take on the responsibilities of a teenaged girl, she was placed into foster care. Lynda wondered how it was possible that someone with means could end up homeless, just like she had been. It scared her to realize that life really never did provide any guarantees, even when you came from roots that offered promises of more.

When spring came with its breaths of fresh air and budding blooms, Lynda showed Hope the small garden behind the cottage. She taught her how to dig out holes and bury bulbs, ensuring the roots were down, the pointy sides were up, explaining that these were dahlias and lilies, and they would bloom in the summer. When Lynda pointed to the rose bush, asking when it would bloom, Lynda smiled to herself at Hope's wish for the most unoriginal of flowers, ones she herself never cared for. She found she was a little more excited for the roses to bloom this year.

Hope proved to have a green thumb as well, and together they worked the cottage's garden, expanding it to include herbs and vegetables. Fresh mint for tea. Basil, cucumbers, and tomatoes for summer salads. The cucumbers grew in abundance, and Hope and Lynda guided the younger girls into slicing them and filling mason jars with a brine of vinegar, water, dill and any other spices they wished to have. The result was their very own homemade pickles to accompany their ham sandwiches.

The girls poured over books in the library on all things botanical. There was something wonderful about getting their hands dirty in the soil. Something powerful in knowing they were capable of manipulating the earth in a way that produces small treasures. Hope expanded their operations to making tinctures, drying herbs and flowers, and experimenting with the right vinegar ratio, wishing she could get her hands on alcohol for the proper recipes. For now, as she was attempting to stay clean, she'd stick with her natural remedies.

Soon the adventure turned to beauty endeavors. The girls saved their money to purchase various oils. They'd stand in the kitchen, heating and blending and laughing at the explosions of beeswax and aloe as they attempted to emulsify concoctions to make lotions and creams. "I'm going to sell these one day," Hope would say. "Figure out the key to eternal youth."

Lynda would nod and say she couldn't wait to see. For both girls, youth had been robbed from them, replaced with hardships the young and innocent should never know.

IT WAS IN THE MIDST of this growing friendship that Hope finally shared with Lynda the rest of her story.

Lynda had always assumed an old boyfriend or dealer had

been Hope's rapist, but instead her friend shared that within a few weeks of being in her old foster home, the man of the house had taken an inappropriate liking to Hope. Midnight groping would leave her disgusted and stunned.

At that house, Hope had shared a room with two other girls, twins who were three years younger than she was. She quietly took the man's abuse, figuring at least she could keep the twins safe. She'd sleep in the bed closest to the door, always ensuring any nights he came in, he'd see her first. It was hell, but it was better than standing by and watching two twelve-year-olds receive this punishment.

She thought about saying something, sure. But she knew it would be hard to get anyone to believe her. Surely not the man's wife, who always sided with her husband when disagreements arose. She could tell her social worker, but Hope feared what would happen when the man would inevitably deny it. Foster families willing to take in teens were hard to find, she had learned. Would the state be desperate to keep this home on the roster, removing Hope from the house but leaving the twins behind? She couldn't take that risk.

When his actions escalated and he was lying on top of her one night, she got through it by imagining the way she'd kill him one day. How she'd get out of the house and find a way to murder him, ensuring no one else would ever endure abuse by this man. It was the only way she could survive, by fantasizing all the ways she'd watch the life disappear from his face. Lynda knew the feeling.

It was two years later when the twins were reunited with their biological family. Hope decided it was time to share her story with the social worker. She was a senior in high school, nearly on her own soon anyway, but she couldn't stand the abuse for a minute longer. While powder and pills had helped her cope, she was determined to find some semblance of the person she once was before the hell of losing her parents, then gaining a rapist.

Hope was removed from the home and placed at Jennifer Grace Cottage, but as suspected, she learned that the man denied everything. The coward blamed the drug-using teen for lying, and so he was able to keep his standing as a foster home.

There was no justice served.

Lynda listened quietly to all of this one summer night when they had snuck out of the house and were perched on a bench in a park, trading sips of rum from a bottle in a brown paper bag, acquired through a sweet smile and friendly wink given to the drunk walking in the liquor store at ten o'clock that morning. The perfect target, the man happily agreed to buy the girls whatever they wanted, taking their money and returning with the prize. They were seventeen and eighteen by then, and would be heading off to college soon thanks to scholarships and a small sum of money Hope was to receive upon her eighteenth birthday. The girls would room together, never leaving one another's side. The bond of sisterhood, brought together by the darkest of circumstances.

Heads spinning and bodies full of booze, they jumped on their bikes and rode around. Hope steered them down the winding streets until they reached the dirt road leading up to the shabby old foster home of her own personal horrors. They giggled, dropping their bikes to the side and sneaking around in the dark, between bushes, peering in at anything they could see. Hope wanted to know if there were any children in the home suffering as she had.

When a light came on in the house, Hope slowly rose from her hiding spot, eyes glued on the man opening the fridge, assembling himself a midnight sandwich. Lynda pulled at her hand, whispering for her to get back down, what the hell was she doing, but Hope was in a trance, eyes laser-focused on the man in the kitchen, now walking toward another room.

A light switched on outside. Lynda watched in horror the moment the man saw Hope. She grabbed her pseudo sister's hand, telling her they needed to go. *Now.* They began running toward their bikes, stashed twenty or thirty yards away, the girls drunk and stumbling in their escape. Lynda's heart was racing. She couldn't believe they had been so stupid.

Lynda made it to her bike, grabbing it and ready to take off, when she realized Hope wasn't with her. She looked behind her, saw the man with one hand clamped around Hope's long hair, the other over her mouth as he pushed her to the ground. In a panic, Lynda raced back to them. She jumped on the man's back, punching with all her might while he gripped his hands around Hope's throat. It was no use, though. Her punches might as well have been mosquito bites to him, nothing more than an annoyance. She scrambled around to find the rum bottle, discarded in the grass. She raised it up, slamming it down on the man's head with all her might, while her friend's blue eyes bulged in shock and horror. Two slams to his temple, blood gushing from his head, and he released Hope. Gasping for air, she scrambled to her feet, telling Lynda, "Come on, we have to get out of here," but Lynda stopped her.

The man groaned on the ground, hands held to his face and covered in blood. "We can't," she panted out, trying to catch her breath. "We were trespassing. He'll tell, and we'll be done for."

Hope was crying, saying they would explain what happened, it was self-defense, he had been strangling her, it would be fine. Everything would be okay.

But Lynda knew better.

She knew that this man's word against the girls' was not a thing to allow to happen. Lynda was eighteen, Hope about to be eighteen herself. They'd be tried as adults, and their lives would be ruined.

Lynda scanned around and found a rock big enough to do

the job. She heaved it in her hands, standing above the man and saying a silent prayer for forgiveness.

Three more blows to the man's head, she gave each one all the force she could, and then he was still.

They waited a minute. Then a minute more. The night around them was silent, save for the quiet hum of the house's condenser unit as the air conditioning turned on.

They were leaning on each other and breathing heavily, scanning for any signs of life from both the surrounding area, and from the man on the ground.

Thankfully, there were none.

Lynda rushed around to grab the remnants of the broken bottle, instructing Hope to do the same. It was dark, they struggled to see, but the dried and patchy grass and dirt of the yard allowed them to collect most of it.

They collected the rock Lynda had used and dropped all the items in the baskets of their bikes before doing one last scan for evidence of their fight. They left the man there and rode along in the dark, far away from the house, eventually stopping at a curbside trash bin. Lynda dug through to find a bag to open, adding in the makeshift weapons with the remnants of someone's pizza dinner.

Then they raced to their cottage and snuck back inside, washing dirt, blood, and sins down the drain.

———

IT WASN'T LONG BEFORE THE news of an investigation into the death of the man, left beaten to death in his yard, hit the newspapers. Lynda and Hope decided that if Hope was somehow identified as a suspect, Lynda should not be tied to her. So, they decided to change the plan. The girls would not go to college together.

"If the police should ever question you," Lynda instructed, "you say nothing. We were home all night, right?"

Hope nodded. "Home all night."

Parting ways was not what they wanted, but it was the safest way to keep Lynda out of jail. "Secret 'til the end," they promised one another. "We take this to the grave." They hugged and cried and assured one another they'd make their way back into each other's lives. Lynda prayed it was true.

When Hope turned eighteen, just a week before the girls were to head off to college, she received some money from her family's small estate. Thirty thousand dollars, ten of which she gave to Lynda.

Lynda tried to refuse it, telling Hope that the money was hers. She couldn't possibly. Hope insisted, smiling through tears and telling her friend she could pay her back one day if she really wanted, but either way, Lynda was going to take the money.

"I will absolutely pay you back," Lynda said as she hugged the friend she was heartbroken to have to say goodbye to. "With interest."

"With interest?" Hope said, blue eyes sparkling.

"Oh yeah. I'll double it. Quadruple it. Hell, I'll pay you back times ten."

Hope laughed. "Times ten? That's a hundred thousand dollars. You really see that kind of money in your future?"

Lynda nodded, zipping the last of her bags and swinging it over her shoulder. "I really do. For us both."

Hope handed her the check and said, "Deal, then. Times ten." They hugged with one last round of promises that when this was all over, they'd reach out to one another again. They'd find their way back. "But I'll be changing my name, just a heads up," she said. "Hope just doesn't feel like the name I want to go by anymore."

Lynda looked at her friend—her sister, really—sad to hear

her say that. "But my girl, we have hope ahead of us. Tell me you believe that." *Tell me I didn't kill a man for nothing.*

Hope shook her head. "I want more than just hope."

Lynda could hardly argue with that. And a name change might be another good safety measure. "Okay, then. What are you going to go by?"

Her blonde sister who looked nothing like her grinned. "I want to be Holly. Like the Holly bush, the symbol of protection and resilience."

Lynda smiled. "It's perfect," she said, before adding, "Love you times ten, Holly."

"Times ten," Hope—now Holly—agreed.

forty

• • •

Discernment

Present Day

taven

Sunday, 1:13pm

I STAND BACK a few steps as I watch my mother and Desiree walk side by side. The pathway winding through the cemetery is quiet and peaceful, and I listen as my mom tells a most unexpected story.

"Your mom and I lived together briefly when she was seventeen and I was eighteen," she tells Desiree. I hadn't been aware of this, and it's clear Desiree hadn't been either. As far as we knew, our fathers had met at a conference or something, and forged the brief Hatson-Carlisle alliance that way.

"You mean after my grandparents died?" Desiree asks. She pauses her steps and turns to my mother, and I can see the confusion on her face. "You knew her then?"

My mom nods. "Very shortly, yes. We lived in a group home for teen girls."

"Like an orphanage? I thought my mom had been in a foster home for that time."

My mother puts her hand around Desiree's shoulder, and guides them to continue walking. "She did for a bit, yes. But it was not a safe home, and so she was brought to the place I lived." I notice my mother doesn't mention where this place was. She's always been dismissive at mentioning much about her past, and I wonder why. No doubt it's because of elements of her past that she guards, not wanting to tarnish her reputation. It's something I struggle to understand. While there are certainly aspects of my past I'm not proud of, I also recognize the importance of being honest with myself. Honest with others, too. It's how we fight the isolation we can otherwise feel. No sense in pretending everything's perfect when it can be helpful to both ourselves and people with similar struggles to hear the hard truths.

But that's never been my mother's way.

Desiree looks back to me as if to confirm I'm still here. I smile and give an encouraging nod. She looks back to my mom. "What do you mean it wasn't safe, what happened at the foster home?"

I see the gentle squeeze of Desiree's shoulder. "Just another man with a will to do harm to young girls."

"Was it ever reported? No matter how long ago it was, we should still report it, he could still be hurting people." There's alarm in Desiree's voice.

My mom lets out a little laugh. "Looks like you've learned a thing or two." I wince at knowing she's referring to what happened to my Dazzle when we were in college. I can't help the involuntary squeeze of my fist I have at the thought. I should have killed that fucker.

My mom continues. "No need to worry about that, though.

Your mom did tell, so it's out there. And the man died of a heart attack soon after."

Desiree's quiet, just nodding and absorbing, I guess, as the three of us continue to walk along. She talks about how close she and Holly were, like sisters who were always meant to be. She shares stories of how they'd dream together of the future lives they'd live—far away from here. How when Desiree's mom came into her small inheritance, she gave my mom ten thousand dollars, and my mom promised to pay her back one day. With interest, times ten.

A hundred thousand dollars.

The check my father had given Desiree all those years ago, after we learned what had happened with Jacqui. I remember being so disgusted with my parents, thinking they were paying off this shithead and his family as a way to stay away, and I hated what I thought to be their belief that money could solve such an unforgivable problem. I thought it was an insult to Jacqui.

But holy shit, that's not what it was. I wonder if Desiree's making that connection, too. The money had nothing to do with Jacqui, it was just my mom keeping up her promise, knowing she'd have to part ways with her old friend again.

"Times ten," Desiree whispers. "My mom's tattoo." She looks at my mother. "My mom had a 'times ten' tattoo on her ribcage, hidden under her breast. I saw it when she was sick. That was because of you?"

My mom smiles. "She did?"

"Yes. Do you have one too? Matching tattoos?"

My mom shakes her head. "Good God, no. Do I strike you as the type of woman who would have a tattoo?" All I can think is hell no. "But I'm glad to hear Holly had that," she says. "I like that."

When we have made a full circle and arrive at our cars, my mom faces Desiree, who asks, "Why all the secrecy about your friendship? I mean, like you said, even in my mother's dying days, you would think she would have told me about how you and her really knew one another. It doesn't make any sense."

My mom takes Desiree's hands. "Suffice it to say that some things are best to remain out of the ears of people who don't need to know. We had our reasons, though, I can assure you."

"What kind of reasons?" I ask. I'm not sure what Desiree's thinking, but I have a feeling there's a whole lot more to the story.

My mom looks back and forth between us both. "Just know that back then, things were often difficult. While your mother and I were lucky to have one another, it was within circumstance that were not the easiest. Memories we'd rather leave behind us, which is why we decided to build new lives for ourselves. But your mother was always in my heart. It wasn't until years later when Bill and I were looking to shift gears in our own careers that I finally reached out to your mom. We arranged to have our husbands meet. I imagined we would likely share about our history at some point in time. But, well—you know the rest."

Desiree drops her head down. "I do know, now. Taven only just told me about what happened with my dad. I don't even know what to say."

I see the expression shift on my mother's face at the mention of Frank Hatson. I can only imagine what she's thinking. "Well, I'm happy to hear that you didn't follow in the plan to join in on his businesses, and that you chose a path for yourself. A pediatrician, I heard, right?"

"Yup," Desiree confirms. "It was something my mom encouraged right as she was in her last days. She wanted me to do my own thing. Even said I should drop out of med school if I wanted," she says with a laugh. "But I knew I loved medicine."

"A science mind, like your mom."

I've remained mostly quiet through their exchange, just allowing them to take this strange moment to themselves, but now I step forward and take Desiree's hand. "A natural healer, I have no doubt." I plant a kiss on her head, and turn to face my mother, daring her to show any ounce of disapproval.

She studies me for a moment, then scans her eyes over to Desiree. "Never in a million years did I think Holly's daughter and my son would end up together. But you two never could seem to stay away, could you?"

"Full circle," I say.

My mother nods, her eyes pensive. "Indeed. The lifecycle of a crush, I suppose."

I smile. "Mom. It's the final phase of a crush. Desiree is the love of my life."

My mom steps forward and gives us both an awkward group hug. I pull her in tightly and slightly lift her off the ground, telling her she can do better than a lukewarm embrace.

She laughs, pulling back and straightening out her blouse, saying, "Maybe all the hell Holly and I went through was for this, then. Right here. Maybe we were meant to have you two. And you two were meant to have each other."

forty-one

. . .

Acceptance

Present Day

desiree

Sunday, 5:45pm

I RELUCTANTLY PACK up the last of my things, sad to have to be heading home and back to reality.

On the other hand, I have a new bloom in my chest in thinking about all that the future holds. Taven Carlisle, back in my life. For good this time, I do believe.

He drives me back in his Bronco, good old Eruption Green. He asks me why I'm laughing, and I tell him Inferno is a good name for a car, but I'm not sure I can be running around and calling this car Eruption. He says that's all he's ever called it, because it made him think of me.

I think about the term, and how it's fitting as a way to describe the events of the past forty-eight hours. I think about what Lynda said, how she described the lifecycle of our crushes on one another, and how perfect the term "crush" really is. To compress to the point of distortion. And if that's the case, I'm glad we made it to the end of the cycle, to an eruption of truths and realizations that are freeing us both from the maddening cycle of emotional torment we've been through. It's been long enough.

If only the actual lifecycle of a crush could be so fast, just forty-eight hours. From intrigue and the initial flutters of excitement, the hope we feel in the start of something new. To capitalizing on moments together and making every second count. Then torturing ourselves with hunger and want that doesn't seem to have an end, or the begging and bartering and grasping wrapped within our emotional desperation. The agonizing that can feel consuming, yet there's no denying the way it can also make us feel beautifully alive.

If we're really lucky, we can eventually land into that final phase—madly, deeply in love. How simple that would be if it all could be just forty-eight hours.

But no real transformation can be so fast, that much I know. Some things you just can't rush. We can tell ourselves we prefer the comforts of what we know, thus avoiding the discomfort brought about by the chances we would take in facing change. That only steers you more off course, effectively prolonging the process, or worse—removing the possibility of reaching the end at all.

I share my thoughts with Taven, and he rubs his hand over his face, his other hand resting on the steering wheel. "I guess you're right," he says. "Just have to courageously ride along and let things run their course."

I tell him that I like where it's landed us.

He drops me off to my condo and walks me in, asking if he could stay the night. Just one last night with me, here in my home, then he'll leave first thing in the morning. I say yes.

As we lie in my bed later, naked and sticky with sweat, he

cradles me in his arms. He's quiet, and I ask him what he's thinking.

He kisses me. "I'm thinking about how you should get a tattoo for your mom, finally. Times ten."

"Under my boob?" I say with a giggle.

"Anywhere you want," he says.

I raise my arm in front of his chest. "How about right here?" I ask, running my finger along the underside of my forearm, between elbow and wrist. "Think I could pull it off? Can I be a tattoo girl? Melissa would be proud."

He sits himself up against the pillows and headboard, scooting me up to look at him. "Desiree, you can be any girl you want to be, don't you know that?"

"You mean woman."

"You said girl," he points out, and I run my fingers over some of his tattoos, explaining to him that I still sometimes struggle to believe that transformation.

He lifts my chin, and his dark eyes are serious on mine. "Dazzle, I may not know everything there is to know in life, but if there's one thing I understand, it's transformation."

"Is that so?"

He nods. "It is."

"And what, dare I ask, do you know about transformation?" I lay across his lap, cradling my head in my hand as I look up to him.

He traces a finger down the slope of my nose, over my lips. "I know that true transformation isn't about changing into anything new, for one thing," he says. His finger trails its way up to my cheekbone, then down to my jawline, then my neck and collarbone.

"So what's it about, then, if it's not changing to something new?"

He locks eyes with me, and I'm so in love with him in that moment, with his seriousness and the wisdom he's trying to impart on me, wisdom he has hard earned. He says, "True transformation isn't about changing—it's about finally allowing yourself to be exactly who you've always been at the core." He raises my hand and kisses it. "It's the thing that I've loved about you from day one, Desiree. That you've always lived that way, even as a kid. Even though you might have been a little different from everyone else. You weren't the loudmouth starved for attention, or the show-off bragging about the latest name brands in your closet. You didn't feel the need to constantly be in a sports uniform to feel power and purpose, like I did for many years, and you never even bragged about the fact that you were valedictorian at your high school. You've always just been you, and I'm so incredibly in love with that uniqueness."

I nod, eyes welling at the simplicity of his statement. "I'm incredibly in love with your uniqueness too," I tell him, planting a kiss on his chest.

My whole life, I've always felt like I was plain, searching for some way to be significant or special. Yet here he was, all this time, in awe of the fact that I didn't try and mold myself into anything to be exceptional in some way. I've just been myself. "Accept yourself and live within that truth," I say with a smile. It's something my therapist Ruth would say. How wise my Taven is.

"Sounds like another tattoo option," he says with a grin.

"Too long."

He shrugs. "Yeah, maybe you're right. But you, Dazzle, are an assertive and strong *woman*," he says, cupping the underside of my face in a gentle hold. "You may not be as vocal and hotheaded as Melissa, or as reckless as I was for many years, but it doesn't mean you're any less fierce or fucking incredible. Got that?" I nod, loving the determination on his face.

I trail my fingers along the lettering of his 'one day at a time' tattoo. "I'm so happy you're back," I tell him. It's a loaded statement, I mean it in more ways than one. I have a feeling he understands.

"I'm not going anywhere," he says. "In fact, I want to spend the rest of my life being here with you, showing you just how exceptional you are to me."

"You don't need to, I already know," I insist.

"So you don't need me to spend the rest of my life with you?"

I let out a giggle, a flutter in my chest at hearing him say that. I poke him in the shoulder. "You can't be engaged to two different people in the same weekend," I tell him.

He shrugs, leaning his head back and closing his eyes. "Fuck that. Yes I can."

I kiss the smooth skin of his stomach, just below his chest. "You're greedy."

"Maybe," he says. "But that wasn't a proposal. Trust me when I say you'll know it when it happens."

"Promise?"

He opens his eyes and looks at me. "I promise it times ten, Dazzle."

epilogue

. . .

Crystalize

Ten months later

desiree

Summertime

THE CROWD WAITING beyond is quietly chatting, and Dylan takes my arm as I rub the small bump of my belly, the pale pink dress I'm wearing stretching out over with just enough room to spare. Not exactly the plan we had, to get pregnant so soon. On the other hand, Taven and I have rarely done things according to plan.

I look up at my big brother as he prepares to walk me down the aisle. He was the obvious choice to have by my side for this moment, as my father is not someone I wanted to give this honor to. I talk to him now and then, a decision I made after initially feeling disgusted by him, thinking I'd never want to see him again.

But when I thought about it, I thought of my mother. She

loved him and chose to stay by his side. She was fiercely loyal like that, and I've chosen not to hold unnecessary hatred in my heart for him. Not worth the energy.

Thankfully, he's off living a new life in Europe, and that's just fine by me. I'll see him for a quick coffee when he's in town, but for the most part, that's about where we stand. And no, he was not invited to the wedding. With Melissa as my maid-of-honor, and Jacqui as a bridesmaid, their comfort and ability to let loose in today's festivities was far more important to me.

The three of us enjoyed a fun-filled weekend holed away in a mountain cabin for a makeshift bachelorette celebration. I watched as they shared a bottle of wine, laughing and crying and forming their own beautiful friendship. Eventually sharing some tales of good old Frank Hatson, then looking at me, startled at their drunken loose lips, worried I would be uncomfortable or offended. I waved them off, ensuring them the only thing that would make me uncomfortable was them holding back. We need to be able to speak up and share our honest and ugly stories now and then. Through those connections, we heal.

Dylan looks down at me and smiles. "You look beautiful," he says as he kisses my cheek. "You ready?"

I nod and tell him I was born ready. Not exactly the truth, but it's not a lie either. We make our first steps down the makeshift aisle in Taven's backyard, the home we now share together. I've opened my own practice just down the street in town, and I like the quiet of our secluded home, with plenty of space for our future kids to roam around one day. We plan on having more little Carlisle cuties. For now though, I'm happy to be starting with just the one.

We walk down and I see old friends and new, some colleagues and some faces that I don't recognize. I think they are friends of Lynda and Bill's, and I loved seeing how excited Taven's mom was to be inviting people from her world to show off her son and his new bride. I have a feeling it's part of her love of control, but I have a better understanding of why she is the way she is. I can respect it.

When Dylan passes me off to Taven before taking his place on the groomsmen side, I smile at my handsome soon-to-be husband, eyes tearing up as he sucks in a deep breath. He's giving me that look that I love. The one that tells me I'm the woman of his dreams, like he can't believe I'm real. That I chose him.

I'm not sure he'll ever quite understand that from the moment I saw him at that first concert so many years ago, he was it for me.

<hr>

IN THE RECEPTION THAT FOLLOWS, under the protection of a white tent and a gentle breeze that offers reprieve from the June heat, Melissa stands up to give her toast. Taven reaches over to squeeze my hand, then reaches in his suit jacket to pull out a small pack of tissues, just in case. I laugh and pull one out, emotional already and my best friend hasn't even said a thing. Taven takes the tissue from me, dabbing at my eyes and then pushing a glass of water over to me.

Melissa stands up tall, ever the performer in front of a crowd. Her cream-colored dress clings to her curves, making her look like the star that she is. Dark curls spill down her back, and I can't help but look over to Dylan to see if he has any kind of reaction to her. I still hold out hope for the two of them being together one day. The football star and the actress, how appropriate. His face is unreadable, but when the guy next to him reaches over to whisper something in his ear, and Dylan doesn't even acknowledge him, I have a feeling my brother might be just the tiniest bit smitten.

Melissa clears her throat, mic in hand, and the guests quiet. "You should all know that I'm Melissa Belle, and I was Desiree's first crush, and she mine," she says, and the crowd politely laughs.

"It's true!" I yell out.

"See?" she says with a winning grin. "Taven, watch out. Your wife always has a backup."

"Not on my life," he shouts back.

Melissa's face turns serious, and she raises the mic once again. "I don't know about you all, but I'm not always the easiest of people to be around. I can be loud, I can speak my mind when no one asks, I can have a temper. In fact, Desiree and I first became friends after she watched me punch a kid that was hurling insults at me. And my darling Desiree called me her hero. Meanwhile, my hand was sore, and I was worried that I just embarrassed myself in front of this cute girl that I had secretly been desperately hoping to make my friend, because Desiree always seemed so cool and unaffected by everything. But damn, my temper got me again." I glance over at Dylan, and see him grinning and nodding his head. "Yet Desiree called me her hero, and that was that.

"Truth be told, it was Desiree that became mine. As I got to know her, I learned that she had this unique ability to do the right thing, even if it was keeping her mouth shut on my violence." I laugh and dab at a tear that manages to escape. "I loved the way she'd have these wildly deep conversations with me about life and what gives it meaning, then in the next breath, say she was craving ice cream. Desiree is the type of person to write me a sweet card, just because. Then dare me to do something wild, just so she could watch, and I'd fall for it every time," she laughs. "Some of those dares I'll just go ahead and keep to myself."

She shifts her weight from one foot to the other and sighs. Her voice holds emotion in it as she says, "Desiree has an incredible ability to love. It's one of her best qualities, and she can hold onto love through thick and thin, something that's not easy to do. She's stood by me when I was making terrible decisions, of which there were many," she laughs. "I've also watched her stand by Taven over the years when he's..." she trails off, then tilts her head side-to-side with a mischievous smile, debating how to say it, I imagine.

Taven fills it in for her. "Just say it, Mel! When I was a terrible drunk," he laughs, and our friends and loved ones laugh too, all well aware of his road to sobriety.

Melissa smiles. "Alright, fine. You heard it from him, not me.

"But the real reason I even bring that up is because of something so important, something we could all learn from looking at this couple before us here today. Because one of the most admirable qualities about Desiree is how she also knew when to choose herself." I watch as she slowly nods, letting that last statement settle. The space is quiet, hanging on her words. "Desiree once had to make the difficult decision to walk away from Taven, a man I know she fiercely loved, but realized he needed to learn how to love himself as well. And that could not have been easy."

I hear Taven quietly laugh beside me. "Oh shit, she's good," he says, and I see him do a few rapid blinks, before giving me a kiss on the cheek. "Smart woman," he whispers to me.

I lay my head on his shoulder and wait for Melissa to continue. "That takes real courage to do that, which makes her my hero."

She looks over to my husband now—*my husband!*—and addresses him. "Taven. Despite me dragging you through the mud a little right now—"

"It's alright, I can handle it," he calls out. I look over to Lynda, wondering how she's liking this hanging-out-the-laundry toast, but her mouth is curved up into a small smile.

"You can handle a lot," Melissa agrees. "You've been a hero right back to Desiree in so many ways. I've seen you push her out of her comfort zone. I've seen you help her break a couple rules now and then. I've seen you protect her from things that would hurt her, and seen you help her heal when she was temporarily bruised or broken. Last year when Desiree was struck by lightning—did you all realize that?" she asks everyone. "Yeah. This girl was actually struck by lightning!"

"Indirectly!" I clarify.

"Potato, pot-ah-to, it still counts," she says. "But when that happened, Taven dropped everything to scoop her up, insisting that when she was released from the hospital, he'd take her back to his place, adamant that he was going to be the one to take care of her. And I actually let him, because that's the kind of guy he is." She looks over to him. "I have no doubt you'd go to hell and back just to keep our girl safe and happy, just as she deserves. And I know you'll continue being that hero to the baby you guys will soon be welcoming. That baby doesn't even know how lucky he or she is to have the two best goddamn superheroes as parents in the world.

"So, raise a glass," she says, and Taven and I raise our sparkling waters. "To the childhood sweethearts turned husband and wife. The heroes every one of us are lucky to have in our lives. Here's to less lightning strikes and crazy drama in the years to come. Salut!"

"Hear hear, salut!" Taven says beside me as I giggle my way through wiping my tears.

I watch as Dylan rises to a stand when Melissa passes his table, heading to me, but my brother stops her. He gives her a kiss on the cheek and whispers something in her ear. She throws her head back and laughs. I can't help but watch the exchange with a new hope blooming in my chest. This one for them.

I look down at my arm, the graceful black lettering of my "times ten" tattoo, and I say a silent prayer of gratitude to my mom. I wish she was here today, of course, but I'm thankful to have a new mother figure officially in my life. A woman I never even realized had meant more to my mom than I could ever understand. A sister. A friend. A keeper of promises and—as

Taven and I suspect—shared secrets that we'll never be privy to. Lynda's a good step-in, and I'm learning to love her, just like my mom would want me to.

I think about the letter I read from my mom earlier today. Given to me right before her death, she instructed me to read it the morning of my future wedding day, if I had one. I was with Parker back then, the surgeon my mom was thrilled to have by my side. I had worried her letter would be referring to him, but thankfully, it wasn't.

Instead, she told me if there was any ounce of doubt in my mind about whether or not to take this plunge, to marry this man, that I shouldn't do it. That I could be a runaway bride, and she'd figure out how to take care of the rest from wherever she'd be. I had laughed and showed it to Taven, watching him put on his suit jacket and giving it a quick tug. "See? Even your mom knew Parker wasn't it for you," he grins. "Think she was hoping it'd be me?"

I shrugged, looking down at her handwriting. "I like to think so."

I reach for my purse now and pull out the letter, reading the rest of it yet again while Melissa is still busy flirting with my brother. I skim down to the part I'm looking for.

You have your whole life ahead of you, and there will be countless decisions to make. Some you'll make the right way, some the wrong way, and some you'll have to live with the questions of what might have happened if you had done things differently.

I've always admired your ability to face things, Desiree. I've always been more of a hand-waver, content to ignore while telling myself

I'd let be what will be. In some ways that can be good, in other ways, not so much. So if there's one thing I want for you, it's to make this choice wisely. A husband is not just a security blanket you hope to be able to hide under when needed. He's not a convenient friend or even a guaranteed lover.

Instead, a husband needs to be a perfectly imperfect human, just as you are, and completely willing to understand and acknowledge his own weaknesses, right along with his strengths. When a person can do that, they can live with integrity and authenticity, free from an internal hunger to self-serve. A self-aware man has the emotional intelligence to approach life with enthusiasm, honesty, and curiosity, even when something is not going his way. That's the key, that's the real test of character. When someone has this, they approach relationships with a faith and courage that allows them to be vulnerable, which is the only way to make truly meaningful connections.

So. If there is any doubt in your mind in your chosen husband's ability to do this, then run, my darling. Run as fast as you can, because you are worth so much more than "good enough."

Don't sacrifice your ultimate peace and happiness just because. Even if you never find the right man, it doesn't matter. Because as I lie here now, it's not your father I'm thinking about the most. It's my children, and it's the other women I've had in my life that I'll be missing. That's what I'm most thankful for. That's what's worth grieving.

If you read this and decide the man you've chosen does exhibit all these qualities that I insist you have, well then, happy wedding day, my darling. May you live out many years together. Have children, or don't. Buy a beautiful home, or not. Travel, or stay put, dream big or dream small, whatever is right for you.

As long as you're courageously loving yourself and living true to yourself, that's all that matters.

P.S—If you ever decide to have children, and you have a girl, would you consider giving her Hope as a middle name?

You should know that once upon a time, it was my first name.

Love always, Mom

Taven looks at me holding my letter. I point out the line at the end and his eyes scan her words. "Think she'd be upset to know we're having a boy?" he asks.

"Nah," I say. "She'd get over it. The hand-waver, never letting anything get to her."

He places his palm on my belly and tells me we should keep trying for a girl. That he's committed to however many kids it takes until we can give my mom her dying wish, even if that means having ten.

I laugh and put my hand on his. I tell him thank you for being a good sport, but that I want to concentrate on the one we're having, feeling lucky that I get even one chance to become someone's mom. "How many times can lightning strike in one person's lifetime?" I ask, looking up at him.

Taven smiles and replies, "Dazzle." He pushes a strand of hair away from my face, dragging his touch down my cheek. "Every single day with you is like lightning."

The End

Want to see what Taven's wedding gift to Desiree is? Go to https://BookHip.com/KLDWDGZ for the bonus scene!

acknowledgments & thoughts

You should know, dear readers, that a lightning strike was not part of my original vision for this tale. Nor was the topic of addiction or even the idea of Desiree leaving the man she loved in his darkest hours.

No. None of that was in my original storyline.

My lovely first broad-strokes concept of this story was all about family meddling (a topic I love and you'll see in some way, shape, or form in most of my books), and I had this grand idea of creating a heroine that learns family boundaries due to a family rivalry. It's a valuable lesson, and one I hope to show in greater depths in some book in the future.

But it wasn't the topic meant for this book.

My stories always seem to take a life of their own, and I've learned to trust that process. My characters have their own tales to tell, whether or not it was part of my original vision. I listen.

I've thought a lot about how this book transformed. It started with the concept of a crush—the longing we can have to feel a deep connection with something we have decided is *it* for us. In life, we sometimes need to trust the process, painful as it might be. While there are certainly far more painful things to go through than something like this, the gift of writing a novel, I have to say, writing this book was *hard* for me.

Why? For one, it's my first standalone, and that in and of itself felt like writing a debut all over again.

The other tough thing, though, was Taven. I hadn't planned on him being someone who struggled with addiction. It was that early hospital scene when Melissa and Desiree share the moment of recognizing that he was at a music festival and sober that created that storyline. The words just wrote themselves, and as I typed out that moment, "*Sober,*" I realized this story was going to be way more than I originally thought. But what a perfect way to depict a crush.

I was scared to write it. I hated that that's what my characters were telling me they needed.

My life's work has always been about exploring the messiness of being human. I love having the opportunity to do so in beautiful love stories meant to entertain, first and foremost, and teach some lessons in the process. When I realized that Taven's current sobriety was going to be *A Thing*, I knew I was going to be tackling something challenging.

I wanted to give a voice to the Desirees of the world that have stood by and tried to help (I'm looking at you, loves!). I consulted with a dear friend who has been in that position to help me solidify the scene at Taven's house where Desiree finally allows herself to get good and mad at the hell Taven put her through. Thank you, thank you, Ky. I imagine doing so was challenging, but I hope it offered some release as well. You are completely amazing. Desiree got her voice thanks to you.

I also wanted to give a voice to the people that have struggled with addiction, and make sure that their take on it was felt and understood. I recognize that there are various views of what it means to struggle with addictive substances, and I'm not sure there's any "right" way to look at it, other than the one that helps an individual achieve the kind of day-to-day life where they can live with pride in themselves, and not regret due to the way their addiction to something may be impacting them.

I didn't want to shame. I didn't want to offer false pleasantries. I didn't want to undermine or brush aside the impact, and I didn't want to glory in the gory just for entertainment's sake. Ooof. Basically, I didn't want to do this.

I did it anyway. I hope someone out there feels some kind of validation in the story, no matter what side of it you may sit on.

And for those of you waiting for the "I set boundaries with my family and it was hard and I'm proud" story? I hope you got a bit of that with the way Desiree and Taven set their own paths.

Now, on to my thank yous, as I could *not* have done this alone.

Lynda and Evelyn Hambright—this baby is just as much yours as it is mine. Yup, I had to name two characters after you both, because it just felt right. I'm so thankful our paths have crossed. Now grab an oxygen mask as I smother you with all my respect and love.

My very best friends, Katja, Christine, Jen, Jacqui, maybe a few more who prefer to be anonymous. You had to get characters named for you as well.

Jacqui Muller, my Jacqui. Readers should know that your impressive early feedback and developmental editing is what breathes so much life into my work. Thanks for coaching me through all my question marks and fears with this one.

Catherine Elaine—for catching all my skipped and extra words and working your proofreading magic as always.

Melissa—is your girl as spunky and fabulous as you are? I sure hope so, because you're a gorgeous soul.

To the alcoholics/addicts in my life, both recovering and maybe hoping you can still get a hold of this thing—you're amazing no matter what. May you get to a place where you firmly believe that.

For those of you that relate, here's a great book for you. My unofficial mentor Peggy Bastianelli informed me of it, and I'd love for any and everyone to read it, because it's damn good. It's *This Naked Mind: Control Alcohol*, by Annie Grace, and it one thousand percent helped me as I wrote this story. Whether you struggle with alcohol or not, it's worth a read. Peggy...I'm not sure you'll ever quite know how meaningful your role in my life has always been. Our conversations are a permanent resource in my memory banks, and I can solidly say I'm a better woman because of your insights. I aspire to be as awesome as you.

To my fearless early readers of my debut, *Midnight to December*...those of you who took a chance on me, a newbie author with zero fame, just hoping to get the VZ word out there —you all read my words anyway without even knowing me. Your messages of love of my work have been EVERYTHING. Seriously. I might not have continued writing if it weren't for you. I'll keep going and keep providing the best characters I can because of you. Any requests for what you want next? I'm all ears, loves.

Thank you B. Williams for weaving the craft in such an inspiring way.

To the author women in my life. We happened to be sharing a house for a retreat when I worked on edits for this book, and being around your badass and creative feminine energy was exactly what I needed. Lydia Michaels, DD Lorenzo, Alexandra Hale, Ellie Masters, Meredith Wild, Michelle Windsor, Samantha Cole, and Willow Winters—YOU ARE THE REAL DEAL. Marisa, thanks for keeping us wonderfully balanced. Oh, and everyone needs an Amber Vasquez.

As Lydia reminded me, I need to thank myself as well, for— as she so aptly said—allowing myself the courage to be vulnerable so I can grow. That courage made this book possible.

And finally, to my husband Matthew and our four babies. I've been selfishly writing as much as my heart wants. And here I am now, releasing book five. I'm already spinning the vision of book six. I jump up from the dinner table when an idea pops in my head. I stare at a screen and click away, and yet, you all still support me with such enthusiasm, it makes me downright emotional. May I be the wife and mom you deserve, because you darlings deserve the absolute best.

One final note—when I was in college, I was a volunteer rape crisis counselor. It was a pivotal point for me, and I became a licensed therapist as a result of my passion for helping others.

To become a volunteer, I went through several weeks of training to learn active listening skills, local laws, and various ways to support someone who has suffered from a sexual assault, and secondary victims. If you or anyone you know needs support, please check out https://rainn.org/resources or call the hotline at 1-800-656-HOPE (4673).

about the author

A believer that life is all about the great stories we live to share, Vanessa Zian loves helping people find the heart and ah-ha moments in their own tales. Her two loves are romance novels and tapping into underlying emotions.

When she's not writing or reading romance, Vanessa works as a therapist, helping clients heal through the powers of introspection. She writes with the same goals in mind—to find value in the conflict and strength of character in beautiful stories, and to celebrate our happy endings.

Vanessa lives in Delaware with her childhood crush-turned-husband, their four kids, and their rescue pup Mikka.

And lots of high heels.

Readers—please consider leaving a rating or review! It's vital to helping get the word out there, and I'm so thankful. Please jump on Goodreads or Amazon and let other readers know your thoughts!

Join my newsletter where I will randomly ask for character name ideas, offer therapeutic tidbits, share sneak peeks, etc! Visit
vanessazian.com
Email: Vanessa@vanessazian.com

facebook.com/VanessaZianWrites

instagram.com/vanessa_zian

tiktok.com/@vanessazian

www.ingramcontent.com/pod-product-compliance
Lightning Source LLC
Chambersburg PA
CBHW030732310726
48969CB00005B/1203